FINDING YOU

THE WRIGHT HEROES OF MAINE
BOOK 3

ROBIN PATCHEN

JDO PUBLISHING.

Published in Austin, TX.

Cover by Lynnette Bonner

Paperback ISBN: 978-1-950029-42-6

Large Print ISBN: 978-1-950029-43-3

Hard Cover ISBN: 978-1-950029-44-0

Library of Congress Control Number: 2024907710

For the Minds...
Hallee, Lacy, Misty, Sharon, Susie, and Tracy.
I don't know if I could do this without you, and I don't want to find out.

CHAPTER ONE

The morning sun glared down at Hasan Mahmoud, and he glared right back. Normally, he thanked Allah for sunshine, but where he lived, the sun did its job properly.

Not like here in Germany, where despite the cloudless sky, the temperature was barely high enough to melt the icicles hanging from the snow-topped buildings all around him.

Hasan loathed Munich—especially this time of year. It was an explosion of red and green and gold, of manger scenes and Santa Clauses. And infidels worshiping their pagan gods.

Father, Son, and Spirit. Even a fool could count the three Gods of Christianity. Heretics, all of them, flocking to the market to pick among cheap knickknacks to decorate their homes and hang on their trees. Spend, spend, spend—proving what they truly loved.

It would be one thing if they believed in something, but Hasan had seen enough of so-called faith to know those in the West worshiped money far more than they worshiped their crucified Jesus.

Christians were almost as bad as false Muslims, who gave lip service while enjoying their evil.

They would all pay. He could almost see it, almost hear the screams. He only wished he could be here when it happened. But he'd be gone by then, on his way back to Iraq before anybody could stop him.

None of it would happen if he failed this morning's mission.

Hasan would never have guessed he'd be following clues like some greedy treasure hunter. Most people believed that Saddam Hussein's stash of munitions had been destroyed—or had never existed in the first place—but Hasan knew they were in Germany. He even knew approximately where.

Approximately.

And that was the problem.

He'd been searching fruitlessly for years.

Finally, the key to locating the weapons had been found, right here in Munich. And he was going to get his hands on it. That would be the first step in securing what the madman Saddam should never have moved out of his country.

Worthy followers of Allah had identified the perfect tool for recovering the item, an American infidel who deceived Muslims into abandoning their faith. She lived in the heart of Old Town, an area crowded on a normal day.

Right now, it was overrun with tourists, thanks to the Christmas market that had been set up in the square.

Restaurants and stores filled the street level of the woman's apartment building, the nearest, a bakery packed with customers. The scents of coffee and baking bread flavored the frigid air. Sandwiched between the bakery and a souvenir shop, a locked door led to apartments on the upper floors. Hasan made it through the crush of people and leaned against the wall beside the door. He forced a contented expression, as if gazing at the scene gave him pleasure.

He only had to wait a few moments before somebody exited

the building. The older man caught his eye and held the door open.

Hasan smiled as he grabbed it. *"Danke."*

"Bitte schön." The fool dove into the crowd.

Hasan moved inside, shutting out the cacophony and the chill that reached beyond his wool coat and leather gloves.

Like so many things in the West, this building was a facade. The exterior had been designed to look old, but inside it was obvious that the structure was much newer than it seemed.

Even their architecture deceived.

In Iraq, the birthplace of the world, there was no need to pretend there was history. It was evident in every corner of the nation.

He found a stairwell and climbed two flights. Checking the corners for cameras—there were none—he walked to the proper door and knocked.

No answer.

He'd been told the woman had traveled to America. He hoped his source had gotten that information correct.

Still wearing his gloves, Hasan dropped his messenger bag beside the door and crouched to pick the lock.

Locks—plural. The first was easy, but the deadbolt proved less so.

He forced patience, thanking Allah that nobody came. It took far longer than it should have, but finally, the deadbolt disengaged.

One hand hovering over the pistol he'd secured in case the intelligence about her absence was wrong, Hasan twisted the doorknob and stepped into a typical European apartment. The living area was mostly colorless except for a giant painting hanging on one wall. It depicted a village square filled with people. Snowcapped mountains rose in the distance.

Hasan studied the painting until he found himself getting lost in it.

The infidel had taste.

The air was stale and silent. She wasn't here. He carried his messenger bag from the hallway and began.

The main room—kitchen, dining table, and living area—was tidy if bland. He flipped through magazines on the coffee table —not fashion but decorator, which surprised him.

There was no desk, but he searched a pile of papers on her kitchen counter. Evidently, she paid her bills on time and kept her debts low. Unusual for an American.

The bathroom was white and shiny.

The spare bedroom held an art studio, and he spent a few moments in there, picking among the canvases. Not only did the infidel have taste, but she had talent. Too bad she wasted it.

Like she wasted her life.

He spent more time in her bedroom, getting to know this enemy to better predict her movements and manipulate her. Her tastes, her habits, her idols. Money, beauty. Self, self, self. Typical Western Christian, clothed in deceit and pouring out her life to deceive others.

He went through her bureau drawers and finally found what he was searching for lying atop silky and shameful under-things. She'd barely tried to conceal it, the little fool.

She would be the first victim in Hasan's operation.

The clue to Saddam's weapons lay in Munich.

Sophia Chapman would help him get it, whether she wanted to or not.

CHAPTER TWO

Every major decision Bryan Wright had made since he was seven years old was based on lies, each new one an extension of the one before. They felt true and solid, stacked like bricks in a wall between the life he was meant to live and the life he'd settled for.

He was tearing that wall down now—trying to, anyway. Which meant everything was changing.

What would happen when the last bricks were tossed away?

Who would he be? Who did he want to be?

Not that he'd find any answers today.

It was Wednesday, the first of his five-day Thanksgiving break. He planned to stay with his parents tonight so he wouldn't have to make the drive down again tomorrow. He was in no hurry to return to his rental house near the Bowdoin campus.

The holiday traffic from Brunswick, Maine, to Shadow Cove had added fifteen minutes to what was normally an hour-long ride, making him late for lunch. Fortunately, he snagged a decent parking spot right around the corner from Webb's Harborside and, umbrella in hand, walked as quickly as his bum leg would take him. He left his cane in the car. He used it when he had to, but if he could manage without, all the better.

The rain had started to let up in the last few minutes, but as he crossed a narrow side street, fat plops landed on his head. He opened the umbrella before he got too wet.

The sidewalks were mostly deserted, but he saw through the windows that the family restaurant overlooking the Atlantic was packed. Halfway up the walkway to the door, a blond woman stood alone, hunched over, arms crossed, clearly freezing. She wore jeans and a teal turtleneck sweater and had a phone pressed to her ear.

"That's not the point," she said. "You had no right—"

The rain picked up, but the woman didn't move.

"*You're* the one who broke in." She paused, then said, "So you say, but how can I...?"

Obviously, this wasn't a conversation she wanted anyone overhearing. But the temperature hovered in the midthirties, and the rain was just two degrees north of ice.

It was a cheap umbrella. Bryan could get another.

He approached her, catching her eye from about ten feet away.

She tilted her head to the side, looking more curious than annoyed at the interruption.

He held out the umbrella as he drew near. "Keep it."

"Oh." She smiled and...wow. She was slender, five-seven or five-eight, with curly blond hair and striking gray eyes. Standing outside without a jacket in November proved her intellect was more summary than analysis, but what she lacked in IQ points, she made up for in beauty.

She took the umbrella. "Thank you."

He started to respond, but she looked down again. "No, not you. I wasn't talking..." Holding the umbrella over her head, she returned her attention to the person on the other end of the line. "Listen, you need to stop..."

Bryan hurried up the handicap ramp. Inside, the area in front of the host's station was crowded with men, women, and children sitting on benches, leaning against walls, blocking the way. He scanned the dining room and saw that his brothers had snagged a round table with six chairs near the stone fireplace in the center of the restaurant. He skirted diners and barely dodged a server carrying a tray of drinks before stopping behind one of two empty chairs. The other had a jacket draped over it already. "Sorry I'm late."

Michael, second-oldest of the Wright brothers, stood and shook his hand. "Glad you made it. I know it's a drive."

"Thanks for inviting me." Bryan greeted Leila, Michael's fiancée, with a kiss on her cheek, then her sister, Jasmine. The identical twins were petite. Not a millimeter over five feet, he doubted either one weighed a hundred pounds. They both had long, silky black hair and wide, almond-shaped eyes. They were gorgeous, no question about it, though not his type. A good thing because, within about five seconds of meeting Jasmine, Derrick had fallen a little bit in love.

Bryan shook Derrick's hand—his younger brother, who of course had chosen a chair next to Jasmine's.

Derrick gave him his trademark happy-go-lucky grin. "Finally. I'm starved."

"You didn't have to wait." Bryan draped his jacket over the back of his chair and sat, enjoying the warmth of the fire just a few feet away. "Where're Sam and Eliza? They're coming, right?"

"Levi's got a cold." Michael had settled between the twins again. "Eliza told Sam to come anyway, that they'd survive without him for a couple of hours, but you know how he is."

Bryan didn't, not really. He didn't see his brothers often enough.

Maybe Michael guessed that because he explained. "Sam missed so much of Levi's life already, and he refuses to miss anything else."

Huh. Bryan didn't figure a four-year-old's sniffles could be that interesting. The old Sam hadn't exactly been involved in the lives of others. The fact that he wouldn't leave his newly found son when Levi was sick said a lot about how much Sam had changed.

Bryan grabbed the arm of the empty chair beside him. "Whose jacket is this? We probably ought to tell the server we don't need this chair. The place is packed."

Derrick said, "Actually—"

"Sorry!" The voice came from behind, and Bryan twisted.

It was the woman from outside, the blonde. His umbrella hung from her wrist by the strap.

Bryan stood. "You could've kept it."

The rest of his brothers stood as well. Mom would be proud to see the manners she'd hammered into her boys.

She met his gaze. "I'm guessing you're Bryan."

"Uh..."

"You didn't know?"

Since he had no idea what she was talking about, he felt confident saying, "Nope."

She held out the umbrella. "Do you make it a habit of giving your umbrellas to total strangers?"

"Do you make a habit of standing in the freezing rain without a jacket?"

He'd expected a grin, maybe a laugh. But her pretty smile wavered. "Extenuating circumstances. I thought it would be a short conversation. It *should've* been a short conversation. It should never have *been* a... Doesn't matter now." She stuck out her hand. "Sophia Chapman. Sophie."

Her fingers were like ice, and he had the crazy thought that he should keep ahold of them and warm them up. Instead, he released his hold and pulled out her chair. "Everything okay?"

She sat and held out her hands to the flames flickering nearby. "Someone broke into my apartment."

"Dang. What'd they get?"

Her lips slid into a frown. "It appears they took nothing."

"Uh, then how do you—?"

"My ex. He's been"—she made air quotes with her fingers—"'watching' the place for me."

That explained the contentious conversation.

Sophie's smile seemed to take some effort. "It's not important. I appreciated the umbrella." After she sat, he and his brothers did the same.

"Sophie is my friend," Leila said in her Arabic accent. "We met in Germany. She has been visiting her parents in California." Leila focused on Sophie. "What is the place called again?"

"Orange County."

"I knew it was a color." Leila smiled at her, then spoke to Bryan again. "She flew here on her way back so she could meet Jasmine and see where we are living."

"I wish the weather were a little less...typical." Bryan nodded toward the wall of windows streaked with rain. "I guess you can be thankful it isn't snowing. Yet."

"I've lived in Northern Europe for years." Sophie twisted and held her hands toward the flames dancing just a few feet away. "Your weather doesn't scare me."

"You're tougher than most California girls, I guess."

"You have no idea." Her light gray eyes sparkled, reflecting the firelight, which highlighted flecks of green and gold.

Wow.

They gave a server their drink orders and scanned the menu. Bryan had been at this restaurant a few times before and chose the first thing that caught his eye—fish and chips—then set the menu aside.

Sophie seemed to be reading every word. She glanced up and caught him watching.

Whoops.

"What do you recommend?" she asked.

"You're in Maine, so the obvious choice is lobster."

"Done." She set the menu down.

After they ordered their meals, the women carried the conversation, Leila telling Sophie about all the things she'd seen in Maine since she'd moved here. She spoke about the rolling hills and rocky coastline as if they were amazing attractions. She told her friend about the new job she'd just started, running a retreat center that Sam owned.

Bryan hadn't known anything about that.

Sophie questioned Jasmine, the quieter sister, about her life and how she liked America, and Jasmine explained things she found intriguing—like the Walmart Supercenter in Scarborough. "You can get anything you want, all in the same store. They have televisions and food and clothing and toys." Her voice was filled with awe, her accent much thicker than her sister's. Considering she'd never left Iraq until a few weeks before, her English was excellent. "All packaged up with pretty colors. We spent an hour there, and still, I did not see everything. Do they have these in Orange County?"

Sophie didn't laugh or tease at all. "We do. And Super Targets as well."

"What is...Target? This is a store, like Walmart?" She turned not to her sister but to Derrick.

"I'll take you there if you like," he said. "There's one in Portland."

She smiled, the expression both hopeful and shy. "I would like, very much."

It might be November, but romance was blooming—at least on Derrick's part. Hopefully, Jasmine returned his feelings. There was something about her that made Bryan wonder. She seemed...reticent. No, that didn't cover it. It was that, plus something else.

Fearful, maybe. Which would make sense.

She and Leila were both in danger from the men who'd hunted them across two continents. But the twin sisters were well-hidden in this little Maine town. Surely, even if the terrorists somehow figured out where they were, they wouldn't be able to get into the States, right? Their names had to be on watch lists.

Of course, anybody could waltz across the border these days. So there was that.

Perhaps fear was all Bryan read in the shy sister's expression. He definitely saw affection for his brother.

In which case, great. Bryan was happy for them.

He was.

It wasn't Derrick's fault that Bryan hadn't met a woman who interested him in years. And the last one had turned out to be so *uninteresting* that he could barely remember her name.

Their meals were delivered—seafood and onion rings and french fries piled high all around the table.

Sophie's lobster, shiny and red, was a beauty.

She looked at him with wide eyes, though, if he weren't mistaken, not wide with wonder but horror, prompting him to ask, "You have had lobster before, right?"

"Of course." But the quick shake of her head indicated the opposite. "I've tasted it, you know, in bisque. And sandwiches and salads. But it's never come"—she gestured to her plate—"like that. It's not exactly prevalent in Southern California. Or

Germany. I expected, you know, meat. On the plate. Ready to eat like...like everything else a person would order in a restaurant." She gazed at the other meals—burgers, fried fish, soup for Jasmine. Yup, all ready to eat.

"You're in for a treat," Bryan said.

She leaned away from her meal like she would an enemy. With its eyes open, its claws aimed as if preparing to attack, it did look a little menacing.

He couldn't stop a chuckle. "Would you like some help?"

Her gaze flicked to his fish and chips. "Do you want to trade?"

"No way am I depriving you of an authentic New England experience." From the table, he plucked the bib the server had left for her. "Put this on."

She unfolded it and held the thin plastic in front of her, smirking at the cartoon lobster. "You're not serious."

"Unless you want to ruin that pretty sweater."

"Fine." She tied the straps around her neck. "I don't think this can protect me if that thing goes on the attack."

On her other side, Michael cleared his throat. "I'll pray for us, and then we can dig in." He asked God to bless their food, then added, "And protect poor Sophie from her dangerous crustacean." Which brought a guffaw from Derrick.

The group echoed his amen. All but Sophie, who didn't seem amused.

"You can do this," Bryan said. "Start by gripping the tail in one hand and the body in the other." Bryan inched closer and reached to demonstrate—not actually touching the shell. "Then twist your hands in opposite directions and pull the pieces apart."

When she looked at him, her eyes seemed a little wider. Her pink lips puffed out in a pout. "Maybe you could just do it for me?"

Oh, man. Where did women learn to do that...that flirty *help me* thing? Were they born with the ability? Did she even know what she was doing?

He was tempted to agree, just to see her smile.

But he'd been resisting tempting women for years. How many pretty coeds had used similar looks in a quest for a better grade? *Couldn't you just add a few points to bring it up to an A so I can keep my perfect GPA?*

He told those coeds no. He could say no to Sophie. "How will you learn if I do it for you?"

"Why do I need to learn if I'm never going to do this again?"

"Maybe you'll love it."

She groaned, which told him she doubted that very much, but she gripped the lobster as he'd said and separated the body from the tail, exposing the beautiful white meat.

She dropped the two pieces and backed away. "Ew, what's that green stuff?"

"That's lobster too." He couldn't help the humor in his voice. "It's called the tomalley. It's intestines."

Her nose scrunched. "Disgusting."

"I hate to tell you this, Sophie, but every animal you eat has intestines."

"I prefer my meat to come on Styrofoam trays from the grocery store. Or like"—she gestured to his fish—"that."

"But this is going to be so much better. Twist off the claws and knuckles, then break them apart." Again, he demonstrated, and she did what he said, setting the pieces aside. "Good. Now grab the tail like this." He put his hands over it, thumbs on one long edge, fingers on the other. "Squeeze until it cracks. Move down the length and keep squeezing until you've cracked it all the way." She did, then opened the shell and dropped the meat onto her plate.

"Well done."

"What's next?" She must've forgotten to be horrified because she grinned at him.

He explained how to crack open the claws and knuckles with the nutcracker, then watched as she separated the meat from the shell.

"Good."

She moved the white meat to one side of her plate, the empty shells to the other. "The meat looks good, once you get it free."

"The best things in life are found on the other side of fear."

"And ickiness?" By the way one corner of her mouth ticked up, she was barely containing a grin.

"You can suck the meat out of the legs." He picked one of them up, squeezing it with his fingers, though the stubborn meat stayed inside. "You'll need to use your teeth. It's kind of like... like sucking toothpaste from a tube."

"There's a lovely picture. Consider the legs your fee for helping me."

"Maybe you'll decide to try it. For the body... a lot of people skip it altogether. You just separate the shell from the meat." She did, exposing a little meat, all the gills, and a lot more intestines. "You want to avoid the gills."

"What about"—she gestured to the tomalley—"that stuff?"

"Some say it's the best part." He leaned close and lowered his voice. "Between you and me, I think it's disgusting."

She laughed, the sound light and fresh, a sound he wanted to hear again.

Sophie Chapman. He had a feeling he wouldn't be forgetting *her* name.

Except...she lived in Germany.

With her fork, she shoved the tomalley over to join the discarded shells. "And the rest of this?" She poked at the body.

"You have to dig out the meat." Which was mixed in with more intestines and gills and membranes.

"I see why people skip it." She added the whole thing to the pile of trash. "That was a lot of work."

"Trust me. It's worth it. Go ahead." He gestured to a piece of meat from the tail. "Dip it in the butter and..."

She did, then placed the bite in her mouth.

Her eyes closed. She moaned loudly enough for the whole table to hear. Bryan figured he was the only one who heard it to his bones.

Her hand stayed by her mouth, and a drop of butter dripped down her long fingers toward her wrist. There was something about that slick butter, and her moan, and the pleasure on her face, that...

Okaaaay.

He forced his gaze away. He needed to focus on...anything else.

Michael gave him a look that said he knew exactly what Bryan was thinking. He nodded toward the table.

Right. Eat. There was nothing sexy about fish.

Bryan's fried haddock was excellent, the skinny french fries crisp and salty. But suddenly, he had a strong craving for lobster.

CHAPTER THREE

E ven the least observant person on the planet could guess these men were brothers. Sophie had known it the moment she'd laid eyes on Bryan outside.

They were all over six feet, all with dark brown hair and dark eyes. All had wide shoulders and strong chins.

But Bryan was the best-looking and easily Sophie's favorite. Any guy who'd give a total stranger an umbrella with no expectation of getting it back—just because she'd been too distracted to remember her coat?

Sophie wouldn't be forgetting Bryan Wright anytime soon.

And as distasteful as breaking into her lunch had been, he'd shown himself to be kind and patient, explaining each step without a hint of rudeness or condescension.

Good thing, because she'd had her fill of rude and condescending men.

She'd definitely had her fill of men who couldn't figure out the meaning of *I don't want to see you anymore*. Men who thought she needed them to help her. To keep an eye on her home. And let themselves in at the first sign that something might be amiss.

As if he had any right.

She tamped down a fresh wave of fury. There'd be plenty of time later to fume at her ex-boyfriend.

And worry about a break-in at her Munich apartment. Unless Felix was lying about the whole thing, which seemed entirely plausible.

She shook off all her suspicions and cut another piece of meat. She had to admit, the lobster was delicious, probably more so because she'd worked so hard for it.

Leila was telling her sister what Christmas had been like in Munich. The snow, the markets, the tourists who came from all over the world.

Bryan and Derrick explained some of their family's traditions. The Wrights, it seemed, celebrated the holiday at a vacation home on an island off the coast. They called the place "camp," but what kind of camp had room for a sixteen-foot Christmas tree?

Which they cut down themselves on the island?

They had to be exaggerating.

The whole Wright family would be there this year, including the brother who lived in Oklahoma with his wife and kids, but who was moving back to Maine soon.

Fun, the things you could learn if you just listened.

Like Sophie, Michael did more listening than talking. He couldn't seem to take his eyes off Leila, whose face was filled with wonder, absorbing the information as if there might be a test.

When Sophie had learned that not only had Leila come to America with her boyfriend, but also that they were planning to get married, she'd worried. Sure, Leila and Michael had dated for almost a year, but what did Leila actually know about the guy? Concern for her friend had prompted Sophie to change her plans and fly to Maine for a quick visit on her way back to Germany.

She needn't have worried. If the look on Michael's face was any indication of his feelings, the man was smitten.

And Leila was clearly in love. The two were kind to each other. They looked at each other with pure adoration. Not patient condescension. Certainly not possession.

Leila had found in Michael what Sophie had been craving for years. A person who loved her for her. Not for what she could do. Not for what she could add to the world.

A person who thought she was worth fighting for.

Not that she'd ever say that aloud. What twenty-first-century woman would admit to wanting to be the princess in the fairy tale?

Excitement danced in Leila's eyes as she met Sophie's. "Can you imagine? A bonfire in the snow?"

That was another of the Wright family traditions. To hear the guys tell it, the flames rose fifty feet into the air.

More hyperbole, surely.

But Sophie wasn't going to discourage her friend's enthusiasm. "Sounds amazing."

"I can't wait to see it." Leila turned to Jasmine. "Michael says we will roast marshmallows and have them with graham crackers and chocolate. They're called some-mores."

Michael chuckled. "S'mores. One syllable."

"I wish to try s'mores." Jasmine said the word slowly, as if she were tasting it on her tongue.

"You will." This from Derrick, whose grin stretched. "You'll love them."

Sophie wasn't sure about that. She'd never been a fan of the squishy, sticky treats. As a rule, she didn't enjoy getting her hands dirty when she ate.

She glanced at the empty lobster shell on her plate. Her

fingers had been within millimeters of intestines. It was a testament to the flavor of the meat that she was still eating it.

Derrick, the youngest brother, seemed happy-go-lucky.

Bryan... Now, he was a different story. Less carefree. More serious. But obviously enjoying the time with his family. Sophie had the feeling the Wrights' Christmas was loud and chaotic, filled with chatter and music and food and presents and discarded wrapping paper strewn across the floor.

Lots of laughter. Lots of love.

Add snow and a crackling fire... All they needed was a sleigh ride to make it the perfect Currier and Ives Christmas.

That was how a family should celebrate the holidays.

And what kind of horrible person compared her own family's traditions to another's? Her parents would've had a houseful of kids, if they could have. If Josie hadn't been born with severe cystic fibrosis that took all of Mom and Dad's attention.

Now it was just the three of them. Even years after Josie's death, Christmas was a day to endure, not enjoy. Like Thanksgiving. And Easter. And pretty much every special day on the calendar.

"Did you like it?" Bryan eyed Sophie's plate.

She'd eaten all the easy-to-access meat and was considering attacking the legs. She wasn't sure she could bring herself to... How had he explained it? Pull out the meat like sucking toothpaste from a tube? And use her teeth? On the shell?

Yeah...no. "I did. Thanks for your help."

"Always a pleasure to introduce a neophyte to the joy of lobster."

She laughed. "Who uses the word neophyte?"

He shrugged, maybe a little embarrassed, if the sudden color on his face were any indication.

"College professors," Michael said on her other side. "People who have to prove they're smarter than everyone else."

"I don't have to prove it," Bryan said. "Everyone already knows. I can't help it if my intellect shines through."

Michael's eyebrows hiked. "Especially when you pick words like neophyte." To Sophie, he said, "You should tell him what you do. I think he'll be interested."

She turned back to Bryan, curious as to why he might be.

"Let's hear it," Bryan said. "I'm interested already." At that last remark, the tinge of pink on his cheeks deepened to red. "In your job, I mean." He cleared his throat and sipped his water.

She had a sudden, almost irrepressible desire to giggle. Could he be interested *in her*?

Not that it mattered, considering he lived here and she lived in Germany. Too far away for a guy like him to bother.

Bryan set his water down. "Well?"

"I minister to refugees in Munich."

His face brightened. "That's how you met Leila?"

"She was volunteering as well. There are tens of thousands of refugees—many from Arab nations, like Leila and Jasmine. The country is generous to let them in, but the people need more than the government can provide. The ministry I work for does what we can for those who walk in the door."

"And tells them about Jesus," Leila added from Michael's other side. "This is why I volunteered there. I don't wish to only give away food and clothes and help people find jobs. I wish to tell people about the One True God."

Bryan's gaze was intense. "That must be so rewarding."

"I can't imagine doing anything else. I've heard the most heart-wrenching stories. What the refugees have endured...it's unimaginable. And then they discover Jesus. There's nothing like watching a former Muslim get baptized and experience the freedom of Christ for the first time."

"Wow." He sounded genuinely interested. "I'd love to be a part of something like that."

Sophie smiled at Michael. He must've understood Bryan's desire to get involved.

But the older brother said, "I meant the other thing you do. Your paying job."

"Oh. That's not nearly as interesting." She turned back to Bryan. "I work at a museum designing art exhibits."

"Really? Which one?"

"I doubt you've heard of it."

"You'd be surprised." Michael's words were droll, almost bored.

Bryan flicked him a narrow-eyed glare.

"I work at the München Meisterwerke Galerie."

"No kidding!" His eyes brightened as if that were the best news he'd heard all year. "They're about to have an exhibit of Babylonian artifacts. I've been dying to get over to check it out."

"Um...why?"

He laughed. "I'm an antiquities professor. Ancient Middle Eastern artifacts are my specialty."

"And here I thought you were interesting." Whoa. Had she said that? Teasing him like they were old friends?

"Wow." He pressed his hands to his chest. "I'm wounded." But he was grinning. "I know it's not the most fascinating thing to study, but I enjoy it."

"He was obsessed with *Raiders of the Lost Ark* when we were kids," Michael said.

"Oh, my gosh," Derrick said. "That scene with the invisible steps and the...what was it, a cup or something? He must've watched that movie a thousand times."

"*The Last Crusade.*" Bryan shook his head, clearly horrified at his brother's ignorance. "It was an invisible *bridge* and the *Holy Grail.* You know, the vessel Jesus passed around at the Last Supper? Have you heard of that?"

Derrick gave Sophie a raised-eyebrow look as if to say, *See what I mean?*

Sophie giggled, then slapped her hand over her mouth.

"Oh, fine," Bryan said. "Join pick-on-Bryan day, why don't you?"

Leila was shaking her head, amusement playing on her lips. Sitting between Derrick and Bryan, Jasmine grinned.

They were all so...happy to be together. So free and unguarded. What would it be like to enjoy that kind of relationship with her family?

Bryan sent his brothers a glare, but he obviously wasn't mad. To Sophie, he said, "Tell me about the collection."

She shrugged. "It was donated anonymously a few months ago, and it's going to Iraq after the exhibit."

"Anonymously?" Michael asked. "That's strange."

She turned to him. "By the provenance, it's clear that the items were looted from the National Museum in Iraq. They've been missing for years."

"Since April of 2003," Bryan supplied.

"That's right." Michael closed his eyes a moment, nodding, "I remember that story."

"It happened after Baghdad fell, but before the US secured the city." Bryan leaned toward his brother—and Sophie, who sat between them. "There was still fighting, or so I've heard. The museum employees abandoned the place for thirty-six hours. In that time, thousands of pieces were stolen and eventually squirreled out of the country. I think they've gotten back"—he looked at Sophie—"about half?"

"Something like that. Our collection came from London. There was a huge bust up there early this year, and a bunch of people were charged and sent to prison. The working theory is that the people who possessed the items donated to the museum decided it wasn't worth the risk of being caught with them."

"Really?" By Michael's smirk, he was skeptical. "I've never known thieves to willingly hand over what they've stolen."

"My understanding," Bryan said, "was that they couldn't sell these pieces. Most of the time, when something like that is stolen, the thieves already have a buyer. But these people were just opportunists, taking advantage of the chaos. They snatched and grabbed and ran. They probably sold everything they could, but the international art community has been searching for the missing items." To Sophie, he said, "I think the items at your museum are some of the most recognizable."

"That's what they say." Sophie had never cared that much about ancient artifacts. They were interesting, of course. Anything that'd been around for thousands of years was historically significant.

But was it *artistically* significant?

Sophie had an art degree. Her interests lay more with paintings. Her favorites were impressionists. Not exactly the coolest style to study these days, but she'd always had a fondness for beauty. She'd take Renoir over Warhol any day of the week.

Not that old clay idols weren't beautiful.

Except...they weren't.

"When are they going to be returned to Iraq?" Michael asked.

Again, Sophie didn't have a definitive answer. "Before the end of the year, I think."

"That soon?" Bryan asked.

Michael leaned toward him. "You should go this weekend. You've got a few days off. Those pieces will be easier to see in Munich than Baghdad." He tipped his head toward Sophie. "And I bet she could get you access to all the pieces, not just what's on display."

Bryan turned to his brother, and from her seat, she could only glimpse a little of the look he gave him, but his eyebrows were raised and his lips were turned down at the corners. He was displeased? Or...something else?

Michael either didn't see it or chose to ignore it. To her, he said, "You could do that, right?"

"For sure," Sophie said. "I'd love to."

Had Bryan even heard her? He seemed too busy glaring at his brother.

Warmth filled Sophie's cheeks. What was she doing, inviting a man to visit her in Europe? A man she'd just met? A guy shows her the slightest kindness—an umbrella and lobster-eating instructions—and now she was throwing herself at him?

No wonder he looked uncomfortable.

But it was too late to rescind the invitation. Not that it mattered. It wasn't as if Bryan was about to buy a last-minute flight to Germany to look at a bunch of old clay jars.

On Michael's other side, Leila said, "You should go, Bryan. You'd like the Christmas market. It is a great time to visit Munich. I'm sure Sophie could show you around." To Sophie, she said, "Unless you are too busy."

Sophie shook her head but spoke to Bryan, trying to make light of the situation. "Do they always work so hard to get rid of you?"

"Hmm. I should be used to it by now."

"If you do decide to travel to Germany someday—"

"Could you really get me access to all the artifacts?"

"Of course. And I'd be happy to show you around the city."

He shifted to speak to Leila. "Do you think I'll be able to get a hotel room? I know it's a touristy time of year."

"I can find you a room," she said. "No problem."

"Seems like all the pieces are falling into place," Bryan said. "Funny how that happens sometimes."

Funny. Yet Bryan didn't seem the slightest bit amused. Leaving Sophie to wonder...what was she missing?

CHAPTER FOUR

After lunch, Bryan drove straight to Sam's house and rang the bell.

A good ninety seconds passed before the door swung open.

"Hey, Bry. Come on in." Sam stepped aside, and Bryan entered the two-story foyer. He had no idea how much money his brother had accumulated, but if this house overlooking the Atlantic was any indication, it was a significant amount.

Bryan couldn't remember the last time he'd seen this brother in casual clothes. Even when they got together as a family, Sam wore expensive-looking jeans, cashmere sweaters, and Italian loafers. Today, he had on sweatpants and a sweatshirt and didn't seem a bit self-conscious about his attire as he gave Bryan a back-slapping hug. "Didn't know you were coming over." He closed the door. "Sorry we missed lunch. Levi's sick."

"Nothing serious, I hope."

"I wanted to take him to the doctor, but Eliza says it's just a cold. You staying here tonight? We have plenty of room."

"I'll go to Mom and Dad's. I just need to talk to Michael."

Sam flicked his gaze toward the kitchen. "I don't think he's here."

"He was going to drop the twins and Sophie off. I'll wait, if that's okay."

Sam grinned. "Anytime. You need food or a drink?"

"Nope." Bryan lifted his laptop bag. "I can keep myself busy if you're in the middle of something."

Sam's gaze flicked to the staircase. "Eliza's taking a nap. I was reading to Levi, but if you—"

"Go. I'm fine."

"If you're sure." Sam started up the stairs, calling back over his shoulder. "Help yourself to whatever you need."

"Thanks." Bryan walked the wide, marble-floored hallway into the gourmet kitchen—all granite and stainless appliances—and set himself up at the table in front of a wall of windows.

On clear days, the view was spectacular, but today the little cove at the bottom of the hill was barely visible through the mist and rain.

He opened his laptop and searched for flights to Munich.

Yikes.

This was not going to be cheap.

But Michael wasn't wrong. It would be much easier to see the artifacts before they were returned to Baghdad. Not only that, but if Bryan didn't take this opportunity, he'd probably only get to see what was on display in Iraq. Sophie could get him access to the entire collection.

Though, honestly, he could get access without her help. He was well known in the community of antiquities professors.

He'd intended to go to Munich during spring break. Last he'd heard, the artifacts wouldn't be returned to Iraq until summer. Since the timeline had changed, he needed to adjust his plans if he wanted to see the collection.

Even considering the cost of flights, it would be wise to go now.

The fact that Michael had seemed to be pushing him into this trip was beside the point.

Mostly beside the point.

He chose a flight that left the following night so he could celebrate Thanksgiving with his family before the long drive south to Boston.

But he wasn't going to book it until he had some answers.

Finally, Michael came in through the door between the garage and the kitchen.

Bryan stood. "Fess up, bro."

Michael didn't seem surprised by Bryan's tone as he closed the door. "Where's Sam?"

"Upstairs with Levi. Eliza's resting. It's just you and me, so don't try to pretend you don't have ulterior motives for pushing me to go to Germany."

Michael snagged a water bottle from the refrigerator. "Want one?"

"I'm fine."

Michael twisted the cap off and took a sip. "Wasn't going to pretend anything. Come on." Michael led the way to the opposite wing—Sam's house had *wings*—to the den.

Bryan had only seen this small, private living area a couple of times, and only when he'd glimpsed it on his way to Sam's office.

Like all the main rooms in the house, a wall of windows overlooked the cove, interrupted by a door that opened to the deck stretching along the back of the house. The main living area near the front door had a formal feel, but this room was comfortable and reflected Sam's personality. An oversize sectional faced a stone fireplace and flatscreen TV mounted above the mantel. The walls boasted, among other things, a framed Celtics jersey signed by one of the legends, a poster of Fenway Park, and a blown-up picture of Sam on his motocross motorcycle. Bookcases displayed well-worn books and auto-graphed footballs and baseballs.

There were photographs everywhere—of the six Wright brothers, of their parents, of a younger Eliza, and seven or eight Bryan had never seen, all showing off Eliza or Levi or both.

"Sam doesn't mind?" Bryan asked. Their brother could be obsessive about his private space.

"He's changed." Michael sat on a recliner.

Bryan settled on the sectional, toed off his shoes, and propped his aching leg on the coffee table. "I guess a woman'll do that."

Michael grinned, but the expression faded fast. He leaned forward and rested his forearms on his legs. "I haven't told you much about my job."

"That's the thing about being a spy, right?"

"Agent."

Was there a difference?

"I can't share much. But I need your help with something."

"Okaaaay." Because really, how could an antiquities professor possibly help a CIA agent?

"It needs to stay between us."

"No problem."

"I mean it, Bryan. You can't tell anybody. Not our brothers or our parents or friends or people you work with."

"I know what 'between us' means."

Michael lowered his gaze to the floor.

When the silence stretched to uncomfortable, Bryan said, "What's going on?"

His brother looked up. "I was ordered not to find Leila."

"I didn't know that." Bryan noticed tension between Michael and his team when he and Derrick had flown to Lesvos to pick up Michael, Leila, and Jasmine. Thanks to Michael, the sisters were now safe from the people who'd been chasing them.

"I didn't feel like I had a choice," Michael said. "The point is, I'm on thin ice with my team leader." He smirked—a trademark look for Michael. "I swear, if I say the sky is blue, Brock'll insist it's red—and call me a fool for not seeing it. Not that I blame him. I did disobey orders. And we still haven't figured out exactly what's going on. To be fair, we've gotten a lot of conflicting information."

"To be fair," Bryan said, "I have no idea what you're talking about."

"Sorry. If Brock found out I was telling you this, I'd be in serious trouble, and the last thing I need is to go against orders again, but I don't see another option."

"I can't imagine how I can help you, but I'll do what I can. I'd be honored, not just to help you, but if I thought I could do something for my country..." Bryan had, once upon a time, wanted to join the military. Of course, he'd been a little kid the first time the notion had come to him. His injury had kept him from fulfilling that dream.

It shouldn't bother him that Grant had been a Green Beret, and now he knew Michael was a CIA agent. Bryan's brothers were living his dream while he taught ancient history to bored college students.

There he went again, feeling sorry for himself.

"I wouldn't ask you to do this if I had another choice."

"Gosh, you know how to make a guy feel important."

Michael chuckled. "Sorry. I don't mean it that way. I'm not in the business of dragging my brothers into my work. It was one thing when we needed to save Leila and Jasmine, but for this..."

"What is 'this'?"

"I've spent a year tracking the movements of a terrorist. Until I rescued Leila from Iraq, I didn't know the guy's real name. He's the one who kidnapped her—an old friend of her father's."

Leila's father was friends with a terrorist? Bryan had known the people chasing her and her twin were bad guys, but terrorists?

"The guy's name is Khalid Qasim," Michael said. "He's working with Leila's uncle, Hasan Mahmoud. We believe the two of them are plotting an attack in Europe. The problem is that the information we have is conflicting. The evidence Brock and the team uncovered—the evidence he thinks is the most telling—indicates that the attack is going to take place in Brussels or Amsterdam. But based on a map Leila saw and some things Jasmine overheard in Iraq, I'm convinced the attack is going to take place in Munich."

In Munich. Where Sophie lived.

Bryan still couldn't figure out how he could possibly help, but at least they were closing in on it. And if Sophie might be in danger, he'd do whatever he could to help.

Because she was Leila's friend, of course. Not because of his reaction to her at lunch.

Michael stood and paced. "The team thinks the map and all the chatter about Munich were related to Leila's family trying to track her down, but I disagree." He wore a path in front of the windows. "I followed Qasim in Munich for a year, and I never sensed that he was looking for someone. He was meeting with locals, some of whom are on the watch list. They were plotting something."

"But he did find Leila."

"Accidentally. I think." Michael paused and studied him for a minute. "As long as I'm telling you things I shouldn't... It's just a matter of time before it's obvious, and I think it'll make more sense if you know..."

It couldn't make *less* sense. Bryan stifled the urge to tell Michael to finish at least one thought before he skipped to another.

"Jasmine is pregnant."

Whoa. "Wait. What?" Didn't even make sense. She'd been held captive—by her family, right? Wasn't that what Michael just said?

"There's more." Michael perched on the arm of the sofa. "See, Khalid Qasim..."

When his voice trailed off, Bryan wondered if this was a test to see if he was paying attention. "The terrorist you were watching."

"Right." Michael blew out a breath. "He's Jasmine's husband."

Bryan sat back, stunned. "She's married. To a terrorist?" At Michael's nod, he asked, "Does Derrick know?"

Michael shook his head. "And you can't tell him. The terrorist part is top secret. And her condition... When Jasmine chooses to reveal her situation is up to her. From what I can tell, she loathes Qasim. Her father forced her to marry him. My theory is that Qasim, while he was in Munich, saw Leila and recognized her."

"Because she's identical to his wife."

"Exactly. He's an old friend of her father, so he knew about Leila and that she escaped her family a decade ago. I think he was in Munich putting together some plot and happened to see her, not that he was in Munich looking for her."

"Makes sense."

"But Brock thinks Qasim was looking for her. And no matter how much I insist..." Michael ran a hand down his short beard.

"You say blue, he says red."

"He's never liked me. Never wanted me on his team. Since I went to Iraq against his orders, he's been dying to find a way to get rid of me. He's just waiting for me to live up to my call sign."

Michael's call sign was *Wrong.*

"Sorry, man. That's unfortunate, especially considering you were saving your girlfriend."

"I should've trusted him."

Knowing how many secrets Michael had kept over the years, Bryan couldn't resist his sarcastic, "Because you've always been so trusting."

A burst of laughter escaped Michael's lips. "That's my superpower. Trust." His amusement didn't last. "I should have trusted my team. I don't know what would've happened, but the way I handled it... Leila and Jasmine could've died—or been lost forever. I'm so grateful to you. If you hadn't seen them—"

"That was all God. I was just sitting there, praying He would reveal them to me."

"But you were *there*. And I can't even..." Michael swallowed hard.

"They're safe. You risked everything, and it worked out. I know you don't want to lose your job—"

"I don't care about that." He pushed up from his perch and paced again. "Now that we're planning to get married, the last thing I want to do is spend my life overseas. Or even in Washington. Another year and I can retire and start a new career. But not until Qasim and Mahmoud are stopped. In custody or dead. Either way works for me."

"Do you think they're still looking for the twins? I know we're keeping their whereabouts secret, but is that just a precaution, or—"

"Jasmine's carrying Qasim's kid," Michael said. "What do you think?"

"Good point."

"I don't think they have any idea where Leila and Jasmine are. From what we can tell, they've given up the search for now, focused on whatever it is they're planning."

"And this is where I come in," Bryan guessed, though he still couldn't imagine how he could help thwart a terrorist plot.

Michael settled on the chair again. "When Leila was in Iraq, she saw a map of Munich on a desk and remembered a couple of intersections that were circled. Those intersections are in Old Town."

Which was where the museum Sophie worked for was located. But so were a whole lot of other things.

"We asked Jasmine about the different businesses and tourist attractions near those intersections to see if she'd ever heard them mentioned by anyone at the compound where she lived. The only thing that she was certain she'd heard was the name of that museum—the München Meisterwerke Galerie."

"You figured out they have all those artifacts—"

"Stolen from Iraq. There must be something in the collection of interest to them."

"Why, though?"

"You tell me."

Bryan shrugged. "*I* think they're fascinating."

"Thank you, Indiana Jones."

Bryan didn't mind being compared to the famous—if fictional—archeologist. "From what I know about what was donated, most of the items in that collection are from long before the establishment of Islam. Of course, Christians are interested in things unrelated to Christianity and Judaism, so it could just be that—it's their heritage and needs to be returned to Iraq. But that's the plan already, so why bother trying to get them back while they're still in Germany?" He shook his head. "These guys are Muslims, right?" At Michael's nod, he pressed. "Are they devout?"

"To the degree that they're willing to kill for their belief, I'd say so."

"Right. But... I mean, lots of Muslims aren't violent. Lots of strong-believing Muslims insist their religion is one of peace. People justify all sorts of evil by claiming they're doing it for God when true believers who really know God understand He'd never approve. I'm sure there're Muslims who do the same."

"Your point?"

"I guess it doesn't really matter whether they are or not. Only that... Do you remember those videos of ISIS destroying statues in Mosel?"

Michael's eyebrows hiked. "I probably don't follow museum news as closely as you do."

"It was 2015. They broke into a museum and took sledge-hammers—even jackhammers—to ancient statues because they were idols worshiped by their ancestors and therefore offensive to Allah. Not all Muslims feel that way about artifacts, but the militants seem to."

"Okay."

"The antiquities at the Meisterwerke Galerie aren't all idols, but a lot of them are. So why would devout Muslims be trying to get their hands on them?"

"Again," Michael said, "you tell me. You know more about those pieces than I do. What's your best guess?"

Bryan considered the question. He wasn't familiar with every piece in the collection, but he knew the more famous pieces. They were historically significant and not without value. But there were certainly *more* valuable things a person could collect. Or steal in order to sell, if that was the plan. "I can't possibly guess."

Michael leaned toward him. "That's why I need you to look at the collection, see if you can figure out what might interest them. Look for something unique or something that doesn't fit."

"You think the big thing they're planning for Munich is a gallery heist?"

"I think the gallery has something to do with it. I wouldn't ask you if I thought there was any danger. But there's no way they'll be able to connect you to me. The only terrorists who got a look at me were killed on that boat in the Med last month, and even they didn't get a good look. I've never used my real name or told anyone where I'm from. My cover is solid."

"Sophie knows."

A dark look crossed Michael's face. "Where we live, yeah. And that wasn't my choice, but Leila..." Again, the smirk. "They're best friends. I've done my homework on her, and there are no red flags. Even so, bringing her here was a risk. Not one I would have taken, but Leila contacted her without telling me."

"Ah."

"She doesn't know what I do, though. Leila hasn't shared that much. And you can't, either. If you get any bad feelings about Sophie, separate yourself right away. And let me know."

Bryan had experienced a lot of feelings about Sophie in the hours since he'd met her, but none of them had been bad.

In fact, he very much looked forward to spending time with her in Munich.

"Also." Michael grabbed an envelope off the coffee table and held it out. "Leila wants you to give this to her friend Aaron. He works at the mission where she volunteered."

Bryan took the letter. "I found a flight that leaves late tomorrow night. I'll head to Boston after dinner."

"I'll pay you back."

Bryan pushed to his feet. "Nope. This is on me, and I'm happy to do it. I just hope I can help."

CHAPTER FIVE

S omething wasn't right.

Thursday morning, Sophie turned in a slow circle in the center of her living room, remembering her conversation with her ex-boyfriend the day before.

Felix had claimed her apartment door had been ajar when he'd stopped by. That somebody must've broken in.

Maybe.

She was exhausted after her overnight flight from Boston, but she needed to deal with this.

She'd hoped the building manager had needed access for some reason and had forgotten to lock it, but she'd texted him the day before, and he'd assured her that he hadn't been in her apartment since she left.

Everything was where it should be. Her TV was still mounted to the wall, the router and modem beside it.

But something wasn't right.

The kitchen counters were clean. The few things she displayed there—her favorite cookbooks, a pretty wooden charcuterie board, and a photo of Sophie and her sister—were exactly where she'd left them.

On the opposite side of the small common room, the throw pillows were propped on her white sofa, as usual. The curtains hung beside the tall windows. The blinds were angled to let in a little light but block the view of people in neighboring buildings. Blankets were rolled up and tucked in a wicker basket in the corner.

She pulled her suitcase down the hall to her bedroom and checked her jewelry box. When she found nothing missing, she opened her bureau drawer.

Her museum badge was exactly where it was supposed to be.

Everything looked untouched.

On her way back to the living area, she glanced into her studio. All her paintings were still there, but...one was sideways.

Her heart rate kicked up.

She returned to the living area, and the magazines stacked on the coffee table snagged her attention.

After she'd finished packing the evening before she left for the States, she'd flipped through the one that had come in the mail that day—the Christmas issue. But based on the pastel flowers on the cover she could see, a summer issue was on top.

A small thing. A tiny thing.

But proof.

Somebody had been here. Somebody had gone through her magazines. And looked at her paintings. And...what else?

She couldn't imagine her sixty-something maintenance man showing interest in old issues of *Elle Decor*. And he was the only other person with a key.

Well, the only other person who was *supposed* to have a key.

A knock had her nearly jumping out of her skin. After checking the deadbolt to make sure it was engaged, she said, "Who is it?"

"It's me."

Felix.

She'd been home approximately five minutes. Excellent timing? Doubtful. She opened the door. "What are you doing here, Felix?"

He stood a few inches north of six feet with sandy blond hair brushed to one side and green eyes. He had a strong chin and a long, Romanesque nose.

She'd once thought him handsome. She was over it.

He worked to hide the hurt in his expression at her harsh tone. "How vas your flight?" Despite his German accent, he spoke excellent English.

"Long." She held out her hand, palm up. "Give me the keys."

"May I come in?"

"No."

He blinked, clearly surprised. Since their breakup, she'd gone out of her way to be nice to him. Too nice, apparently.

"It vas good I had zem. I vas able to lock up—"

"I have a landlord, Felix. He could've locked up."

"You vould not have known about the intruder if not for me. You should thank me."

"I'll thank you to give me my keys."

"You need somebody to look after you."

She didn't respond and didn't lower her arm.

Finally, he dug into his pocket. He took his time removing two keys from his keyring and then plopped them in her palm. "Zis is a mistake. Who vill take care of you?"

She fisted them. "Did you make any more?"

"I am not trying to... I only vant to protect you."

"I don't need your protection. I don't need you to watch my apartment when I'm gone."

His shoulders hunched. "You said ve could be friends."

"Friends don't make copies of friends' keys without their knowledge. Friends don't enter friends' apartments without permission."

"Vat if there had been an intruder? You could have been hurt."

"You could've gotten the building manager. Or called the police. What were you doing here?"

His Adam's apple dipped and rose. "You hadn't been at the center, and I thought... I miss you."

When Sophie had broken up with him, she'd done her best to close the door to a relationship but to keep their friendship intact.

A mistake, apparently.

On the phone the day before, Felix had claimed he'd stopped by her apartment and found the door ajar. He'd knocked, and when she didn't answer, let himself in. Guessing she'd gone to visit her parents for Thanksgiving, he'd taken the liberty of looking around to see if anything was missing. And then he'd locked up for her.

He obviously hadn't realized when he told her the story that she was smart enough to figure out that, if he locked her doors, then he must have made copies of her keys.

Maybe the rules for dating were different in Germany than in the States, but she couldn't imagine that making copies of someone's keys without their permission was acceptable in any culture.

"Is anything missing?" he asked.

"I haven't been here long enough to look. If there is, I'll alert the authorities."

His eyes brightened. "I have a friend who vorks—"

"I don't need your help, Felix. I don't need you to check on me. I'll see you at the center." She gripped the door to close it.

But he blocked it. "I love you, Sophia. You and I are—"

"Done. We're done. It's time for you to accept that." She gave his hand, pressed against the door over her head, a pointed look.

He dropped his arm. "I love you."

"I'm sorry." She stepped inside, shut the door, and engaged the deadbolt, just to be safe.

Except, was she?

If Felix had another set of keys, he could still get inside. Not that she believed he'd hurt her. She'd only ever felt safe with him. Well, safe and smothered, but never in physical danger.

But if he had been the one to break into her apartment, perhaps she didn't know him at all.

She needed to change the locks. And get an alarm with a video camera.

She'd broken up with Felix five months before—and this was why. He'd named his hovering behavior *devotion*.

She named it *possession*, and she wouldn't put up with it.

So, had there been an intruder?

Or had Felix used his key to let himself in and go through her things and then covered his tracks by claiming he'd found the door unlocked?

Had Felix graduated from *devoted ex-boyfriend* to *stalker*?

And if so, what could she do about it?

At the Munich airport the following morning, Sophie climbed out of her car and walked around it to the curb.

Bryan had taken the same flight she'd arrived on the day before, though when he exited the airport into the chilly morning, he looked a lot fresher after the overnight trip than she had.

He pulled a suitcase with one hand, leaning on a cane with the other while he scanned the area. She thought she'd detected a slight limp when she'd met him Wednesday. It was more pronounced now.

She waved, and he headed toward her, smiling.

"Thanks so much for meeting me."

"Happy to do it."

They got his suitcase in the trunk and headed toward Munich. "Did you sleep at all?"

He yawned, then chuckled. "Not enough, I guess."

"Try to stay awake until bedtime. Leila got you a room at the hotel where she used to work, but it won't be ready until late this afternoon."

"No problem. I'll see if they can store my bag and then take in some sights until check-in."

"Or," Sophie said, "we can go to the museum. The curator's already given permission for you to view the collection, but you'll need a badge. We can do that today so tomorrow, once you're rested, you can get started."

"That'd be great. Is there a bathroom where I can change my clothes, at least? I hate to meet anybody looking—and smelling—like this."

"You smell great." Like sandalwood and something uniquely masculine and yummy and... She clamped down on her thoughts as heat filled her cheeks. "I mean, not bad."

"I'll take 'not bad,' I guess."

"But I don't blame you for wanting to change." She could let him use the museum's employee bathroom, but it was barely larger than the one he could've used on the airplane.

She could take him to the hotel. She'd been there many times to visit Leila and had no doubt the new manager would let Bryan use the bathroom in the lobby and store his things until he could check in. But it was public. And unlike the buildings in Old Town, the hotel was *actually* old, having escaped the bombings during the war. Sophie assumed the public bathroom off the lobby had once been a coat closet.

There was one obvious solution. The fact that she was reluctant to suggest it had nothing to do with the man beside her and everything to do with Felix and his weird behavior.

Bryan wasn't Felix.

He was her best friend's future brother-in-law. He'd given Sophie—a total stranger at the time—his umbrella out of pure kindness. Surely, he wasn't the stalker type.

And anyway, he lived in Maine. How much stalking could a guy do from North America?

Even after the mental pep talk, it took a bit of courage to say, "You can get cleaned up at my apartment, and then we'll walk to the museum."

"That'd be great. As long as you let me buy you lunch as a thank-you."

"Deal."

The traffic was heavy but moving. It was a typical November day in Germany, meaning cold and gray. Maybe it would brighten up a little over the weekend, even if the temperature wouldn't reach forty.

"You had a break-in, right?" Bryan asked. "Was much stolen?"

"Nothing, as far as I can tell, but someone was definitely there."

"How do you know?"

"You'll think I'm crazy, but there were a few things that were just...off. A book on the wrong shelf. A canvas that should have been propped up-and-down but was sideways. You know... landscape instead of portrait."

"Why would somebody come in, move your stuff around, but not take anything?"

She had a good idea who'd done it and why, but Bryan didn't need to know about her ex. "I'm having an alarm with a camera installed tomorrow. If it happens again, I'll be able to answer that."

If Bryan had any more questions, he didn't ask. Instead, he gazed out the window at the passing landscape—trees and fields all around, covered with a light dusting of snow. It was flat here, mostly farmland, but if it were a clear day, they'd see the Alps in the distance. They could be on the slopes in Austria in an hour and a half.

He yawned again, then chuckled. "You're going to have to keep me awake. Why Munich? Of all the places in the world you could live, why here?"

"It started when I was a kid. My mom got pregnant with my little sister when I was seven. Before Josie was born, Mom and Dad and I went to Europe for a few weeks. They wanted one last trip before the baby was born."

"A babymoon," Bryan said.

"I love that you know that term."

"I'm up on all the hip things the youngsters are doing these days."

She laughed. "Like you're a senior citizen. What are you, thirty?"

"Thirty-four."

Which made him a year older than she was. Unlike Felix, who was a few years younger.

Not that she was comparing them, as if Bryan might be boyfriend material. She wasn't exactly looking for a new boyfriend, especially considering she hadn't figured out how to get rid of her old one.

"One of my TAs and her husband went to Jamaica when

she was about six months pregnant," Bryan said. "She used the term."

"That makes sense. So my parents wanted a babymoon, though I don't think they called it that. We toured all over Germany, Austria, and Switzerland, and I fell in love. Especially with Switzerland. You ever been there?"

"I haven't. I'd love to go, though. If you fell in love with Switzerland, why do you live in Munich?"

"Switzerland's cost of living makes Munich seem downright cheap. And there were other factors. I got the job offer at the museum, for one. I guess the biggest thing is that I came to the refugee center on a mission trip when I was in college, so I already knew a few people here. I wanted to be a part of the work the center was doing."

"I'd like to hear more about that."

"I'll show you if you want. It's not far from where I live. We can go this afternoon, after the museum. Starting tomorrow, I'll have to dive into work to get ready for the exhibit."

"I appreciate that. I'm sure you're busy."

"Not really." Plus, her boss had asked her to show Bryan around the city. He was hoping Bryan would write a paper about the antiquities and speak of the museum in glowing terms.

She certainly hadn't complained about the assignment. Spending time with Bryan felt like anything but work.

He was quiet as they reached Munich, seeming to take it all in.

Because of the foot traffic, she had to slow down considerably as they entered *Altstadt*—Old Town—the historic city center. The buildings here were originally constructed in medieval times, then rebuilt after the bombings in World War II to look as they had for centuries before.

Sophie's car was barely inching along now, thanks to all the vehicles and people. She pointed down a narrow road. "The Hofbräuhaus is that way. You've heard of it?"

"Who hasn't?" He peered, but it was impossible to see much of the famous beer hall from here.

"It's more crowded than usual because of the Christmas market in Marienplatz."

"Mary's Square," he said.

"You speak German?"

"Did my homework on the flight. The buildings *look* old."

"I assume you know they aren't."

"I read that last night. I love that the city tried to recreate what it was like before the war."

"Since I live in one of those buildings," Sophie said, "I'm glad they're fairly new—and by 'new,' I mean almost eighty years old. But eighty is better than hundreds of years. They have heat and electricity and good insulation and plumbing—and were built with all those things in mind."

"You live here, in Old Town? I'd think it'd be pretty pricey."

"Isn't cheap. Before I moved, my mother came with me to look at apartments. She wanted me within walking distance of work and the refugee center—and in a safe part of town. Not that Munich is a dangerous city, but you know moms. She pays the lion's share of the rent."

"Generous."

"Yeah. Very." That trip to Munich was the most time Sophie had spent with her mother in years. There'd been all sorts of promises at the time about how she and Dad would come to visit often. But they hadn't. Not once.

Her parents were doing their best. Sophie knew that. But there was a tiny part of her that resented their grief. Fourteen years had passed since they'd lost Josie. Her death had devastated all three of them.

But Mom and Dad still had a daughter. Rather than pouring

all the love they'd heaped on Josie onto Sophie, they almost acted as if Sophie had died that day too.

Their family had been buried with Sophie's little sister. Whoever said time healed all wounds had no idea what he was talking about.

So yes, Mom and Dad were generous. They gave her money. They'd bought her this little BMW so she'd have a car in Europe. She never wanted for anything. Except their love.

CHAPTER SIX

The city was amazing, decked out for Christmas. Old buildings, cobblestone streets, colorful shops, and people everywhere.

Bryan hadn't known much about Munich until he'd boarded the night before. He'd spent the first couple of hours of the flight researching, thanks to in-flight Wi-Fi. The city began with a market back in the twelfth century. Ironic, considering the market—the Christmas market, in this case—was still going strong, and in the same place it'd been nine hundred years before.

There were a lot more places to shop than a little farmers market these days. High-end boutiques, clothing stores, and souvenir shops lined the sidewalks, interspersed with coffee shops and restaurants and bars, all offering, from what he could tell, everything a person could want.

Sophie focused on the road, dodging pedestrians who darted across the street—not Germans, he assumed, who were known for their love of order. From the look of the crowd of people crossing in front of them now, hauling sacks emblazoned with store names, he guessed they were Americans.

Sophie parked in an underground garage, and he grabbed his suitcase and followed her to an elevator.

She opened the door to her third-floor apartment, and he stepped inside, taking it in. Parquet flooring stretched across the smallish room that held a couple of white sofas catty-corner to each other with brightly-colored pillows placed just so. Over the longer sofa, a giant painting depicted a little village—Swiss, if he had to guess—with snowcapped mountains in the background. It was mesmerizing. It wasn't old—that was obvious, considering one of the villagers was scrolling on a cell phone. But it was painted in an older style—like a Renoir? Not that he knew much about fine art.

The picture took up almost the entire wall.

The clatter of keys had him shaking out of his stupor. He continued the scan of the room.

A blue blanket that matched the blues in the painting was draped over one arm of the sofa, and though it looked pretty there, he figured it was more for use on cold nights than for show. A round coffee table displayed magazines. A colorful area rug brought the living room together and separated it visually from the kitchen.

The kitchen took up the other end of the room, with white cabinets, stainless steel appliances, and a mosaic backsplash in shades of blue. A rectangular table had four chairs. Beneath each of the three oversize, old-fashioned windows sat a radiator that looked straight out of the fifties.

The space was both elegant and welcoming, like the woman he was getting to know.

Sophie opened the narrow refrigerator. "Water?"

"Sure. I like your apartment."

She handed him a bottle. "It's home."

That was exactly what it was. If he'd had the idea that

Sophie's time in Germany was meant to be temporary, this place belied that.

He palmed open the top of the bottle and downed about half the liquid inside. He hadn't realized how thirsty he was.

She grinned. "Let me get you a towel." She disappeared down the hall and returned a moment later, holding out a fluffy white one.

"Thanks. You sure it's okay?"

"Positive. Feel free to use whatever you find in there."

He dragged his suitcase down the hall. The bathroom was larger than he'd expected, with a giant bathtub, though the glass-walled shower was tiny. It took some maneuvering to get himself clean without spraying water all over the place.

Twenty minutes later, he headed toward the living room. Nothing like a shower to make a man feel like he'd slept—even when he hadn't.

He peeked into a room on his left, then paused and took a second look.

It was filled with canvases. One was propped on an easel. Some hung on the walls. The rest were leaning along the edges of the room. Many of them looked unfinished. A mountain with no sky behind it. Village buildings with no doors or windows.

The canvas on the easel depicted a crowd of people in a park surrounded by houses and businesses with steep roofs and window boxes overflowing with flowers. Trees edging the town square sported light green leaves, and tulips blossomed in patches all around. Snowcapped peaks rose in the background, but the focus of the painting was the people. Some were seated on blankets, enjoying a picnic. Others were rushing past, looking worried or at least hurried.

But where bodies should be, there were only swaths of paint, thick lines waiting to be filled in.

"Now you know my secret."

Bryan cringed. "Sorry. I shouldn't have..." He faced her, relaxing when he saw her smiling. "What secret?"

"I like to start things. I'm not so good at the finishing part."

He turned back to the room and reached for the light switch. Before he touched it, he said, "Is it okay?"

"Go ahead."

He flicked the light on and moved closer to the easel. The detailing was amazing. "You're really good."

"It's just a hobby."

"I think it could be more than that, if you wanted it to." He shrugged. "Not that I'm an expert. But I'd buy one."

He didn't know this woman that well, but he'd guess her expression—slight smile, dipped chin—was pleasure. And maybe a little embarrassment.

"You look refreshed," she said. "Museum first, or lunch?"

"How long will it take to get my credentials?"

"An hour or less, I think."

He glanced at his watch, surprised to find it was barely past eleven. "Unless you're starving, I'd say museum."

They returned to the living room, and he settled his suitcase against the wall. "Should I take this with me? Or leave it here?"

"Leave it. We'll come back for it when I take you to the hotel. Unless you want to drive to the museum." She gave his cane, which he'd left propped by the door, a pointed look. "I wasn't sure—"

"After sitting for so long, the walk will do me good."

She picked the cane up and held it in both hands. "It's amazing."

It wasn't his favorite accessory, but it was unique. "One of my dad's friends is a woodworker. He carved that for me from an applewood branch he got off our property as a high school graduation gift."

She was still studying it. "Just what every teenage boy wants."

"Yeah. It was a little much for my undergrad years. Back then, I still believed I wouldn't need it forever. I started using it when I entered grad school."

She handed it to him. "I'm sure it made you look sophisticated compared to the other students."

"That and the sports coats with the patches." He tapped his elbows.

She laughed, pulling the door open. "Very dapper." In the hallway, she said, "Stairs okay?"

He appreciated her thoughtfulness. "Just do what you'd normally do. Ignore my leg. It'll be fine."

They took the stairs to the ground level and exited the building.

The sound hit him first. Traffic noises. Conversations coming from café tables in front of a bakery right beside the doorway—people bundled in parkas and hats, sipping from hot mugs and nibbling croissants. Beneath those noises, Christmas music played over loudspeakers in the square across the street.

He inhaled the scents of yeast and hot chocolate and...something savory. Sausage?

They joined the crowd, walking to a cross street just a block from the entrance to Sophie's building, where they turned away from the market. Within a few minutes, they'd left most of the noise and chaos behind.

"Do you enjoy this time of year," he asked, "or do the tourists ruin it for you?"

"I like it," Sophie said. "I'm used to the crowds, and since I walk almost everywhere I go, I don't have to deal with the traffic."

"Nice that you have a car, though, even if you don't use it that much."

"My mom wanted me to have the freedom to travel whenever and to wherever I wanted. The trains are great, but if you want to get away from the cities, you need a car."

"Have you?" Bryan asked. "Traveled a lot?"

"As much as possible. I've seen some beautiful places. I like Paris. I love Prague. I ate my way across Italy this past summer." She patted her flat stomach. "Took weeks to burn that off. London is fascinating, though it's a little too...English for me, I guess." She grinned at him. "I prefer going places where I don't speak the language."

Bryan preferred to know what was going on. He preferred to know what people were saying when they spoke to him. And what he was ordering in a restaurant.

He'd always thought of himself as adventurous, but when it came down to it, he did more reading about adventures than actually living them.

Two days before, he'd planned to spend the weekend in Shadow Cove with his family. Yet here he was. This was an adventure he hadn't planned, and so far, he was enjoying it.

Mostly because of the curly-haired blonde beside him.

"Where haven't you been that you want to go?" Bryan asked.

"Oh, gosh. I want to go everywhere. I'm hoping to get to Spain and Portugal this summer. Long drive, which is why I haven't done it yet."

"You'll drive? Not fly?" He imagined a map of Europe. Spain had to be...twelve hundred miles? Maybe fourteen? That would be like him driving from Maine to St. Louis.

"If I have time, yeah. The drive will be half the fun, through Switzerland and France. I could even detour and hit Monaco. I haven't been there yet."

"Let's say you can do it. Where will you go first, once you hit Spain?"

"Barcelona." She answered immediately. "To see the architecture."

"Gaudi, right?" Bryan asked. "Isn't that where he's from? The guy we get the word *gaudy* from?"

"Exactly. His influence is said to be all over the city."

"I've wanted to go myself, but..." There was no good way to end that sentence. He'd spent the majority of his life feeling sorry for himself instead of following his dreams. Not that he was about to admit that to a beautiful woman he wouldn't mind impressing. "Do you travel alone, or do you have friends you go with?"

"Oh, we travel in packs." She shot him a quick smile. "I've got friends who are always up for a trip."

That was one of Bryan's hesitations. He wanted to see all the places she'd mentioned and more, but not alone. It was one reason he'd spent an obscene amount of money taking flying lessons. He'd always wanted to learn to fly, like his little brother. And now that Bryan had his license, he could join Derrick on charter flights. But Derrick's company mostly made trips in the US.

The museum where Sophie worked was small and tucked beside similar buildings on both sides. If she hadn't turned to climb its steps, he'd have walked right by.

It was much larger inside than he'd have guessed from the sidewalk. The foyer was three stories high, echoing their footsteps as they walked to the desk. A Volkswagen-sized chandelier hung overhead.

Sophie spoke to the older woman behind the desk. "*Guten tag*, Betsy." She introduced Bryan, then said, "We're here to get his credentials. Is Herr Papp here?"

The woman jerked her head to the side. "*Da*. In the office."

Bryan followed Sophie down a tiled hallway painted bright white and lined with landscapes that were roughly the size of an efficiency apartment. So far, the only thing he could say about this museum was that their artwork was gigantic.

She turned at the end of the hallway and stopped at a door, digging into her purse for a card. She swiped it in a reader beside the door. Then, she pressed her index finger to a black screen.

The door clicked, and she pushed through. "Come on in."

As spacious as the foyer had been, the office was tiny, filled with file cabinets, boxes, and tables covered in all manner of paper and supplies.

A man stood from a desk. He looked exactly like Bryan would have imagined a German museum curator to look. Wearing a black suit and tie, he was tall and slender with gray hair, a bulbous nose, and round glasses. He stuck out his hand. "Jakob Papp."

Bryan met his palm with a firm handshake. "Bryan Wright. Nice to meet you."

"We are glad to have you." His German-accented English held a tinge of British aristocracy. He didn't smile, and as the man made small talk, asking about Bryan's flight and first experiences with Munich, Bryan had the impression he was going through the motions in an effort to be polite.

Papp requested Bryan's passport and ID and created a badge that would give Bryan access to the Iraqi artifacts—as long as he was accompanied by a museum employee.

To Sophie, the curator said, "You will stay with him when he's on the property."

A slight hesitation was followed by, "Yes, sir."

"And still get the exhibit ready, of course."

"Of course."

Papp had Bryan press his fingertip to a pad, then tapped on a computer. "Please test the card and reader."

Bryan left Sophie with her boss, stepping into the hall and letting the heavy door close behind him.

He slid the card into the slot, then set his index finger on the reader, as Sophie had done.

The door clicked, and he stepped back into the office. "Works. Thanks."

"You will want to get started right away, yes?" Papp asked.

"First thing in the morning." Bryan worked to stifle a yawn. "I'll take the day to see your beautiful city and get some rest."

"*Ja. Gut.* Tomorrow then." To Sophie, he said, "Accompany our guest wherever he wishes to go."

"I will, sir."

Showing Bryan around was part of Sophie's job? The thought brought a sharp twinge of disappointment.

He'd visited other museums and gotten to know other curators and antiquities experts. Sophie was neither of those, and he liked to think she was spending time with him because she enjoyed his company as much as he enjoyed hers.

They left the museum and headed toward Sophie's apartment and the chaos of Old Town.

A kid on a scooter careened toward them.

Bryan wrapped an arm around Sophie's waist and pulled her out of the way an instant before the kid ran into her.

"Sheesh." She looked behind her at the retreating form. "He's gonna hurt somebody."

"You want me to run him down? Beat him up for you?"

"Hmm." She tapped her nose as if considering it. "Maybe not this time."

Bryan realized he still had his arm around her waist. Reluctantly, he stepped away. "Lighthearted fellow, your boss."

Her laugh was bright. "He takes his job seriously. Treats the artwork like his children."

"And his employees?"

"Like employees."

"Does that bother you?"

"Not at all." Her gaze flicked up to Bryan's. "I have friends. Just not from work. What sounds good to eat?"

"German food?"

"I'm pretty sure we can find that." She stopped at a little café with thick canvas in the place of walls and plastic in the place of windows. He assumed those would be pulled back in warmer weather. The restaurant was packed, but within a few minutes, they were seated and skimming the menu.

"If you want the real German experience," she said, "you have to order a beer."

"Unless you want me snoring at the table, I'll take the fake German experience today."

They ordered, then chatted about nothing important until the meals were delivered.

Crispy breaded and pan-fried veal with mushroom sauce, potatoes, and warm red cabbage. Salty, savory, a little sweet. Delicious.

"This is what seafood is supposed to look like." Sophie cut into her flaky fish with the edge of her fork and lifted the bite. "No shells."

"I bet it's not as good as lobster."

She ate the bite and then wagged her head. "You've got me there."

She asked about his job, and he told her about the Bowdoin campus, the students, the classes he taught. She shared her own college experience in Southern California, where they skipped class to go surfing.

"My students skip to go skiing." He leaned forward and lowered his voice. "You ski?"

"I love it. Kitzbühel is less than two hours from here. Great skiing. Do you ski?"

"Oh, yeah. It's a challenge, of course, and I don't have my brothers' stamina, but I can do it."

"Then you should ski Europe sometime. Switzerland is even better than Austria. If you could stay longer, we could head down for a day. Though I'm not sure the resorts are open yet."

"Maybe another time."

Normally, for Bryan, that expression was a euphemism for *thanks but no thanks.*

But he'd love to hit the slopes in Austria or Switzerland. With Sophie.

She was lighthearted and funny. She smiled at the servers and didn't mind when they couldn't be bothered to smile back. She played peek-a-boo with a baby at a nearby table.

The conversation veered back to the places she'd visited.

"What's your favorite so far?" he asked.

"Switzerland."

"Even after you've been all over Europe, you still love Switzerland the best?"

"You have to go there someday. It's...amazing. These charming villages nestled up against the mountains. It's...indescribable."

Like the painting hanging over her sofa at her apartment. When he'd first seen it, he'd assumed she'd purchased it—and it wouldn't have been cheap. But now he asked, "Did you paint that picture in your living room?" At her nod, he said, "It's amazing. You're very talented."

"Well..." She lifted one shoulder and let it drop. "It's finished, anyway, which is more than I can say for most of my work. It's Mürren, Switzerland."

"Did you go there and paint it? I mean, are you one of those people who sets up an easel in the middle of town?"

She laughed. "Nah. When I'm traveling, I just want to see the sights and enjoy the experience. I took a million photos. The painting is a compilation of those pictures. If you went there, it would look familiar, but it's not an exact—"

"Who is zis?"

The demanding words came from a tall, blond man marching up to the table. When he stopped, he braced his legs as if he were prepared for a fight and glared at Sophie, barely flicking a gaze Bryan's way.

Her eyes widened, then narrowed to slits. "What are you doing here, Felix?"

"I see you through ze vindow."

"You need to stop. Now. Stop following me. Stop coming to my apartment. Just...stop. It's over."

Felix speared Bryan with a sharp look. "Zis is why you dump me? For zis...zis cripple?"

She shot Bryan a look. "I'm so sorry."

Bryan wasn't offended. What did he care what this jerk thought?

But Bryan's cane was hanging from a hook beneath his wool coat near the door. Even if this guy had seen it, he couldn't possibly have known it belonged to Bryan and not one of the other diners.

Bryan pushed back his chair, just in case he needed to step in.

But Sophie launched to her feet and glared up at the tall man. "There are stalking laws in Germany. If I catch you following me again, I will report you."

Felix had the nerve to look wounded. "I told you, I see you through ze vindow."

"Then how do you know my friend has a limp?"

He blinked. "I saw...earlier." Felix faltered, then squared his shoulders and aimed his chin at Bryan. "Zis man will never love you like I do."

"Who I spend time with is none of your business. What I do with my life is none of your business. Stay away from me, Felix, or I will have you arrested."

Everything in Bryan wanted to stand up and punctuate her words with a threat of his own. Or maybe a punch, not that he generally resorted to physical violence. If anybody had ever been asking for a black eye, it was this guy.

But Sophie was handling herself. He doubted she'd appreciate his stepping in to play the rescuing knight.

Besides, Bryan didn't want to add fuel to the guy's obvious rage.

Felix didn't move, though his hands curled into fists.

She didn't move, either, just glared at him.

Bryan gripped the edge of the table. He wouldn't get involved unless she needed him to. But staying seated was killing him.

After a few very tense moments, Felix swiveled and marched to the door and outside into the gray day.

Sophie waited until he was gone, took a deep breath, and then settled in her chair.

He could see an apology forming in her expression.

As if she owed him one.

"He seems nice," Bryan said.

She let out a quick burst of laughter. "Oh, yeah. He's dreamy."

"Let me guess. He's the reason you nearly caught pneumonia Wednesday?"

She sighed, her amusement fading. "We've been broken up longer than we were together. I knew he was having a hard time with it, but..." She pushed her plate away and forced a smile he wasn't buying. "It's fine. Thank you for not...running him down and beating him up."

He'd been seriously tempted. "You had it under control."

"I hope so. It's better if I handle it myself." She shook her head. "It's nothing."

"It's not nothing," Bryan said, "and you should report him. Don't wait until the next time. You said they have stalking laws here?"

"According to the internet, and you know how reliable that is."

Bryan's gaze flicked to the clear plastic windows. He didn't see Felix skulking, but that didn't mean he wasn't there.

"He does this a lot?"

"This is the first time he's confronted me in public."

"As opposed to in *private*?"

She sipped her drink and set it down, and he had the distinct impression she was considering telling him more.

Rather than press her, he took a bite of his Wiener schnitzel.

"He copied my apartment keys."

Bryan swallowed, his adrenaline spiking. He kept his tone casual. "Without your permission, I assume."

"I'd given him a set when we were dating so he could water my plants when I was out of town. He gave them back, but—"

"Made a copy first." Bryan put that together with everything else he knew. "You're thinking he's the one who broke in?"

"He swears not, says that he went over there to check on me and found my door ajar, but after this..."

Bryan set his hands in his lap so she wouldn't see his clenched fists. "There was a student on campus. Twenty-one. She worked in my department, so I got to know her a little bit. She broke up with a boyfriend, and he started following her. He sent her flowers. He called and texted her hundreds of times a day. She started getting messages through social media that she was convinced were from him. She reported him to campus police, and he got expelled from school. She took out a restraining order against him."

Sophie's expression shifted from interested to wary. "What happened?"

"She had one of those personal alarms, which she carried when she was in public and alone. She saw him coming one night and set it off. It was after dark, but not late. Just winter. The alarm didn't make him go away. He attacked her."

Sophie leaned back against her chair as if distance might help.

"She pepper-sprayed the guy before he could do much damage. But if she hadn't... I have no idea if he'd have raped her or killed her or...both. The point is—"

"I get it. I need to report him."

"She reported her stalker, Sophie. You need to assume that won't scare him off. Meaning, you need to have a way to defend yourself."

"I can't imagine Felix hurting me."

"Before this, could you have imagined him stalking you?"

She opened her mouth, then closed it.

He didn't press his point, just sipped his water and waited.

Finally, she said, "I see what you're saying."

"You need to find a way to defend yourself." The sooner, the better. There'd been other stalking cases on campus, and the first that had come to mind hadn't ended as well as the story he'd told her.

That young co-ed had landed in the hospital. Her stalker was in prison.

Maybe Felix wasn't violent, but the fact that he'd confronted Sophie, in front of Bryan, in a public place...

Bryan had a bad feeling about that guy.

CHAPTER SEVEN

S ophie was still shaking when Bryan paid for lunch, and they headed for the refugee center.

She'd been skeptical of Felix's story when he'd called to tell her about an intruder, but there'd been a small part of her, that hopeful, always-assume-the-best-about-people part, that wanted to believe he was telling the truth.

Now she knew better.

Bryan was right. She needed to call the police. And he was also right to assume the police wouldn't do anything. What *could* they do? Felix hadn't hurt her or threatened her. She could tell them about the copied keys, but he'd claim she'd given them to him—which she had, at one point.

Her word against his.

Her previous relationships had been casual and ended with see-you-laters and let's-be-friends.

Not that she ever saw those guys later. Not that they remained friends. She'd forgotten them, and they'd probably forgotten her. She'd expected the same when she ended things with Felix.

"You all right?" Bryan asked.

"I'm fine."

Bryan was leaning more heavily on his cane than he had been earlier. She'd been so distracted, she hadn't considered his leg.

"You don't seem fine," he said.

She wasn't sure what to say to that. "The center is on the other side of the Marienplatz, at least a mile from here. Want to get a cab?"

His brows lowered. "I can walk." The words didn't come out angry, but there was no kindness in them, either.

They pushed through the crowd near the Christmas market, past the festive music and happy tourists, which didn't bring the joy they normally did.

When they were out the other side, meandering along a narrow cobblestone road that was closed to traffic, Bryan bumped her shoulder.

"Sorry. I sometimes get...defensive about my limp."

"No problem."

"You haven't asked me what happened."

"I'm interested if you want to tell me."

One corner of his lips ticked up. "Another time."

They reached a busy street and crossed at the corner, then turned west, away from the river. Office buildings rose on both sides. A few shops were interspersed here and there. A pharmacy. A small grocer. A deli.

Though the traffic was steady, it was quieter here than in Old Town. Fewer people. She was glad for the relative peace in her environment, considering her mind felt more chaotic than the Christmas market.

"What are you thinking?" Bryan asked.

"Nothing important."

He stopped and faced her. "Sophie."

She stopped, too, reluctantly. "I'm fine."

He crossed his arms. "Not that it's my business, but..." There was a slight pause, and he said, "I'm interested if you want to tell me."

Ah. Parroting her words. She could parrot his and put him off to another time.

His eyebrows rose. If she could hear his thoughts, she was pretty certain she'd hear, *You can trust me.*

Not that this was about trust. It was just...she wasn't sure what she was thinking.

Maybe it would help to articulate it.

She started walking again, and he fell into step beside her.

"I was trying to figure out how I didn't see it. How did I not know Felix was going to start...behaving like...?"

"A stalker?" At her nod, Bryan said, "You think you should have?"

"Don't you?"

"I assume you started seeing him because he was a nice guy. And remained a nice guy, for a while, anyway."

"Yes. He sort of fawned over me, you know? But not in a smarmy way, like a flatterer. More like...like he thought I was special."

"I can see that."

She glanced at the man beside her, expecting to see teasing in his eyes. But she didn't. Bryan seemed serious. Contemplative.

"At first, it was great. We had fun together, laughed together. You know how it is at the beginning of relationships."

"Sure."

"He's younger than I am. He turned thirty this year—I wasn't robbing the cradle or anything. But he's a little condescending." Understatement of the century. "He talks to me like I simply can't understand the ways of the world. I don't know if it's because I'm a woman or I'm American or...I don't know.

But he acts like he's so wise and I'm so naive. It got on my nerves."

"I can imagine."

"Back at the restaurant, you didn't jump to my defense. You gave me counsel after, but you didn't act like I didn't understand what was going on. If the situation had been reversed, Felix would have lectured me, told me what to do, and then nagged me until I did it. He also wouldn't have let me handle it. He'd have taken over—to protect me. Which...maybe I'm being petty. That's nice, right? That he wants to protect me?"

"You're not petty. Your feelings are valid."

Yes. Her feelings *were* valid, but Felix had always acted like they weren't important, certainly not worthy of consideration. Because she was just a naive little American girl who had no idea what to think. Or feel. Or believe.

"He got to where he wanted to know where I was at every moment of the day. He claimed he was worried about me—you know, because I'm so incompetent." She heard bitterness in her voice. "I'm not being fair. I'm annoyed with him right now, so I'm seeing things differently. I don't think I saw it that way at the time."

"Makes sense."

She paused the story to grin at the man beside her.

"What?"

"You're good at that, saying just enough to get me to keep talking."

"It's a gift. Go on."

She almost did, then stopped herself. "Wow. I know you're doing it, but I can't seem to resist."

"My evil plan is working." He waggled his eyebrows and added a sinister "Mwah-ha-ha."

She laughed, happy to forget Felix for a moment.

But her ex-boyfriend was hovering at the edges of her mind.

Maybe hovering right around the corner.

It was just...creepy.

"Will he be at the mission?" Bryan asked.

"Shouldn't be. He usually takes Friday off so he can work the weekend." She turned onto the street where the mission was located. "When I planned my trip to Italy last summer, he tried to invite himself along. But that would have been awkward with my girlfriends. And we need the extra seat for all our luggage."

"Wow. Over-pack much?"

"Not me, but they do." Sophie attempted a smile, but she wasn't feeling it. "That was just an excuse. I didn't want him to go. I was looking forward to the break."

"Not a good sign."

"That's when I broke it off. He argued with me, actually argued, as if I didn't have the *right* to make that decision. As if I owed him something. I was not sorry to leave Munich for a couple of weeks. I thought he'd have moved on by the time I got back."

"That was when?"

"July. We'd only dated since April. It shouldn't have been a big deal. But here we are, four—almost five months later. And he still hasn't accepted it. I just feel stupid that I didn't realize what kind of a guy he was."

"How would you have?"

"I assumed, since he works at the mission and loves the people there so well, that he had to be a good guy." She stopped before they reached the glass-fronted center, not wanting to take this conversation inside. "You asked what I was thinking, and there it is. I was wondering how I didn't pick up on his issues before. What did I miss?"

Bryan tilted his head, seemed to think her question through. "Did you find an answer?"

"Not yet."

"Is it possible you didn't miss anything? That the thing you needed to see, you couldn't see yet? We date to get to know people better. You didn't know Felix well enough before because you hadn't started dating him. Right?"

"I'd worked with him a lot, though."

"Did he show that side of himself at work?"

"No."

"Then how could you have seen it?"

She couldn't argue with Bryan's logic.

"Maybe you'll be able to pinpoint some...clue you missed. From what I can tell, when you realized he wasn't the guy for you, you broke it off. I assume you were clear about what you wanted? That it was over?"

"Tried to be, though I told him I hoped we could be friends. We see each other all the time, so I wanted to end things on a positive note."

"There's no harm in being kind, Sophie." His tone was gentle, containing no censure. "Felix's behavior isn't your responsibility. Not that you asked for my opinion."

She got the sense there was more. "I'm asking."

"Okay. I think..." He seemed to consider his words carefully. "You're being hard on yourself. Felix has to own his behavior. You can only own yours. And yours seems...fine."

It was ridiculous how much Bryan's words affected her. She'd needed to hear that what Felix was doing wasn't her fault. Not that she'd known she needed that.

But Bryan had.

She rested her hand on his arm. "You are a very wise and insightful man."

He chuckled, the sound lighthearted—and maybe a little surprised—though at the compliment or the touch, she didn't know.

He shook his head. "You're easily impressed."

Flippant words, but not true.

She'd liked Bryan at their first meeting. Not just because of the umbrella. And the lobster. And the fact that he was handsome. She'd liked his kindness. His humor.

The more time she spent with him, the more she liked him.

Did the man have any faults at all?

CHAPTER EIGHT

It probably wasn't okay that, while Sophie was telling him about her creepy ex-boyfriend, Bryan had to force himself to focus.

Because, wow, he wanted to kiss her.

Definitely not okay.

And when she touched him—that slight grip on his arm? He felt it to his toes.

He was tired. That was all it was. And she was gorgeous. Her curly hair looked so...soft. Her gray eyes—had he ever seen gray eyes before? They were mesmerizing.

Thank heavens she couldn't read his mind as she dropped her hand and continued down the sidewalk, then stopped beside a door in the middle of a glass-fronted shop. The glass was dark, making it impossible to see inside.

The Arabic writing etched on the door was a clue, though. This was the mission.

"No photographs," she said. "That's very important. A lot of people here are hiding."

"Like Leila. I get it."

"Right. Of course you understand."

She reached for the handle, but he got there first and pulled it open, then followed her inside.

He wasn't sure what he'd expected, but this looked like a doctor's office waiting room. With the linoleum floors and faded plastic chairs, it was drab except for beautiful paintings on the walls. They depicted various European settings—the Eiffel Tower, rolling green hills that brought Ireland or Scotland to mind, and the Glockenspiel, the famous clock right here in Munich. There were mountaintops and chalets and seaside villages, all the sights being admired by beautiful people of all shapes and sizes.

Sophie's paintings. He'd bet a month's pay on it. Amazing how a little beauty could transform a space.

The area was packed with people—men, women, kids. Most wore traditional Arab garb, but a few wore jeans and sweatshirts or sweaters. Children played in one corner, where toys lay scattered across a dingy rug.

The walls were a dull beige, the woodwork scuffed. There was a worn wooden table at one end. A woman sat behind it talking to a young couple with a few kids crowded around them.

Bryan was still taking the room in when a few of the people turned to see who'd arrived.

Children bolted in their direction and flocked to Sophie, all chattering at the same time in multiple languages. The kids were dark-haired and dark-skinned with bright, joyful eyes.

Sophie dropped her purse on an empty chair, crouched down, and responded in what had to be Arabic.

What had Bryan said about her intellect when he'd first seen her? More summary than analysis?

Who was the idiot now? Because obviously, this woman was brilliant.

She grinned up at him and switched to English. "Bryan, meet my friends."

"Hi." Unsure what to do, he waved, and a few of them waved back.

One little girl—probably four or five—wrapped her arms around his legs.

He would bend down to meet her, but she was attached to him. Instead, he said, "Hey there."

She ducked her head, looking embarrassed but still hanging on. What was he supposed to do? He wasn't about to scoop the child into his arms. Her parents might not appreciate that. Instead, he patted her kinky-curly hair. "Do you speak English?"

She nodded, glancing up with wide, black eyes.

"My name is Bryan. What's yours?"

This time, she held his gaze. "Bishaaro."

"Bishaaro. What a beautiful name."

Watching him, Sophie looked pleased. "Bishaaro and her parents are good friends of mine."

"Well, then. I'm honored to meet a good friend of Sophie's."

Bishaaro grabbed his hand and tugged. She was a tiny thing, but he was powerless to refuse those gorgeous black eyes as he followed her to a corner. She plopped down in front of a table covered with toy trains similar to the ones he and his brothers had had when he was a boy.

Bishaaro pushed a train car along the wooden track.

Bryan added another car to the back of hers and made the appropriate noise, high-pitched and whistle-like. "Choo-choo!"

She mimicked him, eyes bright. "Choo-choo!"

Other children joined them, pushing trains around the track, all calling "Choo-choo!" until the sound was deafening.

Bishaaro didn't seem to mind sharing. She stayed right at Bryan's side as if he were her new best friend, and he had to resist the urge to gather her up and squeeze.

A throat cleared behind him, and he turned to see Sophie

71

watching, amusement on her face. "I thought I'd show you around."

"Right after this next delivery, ma'am."

Bishaaro giggled, and they pushed the train into the station together.

"There we go. Now the town has all the cookies and hot chocolate they need for Christmas."

"And pudding!" Bishaaro yelled.

"Of course, pudding! How could I forget?"

Sophie crouched down. "Bishaaro, will you introduce Bryan to your parents?"

She hopped up and took his hand.

Bryan stood, careful not to pull the girl over as he did. He let her lead him among the chairs and people—all watching with keen eyes—to a couple near the windows, who stood as they approached.

They both greeted Sophie, the woman hugging her quickly.

"These are Bishaaro's parents," Sophie said. "Koombe and Tisa, meet my friend Bryan."

Bryan guessed Koombe was in his forties. He had very short black hair and black eyes and a scar running from his cheek to his ear, lighter than his dark skin. He held out his hand, and Bryan let go of Bishaaro's to shake it.

"It is a pleasure to meet a friend of Sophie's." Koombe spoke excellent English with an African accent.

Tisa offered a shy smile. Her daughter looked a lot like her—dark skin, curly hair, wide black eyes. She was beautiful.

"Pleasure's mine. Your daughter is very sweet." Bryan grinned at the child. "We're good friends now."

The girl, seemingly shy again, tucked against her mother's skirt.

"We are blessed that she is with us," Koombe said. "Our

others are with God." Despite the words, the man spoke with peace in his voice.

"I'm so sorry."

"They are waiting for us in Heaven, so do not be sorry. We will see them again."

"You're right, of course. Still, I can't imagine." Yet this man's faith seemed firm. And by his wife's expression, hers was too.

Sophie squeezed Tisa's hand. "I'm going to show Bryan around. Let's have coffee next week, okay?"

Bryan said goodbye to the adults, then addressed the little girl. "It was a pleasure to meet you, Bishaaro. Thank you for playing trains with me."

She grinned. "Choo-choo!"

He laughed as he followed Sophie through the crowd. She smiled at people, kissed a couple of women's cheeks. She was well loved here, and he could see why.

She was amazing, after all.

Some gave Bryan squint-eyed looks. They'd been through so much, and most of them still weren't settled. From what he'd read on the flight—after his study of Munich—many of the refugees in Germany lived in camps or multi-family homes, waiting for visas so they could work. Even those already working didn't have the funds to move into their own places.

He followed Sophie past the table where the woman was checking in families and through a door. He closed it, leaving the cacophony and chaos on the other side. Back here, voices were low and murmured.

Short cubicles filled the dingy space. In one, a dark-haired woman held a baby on her lap, a little boy sitting beside her. They were holding hands with a sandy-haired man on the other side of a desk. Their heads were bowed in prayer.

Sophie continued through the room. "We meet privately

with everybody who comes in." Her voice was low. "We find out what they need and pray with them."

She led him down a hallway and paused at an open doorway that led to a room packed with shelves and shelves of food. Inside, a few people perused the selection.

"Some food gets donated," Sophie explained. "A lot of it we have to buy. Nothing fancy. Rice, lentils, canned fish, canned chicken, salt, sugar. That sort of thing. They aren't eating like kings, but they won't starve."

"Amazing."

She gestured toward the end of the hallway. "We keep clothes and other household items in a room back there and give them out as needed. We're here every day, though only in the morning on Sunday for church. That's one of Felix's jobs—he preaches. Some of our converts are afraid to attend services in a Christian church. If their families find out they converted, it could cause them trouble, even here in Germany."

Bryan couldn't imagine fearing his own family, but Leila had—enough that she'd escaped Iraq so they wouldn't discover she'd become a Christian.

Sophie knocked on a door that stood slightly ajar.

"Come in," a man called.

They entered a small office.

On the other side of a desk, a Middle Eastern man, probably in his midsixties, stood. He wore a suit and tie. His graying hair was cut short, and he had a trimmed beard and mustache. He smiled at Sophie. "Welcome back." He had a thick accent, Arabic, Bryan guessed. "How was your holiday?"

"Excellent. Aaron Driscoll. I'd like you to meet Bryan..." Her voice trailed, and he realized she wasn't sure if she should use his last name.

Smart woman.

Bryan stepped forward, hand outstretched. "It's great to meet you. I've heard a lot about you."

"Really?" The man's eyebrows hiked as he looked at Sophie.

"From a mutual friend," Bryan said. "She said she can't imagine where she'd be if not for you." He reached into his inside jacket pocket and pulled out the letter Leila had written. He didn't hand it over, though. "This has to stay between us. You can't tell anybody you heard from her. You definitely can't tell anybody who gave you this letter. I'd like you to destroy it after you read it." He had no idea if there was anything telling in it, but better safe than sorry.

Aaron's gaze flicked to Sophie, who said, "I'm guessing it's from Leila."

"Oh." He held his hand out, but Bryan was reluctant to hand it over.

His future sister-in-law's safety—and that of her twin sister—were on the line here.

Of course, Michael had given him the letter to pass along, so it should be fine.

Sophie rested her hand on Bryan's arm, and he felt the same zing he'd felt earlier. "You can trust Aaron. He's the keeper of many secrets."

He handed the letter over.

Aaron held it to his chest almost reverently. "She is okay?"

"She's safe and healthy."

He looked at the ceiling. "Thank You, Jesus, for delivering our sister to safety. You are so good to us."

Bryan felt a sting of tears. Since when did he cry? In public, no less?

But there was something so...real and unafraid about offering a prayer, aloud, the instant the gratitude hit.

Bryan needed to learn from this guy.

And, considering his weird emotional reaction, he also needed to sleep.

"Aaron runs this mission," Sophie said. "He and his wife have led...gosh, how many, Aaron? Hundreds of Muslims to the Lord?"

"I do not count, but the Lord knows. He works through me. I am only a mouthpiece."

Shaking her head, Sophie looked at Bryan. "He's a good mouthpiece. He's fearless—and in this crowd, that's saying something. In the States, our biggest worry sharing the gospel is that someone might ridicule us. Here, the danger is much more serious. Deadly serious."

"My life is in God's hands," Aaron said. "I will do what He tells me to do, and He will do with me what He chooses."

"I love that faith." As Bryan said the words, he wondered what it would be like to be so fearless. To go after what God wanted without counting the cost.

To simply trust that God knew better. Bryan had never had the faith to do that. Between his bitterness, his feeling less-than for most of his life, and his fears, he'd taken the easy road.

Some might not consider earning a doctorate easy, but for Bryan, it'd been the coward's way out. Hide in a classroom. Hide behind books.

Never live the life he'd dreamed of...and then resent those who did.

He was getting better, but seeing what a life truly dedicated to God could look like highlighted for Bryan how far he had to go.

Aaron came around his desk and faced him. "Our Lord has something good for you." The man was inches shorter than Bryan, but his words held strength and authority. "Our God has a plan for you, and it is good. And He wants you to stop berating yourself. This is something you do, yes?"

Bryan couldn't help the smile he felt on his face. "Yes. A lot. As in, ten seconds ago."

Aaron grinned. "You see? He loves you. You are forgiven. It is time to go forward." He nodded as if he'd said his fill, then rounded the desk again. "There is nothing else?"

"I just wanted Bryan to meet you," Sophie said.

"I am glad. Please, give my love to Leila. Tell her she is in my prayers every day."

"As you are in hers, I'm sure." Knowing his future sister-in-law, Bryan felt confident with that statement.

Sophia and Bryan said goodbye and returned the way they'd come. He held open the doorway to the waiting room, surprised to find there were more people, different people.

Again, Sophie was assailed by children.

Bryan scooted past the crowd to the door and turned to watch Sophie. She was such a natural, not only with the kids but with their parents. Her love for them overflowed.

And they admired her, if the looks on their faces were any indication.

Except one.

A man, seated against the wall. Dark skin, western clothes. Balding. He wore glasses on his round face and had a long, thick nose.

He was staring at Sophie. Though his eyes were relaxed, almost bored, his mouth was tight at the corners. Was that anger? Something else?

Clearly, the man wasn't feeling anything close to admiration.

Bryan angled toward the blacked-out windows—darkened to protect the people inside from being seen by passersby. Because not all Muslims took kindly to their brothers and sisters seeking refuge in a Christian mission.

Thanks to the bright lights inside, Bryan was able to watch the man in the reflection. There was no doubt in his mind.

He was one of the terrorists whose photos Michael had forwarded to him, a man plotting something at the museum where Sophie worked.

Hasan Mahmoud. Leila's uncle.

He was watching Sophie.

Bryan itched to grab Sophie and run. But he waited by the door, unwilling to give Mahmoud any indication that he recognized him.

When she finally tore herself away, he held the door open, forcing a smile he definitely didn't feel. She was walking toward him when Hasan stood and bumped into her, ostensibly on his way to the desk.

Bryan wasn't buying it.

"Pardon me, madam." The man's words were spoken in perfect English.

It was all Bryan could do not to yank Sophie away.

She smiled at the terrorist. "No problem. Have a good day." She continued outside, her joyful expression fading when she saw Bryan's face.

As soon as the door closed behind them, he gripped her arm and hurried down the sidewalk.

"What's the rush?" She practically jogged to keep up, sounding curious, maybe a little amused. "You could've used the bathroom there, if that's the problem."

He didn't answer and didn't slow. They reached the corner, and he turned, glancing back the way they'd come.

Mahmoud wasn't following.

"This is the wrong way."

But he kept moving.

"Bryan, what's wrong?"

He slowed to a normal pace. "There was a man in the lobby. The guy who bumped into you."

"What about him?"

Bryan stopped to face her. Because he had ahold of her arm, she had no choice but to stop as well. "Does he go there a lot? Check your purse. Is anything missing?"

She opened her small bag and poked around inside. "I have my wallet. Keys. Museum badge." She looked up. "What am I looking for?"

"You sure he didn't take anything. Or leave anything?"

"Nothing."

"It's important. Look again."

She shot him a quick look—glare, more like—but did as he asked. Her purse wasn't that big.

While she searched it, Bryan scanned the road behind them and in front of them. Just in case Mahmoud was coming after them.

When Sophie was finished, she looked up. "Nothing's missing." Her tone was short. "There's nothing here that shouldn't be. What's going on?"

"That man is a terrorist," Bryan said.

He wasn't sure what he'd expected, but not the anger that crossed her features. "Not every Arab is a terrorist, Bryan. You should know better. Your future sister-in-law is Iraqi."

"I'm not a bigot, Sophie. But that guy—"

"And you know this how?"

He couldn't say. He'd promised Michael. But Michael hadn't known Mahmoud would show up at the mission where Sophie worked. He hadn't known Sophie might be a target.

But everything in Bryan told him Sophie *was* a target.

There was a reason that man had been watching her—and with such vitriol.

"I can't say."

"Right. Well..." She looked around, shaking her head. "This isn't the right way." She started to turn around, but he didn't let go of her arm.

"Let's keep going this way. We'll catch a cab."

"Whatever."

She was annoyed. He hated that, but there was nothing he could do about it until he could explain to her what was going on. Which he couldn't do. Yet.

They flagged down a taxi and rode in silence to her apartment. When they climbed out, he paid the driver and sent him on his way.

She started toward the door.

"Would you mind doing me a favor?" he asked.

She stopped and smiled at him—a little smile, but maybe it meant she wasn't really angry. "Sure."

"Would you get my suitcase for me? I need to make a phone call."

"Oh. Okay." She gave his leg a quick look, probably assuming it was aching—which it was. He didn't usually do so much walking in a single day. But that wasn't the reason he'd asked the favor.

After she'd gone inside, Bryan paced away from the bakery and all the people seated outside as if the temperature were in the seventies, not the forties. He dialed Michael.

His brother answered with, "Everything okay?"

"I saw Hasan Mahmoud." Suddenly feeling paranoid, Bryan glanced around, but there was nobody close enough to overhear, especially with the traffic, the Christmas music, and the dull hum of a hundred conversations coming from the square. "He was at the mission where Sophie volunteers. She took me there to show me around. He was in the waiting room."

"How sure are you?"

"It was him. He bumped into her. On purpose."

"Not that I doubt you, but maybe you just think it was him."

"I don't forget faces, Michael. I am absolutely positive. He was watching her. I'm thinking, if he's been surveilling the museum, he must know she works there. What if she's a target?"

"The museum is, but I doubt Sophie—"

"But you don't know. This guy must be aware that she works at the museum—and she volunteers at a mission that tells Muslims about Christ. If he's a radical Muslim, then he has two reasons to target her."

"I see what you're saying." Michael's words were followed by a long pause. Finally, he said, "I need to reach out to our guy in Munich, see what they know. I hadn't heard Mahmoud was there."

"Does the museum curator know about the threat? He should. He needs to increase security."

"It's...delicate," Michael said. "We had someone at the embassy share what they could. I know they're planning extra security once the exhibit starts."

"The pieces are at the museum now, though. They need to know—"

"Bryan." Michael sounded impatient. "Look, it's not that I don't appreciate your input, but we know what we're doing. If Brock knows Mahmoud is in Munich, he hasn't shared that information with me. But he probably wouldn't. I'll pass this along. You do your part—look at those items and figure out what Mahmoud is after. We'll remove it—remove anything you think could be the reason for all of this. Once we do that, the threat will be mitigated."

"You'll have accomplished *your* purpose, to keep Mahmoud

from getting his hands on what he's after. But what about Sophie? What about the other museum employees? Are they safe?"

"We can't protect everyone. We're trying to—"

"I'm going to tell her what's going on."

"Absolutely not." Bryan's older brother had always been bossy, but Bryan had never heard the ring of authority in his voice like he did today.

Bryan might be seven years younger, but he wasn't a little kid anymore. "You'd just have Sophie walk around, vulnerable, and do nothing to keep her safe?"

"That's not the mission. The mission is—"

"Were you worried about the *mission* when it was Leila?"

"That was different." There was a long beat of silence before Michael asked, "Wait. Do you have feelings for her?"

"Even if I didn't, she's a human being. An American, if that matters. And your future wife's best friend. I'd think you'd care."

"It's not that I don't care." Michael's voice rose to match Bryan's. "I don't know if she can be trusted. What if she can't?"

"She can."

"Bry, you don't know that."

"Her apartment was broken into, but nothing was stolen. She thinks her ex-boyfriend did it."

"Why would she think—?"

"He's stalking her."

"Oh, wow. That's—"

"But what if it was Mahmoud or one of his cohorts? Are you really telling me not to warn her? Are you really so...heartless?"

Bryan expected his brother to fire back, but he heard nothing but silence for a long time. Long enough that he glanced at his screen to make sure they were still connected.

"If you tell her"—Michael's voice was low, almost a whisper

—"and word gets back to Mahmoud that we're on to him, the mission will fall apart. What they're up to... We don't know all of it, and Brock is convinced it's going to happen elsewhere, but I think Munich is the target. We think they're planning some kind of bombing. You're there now, Bryan. Imagine a bomb going off in the middle of the square at the height of the Christmas season."

He closed his eyes, trying to squeeze out the image that presented itself. All those innocent people running for their lives. Screaming for their children. "The bombing is going to happen that soon? Before the new year?"

"There's a reason I want you home on Sunday. According to the spotty reports we're getting—and these things are never perfect—they're planning it for next weekend. Think of it. All those shoppers. How many would die? Are you really willing to risk that?"

"Sophie's not going to tell anybody. She's a believer. She works at a Christian mission. She's a good person."

"She hasn't been vetted."

"Here's the deal, Michael. I'm telling her, or I'm leaving."

A long sigh. "You're going to get me thrown into prison. And that'll be the least of our problems if this gets back to Mahmoud."

"Sophie can be trusted."

"You'd better hope you're right. Don't tell her about the bombing. Don't give her any names. Don't tell her about me being in the CIA. Don't tell her—"

"I'm going to tell her I've been tasked with going through the artifacts to find out what they might be looking for and that I saw a terrorist at the mission. But the museum needs to know. They need to be prepared."

"I'll take care of the museum. Tell Sophie what you think you must, but impress upon her that—"

"It's a secret. I know."

"If anything else happens, call me. I'm not far."

Not far? Meaning... "You're in Europe?"

"Like I said, we think this thing is imminent."

Michael ended the call, and Bryan turned toward the door.

Sophie stood a polite distance away, far enough that she wouldn't have overheard. He hoped.

"You ready?" she called.

He approached and took his suitcase. "I need to talk to you about something before I head to the hotel."

She squinted, trying to read his face. Not that she'd ever be able to guess what he was about to share. That there was a plot brewing—and a terrorist might be watching her.

CHAPTER NINE

"We can talk in the car." Sophie had no idea what that phone conversation had been about, but obviously it was private. Was he talking to a girlfriend?

Not that she should care. It wasn't her business, but if he had a girlfriend, wouldn't he have mentioned her? Or was he one of those guys who liked to keep his options open?

She started back toward her building to access the garage, but Bryan stopped her with a grip on her arm.

"I'll take a taxi to the hotel after we talk."

"Let's get coffee then." She nodded toward the bakery.

"I'd rather we go up to your apartment."

If they were going to do that, then why did he have her retrieve his suitcase?

Weird.

But whatever. She unlocked the exterior door and headed down the hall toward the elevator, nothing but the sound of Bryan's rolling suitcase and the thump of his footsteps and cane behind her.

Upstairs, she unlocked her apartment door and stepped inside. She'd flicked the lights on when she'd come up earlier. It was after four, and the sun was already dipping below the horizon. As much as she loved Germany's long summer days, the short winter days got to her, especially when so many of them were gray. She'd been spoiled by perfect, sunshiny weather growing up in Southern California.

She settled on the couch. "What did you want to talk about?"

Bryan left his suitcase and cane by the door and sat on the loveseat adjacent to her. "You're going to have to trust me, even though there's a lot I can't tell you."

That didn't bode well.

"I do want to see the collection in your museum, but that's not the only reason I'm here."

"Okay."

He leaned toward her, resting his forearms on his legs. "There's been...chatter." His words came slowly, as if he examined each one before he spoke it.

"On the internet?"

He shrugged. "I don't know any details. Certain powers that be believe terrorists are after something in your museum—they assume it's in the collection of artifacts. I've been tasked with studying them. The thinking is that there is a specific piece that terrorists are looking for. It is believed that I might be able to figure out which artifact and why."

She didn't miss how careful he was not to mention *who* had tasked him, and *by whom* these things were believed.

"Are you some kind of...spy?"

"I'm an antiquities professor at Bowdoin, just like I said. It's not a cover. Being a professor is my day job and my only job." He paused, dipped his head side to side. "Well, I'm also Derrick's copilot sometimes. He owns a charter jet, but I just do that for fun."

He moonlighted as a *pilot*? For fun?

Interesting side gig.

"Who are these powers-that-be?"

"I can't tell you that."

"How do you know them?"

He pressed his lips closed. After a long moment, he said, "I can't tell you that."

Sophie stood and paced. "I don't understand. Why are you telling me this?" She swiveled and stuck her hands on her hips. "Is this why you were suspicious of that guy in the mission? You think there are terrorists in Munich, and that guy...what? Had the look of one?"

"He *is* one, Sophie. I saw his picture. I even know his name."

"What is it?"

"I can't tell you—"

"Of course you can't." Her volume rose with her frustration. Was this some big...lie? What did she really know about Bryan except that he was the brother of her friend's fiancé? "You expect me to believe this?"

"I'm not sure I expect it." He didn't return her irritation with his own. Instead, his tone was calm, his words still coming slowly, thoughtfully. "I *hope* you'll believe me, even though I can't prove anything I'm saying. Or back it up with evidence or even tell you how I know. It's a big ask."

"I'll say."

"Sophie." He gave the couch a pointed look. "Please?"

She sat. "What *can* you tell me?"

"I know who that man at the mission is, and I know he's a terrorist, and I believe that he's planning something—something at *your* museum. And today, he was watching you. Which is why I'm telling you this."

"I was surrounded by people. How do you know he was watching me, specifically?"

"While you were playing with the kids, he couldn't take his eyes off you. And not like... It wasn't attraction. What I saw on his face was much darker. I'm only guessing here, but if he is planning a...heist or something, he's probably been watching the museum and its employees. Meaning, he knows who you are. Maybe he even knows where you live."

The thought sent fear like ants skittering over her skin.

A terrorist knew her name?

There was already Felix. Her ex was watching her—his behavior today proved it.

And now a terrorist was watching her as well?

She was being stalked by *two* men? The image of them together, sipping coffee, staring at her window and sharing notes, raised both fear and amusement. It was ridiculous, of course.

"I'm not trying to freak you out." Bryan was serious, and her amusement faded. "You need to understand what's going on. That was the call I made. I needed to inform...them...that I was going to tell you this. I want you to be on your guard until the exhibit is over and those artifacts are returned to Iraq. That's why I didn't have you drive me to the hotel. Well, that and the fact that you've escorted me all over town today." The slightest smile played on his lips, but it didn't hold. "I can't tell you what to do, of course, but you're not going to be out—by yourself, after dark—on my account."

"I can't not go places alone, Bryan. I live alone. How would that work?"

"I'll be here for a few days. I can accompany you to work and home. After that..." He shrugged. "You have friends."

"I'm not going to hide from some..." She waved into the air, not knowing how to talk about this phantom terrorist. "You don't even know if it's true. Maybe that guy you saw isn't who you think he is."

"I'm certain."

As if Bryan weren't capable of making a mistake. Even if he was right... "Maybe he wasn't watching me. Maybe—"

"He was watching you. I *watched* him watching you for two or three minutes. He didn't take his eyes off you, and he looked...dangerous."

"It's possible you're reading into the situation."

"Okay." The word emerged stretched. "Is it also possible you don't want what I'm saying to be true?"

More than possible. She didn't even want to consider it. "The point is, the guy hasn't done anything to me. There's no reason to believe—"

"Are you sure about that?"

"What do you mean?"

"Your apartment was broken into. What if it wasn't Felix? What if he was telling the truth?"

"You're saying you think a *terrorist* broke into my apartment...and stole nothing?"

"Nothing that you've discovered. Yet. And I'm saying we don't know."

Sophie stood and walked into the kitchen, where she watched him from the far side of the table. She needed distance from Bryan and all his bad news.

This was crazy. Why would a terrorist break into her place? "To what end?"

"I don't have any idea."

"What about whoever those powers-that-be are? What do they think?"

"That I'm probably wrong or seeing things. But they weren't there. They didn't see what I saw. I'm not nuts, Sophie. And I'm not wrong."

At least Bryan told her the truth about that, but... Wow. Confident much? Or should she name it arrogance?

Felix was arrogant, certain he always knew more than she did.

She hated that.

She walked to the window and stared out at the dark night.

Was Bryan just trying to make her feel vulnerable? Did he have some ulterior motive?

What did she really know about this guy? Maybe he'd fabricated the whole thing. Or maybe he was a conspiracy theorist who'd cooked up all this craziness in his head.

She didn't want to consider that he might be right. Thanks to Felix, she already felt unsafe. And now Bryan fed her this cockamamie story.

She turned to pace again and found him standing a few feet away. When she started to walk past him, he took her hand. His touch was gentle and warm.

"I'm sorry," he said. "I'm not trying to freak you out. I'm trying to protect you."

Like Felix was always trying to protect her. Telling her what to do, where to go, how to behave.

Something must've played across her face because Bryan dropped her hand. "Sorry. I'm sure you have questions."

"I asked them. You refused to answer."

His lips pressed into a frown. "It sounds melodramatic, but it really is a matter of national security. I'm trying to figure out how to balance honoring my contact's boundaries and warning you." He took a step back. "It's been a heckuva day. I know I need to rest, and you've only been back in this time zone twenty-four hours longer than I have. Between this news and your ex-boyfriend and playing host to a virtual stranger, I'm sure you need a break." He started toward the door.

"You really think I might be in danger?"

He turned to face her again. "I didn't—until I saw that guy watching you. Did you get your locks changed?"

"The maintenance man did that yesterday."

"So Felix shouldn't be able to get in. But if someone else was responsible for the break-in, then they got in without a key the first time. Chances are—"

"The alarm will be installed tomorrow."

"Good. If you're nervous..." His gaze flicked to her sofa, and she had the impression he was about to offer to stay on her couch.

No way.

Was that the true motive here? To get her to let him stay over? To put her trust in him so he could take advantage of her?

"Maybe you could hang something loud on the doorknob," Bryan suggested, "or put something in front of the door, so if someone opens it, you'll hear. Like...pile up a bunch of pans, so if the door opens, they'll fall over. That'd make a racket and wake you up and hopefully scare away a would-be intruder."

"Good idea." An idea that didn't require his help—or his being there.

His story was nuts, but he was a decent guy. He probably believed everything he was telling her. This wasn't some scheme to get her to trust him.

Yes, he'd been less than forthright about his reason for coming to Munich, so there was that. But, if his story was true, then he hadn't had any choice.

The whole thing felt too weird.

"You're not planning to go anywhere tonight, right?" He ran a hand over his short hair. "I mean... Not that it's my business. I don't mean to be... Dang. I'm acting like your ex."

"It's fine." She needed to quit comparing Bryan to Felix. "I'm staying in tonight. I'll be safe here."

She hoped, anyway.

"I'll Uber over tomorrow and walk to the museum with you."

"I'm sure I can make it alone. I do it every day."

He smiled, the expression playful, highlighting how serious he'd been a moment before. "Humor me."

"Okay. If you insist."

He reached for her hand, but she pulled it back.

A look of hurt crossed his face. "Is it all right if I pray for you?"

Oh.

"I guess."

His palms were warm as they wrapped around her smaller hands. He prayed for her safety, and he prayed God would give him wisdom as he searched the antiquities the following morning. "Open my eyes, Lord. Help me find what I'm looking for. And keep us both—and this whole city—safe."

She loved that he'd prayed for his own safety too. It wasn't easy for people to admit—aloud and in front of another person—that they needed help.

She liked Bryan's humility.

"Anything to add?" he asked.

"Only... Thank You, Lord, for bringing Bryan here, and for showing him that terrorist at the mission. Protect the people there. And my coworkers, and the museum."

Bryan squeezed her hands, spoke the "Amen," and stepped away. "You'll be all right?"

"I'm safe here, but that guy saw you with me, so you need to watch your back."

"I will. Don't worry. What time should I be here?"

"I usually leave at seven thirty, but if that's—"

"It's perfect." He leaned down and kissed her cheek, the affectionate move taking her by surprise. "Good night, Sophie." He stepped out and headed down the hall, dragging his suitcase and leaning on his cane for support.

She'd had a million thoughts about Bryan that day, and in

the last hour, they hadn't all been good ones. But as he walked away, she decided her first impression of him was the right one— if incomplete.

He wasn't just a good man. He was a respectful man. And a praying man.

Even if maybe he was a little paranoid. Despite the anxiety his story raised, anticipation bubbled inside her.

She couldn't wait to see him again.

CHAPTER TEN

A mazing what losing a night of sleep would do. Bryan had slept like the dead for... how long? He snatched his phone off the nightstand. A little after five o'clock. Despite his worry for Sophie, he'd slept ten straight hours. The Lord knew he needed it.

His hotel room was tiny. It held a queen-sized bed, a nightstand, and a small upholstered chair beside the wardrobe where he'd hung his clothes the night before. With all the oversize furniture, there wasn't much room to move. It was similar to other rooms he'd seen in Europe, especially for hotels constructed in the previous century.

He showered, dressed, and headed for the lobby, which was as spacious as his room was cramped. Little seating areas were interspersed all around. The woodwork was dark, the walls painted a calm white, and vases filled with flowers rested on many of the surfaces. It wasn't a huge hotel, but it was fancy. If not for the fact that Leila had worked there and gotten him the room—and the fact that the city was overrun with tourists—he'd have chosen something a little more run-of-the-mill.

There was a store with incidentals and snacks. Beside that, a restaurant filled with small round tables. He was hungry but didn't want to take time to eat there. He ordered an Uber and headed out, using his cane for support. His leg ached after all the walking the day before.

When he reached Sophie's building, he ordered two cups of coffee and two pastries at the bakery, thankful they had a drink carrier and a bag with handles, and headed to the apartment entrance. He pressed the button for the intercom.

"Yes?"

"It's Bryan."

The door buzzed, and he made his way to her apartment.

When she opened up, her hair was damp with springy curls. She wore a navy suit with a silky white shirt and...fluffy pink slippers.

"Nice shoes."

She grinned. "I'm not quite ready for the day. How's the hotel?"

"Great. I need coffee, though." He lifted the drink carrier. "Thought you might too."

"Always." She took a cup and stepped back. "I was planning to meet you outside, but you're early."

"I was afraid you'd planned to meet me outside." He winked. "I can see trying to keep you safe is going to be a full-time job."

She shook her head, then sipped the coffee. "I need two minutes. Enjoy your pastry." She nodded to the bag he'd tucked under his arm.

"Got you one too. I heard you say yesterday you liked croissants, so I thought I'd give them a try. I hear they're better in Europe."

"You're in for a treat. Next time, try *Spritzkuchen*."

"Which is...?"

"Like a German donut." She grabbed plates and knives and

set them on the table, along with butter and jelly. "Be right back."

She disappeared down the hall, and Bryan slid the flaky treats onto the plates. The pastry was still warm, and he broke off a piece and spread some butter and strawberry jelly on it.

Oh, yeah. There was nothing like that in Maine.

He was on his second bite of sweet and salty deliciousness when Sophie returned. She'd changed out of the slippers and into navy shoes with short, sturdy heels. He was glad to see she wasn't the type to don stilettos for a full day of work. She'd added gold hoop earrings that hung lower than her springy curls.

She sat across from him, prepared a bite—butter, but no jelly—and popped it in her mouth. "Thank you. This is perfect."

He was already finished and wishing he'd gotten more. "If I lived here, I'd weigh four hundred pounds."

She gave him a quick once-over. "I doubt that very much. You obviously work out." Her cheeks flamed red. "Not that I... I mean..." She focused on another bite of croissant.

He worked to temper his smile.

She finished her breakfast, and they headed out.

Outside the museum, she led the way down an alley to the rear of the building, where she swiped her badge and pressed her fingertip on the panel. The door sounded with a low buzz, and she pulled it open.

Bryan followed her into a room roughly the size of a house. Except the ceiling was higher, and there were no windows. The only light came from fluorescent fixtures far above.

Shelves jammed with crates and items wrapped in canvas lined the exterior walls and created corridors like stacks at a library. Bryan had been in similar rooms all over the world. He'd never seen one so...clean.

As they walked between two shelving units, he ran a finger along one of them, just to see. Sure enough, not a speck of dust.

Impressive.

They rounded a corner and saw Herr Papp beside a rectangular table against a side wall. The table held a lamp, a notebook, a pen, a loupe, and a larger magnifying glass. To the side of the table, three piles of crates were stacked to about four feet high. Beside those, canvas tarps covered larger, oddly-shaped items.

Bryan's fingertips tingled with anticipation. It'd been a long time since he'd been so eager to get his hands on artifacts. When he'd first chosen his area of study, he'd been thrilled with every opportunity to study the ancient world.

Over the years, his excitement had waned. He was tired of piecing together the lives of ancient people. He was ready to live his own life.

Today, he was glad to have a little bit of that old anticipation back.

Papp turned when they approached. He barely gave Sophie a glance. "I trust you had a good night's sleep."

"I did," Bryan said. "Thank you."

"Miss Chapman will remain with you and provide you with anything you need. We must be vigilant about security. There have been threats, apparently, regarding these items."

Sophie shot Bryan a surprised look. Good. Maybe now that Herr Papp had confirmed at least part of Bryan's story, she'd take her own protection a little more seriously.

"You must remain with Miss Chapman or another museum employee while you are with us," the curator was saying. "This is no reflection on you. It is simply protocol."

"Of course. I understand."

Papp nodded to him, then to Sophie, and walked away, his

shoes clicking on the concrete floor. Bryan half expected his arms to stiffen and swing like a soldier's.

The door slammed shut behind him, and Sophie's serious expression morphed into a smile.

"Is he always so joyful?"

"For him, that was pleasant."

"I guess there are worse things than taking one's job seriously." Bryan regarded the crates and other items, rubbing his hands together. "We'd better get started."

She found a pry bar and handed it to him. "You're actually excited about this."

"Aren't you?"

She shrugged. "I guess it's interesting."

Bryan bumped her shoulder. "By the time we're done with this project, you will be impressed. Trust me."

Whether she was impressed by what Bryan did or didn't do wasn't the point, though. He needed to remember that. They were trying to stop a terrorist attack.

Suddenly, the wealth of items didn't excite him at all. What if he couldn't figure out what the terrorists were after?

Bryan had always been the sideline guy. The fifth guy on the Star Trek away team. The extra on the set who got knocked off long before the big climax.

He'd never been the hero, and there was a good reason for that.

He wasn't hero material. What had Michael been thinking to ask him to do this?

Lord, help me figure it out. There's no way I can do it on my own.

If he failed...people would die. And it would be all his fault.

CHAPTER ELEVEN

They'd been studying the different artifacts for more than an hour. Well, Bryan had been studying them. Sophie had been making notes in a notebook and trying to keep her eyes open.

She hadn't slept well.

The pots and pans she'd stacked in front of the door had brought a little comfort. Even so... Had terrorists been the ones to break into her apartment? Or just her creepy ex?

Neither option had led to a restful night, and she yawned.

Bryan turned from the artifact in his hands and smiled. "Am I boring you?"

"Not *you*." She glared at the shelf full of stuff he'd already uncrated, studied, and set aside. "Those things aren't exactly riveting."

"I'm offended." He affected a tone to punctuate the comment. "That's my life's work you're insulting."

"It's not like you made them."

"True." He lifted the thing in his hand as if it held the key to the universe. "Look at this. Isn't it something?"

It was a little clay man with a huge head and a tiny body, not so different than the other pieces he'd pointed out to her.

Her face must've registered her lack of interest.

"I can tell how impressed you are."

She put on her gloves, took it, and turned it over. The proportions were all wrong, but that wasn't unusual for the timeframe. "It's...interesting, in its own way, I guess."

"You know how old that is?"

"Is it older than dirt? Because I see dirt every day."

He laughed. "I can't argue with that. But think of it. Thousands of years ago, hands fashioned this. Fingers pinched here and there." He took it back and showed her the creepy, oversize eyes. "A real person took a lump of clay and formed this, maybe sitting on a rock. Maybe meat was roasting nearby."

"Mammoth meat. Or a saber-toothed tiger."

"I think tiger meat would be tough." Bryan looked at her, one eyebrow lifted. "And I'm pretty sure ancient Babylon didn't have a lot of woolly mammoths. They weren't cavemen, after all."

"Cave *people*," she corrected.

"Right. I wouldn't want to offend all the cave *people* I run into on a daily basis." He set the item aside and reached into the crate for another.

"So that wasn't the...thing the terrorists are after?"

He lifted a shoulder and let it drop. "I have no idea. So far, they're all so similar."

"Phew. I'm glad you think so too. I thought maybe I was missing something important."

He nodded to her notebook. "You're writing down everything. Do you see any patterns?"

She glanced at the notes. "Nope. They've all been from the same time period, give or take a couple hundred years. Same region. They're all everyday items, except the idols, which... Why would Muslims want ancient idols?"

"They wouldn't." Bryan took the next piece, a bowl, gave her the details he surmised about it.

She made her notes. "Exciting job you have."

He must not have heard the sarcasm in her voice because he said, "I like it," with no hint of irony.

But she picked up something in his tone. He almost sounded...resigned.

"Do you?" she asked.

He stilled, then carefully set the bowl aside. "Yes." But the word was drawn-out, hesitant. "I used to love it. Now, I enjoy teaching more than I enjoy the subject matter."

"Does that surprise you?"

"I became a professor because, really, what else is a guy with a doctorate in ancient history going to do? There isn't a plethora of choices. I had this idea of what my life would look like. I'd have my TAs do a lot of the class work, and I'd spend my time doing"—he nodded to the mountain of stuff they still had to go through—"this. Now that I have tenure, I could have the life I'd dreamed of."

"But?" Because she could hear the unspoken word in his tone.

"I don't love it like I used to." He gave her the details about the piece he'd been looking at, then set it aside while she made her notes. "I don't hate it. Don't misunderstand. It just doesn't excite me anymore. But we don't all get to have exciting jobs. Somebody has to do this."

Did somebody? She didn't know the benefit of what Bryan did but figured saying so might insult him.

Her work designing art exhibits wasn't changing lives. But her work with the refugees was. That was her true calling. She was employed at the museum because she had to have a job to stay in the country. If she quit—or worse, got fired—she'd lose her visa.

Would that she could work at the mission full time.

"What's the new dream?" she asked.

Using the pry bar, he opened another crate and propped the lid against the table on the floor. He dug inside and pulled out a dirt-colored lump about the size of her fist.

He didn't say anything for so long that she started to wonder if he'd forgotten she'd asked him a question. But Bryan didn't seem the type to toss out flippant words. Maybe he was thinking.

He rattled off the details about the piece and grabbed another.

But he barely glanced at it before he faced her. "I've had this...feeling that the Lord has something different for me. But I don't know what, or where, or with whom."

"When you pray about it...?"

"He tells me to wait. I feel like I've been trapped in a waiting room for years. Just...languishing."

Bryan seemed like such a take-charge guy. Tall and broad and strong. And confident. She admired his confidence. Admitting his uncertainty about the future showed a depth of humility Sophie admired.

Just one more reason to like this guy. Not that she'd needed one. When she could shove Felix and the bad taste he'd left aside, when she could see Bryan clearly, she saw him to be...

Rather amazing.

He studied the thing in his hand.

"So you're in a waiting room," she said. "What do you see in there?"

He shot her a confused look. "I don't know what you mean."

"Describe this waiting room. Is there a door? Are you

waiting for that door to open? Are you there alone or with other people?"

Chuckling, he gave her the details about that artifact and reached for the next. "It was just a metaphor."

"*Your* metaphor. I think we should examine it."

"I never thought that much about it."

"Think about it now."

After he'd given her the facts about the ugly lump—a tool of some kind, he'd guessed—and she'd written them down, he leaned a hip against the table to face her. "It's stupid, but I guess it feels more like a room with doors all around. One of them leads back to the life I've been living—professor at Bowdoin."

"Do you want to go through that door?"

"No."

No hesitation.

He seemed to realize that. "It's not that I don't like what I do. It's just that I'm excited to do something else."

"Are you sure? Are you sure it isn't a little bit of both?"

His eyes narrowed the slightest bit. He grabbed the next thing out of the crate. "This is the last item in here. Would you—?"

"Sure." She bent over the final crate in the stack and worked the pry bar. The nails screeched as the lid rose. She pulled it off and set it aside.

Bryan gave her the facts about the thing he was looking at and shelved it. "Like I said, I like teaching. So I don't hate my job. But I don't want to keep doing it."

"Where do the other doors lead?"

"That's the question, isn't it?"

"This is your metaphor, Bryan. I'm just asking you to examine it."

They worked in silence for a few minutes, finishing up that crate.

She was opening the next when he spoke again.

"When I was a little boy, we went to a parade. Soldiers were marching, and I thought they were so...cool."

She set the lid aside and looked up at him.

He gave her a sheepish look. "I wanted to carry a big gun, just like them. And then this happened." He tapped his wounded leg. "And that dream died."

"What happened?"

"My brother Grant—he's the next older brother, number four—wanted to show me how he could climb a cliff near our family's vacation house."

Ah. The one on the island they'd talked about at lunch the other day.

"He told me to watch from the dock. He was nine, and I was seven, and we were not supposed to be down there. But Grant wanted to show off. He started up. He made it look easy. Like an idiot, I followed him."

She could imagine it. Two little boys, climbing a rock wall. She'd heard enough about the vacation home—"camp," they'd called it—to picture the cliff, the rocks, the raging ocean below.

"He made it to the top," Bryan said. "I made it about halfway—over twenty feet up. And then I fell."

She winced, seeing in her mind's eye that little boy falling. The terror he must've felt. The pain. "You broke your leg?"

"I hit the rocks. Crushed my ankle and part of my tibia. There were internal injuries and..." He waved the rest of the story away. "I spent weeks in the hospital, then in a wheelchair and a cast. There were years of physical therapy."

"I'm sorry that happened."

He grabbed another artifact but barely glanced at it. "I'm sorry about how I reacted. Grant felt responsible. Michael was supposed to be watching us, but he'd gone to do something else, and he felt responsible too. And I..." Bryan looked down, turning the clay object in his hand, though she didn't think he was really seeing it. "I blamed them. I blamed Grant especially. I was angry with him for years. And bitter. He joined the Army right after high school, mostly to get away from the family. From me. Later I learned he joined because he was trying to honor what I'd once wanted. But I didn't see that at the time. It just made me even more furious with him. In my head, he'd stolen my chance to be a soldier and then stolen my dream. Not only did he steal it, but he excelled at it. He was a Green Beret. The better he did, the more I hated him."

Huh.

Sophie didn't know what to say to that. She couldn't imagine this man—who seemed not only confident but spiritually mature—behaving that way.

He met her eyes. "I thought I was a believer, but I didn't understand the whole *All have sinned and fallen short* thing. I thought Grant was bad, and I was good, and he owed me something." Bryan shook his head. "I've repented and apologized. Grant avoided our family for years because of me, because I made him feel unwelcome. It was terrible and... I was so selfish."

"Are you and Grant on good terms now?"

"Yeah. He's a better man than I am."

"You're doing that thing Aaron called you on yesterday, aren't you? Berating yourself?"

Bryan chuckled. "Curses. Caught again. I seem to find comfort in wallowing."

"Berating yourself for wallowing is just another way of wallowing, Bryan."

"Wow. Tough room." But his eyes danced, making it clear he was kidding as he focused on his work.

She wanted to question him more about what his future might hold, but they had a job to do. Well, he did. Her part was pretty small.

"Still no idea what the terrorists are after?"

He glanced at the shelves where he'd set all the items they'd gone through. "Nothing stands out." He shifted to the shrinking stack of boxes. "And we're running out of options."

She ordered sandwiches to be delivered, and they ate a quick lunch in the office, then returned to the storeroom. It was chilly —never more than seventy degrees, and the humidity was kept at fifty percent, which was best for the preservation of paintings. Not great for her as she shivered, writing notes for Bryan.

By late afternoon, she felt a growing sense of urgency.

What would happen if Bryan couldn't figure out what the terrorists were after?

Maybe the Americans—whoever the people were who'd gotten Bryan involved and called Herr Papp—would ask him to cancel the exhibit, maybe even turn over all the artifacts.

But she doubted the curator would consider it. Which meant that, if Bryan didn't solve this puzzle, then the entire city could be in danger.

She opened the final crate in the stack. So far, all the items had been similar.

But when she dug into the bottom of the crate, what she pulled out was heavier than she'd expected.

She unwrapped the canvas to reveal an off-white box—ivory, she was almost certain—about the size of a thick paperback novel. It had a rounded lid like a treasure chest. The top bore the carving of a man beside a horse pulling a chariot. Around the sides of the chest were square frames, each surrounding a man wielding a weapon. Javelin, spear, sword, and other menac-ing-looking things Sophie didn't have names for. She guessed the handle on top and the corner pieces were made of brass.

Unlike everything else she'd seen that day, this was... beautiful.

"Whoa." Bryan sounded awed. "Where did you get that?"

"In the crate."

He reached for it. "May I?"

She handed it over, and he turned it, studying each side. "This is amazing."

She made notes as he rattled off facts about it. Ivory and brass. So she'd gotten those right.

"Byzantine, eleventh century."

"AD?" she asked.

"CE. Common Era," he corrected without looking up.

Right. She knew that.

He studied the inside and the underside of the lid. "Hm."

"What?"

He held the chest beneath the lamp.

"You see something?"

She was pretty sure she was talking out loud, but he was definitely not hearing her.

"Huh."

She bit her tongue to keep her questions inside. He'd tell her when he was ready.

He studied the bottom of the object, then the underside of the lid again.

Minutes passed. Long minutes with no sound but the humming of the heater and Bryan's unintelligible murmurs.

Finally, he faced her, the little ivory chest held in both hands like a treasure. "The tulip in the onion patch."

"Meaning?"

"This is it, the thing my...people asked me to find." He donned the loupe and returned his focus to the box. "I'm... eighty-five percent sure."

"I love your confidence."

He didn't seem to hear her. He didn't react at all. Clearly thinking hard.

Another moment passed, and he said, "Write this down."

She was already poised over her notebook, but since he didn't look up, she said, "I'm ready."

He rattled off a series of numbers—sixteen, to be exact.

"What does it mean?" she asked.

"I have no idea."

Then... "Where did they come from?"

"Oh." He looked up then, his lips ticking up at one corner. "Sorry. I'm a little absorbed. Come here."

Not that she was far away, but she moved to stand beside him.

He opened the chest, angled the lid so she could see the bottom of it. "See what I mean?"

She leaned in, seeing nothing but smooth ivory. "No."

Bryan inched close, his shoulder brushing hers. He was engrossed with the artwork.

She was focused on his closeness. His warmth beside her. His scent. Was that sandalwood?

She liked sandalwood.

"Take it. Get closer."

She did and... Sure enough, there were scratches in the ivory. "Can I have the—?"

"Here."

Bryan handed her the magnifying glass, and she looked through it at the smooth surface.

A string of numbers had been etched on the ivory. Though... was that a seven or a one? And one of the numbers looked like it could be a six or an eight.

"What does it mean?"

"I have no idea."

She studied the rest of the box but didn't see anything else that jumped out. She set the chest down and faced him. "What *do* you know?" By the look on his face, he had some ideas.

His gaze flicked from her face to the chest on the table. "I know it's not Babylonian, and it's not ancient. I have no idea why it would be paired with these items."

"It must've been stolen from the Iraq Museum, right?"

His head bobbed slowly. "Why would it be there? My understanding is that the museum holds Babylonian art. I didn't realize they had items from other regions. Maybe I just... assumed."

That didn't sound like Bryan, though. He was an expert at this stuff. Wouldn't he know?

"What about the numbers?"

"Definitely *not* from Byzantine."

"Based on...?"

"Byzantine numbers are similar to Greek. They look nothing like these. These"—he nodded to the chest—"are Arabic, adopted in the West in the twelfth century, and even then, they didn't look like that. Those are modern. They had to have been etched later, much later."

"What does that mean?"

"It means... I think it means this is what the terrorists are looking for—and those numbers must be the reason. We were assuming it was the artifact itself they wanted, but whatever they're planning has nothing to do with that chest. I think it has everything to do with those numbers."

He reached for Sophie's notebook resting on her chair, but before he grabbed it, he said, "I need this. I need to pass along the numbers."

"Take it."

He did, then pulled his phone from his pocket. "I need to get a picture of the chest. Would you open it up and angle the bottom of the lid my way?"

She did, and he took a couple of shots. Then, he got one of the notebook page with the numbers.

After ensuring the images were clear, he walked away. He was halfway to the door that led not into the museum but outside into the cold afternoon when he turned. "See if there's anything else in the last crate, please. And...don't say anything to anyone. And don't go anywhere with that piece. Or let anyone else go anywhere with it. If Herr Papp comes back, hide it."

"From my boss?"

"While I make this call. Please. I just don't want him to take it anywhere."

"I'll do my best."

Bryan stepped outside, and the door slammed behind him, leaving her with the mysterious little ivory chest.

Which might be the key to a terrorist operation.

CHAPTER TWELVE

Bryan cursed his brother's voice mail. He left a quick—"I've got something"—and ended the call.

He stared at his phone, certain Michael would respond immediately. When he didn't, Bryan's anxiety ticked up.

He should feel elated. He'd discovered what the terrorists were after. Instead, he was slightly nauseated. What if he was wrong? What if those numbers had nothing to do with anything?

What if the piece the terrorists wanted was one of the other fifty things he'd already looked at? It was only dumb luck that he'd seen those etched numbers. Were numbers etched on anything else? Or words?

What if he'd missed something important?

Another fear overshadowed the rest. Where was Michael? Why wasn't he calling back? Was he hurt?

Bryan's brother was hunting terrorists. Anything could've happened.

Bryan leaned against the brick wall of the museum, closed his eyes, and prayed for guidance and wisdom and peace. *Lead me, Lord. I don't know what to do now.*

He forced his mind to stop churning on all the what-ifs and focused on the God who had all the answers. The Omniscient One. All knowing, all powerful, all sufficient.

Bryan breathed in the truth and blew out all his fears.

Michael had asked him to do this, and he had done it—and would keep doing it to the best of his abilities. And where his abilities lacked, God would fill in the blanks.

Peace washed over him.

And his phone rang. Michael. Thank God.

"Hey, you all right?" Bryan asked.

"Yup." Michael, loquacious as ever. "What'd you find?"

Bryan described the ivory chest and gave Michael the string of numbers. "Even if not for the numbers," he said, "I'd think this was the piece. It's not Babylonian but Byzantine."

"I don't speak *boring*. What does that mean?"

"Babylonian artifacts are from Babylon." Maybe that was dumbing it down a little too much, especially when he added the patronizing tone. "Think two thousand to sixteen hundred years before Christ. The Byzantine Empire stretched from about 330 to 1400 CE. Common Era. After—"

"I get it," Michael said.

"Byzantine was centered in Constantinople, modern-day—"

"Istanbul. So the ivory chest is from Turkey, after Christ, and the rest of the stuff you're looking at—"

"Is much older. Completely different in every way. So obviously, the chest stood out."

"You were surprised to see it in the collection?"

"I'm almost certain that the Iraqi museum displayed items from Mesopotamia. There's no reason why a Byzantine artifact would have been there."

"Any chance it was donated by accident? The thieves didn't realize—"

"And accidentally included another valuable piece of art? Unless they're total morons, I can't imagine that would be the case. It came in the crate with Babylonian artifacts. It wasn't there by accident."

"Okay." Michael was quiet a few moments. "So...I was right. We should be in Munich, not...here."

Seemed Michael couldn't say where *here* was.

"Brock is not going to be happy," he added.

That didn't make sense. "This could be the key to stopping a bombing that could kill or harm thousands of people. Why wouldn't your boss be happy?"

"Because it means I was right. Even worse, it means *he* was *wrong*." After a loud exhale, Michael said, "Can you remove the item from the museum?"

"Uh, no."

"Maybe just...tuck it into your sweater and—"

"Oh, sure. I'll just steal it. I mean, what would be the big deal if I got caught? I'd lose my job and all the authority I've gained as an expert in antiquities. Probably end up in a German prison. At least it would be clean."

"Okay, okay. I get the point. I'll send somebody to pick it up. I'm not sure when that'll happen, though. It's almost five o'clock. One sec." There was a pause, and then, "They close in an hour. I don't have any pull with the guys in Munich right now, so Brock will have to make the call. Meaning, it's time for me to fess up to him that I brought you in."

"Are you going to get in trouble?"

"Yup. But at least this time, I tried to get him to do the right thing first. Who knows? Maybe I'll be the one to lose my job. Or end up in prison."

Bryan hoped his brother was kidding. "What do I do in the meantime?"

"Put the item somewhere it won't be easily found. I don't want anyone seeing it."

"I'm sure the curator cataloged the items when they arrived, so he's seen it."

"And Sophie knows, I guess."

"I told you I was going to tell her, and I'm glad I did. She understands the gravity of what we're doing. She's an ally."

"Let's hope you're right. I'm going to tell Brock, hopefully get the team working on those numbers. But things are crazy right now, threats all over Europe. I'll try to get someone in the Munich office to pick up that chest. Assuming I can, will the curator be amenable to giving it to us?"

Bryan thought about Herr Papp. The man was a lot of things, but amenable wasn't one of them. "You need to have all your ducks in a row. You'll need the proper paperwork signed by the proper authorities. He's not going to just hand it over."

"Is it valuable?"

"Of course. Not only because it's ancient and rare but because it's beautiful." He remembered the look of awe on Sophie's face when she'd first seen it. "Even if it weren't valuable, a guy like Papp isn't going to just hand it over because some American shows up and demands it. In fact, if anything, he'll probably dig in his heels."

"All right. I'll let Brock know. It makes me very nervous to leave it in the museum overnight, but I don't think we can get this done before tomorrow. I don't see another option. I'll get back to you when I know more."

Michael ended the call, and Bryan climbed the steps, only then realizing he wouldn't be able to get past the door with his visitor badge's limited access. He knocked.

A moment later, it swung open, and Sophie stepped aside. She held the chest in her hands. "Everything okay?"

"They're going to send someone to pick it up tomorrow."

"Oh, good."

He followed her back past the shelving units to the table. "Any chance you could hide it?"

She turned to him, eyebrows lifted. "What do you mean?"

"Misfile it, so to speak. Stick it in a box marked...anything else. If, God forbid, the terrorists get access to this room, we don't want them to find it."

She bit her lip, considering the question.

He hated that he had to leave the following day. How had this trip passed so fast? He should've planned to stay longer.

"It won't work," she said. "Herr Papp plans to look at the notebook and all the pieces this evening. We're going to plan the exhibit, and he'll need to see everything."

"But this piece probably won't be part of the exhibit." Seeing the other problem, Bryan studied the little notebook in his hands. "We could recreate this. Rewrite all your notes—"

"No. Look, I know what you're saying, but it won't work. For one thing, Papp is going to be here"—she glanced at the time on her phone—"in about five minutes, so there's no time. Also, when your people come to collect it, he'll know I hid it from him."

"You could say it was a mistake."

"I don't make mistakes like that, Bryan." Her volume inched up. "I'm conscientious. I have to be when the things I handle and display are worth thousands, sometimes hundreds of thousands of dollars. I'm sorry, but if I lose my job, then I lose my visa. I can't risk it."

Right.

He understood her point. Hadn't he just refused to take the artifact for the same reason? Prison, sure, but he figured Uncle Sam could get him out of the charge. But if his peers got wind of what he'd done, he'd lose the respect of the community. And his job.

"The museum has top-notch security," Sophie said. "The piece has been here for months and nobody has tried to get to it. It'll be safe for one more night. It'll be fine."

Bryan hoped and prayed she was right.

CHAPTER THIRTEEN

Sophie stifled a yawn, then continued painting the display wall in the exhibit room. Her phone, propped against the paint can, played songs from her youth. She sang along to an oldie by the Backstreet Boys that had been one of her sister's favorites.

After Bryan left, Sophie and Herr Papp had gone through the artifacts to decide which should be displayed in the exhibit. It hadn't taken him long to show her the pieces he wanted to highlight.

All the items to be exhibited were currently locked away in a closet attached to the office, which was standard protocol. No sense risking those pieces getting mixed up with the others.

Bryan had told Herr Papp that the ivory chest might be of interest to the Americans, though he'd not explained why. Herr Papp wanted it easily accessible, though he hadn't seemed pleased to learn the Americans planned to take it away, so he left it in the office closet as well.

The rest of the pieces in the collection had been crated and returned to the storeroom.

The museum was quiet now. All the visitors and employees —including Herr Papp—had left.

Only Sophie and the security guard remained. She preferred working on the exhibit spaces at night when nobody was there to bother her, but not because she didn't love people. More because she did, and the presence of visitors and employees distracted her.

Usually, when she knew she'd work late to design an exhibit space, she didn't come to work until noon or later. But Herr Papp had expected her to stay with Bryan while he went through the artifacts as if the renowned professor might shove one in his pocket and run.

Ridiculous.

Not that she'd complained. Cataloging the artifacts had been mostly dull, punctuated by that one moment of excitement when they'd found the ivory chest.

But she'd enjoyed the day because she'd gotten to spend all those hours with Bryan. Hours and hours that should have been as boring as watching cement harden were enjoyable in his presence. The more time she spent with him, the more she liked him. He was humble and honest and smart and serious and funny and...

Yeah.

She was attracted to him in a way she hadn't been attracted to a man in a long time. After knowing him just a couple of days, she already felt more for him than she'd ever felt for Felix.

Well, unless one counted anger. She felt a lot of anger toward her ex.

She set the paint roller in the pan, stretched, and tapped her phone with her knuckle to check the time. She should probably wear gloves when she painted, but they got so hot. At least it was water-based paint and would clean easily. Between her work at the museum and her hobby, she was used to scrubbing multicolored freckles from her hands and arms.

According to her phone, it was nine thirty.

Though she'd told Bryan she could get back to her apartment by herself, he'd insisted on returning to see her home. He'd be there in an hour.

She'd already painted most of the walls a soft blue. When she finished that, she'd work on the accent walls, which would be a creamy white in a satin finish, best to highlight the more remarkable pieces. She was making good progress and would finish the walls on Monday, leaving the rest of the week to add display cases and placards.

She covered the roller and went back to work, thinking about Bryan. She'd done a lot of that. And hoping the two of them could spend a little time together tonight because he was leaving the following morning.

A pang of sadness hit.

She'd see him at Leila and Michael's wedding, but would that be it?

Of course she knew that nothing could come of their... friendship. And that was all it was, a friendship.

Even so, she already missed him. It was as if he'd filled a hole in her life she hadn't realized existed. Now she knew the hole was there, a chasm only Bryan could fill.

Which was ridiculous. She'd just met the guy three days before. Even that seemed impossible. How had they not known each other for years?

She didn't want to say goodbye to him so soon. Her life had felt full before Bryan came into it. Now the thought of him leaving made her feel...lacking.

Lord, You have a plan, and it's good. Help me not to want anything You don't want for me.

The song faded, the quiet almost holy as she sought the

Lord. His plan was good, both for her and for Bryan. Maybe He had—

A distant sound arrested her thoughts. Was that a door closing?

The guard wouldn't be opening and closing doors. Gunter only patrolled the main areas. He steered clear of the storage room and the office.

The next song started.

She climbed down from her step stool, laid the roller in the pan, and moved out of the brightly lit exhibit space into the dimmer corridor. Without the overhead lights on, the place had an eerie feeling she'd never quite gotten used to.

Had Herr Papp returned? She couldn't imagine why he would have, but she, the curator, and the security guard were the only ones with access to the building after hours.

Maybe Gunter had dropped something. Or Sophie had imagined the sound. Maybe her mind was playing tricks on her. Bryan's fear that somebody would break in and steal the ivory chest was getting to her.

Even as she told herself she was being silly, her pulse raced. She moved as quietly as possible through the modern masters exhibit, her music fading as she put distance between herself and the exhibit space. By the time she stepped into the foyer, she couldn't hear her music anymore.

She peeked into the security office, looking for Gunter.

Empty. The guard wasn't at his desk. He was probably patrolling on the other side of the museum.

Should she call out to him? Surely he'd hear her in the echoing museum, but... No. Something didn't feel right.

She continued to the office, where she swiped her badge, pressed her finger to the pad, and opened the door, her stomach swooping with irrational fear. She flicked on the light.

Empty.

She checked the closet where she and Herr Papp had stored the items for the exhibit. All of them—including the ivory chest —remained where they'd left them. Of course.

Bryan's paranoia was getting to her.

She locked the closet and left the office. After assuring herself the door was secured, she continued down the hallway, peeking into the various exhibit halls as she passed. Empty, empty, empty.

She turned the corner at the end of the hall.

All was silent.

But not the holy silence she'd experienced back in the exhibit space.

She reached the storeroom, where she repeated the process with her badge and fingerprint, and pushed the door open.

The light was on.

Movement to her right.

A man. Swarthy. Bald. Round face. Glasses.

Eyes wide.

Other men looked up from where they dug into crates.

Looking at *her*.

She jerked back. Slammed the door and ran.

"Gunter!" she screamed.

Maybe he would come. But she feared he wouldn't. Because those men would've taken care of the guard.

She had to get out of there. Everything in her told her to run. Run as fast as she could. To the door. Out to the cold night.

Get lost in the maze of streets.

Leave those men behind.

But...but.

The chest.

"Stop!" The man's voice was too loud.

She ran faster.

Rounded the corner. Reached the office. Swiped her badge, pressed her finger. Pushed inside.

And closed the door as quietly as possible.

Footsteps thumped, passed. Had he seen her come in here? She didn't know. Prayed he hadn't. Aside from the electronic lock, there was no way to secure the door. And if those men had made it into the storeroom, they must have a way past the electronic lock.

But they'd assume she'd run for the nearest exit. Wouldn't they?

What to do? What to *do*!

She shoved her hands into her pockets, but her phone wasn't there. It was playing music back in the exhibit space.

She grabbed the outside phone and dialed 911.

No, that wasn't it.

What was the number?

She couldn't remember how to reach the police in Germany. And she didn't have time to figure it out.

She grabbed the ivory chest from the closet. She couldn't leave it for the terrorists to find, which meant she had to take it away.

The curator would think she'd stolen it.

She'd explain. If this thing could enable a terrorist attack... What choice did she have?

She listened for footsteps in the hallway.

It was quiet. But somebody could be right there, just waiting for her to open the door. Unfortunately, there was no other way out of this room.

And nowhere to hide.

She knew the museum, inside and out. If she could cross into the exhibit hall on the other side of the hall, she could make her way to an emergency exit.

Maybe she could do it without being seen.

Please, Lord. Help me!

She had no options. It was her only chance.

CHAPTER FOURTEEN

B ryan stood and stretched. He'd been sitting in the lobby of his hotel for hours and still didn't have any information worth sharing.

In his Uber on his way back to his hotel, Michael had called to tell him the bad news. Despite what Bryan and Sophie had found at the museum, Brock thought the Munich connection was weak, the numbers on the chest irrelevant.

Michael hadn't gone into detail, but Bryan got the impression that wherever they were, they'd uncovered more important —or at least more pressing—information.

"Just leave the chest where it is," Michael said. "We'll have to trust the museum's security to keep it safe for now. Get on that plane tomorrow." Michael had ended the call.

And hadn't answered his phone since. After Bryan's third attempt to reach him, his brother sent a short text. *Get on the plane. I'll be in touch soon.*

Frustrating.

Bryan ate a quick dinner in the hotel restaurant, then started researching the Byzantine chest. People moved through regularly. Singles, couples, families, even a huge group of tourists—had to be twenty-five or thirty of them. The noise didn't bother him. He liked it, actually, the feeling that he wasn't alone.

He learned nothing new about the chest except its provenance—where it'd been prior to ending up in Munich. It'd been in Baghdad until it was stolen from the National Museum of Iraq in 2003. That much he knew, but how had it ended up at the museum?

That information wasn't available.

He turned his attention to the numbers. How hard could it be to figure out what they were?

He'd checked the photos he'd taken of the underside of the chest's lid and that of the numbers he'd had Sophie write down and compared them. The etching was faint and hard to read, even when he magnified the image.

There was a one that could be a seven, a six that could be an eight.

The four could be a nine. And vice versa.

By the time he noted every iteration, he had way too many possibilities.

He googled all of them and got obscure serial and manufacturing numbers—none of which matched exactly. One of the possibilities led him to a company that manufactured safes.

Except the number was off. Too few digits. But at least that would have been something. Not terribly helpful, though. What safe and where?

Could the numbers be a combination?

He followed that rabbit trail for too long before figuring out that there was no safe in the world with sixteen digits in the combination.

He'd tried dialing the numbers, but that led nowhere.

He tried dashes in between every two digits. Every three. Every four.

Didn't help.

Too many digits to be airplane tail numbers, train numbers, flight numbers.

Too many digits to be times or dates.

So far, he'd gotten exactly nothing. Nada, zippo, zilch, as Derrick would say.

A new thought occurred to him, and he was about to dig into it, but his timer went off.

He needed to leave to meet Sophie and see her home. Hopefully, stop for coffee or a snack or something, because he wasn't ready to say goodbye to her yet.

He'd work on figuring out what those numbers meant later. He ordered an Uber and headed for the door.

CHAPTER FIFTEEN

S ophie prayed for safety as she stepped into the corridor. Empty, thank God.

From both sides, men called out to each other from around corners, speaking Arabic, their voices echoing on the hard floors.

"She's not here."

"We can't let her sound the alarm."

"Find her!"

Sophie dashed into the darkened exhibit space across the hall.

Also empty. So far so good.

Keeping to the shadows, she hurried to the far end. The galleries had openings between them, and she passed through the first and into the second, moving toward the side. Though rarely used, there was an exit into the alley over here. It was wired, as were all the doors in the museum. As soon as she opened it, the alarm would sound.

Which was what she wanted. Except it would alert the men that she'd escaped. Would they search for her?

If they knew she had the artifact, no doubt they would.

She passed through the second gallery and was halfway

across the third when a man shouted, "Stop!" Then, "She has it!"

She broke into a run, but the man was too close and getting closer.

She reached the emergency exit and pushed it open.

The alarm screamed.

She bolted into the alley and turned toward the nearest street, a good fifty yards away.

The frigid air bit as wind funneled between the buildings, bringing tears to her eyes as she ran, ran as fast as her feet would carry her.

She could see the street ahead.

Feel the man behind.

Men.

They were coming. They were all coming. Shouting. Running. Screaming threats.

Terror and panic rose, but she pushed them down.

A figure stepped into view ahead of her, silhouetted by the lights on the main street.

"Help!" She tried to scream the word, it came out raspy and quiet, blocked by the fear in her throat.

The person made no indication he'd heard as he continued past.

But she was almost there.

She reached the mouth of the alley. Crossed the sidewalk. Ran into the street.

A driver slammed his brakes to avoid hitting her.

She barely gave the vehicle a glance, running toward the corner. Activity. People.

Buildings rose on both sides.

Music thumped ahead. Maybe...maybe...

She risked a look behind her.

Still there, crossing the street. Walking fast, eyes on her.

She was thirty or forty feet from the establishment at the corner. A nightclub, she guessed.

A man stood outside, bare arms crossed.

"Help me!" Her voice was stronger. She screamed the words in English, then switched to German. "They're following me. Help!"

The bouncer saw her, looked beyond her. He said something as he walked her way, but she didn't hear over the fear roaring in her head.

"*Danke.*" She passed him and slipped into the nightclub. Hopefully, that man would slow her pursuers down, at least. Give her time to hide.

Darkness. Lights flashing. Music throbbing. Bodies shoving, people bouncing, dancing, laughing.

The stench of alcohol and cologne and perfume.

A blond-haired woman in a too-tight dress bumped her. Giggled. Looked her up and down, gaze falling on the ivory chest Sophie protected like an infant, and said something in a language Sophie didn't understand.

Sophie pushed through the crowd to the back. There had to be another exit.

She reached the long bar, where people stood two and three deep to get their drinks. The bar was one step up from the rest of the room, giving Sophie a slightly better vantage point.

She made her way past a group of young people, then peeked between them toward the door.

A man stood there, surveying the space. Dark skin. Balding. Round face and glasses.

It was the man she'd seen in the storeroom.

The man, she now realized, she'd seen at the mission the day before. The one Bryan insisted was a terrorist.

Right again, professor.

Somehow, despite the people between them, his gaze locked on hers.

She started moving again.

Get me out of here, Lord. Get me to safety.

She reached the far end of the bar, dove into the press of bodies on the dance floor, and pushed through them, working to protect the chest and keep from getting elbowed in the face or bumped hard enough that she fell.

Finally, she hit the opposite side, where circular tables were surrounded by lounge chairs, men and women drinking and laughing and flirting.

Finding a spot between them, she shoved past and into a hallway leading to the restrooms.

And—*thank God*—an exit.

She pushed outside into the frigid air.

Another alley, this one empty. She ran to her left, away from the museum.

Made a right at the corner, then another left.

And kept running, choosing her route randomly, praying they wouldn't catch up with her.

CHAPTER SIXTEEN

As soon as his Uber turned the corner, Bryan saw flashing lights.

Police cars lined the street in front of the museum.

His stomach jumped into his throat. Where was Sophie?

The driver said something as he hit the brakes, blocking traffic. Bryan didn't pick up the man's words, uttered in a thick German accent.

"This is fine." He climbed out of the sedan and limped toward the melee, leaning heavily on his cane. His stupid leg always hurt more later in the day, and it was nearly half past ten. Cold wind seeped through his wool coat and leather gloves.

He hurried toward a man wearing a dark uniform and a knit cap. His jacket read POLIZEI on the back.

Bryan was five feet away when he asked, "What happened?"

The cop barely glanced in his direction. "Move along, sir."

"I was supposed to meet my friend here. She works at the museum. Sophia Chapman. Do you know if she's all right?"

Now, the cop gave him a squint-eyed look. "Do not move." He walked away and spoke to another man in a similar uniform.

The second man approached Bryan. Older than the first, and a few inches shorter than Bryan. He had small dark eyes that looked even smaller compared to his chubby cheeks. "Who are you?"

"My name is Bryan Wright. I'm an antiquities expert in Munich studying some of the museum's collection." No point getting into the details. "Where is—?"

"Vere are you staying?"

Frustrated but feeling it would be faster to answer the man's questions than argue, Bryan gave him the name of the hotel, then his phone number, his current address, and the name and address of Bowdoin College. He half expected the guy to demand his social security number and bank accounts. After the cop wrote down all of that, he asked, "How long are you here?"

"I'm supposed to leave in the morning. Where is Sophia Chapman? She was working here tonight."

"She verks at the museum?"

"Yes." Bryan worked to keep his frustration out of his tone. "She's an exhibit designer. Tonight, she was...designing an exhibit. I was going to meet her. Is she the one who called you?"

"Vy vere you to meet her?"

"I didn't want her walking home alone."

The cop gave Bryan's cane a pointed look. "You valk her home every night?"

"I live in the States, so what do you think?"

The man's beady eyes narrowed. "You expected her to meet you here?"

Patience, Wright. "Yes. At ten thirty."

"Inside or outside?"

"Around back, at the rear door."

"She has called you since you made zese arrangements?"

"I don't think so." He checked his phone to be sure. "I

haven't heard from her." Which was strange. Wouldn't she have texted or called to tell him what was going on?

If she was all right, she would have. The worry that'd hummed since he'd first seen the police lights rose to a roar. *Where are you, Sophie?*

Hasan Mahmoud's men must've broken in to get the artifact.

Had they found it? Had they taken it? Had they hurt her?

Michael had told him not to say anything to anyone about what he'd told him, but...

There was no *but*. Bryan needed to call Michael. It would be up to him and his people to inform the local police about what was going on. "Did she report the break-in?" he asked. "Is she safe?"

"Ve vere alerted by ze alarm. Ze museum vas...heisted."

His fears confirmed, acid filled his stomach. Had Sophie been inside? Had Mahmoud and his men found her? "Where is she?"

"You say she vas there?"

Was. Past tense. "Yes. Working. Have you searched inside?" He couldn't bring himself to ask if a body had been found. If someone had been killed. *Please, let her be okay.* "Where is she?"

"I do not know." The man pressed a finger to his ear, walking away. He paused and turned. "Do not leave, Mr. Wright."

Great. Super helpful.

Bryan scanned the faces all around. There were cops and passersby, though not many of those at this time of night.

But no Sophie.

The cop had told him not to leave. He *hadn't* told him not to move. Not to get closer. Not to listen.

So he did, inching toward a group of police officers gathered nearer the museum entrance. But they spoke German, of course.

He backed off, yanked out his phone, and dialed Michael.

It rang four times. Then went to voice mail.

He hung up and dialed again.

He'd keep dialing until his brother answered.

Because something needed to be done. *Now.*

And Bryan wasn't the man for the job.

CHAPTER SEVENTEEN

Sophia had no phone. No money. No coat. No plan.

She did have a stolen Byzantine chest made of ivory and probably worth more than she earned in a year. Which she'd stolen.

To keep the bad guys from getting it.

That excuse had worked for Ben Gates in *National Treasure*.

She doubted the German police—or Herr Papp—would be so forgiving, at least not if they didn't know about the terrorists. Would Bryan tell them?

Or would the Americans hang her out to dry, even though she'd only been trying to help? And maybe had almost gotten herself killed in the process?

She crouched in an alley a few blocks away from the museum, hiding between a short stack of stairs and a trash bin.

Teeth chattering. Body trembling. Trying not to freeze to death.

She was afraid to go home. If what Bryan said was true, then the terrorists knew where she lived.

Maybe they'd given up. More likely, they were waiting for her outside her building.

What should I do?

Go to the police, of course. Even though it might get her thrown in jail, at least the chest would be safe. They'd hold onto it, wouldn't they? As evidence? They would in the US, and she figured the procedures in Germany would be similar.

She wasn't sure where the closest station was but figured there'd be cops at the museum by now. She headed in that direction, taking a circuitous route, terrified she'd run into the terrorists along the way.

Fifteen minutes later, she reached a corner just a block from the museum. She'd expected police.

She hadn't expected quite so many. There were four...no, six police cars, one just a few feet from where she stood. Uniformed men milled about everywhere.

And there was Bryan. He looked furious, arguing with a police officer. Pointing at the museum. Voice raised. She strained to hear...

"I've been waiting long enough. Is she here or isn't she? If she's not, then you have to find her."

She started toward him, keeping to the shadows, knowing that as soon as she showed herself, she'd be arrested. At least it would be warm in the back of a police car.

The cop responded to Bryan, but he was facing the other direction—and speaking at a more dignified volume.

She had no trouble hearing Bryan's response. "She's not a thief. I don't care what Papp says. Obviously—"

The cop cut Bryan off.

Sophie froze on the sidewalk.

Of course they thought she was a thief. But even her boss hadn't given her the benefit of the doubt?

If she turned herself in, she could explain everything.

She took a breath and blew it out in a puff of white vapor.

That was when she saw him.

The man from the nightclub.

From the museum.

From the mission.

Dark skin. Round face. Bald head. Glasses.

The terrorist.

Talking to...Herr Papp. And a police officer.

Oh.

Oh, no.

Was Herr Papp part of this...thing?

No. Certainly not. But the terrorist knew him. Maybe he knew all the cops. Would any of them believe her story?

Even if they did, would they protect the ivory chest from that man? Or did they trust him?

The terrorist didn't need to take it, just examine it. Just see the numbers, maybe snap a photo of them.

And Papp was acting like they were friends. Acquaintances, anyway.

What should she do?

She turned back to Bryan. They locked eyes.

His head shook, the slightest movement, before he spoke to the cop again. "I'm telling you, Sophia Chapman isn't a thief. Whatever happened here tonight, she's a victim."

Run.

She had to run.

She backed up, returned to the alley where she'd come from, and dashed away.

From the cops. From her boss. From Bryan.

From warmth. And safety.

And into the cold, cold night.

CHAPTER EIGHTEEN

Bryan paced across his postage-stamp-sized hotel room. He'd thought maybe Sophie would call him here, but his phone hadn't rung.

Had he made the right decision?

Maybe he should've urged Sophie to come forward back at the museum. But after Hasan Mahmoud had shown up, Bryan hadn't known who to trust.

The terrorist had arrived a few minutes after Bryan. He'd talked to the curator—in German, so Bryan had no idea what he'd said—but it had been obvious that he and Herr Papp were acquaintances. They'd greeted each other with a handshake, and then they'd spoken to a police officer together, a united front.

Was Papp working with the terrorists? If not, how could they know each other?

What were the options?

And how was Bryan supposed to know?

He dialed his brother for the ten thousandth time in the last hour. *Answer the phone!*

But, once again, it went to voice mail.

Adding a new layer of worry. He'd promised to be available if Bryan needed him, so something must've happened.

Was his brother lying dead on the street in some European city?

He tossed his phone on the bed, frustrated.

Where was Sophie?

Was she safe? Warm?

She hadn't even had a jacket on when he'd seen her. No hat. No gloves. Just a light sweatshirt and yoga pants, clothes perfect for painting.

But she'd been alive. Praise God.

Unlike the museum guard.

At first, all the cop had told him was that a body had been found, and the image of sweet Sophie, lying dead on that cold marble floor, had filled him with horror and dread.

"The guard." The cop must've picked up on Bryan's shock because he hurried to add, "A man named Gunter Wagner. Not your friend. She is not here."

And then the cop had told him she was not only a suspect in the robbery, but in the guard's murder.

Protect her, Lord. Please, protect her.

How could he find her? What should he do?

He had no idea. He was no spy. No cop. No detective.

It was two o'clock in the morning. The hallway was quiet as he let himself out of his room and took the elevator to the lobby.

He'd grabbed his wool jacket and a thick fleece sweatshirt. Just in case Sophie showed up or called. Maybe he'd have an opportunity to give his coat to her, along with the gloves and hat tucked in the pockets. He could do that little thing. If he saw her again.

In the lobby, he found the night clerk at the desk. The woman had a straight-backed posture and wore a burgundy suit —the hotel uniform—with her name embroidered on the pocket.

"Good evening, sir." She spoke with a British accent. "May I help you with something?"

"If somebody tries to reach me on the phone in my room, will they talk to you or an operator, or does the call connect directly there?"

If the question surprised her, she gave no indication. "The main line will ring, and I will transfer the call personally."

"Good. I'm going to be in the lobby." He gave her his name and room number. "If anyone calls for me—"

"I will find you immediately. Do you need anything? The coffee is fresh." She nodded to the little coffee-and-tea station beside a giant flower arrangement. "I could find you a biscuit if you're hungry."

He was a little. And he figured by *biscuit,* she meant cookie. "I wouldn't turn that down."

"I'll see what I can do."

He filled a cup with coffee, settled on the far side of the lobby—in view of the doors—and flicked on a lamp. The overhead lights were off, and the little bulb didn't do much to chase away the shadows, but it was something.

He dialed Michael again.

Again, no answer.

Think, Bryan.

What should he do?

He had to find Sophie, but where would she go?

She was smart enough not to go home. Surely the terrorists would be watching her apartment.

Would she go to the mission where she volunteered? The terrorists knew about that place, too. She probably wouldn't go there. Would she go to Felix?

The thought brought the slightest twinge of jealousy, as if that had any place in this moment. And anyway, he seriously doubted she'd go to the home of a man who was stalking her.

She had friends, but Bryan didn't know any of them.

She would want Bryan to find her, wouldn't she? Assuming that was a yes, then maybe she'd go to somebody they had in common. The only person in Germany they had in common—besides Herr Papp—was Aaron.

Yes, the more he thought about the man who ran the mission, the more convinced he was that Sophie would reach out to him.

What had she called him? The keeper of many secrets. Aaron would protect her.

Bryan needed to find Aaron Driscoll. But how?

Oh, man. He was dumb. They had someone else in common. The most obvious someone.

Leila.

It was six hours earlier in Maine, meaning about eight thirty in the evening. Bryan dialed his future sister-in-law.

"Hello?"

"Hey, it's Bryan. You haven't heard from Sophie, have you?"

"No. Has something happened?"

"We got separated." He wasn't sure how much he should tell her. Of course, she knew about the terrorists. She was related to some of them, after all. She'd crossed continents to escape them.

But did she know about Bryan's mission? About Sophie's part in it? He needed to walk a fine line.

Leila must've guessed his thoughts because she asked, "Does it have to do with my uncle, Hasan?" Her voice was filled with concern. "Has he hurt her? Has he done something?"

"Sophie is all right. At least, I think she is. But the museum was broken into. Do you know about the connection to the museum?"

"Michael said he thought Hasan might be after something there. He questioned my sister extensively, but she had no information. And I assume you went over there to help Michael, yes?"

"Yeah. I found something at the museum today. Tonight, the museum was broken into. Sophie escaped with it." That much he knew—he'd seen the chest in her hands. "The problem is, the police think she's the thief"—and murderer, but he left that part out—"so she's running from them and your uncle and his men. If you know where she is—"

"You have tried to call her?"

"She must not have her phone." Or her purse or her coat, wandering the streets of Munich in the frigid cold, with nowhere to go.

His gaze flicked to the door. Maybe she'd simply walk right in.

But she didn't, and that didn't surprise him. She'd seen him talking to the cops. Maybe they'd look for her here. Maybe they were staking out the entrance right now.

"But I was hoping she'd call you from a payphone or...a borrowed phone or something."

"She would call you, no?"

"She wouldn't remember my phone number. But she might remember yours." Who knew phone numbers anymore? Bryan had a great memory, but he knew very few from memory.

"I doubt she would remember mine," Leila said. "It is a new number."

Right. That would've been way too easy.

"Do you think she'd reach out to Aaron Driscoll?"

"Yes, yes. I think she would." Excitement filled Leila's tone. "Did you meet him?"

"Friday. Can I have his number?"

"My old phone, with all my numbers, was taken away from me. I never got it back."

"Right. Of course. Can you tell me where he lives? I'll just go to his house."

"I do not know, Bryan. I never went there."

Dang. That thought brought another. "Would Sophie know where he lives?"

"I believe so, yes. He was my mentor, but he and his wife are her friends. Have you talked to Michael? He could probably find Aaron's address for you."

"I haven't been able to reach Michael." He heard a quick intake of breath and hurried on. "He was in the middle of something. I'm sure he's fine. He just can't talk."

"Yes. Yes. That is probably true." Though Leila didn't sound convinced. "If I speak with him, I will have him contact you."

"And if Sophie calls you, give her my phone number. Tell her to call me. I'll be here, at the hotel."

"You are not returning tomorrow?"

Technically today, for Bryan, anyway. "I'm not leaving Munich until I know she's all right."

Leila didn't speak for a long moment. When she did, she said, "I am grateful to you, Bryan, for taking my friend's well-being seriously."

"Yeah, well... I like her. She's..." Amazing. Beautiful. Special.

Missing.

"I'll do my best to make sure she's safe."

He was about to hang up when Leila broke into prayer. Like her mentor, she didn't bother to ask if it was all right, didn't waste her time with so many of the rote words Christians used when praying aloud, just started talking to God as if He sat beside her on the sofa.

Bryan closed his eyes and bent over his knees, not adding anything to her sweet and simple request that God protect Sophie and help Bryan find her. That He protect Michael and his team. That He give all of them wisdom and knowledge and insight that only He could provide.

When she uttered the *Amen*, he echoed it. "Thank you for that."

"I will continue to pray for all of you. Please, let me know when you find her. And if you speak with Michael before I do—"

"I'll tell him to call you. Thanks, Leila."

He set his phone on his lap but kept the prayer posture. He needed the Lord now, more than he'd ever needed Him before. So he stayed just like that, and waited for God to answer Leila's prayer.

For the wisdom, knowledge, and insight He could provide.

Because Bryan had no idea what to do.

Bryan stayed in the foyer, only going back to his room long enough to shower and change his clothes. He packed his suitcase and left it on his bed. After booking the room for one more night, he settled in his chair in the common area.

At five o'clock, the overhead lights came on.

Clanking dishes and jingling silverware told him the restaurant was preparing for customers.

The sun rose beyond the windows.

By six, people were exiting the stairwell and elevator, dragging suitcases toward the desk.

They were checking out and grabbing shuttles and cars to the airport for their flights home. Some chattering like it was midday, despite the early hour.

Most yawning, looking ragged but content.

Bryan would have been among them if the visit had gone as planned. He'd reached out to the airline in the middle of the night, explained that he'd had an emergency, and put off his return flight.

Later, he'd call his department head and TAs and make arrangements for his classes this week. He had no idea how long this...thing would last, but he wasn't leaving Europe until he found Sophie.

Not that he had any idea how to manage that.

The front doors opened, and a crowd of people exited into the chilly morning.

One man slipped in.

Bryan watched as the man surveyed the foyer, the check-in desk, the restaurant, gaze skimming past the tourists. Then the stranger continued deeper into the room. He wandered to the beverage station and made himself a cup of coffee.

He wore no uniform, but by the way he held himself—and the way he surveyed his surroundings—Bryan pegged him as a cop.

He looked down at his laptop before the guy's gaze reached him. If the cop wanted to question him, he'd approach.

More likely, he was there to watch for Sophie.

A few moments passed before Bryan reached for his coffee. Sipping, he scanned the room.

Sure enough, the detective had chosen a chair in the corner, back to the wall. Perfect place to watch the door—and Bryan.

Excellent. Not that he thought Sophie would walk in, but if she did...

She'd be caught.

And maybe...maybe that would be a good thing. Mahmoud wouldn't be able to look at the chest if she turned it over now. It would be better for her to turn herself in than to be caught trying to evade the police.

But she'd be charged with murder.

At nine fifty, he ordered a car but didn't head for the doors until the driver texted he was there. At that point, Bryan stood, grabbed his laptop in one hand, threw his bag over his shoulder, and using his cane, hurried outside.

Once he was loaded in the backseat of the silver Mercedes, he greeted the driver, whose image in the rearview matched the one on the app. Middle Eastern, probably in his thirties. Ervin something.

As Ervin navigated away from the hotel, Bryan twisted to look through the rear window.

Sure enough, the cop had followed him.

Bryan turned back before the guy caught him looking.

He'd lost him. For now.

Unless another cop was in a car idling at the curb, just waiting for him to make a run for it. Was Bryan being...tailed?

How had he gotten himself into a situation where he was worried about *tails* like he was trapped in some Hollywood script?

It was Sunday morning, and traffic was light as they wove through town and neared the mission.

When the driver parked, Bryan handed him three twenties and asked him to wait, earning an eager head-nod.

Bryan went to the door, laptop bag slung over one shoulder, leaning on his cane with the opposite hand.

The door was locked.

He knocked. Had to try a couple of times before the door swung open.

Felix stood on the other side.

Bryan was tall, and it was a rare day he had to look up at someone. Felix was a good three inches taller. He wore navy trousers and a pale gray cardigan over a white button-down and a red tie, looking very *GQ*-meets-nerd, young and lean with a strong chin and icy blue eyes that narrowed when he saw Bryan.

He squared his shoulders and crossed his arms, blocking the entry and Bryan's view past him.

"Vat are *you* doing here?"

"Looking for Aaron."

"He is not here on Sundays." Felix backed up.

About to slam the door in Bryan's face.

"Sophie's in trouble."

The door froze in Felix's grip. If anything, the man looked more menacing than he had before. "Vat did you do?"

"Had nothing to do with me. There was a break-in at the museum last night. Sophie was there when it happened, and now she's missing."

"How do you know this? Vy would the police talk to you and not to me?"

"I was there to meet her and walk her home."

If the fiery look Felix gave him were an actual flame, Bryan would be reduced to ashes.

"We've developed a friendship—nothing else." Not that Bryan wouldn't like more with Sophie, but he wasn't stupid enough to say so, not when he needed this jerk's help. "I was hoping we'd have one last cup of coffee before my flight this morning."

"If you have a flight this morning, then vhy are you still here?"

"Because she's missing. I can't leave until I know she's all right. My guess is she went to Aaron's house. Can you give me his phone number?"

"You go back to verever you came from. I vill take care of Sophie."

Felix slammed the door.

Bryan limped back to the Uber and climbed in. "You're okay to wait a few minutes with me?"

"Yes, yes." His accent was not very different from Leila and Jasmine's. "We wait as long as you want."

Fortunately, it didn't take that long.

Eight minutes later, Felix hurried out of the building and practically ran down the sidewalk to a hatchback, one of those tiny energy-efficient things that would probably fold like an envelope in a fender-bender.

Once again feeling like the protagonist in a bad movie script, he said, "Follow that guy."

Ervin yanked the car into drive and angled onto the quiet street.

"I'd rather he not know we're behind him."

"I understand." He eased the gas, putting more distance between them. "You are like Jason Bourne, yes?"

He couldn't help the bark of laughter. "Not even close, man."

Jason Bourne might not have known who he was, but he knew what he was *doing*.

Bryan hadn't the slightest idea.

He hoped this play wouldn't get himself—or Sophie—killed.

CHAPTER NINETEEN

Sophie was sweating, but she stayed curled under the blankets, afraid to move. Afraid the terror would return.

Freezing.

Running for her life.

A man on her heels.

Gripping her shoulder, yanking her around.

No!

She shook herself awake and opened her eyes.

She was safe. And warm. And hidden.

The men only caught up to her in her nightmares.

After Bryan had warned her away from the museum the night before, she'd run and kept running, the slap of her sneakers echoing off the buildings in the silence. She ran for fear of being caught. And then she ran because it kept her warmer than walking.

She'd headed toward Old Town and the tourists and crowds, carefully avoiding the blocks surrounding her apartment. It was eleven thirty by the time she reached the Hofbräuhaus, but the famous beer hall was still hopping. She slipped into the blessed warmth and scanned her surroundings, afraid somehow the terrorists had guessed her play. Which was silly, of course.

The famous tavern was three stories high. It'd been built in the seventeenth century, then expanded late in the nineteenth. Like everything in this part of the city, it had been damaged during the World War II bombings, but since then it had been repaired, refurbished. Renewed.

Under different circumstances, she'd pause to admire the architecture, the dark woodwork and rounded ceilings and arched windows. The artwork on the ceiling had been recently completed, the painters careful to make it look old.

The room took up almost all of the ground floor and was filled with long tables and hard benches, typical of a German tavern. It was beautiful and historical and unique.

The crowd was different here than it'd been in the night-club. No hopping, flirting, drunken dancers. The customers were mostly older, more relaxed, and not out to prove they were important or desirable. This place was less about hooking up and more about friendship and comradery.

In all the years she'd lived in Munich, she'd only been to the Hofbräuhaus once, preferring coffee shops and bakeries to beer halls and bars.

She headed for the bathroom, where she used the facilities and checked her reflection.

The day's makeup was long gone, dripped away by cold-induced tears. Her skin was pink, her eyes red-rimmed, her lips pale. Her curly hair had been whipped by the wind and now frizzed out in a puff.

She was a mess.

But at least she had a plan.

Without her cell phone, she had no way to reach...anybody. Aside from her parents, she didn't know anybody's phone number.

And Mom and Dad couldn't help her out of this jam. She needed to reach Bryan and the "powers that be" who'd told him about the terrorists and the plot and the craziness that had led to this moment.

She'd considered, during her long jog, heading to Bryan's hotel. But it seemed she was the number-one suspect in the museum heist, and Bryan her only defender.

Maybe the police would watch him.

Maybe she was being paranoid, but it seemed foolish to just...waltz into his hotel and hope nobody would see her.

The answer was to reach out to the only person both of them knew in Munich who wasn't involved in all this mess.

She lingered in the bathroom until a fifty-something American walked in. She had a brown-haired bob and kind eyes. She wore skinny jeans, an oversized sweater, clunky silver jewelry, and Adidas sneakers.

The woman glanced at Sophie on her way to the stalls, offering a quick, "Hey, there!" with a Southern accent. Texas, maybe.

When the woman emerged and washed her hands, Sophie gathered her nerve and spoke to her.

"I could use some help."

The woman peered at her in the mirror, suspicion flashing in her eyes as her gaze flicked from Sophie's face to the ivory chest she held beneath her arm. "What do you need?"

"Could I borrow your cell phone? Just for one call?"

"What happened to yours?"

"I left it at work, along with my wallet. And the place is closed, so I can't get back in."

All of which was true, if sans a few pertinent facts.

The woman dried her hands, then turned to face Sophie fully. She opened her mouth, and Sophie braced for the obvious questions. Like what she was doing at a bar at almost midnight, alone, without a wallet, phone, or even coat, and carrying a priceless work of art.

"Are you going to call for a ride?" she asked.

"A cab."

"How are you going to pay for it?"

Oh. Right. "Uh, I think my friend will loan me some money when I get to his house."

"You're not going home?"

"I-I can't go home."

"Mmm-hmm." Her lips pressed closed. "I'm guessing there's a man involved. And I'm guessing he's not as nice a guy as you once thought."

More than one man, and they were definitely not *nice*. Sophie nodded.

The woman dug in her purse, pulled out an iPhone, and unlocked it. "Where you going?"

She didn't remember Aaron's phone number, but she could picture his address. She told the woman, who tapped it into the phone, then looked up. "This isn't the address of the not-nice guy?"

"No. It's not."

"You promise?"

"Yes, ma'am. I'll be steering clear of him."

"Okay, then." The woman focused on the phone, then said, "Your Lyft will be here in five minutes."

"Oh. That's so kind of you." Sophie couldn't help the tears that filled her eyes. "I don't even... If you write down your name and address, I'll send you a check."

"Not a chance. We ladies have to stick together." She hooked her arm with Sophie's and started for the door. "I'll wait with you."

Sophie had arrived on Aaron's doorstep a half hour later.

As she'd known he would, he ushered her inside. He and his

wife, Mary, warmed Sophie up with a cup of tea. Aaron fed her cookies while Mary prepared a place for her to sleep.

Now, in the dim light that shone through a tiny window, she surveyed the space she'd barely glimpsed the night before.

The room was in the attic, barely large enough for the twin blow-up mattress Mary had made up for her. The exposed rafters were so close that, when she sat up, she could touch them.

Though there was no heat in the space, the area was warm enough, the air seeping upward from the lower floors of Aaron's two-story house.

When Mary had first brought her up the night before, Sophie had imagined herself sleeping on the stack of boxes stored in the large space. But Mary had walked between them, around luggage, and to an old, worn bookshelf.

And then she'd swung the bookshelf aside to reveal a short staircase that led up to this hidden space.

"I closed it so you'd understand that you're safe here," Mary had said. "A hiding place from Nazis."

Oh. *Oh.*

A place originally used by Germans to hide Jews was now being used by former Muslims to shelter an American Christian from German police. And terrorists.

There was probably some irony in that, but she was too wrung out to process it.

Aaron, after hearing Sophie's story, had thought the hiding place best, in case the police came knocking. He had enough experience with untrustworthy authorities to fear anyone in a uniform.

Hidden and warm for the first time in hours, Sophie had slept. Late, if the angle of the sun was any indication.

Banging below had her sitting up. Was that what had woken her?

She shoved on her sneakers, descended the short stairs, and pushed the door open, swinging the bookshelf aside. She tiptoed across the attic to the staircase.

The banging came again—insistent knocking.

And then, "Felix, my friend." Aaron's voice was barely audible as it carried up from the first floor.

"Is she here?"

The night before, Sophie had told Aaron the whole story about the terrorists and the museum. She'd also mentioned the break-in at her apartment—and her suspicion that Felix had done it—and was stalking her.

"I am surprised he would behave that way." She'd been about to press her case, but Aaron continued. "Do not worry, my friend. I will not tell him you're here."

At the door two stories below, Aaron asked a question Sophie couldn't make out.

"Sophia." Felix's voice was perfectly audible. "She's in trouble."

Aaron must've asked a question because Felix shouted, "Where is she? Sophia!"

"Friend, friend." Aaron's voice rose a little. "Please, do not shout. My neighbors—"

"Sophia! Where are you?"

"That is enough." Aaron's voice rang with authority. "I understand you care for her, but if she wanted your help, then she would have asked you for it. Go back to the mission and fulfill your duty."

"I need to find her."

"You will not find her here."

Which was true enough, or would be when Sophie returned to her hidden room.

At the sound of Felix clomping through the house two stories below—accompanied by his insistent, "Sophia!"—she did just that, pulling the bookcase closed, thankful that it didn't creak or scrape against the floor.

A few minutes later, Felix burst into the attic. "Sophia!"

"I told you that you would not find her," Aaron said, "and you have not."

Sophie noticed how careful the man was not to lie.

"If she shows up," Felix said, "call me."

"If she chooses to call you, then she will. I will not betray her to you or anyone else. You are needed at the mission now. Go fulfill your duty."

Whatever Felix muttered in response, she didn't hear. The door slammed, and their footsteps faded as they returned to the first floor.

Leaving Sophie to wonder how her ex had heard she was in trouble. And missing.

Had Bryan contacted him? Or had the police?

Fifteen long minutes passed. Sophie didn't leave her hidden room, and Aaron didn't come to tell her all was well. Did he believe she was in danger?

Was she?

Knocking came again, fainter.

It stopped almost immediately, and she heard no voices.

But footsteps sounded, up the stairs and then in the attic.

The bookshelf slid away, and Aaron poked his head into the room. "You have a visitor."

"Not Felix?"

"He is not happy with me, but he is gone." Aaron disappeared.

There was only one person Aaron would bring to her.

She scooted off the bed and started down the short staircase.

A hand reached out to help her the last couple of steps, and she took it.

When she emerged from the dark space, it wasn't Aaron standing beside her, but Bryan.

Thank God.

He pulled her against his chest and wrapped her in his arms.

She gripped fistfuls of his soft knit sweater, too overcome with relief to speak. Afraid to let him go.

Maybe he felt the same because he said nothing. The only sound was the low thump of his racing heart against her ear. He was warm and comforting, and she felt safe with him. Safer than she'd felt since this whole crazy thing began.

Too soon, he backed away just enough to peer down at her, keeping his arms around her back. "You're all right?"

"How did you find me?"

"Felix. I went to the mission, told him you were in trouble, and demanded to see Aaron."

"He brought you here?" She couldn't help the shock in her tone.

One side of Bryan's mouth ticked up. "Not exactly. I figured he'd finish the service first and planned to wait him out. But he left within a few minutes. I had my driver follow him."

Smart. Very smart.

"I was outside when he got here, hoping Aaron would send him away without my having to get involved." He looked around, then toward the staircase where she'd emerged. "Obviously, your friends had the situation well in hand."

"They hid me last night."

"You still have the chest?"

She nodded. "I didn't let it out of my sight."

"Tell me everything."

Behind Bryan, a throat cleared.

Bryan dropped his arms and backed away, suddenly seeming embarrassed. Maybe she should feel the same, but her relief overpowered everything else.

Aaron stood near the attic door. "I am afraid it was not only Felix who was followed here. There's a car I believe belongs to the police. And if *they* followed you, then it's possible the terrorists Sophie spoke about followed as well. What can you tell me about them?"

"The only one I know is called Hasan Mahmoud. He's Iraqi. Leila Amato's uncle, as a matter of fact."

"Whoa." Sophie backed a step away from Bryan to see him better. "Leila's *uncle?*"

"I don't know how much she told you about what happened to her."

"She told me that a family friend spotted her and took her back to Iraq. She had to escape again."

Bryan was nodding slowly. "Yeah, that's true. There's a pretty interesting story, much of it involving her uncle and a... protégé of his, I guess, a guy her father planned for her to marry."

Leila had almost been forced to marry?

"Anyway," Bryan continued, "the family friend and her uncle are terrorists. I'm not supposed to tell you this, but considering you're in the middle of it now, you have the right to know. Hasan Mahmoud was the guy at the mission—"

"*My* mission?" Aaron asked.

"I saw him there Friday."

Sophie said, "I did too. And it was he who broke into the museum yesterday."

Bryan described Mahmoud, but Aaron showed no sign of recognition. "He was watching Sophie. It's very possible that they followed me." He stepped away from her, running a hand over his hair. "I was thinking about finding her and evading the police. I didn't think about the terrorists watching. I shouldn't have led them to your house."

"You mustn't apologize to me," Aaron said. "I'm certain you haven't given them any information they didn't already have."

Sophie had known Aaron a long time, but she'd never seen the grim expression he wore now.

"If they know about the mission, then they know about me and all I've done to spread the Good News to Muslims. If that is the case, then they already know where I live. And all about my family." His Adam's apple dipped, but he squared his shoulders. "My life is God's. Mary's life is God's. Our children have moved out of Germany and should be safe. Mary and I knew the danger when God called us to this. He can protect us. If He does not, then 'To live is Christ, to die is gain,' no?" He nodded, answering his own question. "We will not fear."

"Even so," Bryan said. "If I put you in danger—"

"My life *is* danger, and my God is good. How do we get you two out of here?" Before Sophie could offer an idea—and she had nothing—Aaron said, "Mary and I will prepare breakfast, and we will pray, and you will eat. God will provide a way. He always does."

Sophie admired his faith. Most of the time, she shared it. But after her terrifying dash through Munich the night before, knowing she was being hunted not only by the police but by terrorists...

She had a feeling her faith was about to be tested like it had never been before.

CHAPTER TWENTY

Aaron had insisted Bryan remain in the attic with Sophie, just in case. From here, they could scramble up the short staircase to the secret room if anyone came looking for them.

The space was warm, if not cozy. Exposed rafters overhead, worn plywood floors beneath his feet. Old furniture, boxes, chests, and luggage filled the bulk of the area. Dust motes danced in the light from the small dormer window.

He shoved a few things aside to make room, then dragged an old rocker and a moth-eaten upholstered chair to create a seating area. He pushed a metal trunk—by the weight of it, it was filled with rocks—to use as a table.

While Sophie used the shower downstairs, Bryan settled on the rocker, bent over his knees, and prayed. How had he gotten himself and Sophie into this crazy situation?

More importantly, how was God going to get them out?

Guide us, Lord. We have no idea what we're doing.

Sophie returned from her shower, curly hair wet and springy, gray eyes brighter. She looked fresh and clean and lovely. Mary must've loaned her the black leggings and sweater. But Aaron's wife was short and skinny, lacking Sophie's height and beautiful curves. The leggings barely reached her ankles, and the sweater was snug.

Her outfit hid nothing.

Oh, boy. He was in trouble. Not only was this woman kind and generous and brave and beautiful. She was sexy.

He forced himself to focus on her face. "You look...awake." Yeah. That's what he was thinking.

She didn't seem to pick up on his turmoil as she settled on the cushy chair—though by the way she squished down into it, he wasn't sure how much cushion was left. It nearly swallowed her. "I needed the shower. And a few minutes to process."

"What do you think?"

"This whole thing is nuts. But also real, and we have to deal with it."

Pretty much what he'd been thinking.

Mary delivered a tray of food, setting it on the trunk. She was Iraqi, like her husband and Leila and Jasmine, taller than the twins, but only just, with a kind face and graying hair she'd pulled back in a knot. "Aaron is praying. He will be up in a few minutes."

She started to walk away, but Bryan caught her hand before she could.

She looked down at him, a curious expression in her eyes.

"I can't tell you how much we appreciate this."

Sophie added, "You've been more than generous." She plucked at her sweater. "I'll get this back to you."

The older woman squeezed Bryan's hand, smiling at Sophie. "It is an honor to serve the people of God. I do it for you, but mostly, I do it for Him." She slipped out of the attic, closing the door behind her.

"They're an amazing couple." Bryan pushed to his feet, quelling a smile as he watched Sophie attempt to wiggle out of the chair that'd swallowed her up.

"I'll get it." He held the tray in front of her, and she took a plate and chose from the smorgasbord Mary had delivered.

Pastries alongside butter and jelly, slices of meat and various cheeses, plus a couple of boiled eggs in those little egg cups.

When Sophie had what she wanted, Bryan filled a plate, his stomach growling as he made his selections.

Between bites, Sophie told him about her night. About her harrowing escape from the museum and her dash through a nightclub.

Just thinking about all she'd been through sent fresh fear to his veins. "You were smart to dive into that crowd."

"I lost them, anyway. And then decided to head back to the museum to turn myself in."

"Maybe you should have." He still questioned his decision to send her away.

"With Hasan Mahmoud there? I was afraid he'd get access to the chest. He wouldn't have to take it, just look at the numbers. Which...that would've been easy, right? He could've just acted like he wanted to look at the thing. Maybe he could've memorized the numbers."

"And you'd have been arrested for murder."

She froze, a bite of the soft-boiled egg halfway to her mouth. The healthy pink in her cheeks faded to a pasty white.

Uh-oh.

"Murder?" Slowly, she lowered her fork. "Who was murdered?"

"Sorry. I assumed you knew, though how you could have... Sorry. It was the guard."

"Gunter?" Her eyes filled. "Gunter was killed? How?"

"The police didn't tell me much. All I know is that his body was found where he worked."

"I looked for him. He wasn't... I didn't go into the security room. He must've been behind the desk. I can't believe it." Her voice was a whisper. "They killed him."

Her plate started to slip off her lap, and Bryan grabbed it. He set it and his own on the trunk.

Sophie's lips trembled. She seemed unaware of the tears dripping down her cheeks and off her chin. When she lifted her hands to cover her face, they trembled.

"I'm sorry. I'm so sorry." He knelt in front of her, not sure what to do but wanting to be there, close. Of course she'd known the guard. Of course she cared enough about him to weep at the news of his death.

Sophie loved everybody. Her heart was big enough to cherish all the people in her life.

He cursed himself for being so callous. He pushed forward, wrapped his arms around her, and pulled her into an embrace. He had no idea what to say. The *it's okay* stuck in his throat. It wasn't okay. A man was dead, which was certainly not *okay* for the family who loved him.

And Sophie, who seemed heartbroken.

She tucked her head into his chest and gripped his sweater in a fist and wept.

He held her until she seemed to have cried all the tears she had.

Minutes passed before she managed a few shuddering breaths that weren't interrupted by sobs. She backed up and swiped her fingertips beneath her eyes. "Sorry."

"You two were close?"

Her laugh was watery as she shook her head. "No. Not at all. He was... He wasn't a very nice man. I tried to be friends with him, but he didn't like me. Or anybody, I think."

"Oh." Bryan was confused. Which she must've guessed.

"It's just...he's dead. I feel like it's my fault. I should've alerted him." She tucked her chin and hid her face. "It's arrogant to think I could've changed anything, but even so... I wish we'd told someone. I wish...I wish all those things hadn't happened."

Regret. There was an emotion he was intimately familiar with, though in Sophie's case, she had nothing to regret. She'd done nothing wrong. She'd made no bad choices.

She sniffed. "I don't know what I'm saying. I'm sorry."

He shifted back onto his heels. "You don't owe me an apology. This whole thing is...bizarre. Gunter might not've been your friend, but he was a human being. It's okay to cry for him."

A short sob burst from her. "It's more than that. I was there. They must not have heard my music or even checked that wing. If they had, they'd have killed me too. I guess the gravity of the situation just...hit me. I ran on adrenaline all night. Then collapsed and slept. In the shower, I thought about my escape, but even then... I don't know. Hearing about his death, all I can think is, that could've been me." She shook her head. "How incredibly selfish."

Bryan hooked a finger beneath her chin. "Sophie, look at me."

She did, blinking. Even with all the sadness and worry in her big gray eyes, she was captivating.

"Your life is valuable," he said. "There's nothing selfish about your reaction. Those men could've killed you. They would have, if they'd had the chance. I'm just thankful you escaped. I can be thankful that you escaped and be sorry the guard didn't. And so can you. That doesn't make you selfish. It makes you...smart. And honest."

She nodded, though the motion was slight.

"And I agree. I wish we could've done more to prevent it." But what could they have done differently?

What happened the night before was on the CIA. On Michael. Or, more accurately, on Michael's boss.

If only his brother would call him back.

Something must be terribly wrong. Bryan prayed for him and his team, wishing there were more he could do.

Maybe he couldn't help his brother, but he was going to do everything in his power to see that Sophie was safe and the chest kept out of the hands of terrorists who were willing to kill for it.

~

Bryan had finished his breakfast when footsteps sounded on the stairs. A moment later, Aaron knocked and then stepped in through the attic door. "It is time you tell me everything."

Everything?

He knew what Michael would say. *Tell him nothing.*

But Michael wasn't here. And Aaron had earned Bryan's trust.

Bryan stood. "Take my seat." After the older man settled on the rocking chair, Bryan perched on the metal trunk and told him what he'd told Sophie two days before. About the *chatter* the powers-that-be had picked up. About the artifact the terrorists were after and the potential bombing in Munich.

"But obviously, those so-called powers aren't that worried about it," Sophie said after Bryan finished. Her tone was tinged with bitterness. "If they were, they'd have picked up the chest when you called them yesterday afternoon. They'd have made sure the museum was secure."

Bryan needed to tread carefully. "I think there was some disagreement among the decision-makers about how important the chest was. It's all very...jumbled."

Aaron leaned forward, elbows on his thighs, hands clasped together. The wrinkles on his age-worn face seemed more prominent in the sharp light from an exposed bulb hanging overhead.

Was the man as old as those wrinkles made him out to be, or had danger and difficulty added years to his face? "What do they say now, your powerful friends?"

Bryan hated to tell them this. He hated to tell them how... unsupported they were.

That they were on their own.

But Aaron and Sophie deserved the truth. "I haven't been able to reach them."

Sophie's eyebrows shot up.

Aaron's lowered. "What do you mean? You told them about the chest, and then they quit answering your calls? Do you think perhaps it is all connected?"

Sophie asked, "What are you saying?"

"Perhaps the men who got you involved are working for the terrorists."

"Impossible." The accusation made Bryan's pulse thump in his throat. "There is no way—"

"It is a strange coincidence," Sophie said. "The very night you alert them to which artifact the terrorists were after, people break into the museum. What if Aaron's right?"

"He's not." It was ludicrous. No way Michael was working for the terrorists who'd almost killed his bride-to-be.

Although, were the people he worked for? Was it possible Brock or one of the other guys on Michael's elite team was playing for the wrong side?

He thought about the men he'd met in Greece when he and Derrick had gone to pick up Michael, Leila, and Jasmine. Bryan hadn't had that much interaction with them, but they'd all seemed like true-blue Americans.

They'd risked their lives to save Leila and Jasmine, and in the process, gotten a whole boatload—literally—of terrorists killed.

Bryan couldn't imagine that any of those men was working against America—and *for* terrorists.

And even if they were, Bryan had given Michael the numbers he'd found on the chest. If Michael shared those numbers with his team, and if one of them were working with the terrorists, then there'd be no need to steal the artifact.

Bryan was certain—nearly certain, anyway—that nobody on Michael's team was compromised.

"Your loyalty is commendable," Aaron said, "but sometimes, loyalties are misplaced. I believe you should consider—"

"You're barking up the wrong tree." Maybe Aaron hadn't ever heard the idiom because he looked more confused than anything. "They asked me to come this weekend because the attack is imminent. We're fortunate the chest was moved last night or else Mahmoud and his men would've gotten their hands on it." To Sophie, he said, "You told me they were digging through crates in the storage room, right?" At her nod, he continued. "If they'd known we found the chest, then they would've known it wouldn't be with the rest of the stuff." Again to Aaron, "There's no way my contact betrayed us."

Sophie was nodding slowly, though it was clear her focus wasn't on what he'd said. Her gaze seemed far away, unfocused.

And then she fixed her eyes on him. "Your trip here was Michael's idea."

Uh-oh. "That's not—"

"Unless you set up that whole lunch to fool me into believing you were coming because of professional curiosity, in which case... You lied to me."

He knew where this was going, but he didn't know how to stop the train of her thoughts. "I didn't lie to you. I told you everything. I mean, not at first, but the other night."

"Not everything." Sophie stared at him, not angrily. More like she was trying to solve a puzzle.

In the sudden and growing tension, Aaron looked from one to the other.

"Okay, then. Michael is involved." Sophie's words were tentative. "He was the one who encouraged you to fly to Munich this weekend. He told you that if you waited, you'd end up having to go to Baghdad. And when we left the restaurant that day, you asked him where he was going and then told him you'd meet him there. At your other brother's house. Right?"

Bryan could steer her away from those ideas. He could come up with a plausible story, but he didn't want to lie.

Honestly, he wanted somebody to know what was going on.

"Michael rescued Leila when her family imprisoned her," Sophie said. "From Iraq. Was he in the military? Special forces or something? But...that wouldn't explain how he knows about Mahmoud. Is he still in the military? Or—"

"I can't answer your questions." There was only so much he could tell. "You're on the right track." To Aaron, he said, "Michael is my brother, Leila's fiancé. I'm not supposed to tell anybody this, but you two are involved. You have to promise to keep this to yourselves."

"Of course," Aaron said.

Sophie's eyebrows hiked. "More secrets?"

Bryan sighed. What choice did he have at this point? She knew enough to cause trouble. Now, she needed to know enough to keep quiet. Not that he doubted her loyalty, but she needed to understand the enormity of what was happening.

He closed his eyes, prayed for wisdom, felt no check in his spirit about what he was going to do. When he opened his eyes, he focused on Sophie. "Michael is a CIA agent. He works for an elite team assigned to the White House. Everybody on their team was hand-picked, chosen for their skills—and their loyalty." To Aaron, he said, "They can be trusted. I have no doubt. Michael sent me here to figure out what the terrorists might be after because they think an attack is imminent and there was something of interest at the museum. The break-in last night might've been exacerbated by my presence—Mahmoud saw me at your mission on Friday and saw Sophie showing me around. Maybe he assumed...something. I have no idea. More likely, the break-in was already planned for Saturday night."

He allowed that thought to germinate. "Sophie, do you usually work on Saturday nights?"

"This was the first time, and I was only there because I was out of town earlier in the week."

"Are there other nights you work late?"

"Sure, if I'm getting ready for an exhibit." She seemed to see where he was going. "Herr Papp stays late a lot of nights too. But never Saturday. He and his wife have a standing date on Saturday nights."

"So if someone wanted to break into the museum...?" Bryan prompted.

"Saturday or Sunday nights would be the best options," she said. "The weekend guard, Gunter, wasn't as experienced as the weekday guard. Gunter only worked two nights a week. And no other employees are usually there. But why wait until now? The items have been at the museum for months."

"Easy to find?"

"Oh. Good point. They were stored among all the other things, high on the shelves. Some were in an offsite storage area. But Herr Papp had them all moved Friday because of the exhibit next week. And your visit."

"How could they have known that, though?" And then Bryan remembered Mahmoud and Papp talking on the street the night before and getting the feeling they'd already known each other. "Maybe Papp told him. Maybe they're friends or something. I don't know, but somehow, Mahmoud must've known. Which explains why he waited until this weekend, the weekend before the exhibit."

"Where is your brother?" Aaron asked. "Why has he not contacted you?"

"I don't know. I do know he said there's a lot going on this weekend. Other threats around Europe. He'll reach out when he can."

Bryan preferred not to consider the alternative.

Sophie stood and paced to the bookcase, which was standing open, revealing the stairway to the secret room. She turned and propped her hands on her hips. "What are we supposed to do now?" She sounded frustrated, but he heard the tinge of fear behind that.

"I don't know. I had an idea about those numbers last night." Bryan scooped his laptop from the bag he'd dropped at the entry to the room when he first entered.

"What idea?" Sophie asked.

"What numbers?" Aaron asked.

"Maybe they're coordinates." He answered Sophie, then let her explain the rest to Aaron while he opened his laptop and started searching.

He'd typed the numbers into a note. Now he pasted them and searched the internet, assuming they were geographic coordinates.

Middle of the ocean.

Probably not it. He tried the next iteration, changing the first number from a nine to a four.

This time, the location popped up in Germany, not too far to the west of where they were.

His scalp tingled.

Had he discovered something important?

To be on the safe side, he checked all the other possible iterations of the number, but either they were close to the first Germany location, or they were implausible.

He went back to the coordinates nearest Munich and checked Google Earth. The spot was in the foothills of Bavaria, not far from a highlighted attraction.

Neuschwanstein Castle.

He searched for it. Yes, he'd seen images of the picturesque castle nestled in the mountains southwest of Munich, near the Austrian border.

Less than two hours away by car.

He looked up when he realized Sophie and Aaron had grown quiet and found them both watching him.

"What have you found, friend?" Aaron asked.

Bryan turned his laptop so they could see the map. "If I'm right, the numbers are geographic coordinates, and they lead here."

Aaron leaned close. "What is it?"

All the map showed was a bright red dot in the middle of nowhere.

"You've done a lot of traveling," Bryan said to Sophie. "What do you think?"

"I think it's a random spot." She tapped the screen. "I've never been to the castle, but I've wanted to go." To Aaron, "Have you been there?"

"Never."

"Why would terrorists be interested in this place?" Bryan asked. "Any ideas?"

"No clue."

Aaron's eyes were narrowed, his lips pressed together in a white line.

"What?" Bryan asked.

"It is not...I hope it is not what I fear." He looked from Bryan to Sophie and back. "There were stories, back then.

When Saddam Hussein was still in power."

At the mention of the name, Bryan's chest tightened. What could this have to do with the dictator who'd been killed almost two decades before?

"What stories?" Sophie asked.

"The entire world believed he had weapons of mass destruction. Considering that he used them against the Kurds, it made sense. But when the Americans and her allies invaded, no stockpiles of weapons were found."

"A lot of people believed they'd gotten the intel wrong." Bryan considered what he'd said and amended it. "Actually, many came to believe the administration had lied to the American people. But that never made sense. America didn't invade alone, and the other nations that did had their own intelligence, which told them the same thing."

"Yes, yes," Aaron said. "Everybody was convinced he had them. When they weren't found, there seemed few options. Either the intelligence had been wrong, or Saddam and his people had destroyed them, or—"

"They were hidden." The tightness in Bryan's chest only worsened. "What are you saying?"

"Rumors were that Hussein found a way to get some of the weapons out of the country."

"Chemical?" Bryan asked. "Biological?"

Aaron shrugged. "To be honest, I do not know the difference. They are both deadly, yes? Some work fast, some more slowly. I heard one called...mustard gas? And I think anthrax? It was well known he had stores of that. I think it is biological."

Like Aaron, Bryan didn't know much about weapons of mass destruction, only what he'd heard on the news, and that only if he was paying attention. There'd been a lot of talk of them back in the early two thousands, but Bryan had been a kid.

Sophie stood and paced again. "What are you saying? That

Saddam Hussein hid weapons in the German Alps? Why here?"

"Why not here?" Aaron asked.

"Because... What connection did he have to Germany?" She directed the question to Bryan.

"No idea. Wouldn't that make it the perfect place to hide them? Wouldn't he want to hide them somewhere nobody would ever think to look?"

"But here? Why here? And why...? What a strange coincidence, that the chest is here, and the coordinates are here, just a couple hours away from Munich." She looked at Bryan, as if he might have an answer, then at Aaron. When neither of them answered her questions, she shook her head. "It doesn't make sense."

"Maybe it's a coincidence," Bryan said. "Or maybe the people who donated the pieces to your museum knew something about that one piece. But if that were the case—"

"Why not just send it directly to Hasan Mahmoud? Why go through all this trouble?"

"Maybe the thieves didn't know who to get the information to," Bryan said. "Maybe they sent it and hoped the right person would figure it out. Many of the contents of the donation were published, and probably the chest was among those mentioned, if for no other reason than the fact that it was so different from everything else. If someone were looking for it.... Maybe that was the point of the donation in the first place—to signal to someone where it was."

"I do not know." Aaron's lips twisted, that Middle Eastern lip shrug Bryan had seen a few times. "Maybe it is just what it seems, a coincidence. They happen. Or, even more likely, maybe the hand of God is on this. He brought it here. And He brought you two to a place where you could intervene."

Was that thought reassuring or terrifying?

Terrifying. Definitely. Because Bryan didn't have the slightest idea what he was supposed to do.

Sophie and Aaron both watched him as though he should.

"I need to call—"

Banging downstairs cut off his words.

Aaron launched to his feet, glancing at the chairs and chest, all arranged in a seating area for three.

Bryan saw exactly what worried him and lifted the rocking chair, settling it in the corner facing the wall as quietly as he could. By the time he turned back, Sophie had slid the upholstered chair in front of the chest. Now it looked like a seating area for one—with a table alongside.

"Hide," Aaron said. "Do not come out until I come for you."

CHAPTER TWENTY-ONE

Sophie took the tray and plates into the hidden room, set them on the floor—there was barely enough space—and crawled onto the air mattress. She propped her head on an elbow, her back to the exposed wood behind her, taking up as little of the narrow bed as possible.

Bryan pulled the bookshelf closed until the metal latch clicked in place, then climbed up the steps. Because of the low roof, he was bent double as he surveyed the room.

"Who do you think it is?" she whispered.

He glanced behind him. "Police, I think. I doubt terrorists would knock. Even better if it's the mailman or something." He looked around at the tiny space. "I knew it was small, but this is..."

"Come on." She patted the mattress beside her. "You can't just stand there like the Hunchback of Notre Dame."

"I don't want to be lying down if we're caught."

"We're not going to get caught. This room is well-hidden."

"Don't you suppose German police are used to hidden rooms?"

"Oh. Right." Fear, hot and thick, pressed down on her.

She must've shown it in her expression because Bryan's eyes widened. "Dang. Sorry. I didn't mean to... Would they really search? Even if it is the police, don't you figure they're just asking questions?"

She shrugged. "No idea. Maybe. Either way, you can't just stand there." She patted the space beside her again, and Bryan set his laptop bag on the floor by the plates and crawled onto the mattress beside her. He sat, even though the ceiling was so low that his chin practically touched his chest.

Faint voices carried up from downstairs. She picked up a few words in German, but not enough to figure out what they were saying.

Police, though. Not terrorists.

She didn't hear footsteps or pounding, and she didn't think anybody was moving around the house, so maybe Bryan was right.

Beside her, he banged his head on a rafter.

"Shh."

He glared, whispering, "Forgive my loud injury."

"Sorry." Despite the situation, she had to stifle a smile. "Just lie down, would you?"

"It feels a little..."

Intimate? Yeah, but she didn't say so. Saying it wouldn't make it *less* intimate.

"I think we can control ourselves," she said. "Don't be a chicken."

He chuckled, then clamped his lips shut.

She managed to stifle her own laugh. Not that anything about this was funny. It would be, if they weren't hiding from Al Qaida and the Gestapo.

Bryan scooted down and faced her, propping his cheek on his fist.

"Better?" she asked.

"More comfortable. Thanks."

"Sure." And then, because he was so close and she wasn't sure what else to say, she added, "I think they're still at the door."

"Can you make out what they're saying?"

"No. Sorry."

"It's okay. I can barely hear them."

"Yeah. They're...um..." She'd lost what she was going to say.

Bryan was so close, and she couldn't seem to break his eye contact. Though they didn't touch, his body heat enveloped her. He was right there. Tall and broad and strong, looking down at her with those warm eyes that seemed to take her in, seemed to be as enthralled with her as she was with him.

It was a strange, heady feeling. The world suddenly seemed to tip toward him, and she had to focus on not leaning forward and falling against his chest.

Though she didn't think the police left or anything really changed, the faraway sounds faded, muffled by the desire rising inside her. Silence hovered until it felt like she and Bryan were the only people in the world.

Danger lurked two stories below, and yet all she wanted was Bryan's arms around her.

This was insane.

She needed to say something, anything, to break the tension. "Cozy."

Yeah. No.

Not that.

"Hmm." The sound rumbled from him. "Like torture chambers are cozy."

This was anything but torture. His warm brown eyes had twinkled with amusement earlier. They'd searched hers with concern. But she saw something else there now.

Something that lit a spark inside her. Needing to focus

anywhere but on those eyes, smoldering, she forced herself to look away.

Her gaze landed on his lips. Pink, very kissable lips.

Now she understood what he meant by torture.

He chuckled, the sound barely audible. "Okay, then." As if all her thoughts had floated in cartoon balloons over her head, and he agreed completely.

At least she hadn't gotten on this crazy train alone.

Suddenly, boots thudded downstairs.

Her heart lurched and raced. She whispered, "They're coming." Just in case Bryan had gone deaf.

His lips pressed closed. He dropped onto his back and stared at the ceiling, though she guessed his thoughts were on what was happening below, not above.

If they were caught, she'd be arrested.

And so would Aaron and Mary. And Bryan.

She shouldn't have come here. Coming here had been foolish and stupid and selfish. Sure, she'd had a warm bed to sleep in, but at what cost? That of her friends' freedom.

Would Aaron and Mary be deported?

Had the police followed Felix here, or Bryan? Or had they been watching Aaron's house all this time?

Why had they come inside now? Did they get impatient? Had something happened?

Would the people—those powers-that-be—who'd gotten Bryan involved in this mess help him if he was arrested? Would they help Sophie?

What about Aaron and Mary? Would Bryan's friends care about them?

She wanted to ask Bryan, but his eyes were closed. His mouth was moving. He was praying.

They should have been doing that all along. Stupid, stupid, stupid mistake.

Protect us, Lord.

Protect Aaron and Mary and this home.

The attic door banged open, and she jerked.

Bryan's hand found hers on the bed and squeezed. He didn't move, just continued to stare upward, eyes closed.

It was okay. It was going to be okay. She didn't know how, but God was with them.

Silently, she translated the words that carried through the bookshelf/doorway.

"Who was here?"

"What do you mean?" Aaron sounded genuinely confused.

"People were here." Something scraped against the floor. The chair, maybe? "Who was it?"

"Ah, I see." Aaron's tone was conversational, as if he were chatting with a client at the mission. "I use this space sometimes. Jesus says that, when we pray, we should go to a closet and hide ourselves. This is my prayer closet."

"You have two empty bedrooms," the cop said. "Why here?"

"In this space, I feel close to God."

Close to God.

Such a funny thing, but in that moment, Sophie felt close to God. As if He were right there, watching over them, protecting them.

Loving them.

Maybe she'd pleased Him when she'd escaped with the chest the night before. Maybe God smiled on her because of that.

And Bryan obviously pleased Him. He'd done everything he could to protect her. Not just her, but the people of Munich. It was why he was in Germany, after all.

Was it possible that God had brought her and Bryan together? Was all of this part of His plan?

Outside the room, more scraping.

Furniture was being moved.

Oh, no.

If they tried to move the bookshelf, they would discover the door, the room.

Lord, help.

We need You to intervene, please.

As if Bryan heard her prayer, he squeezed her hand again.

Whatever happened, they were in this together.

Minutes ticked by, measured only by the rapid beating of their hearts as they waited, waited.

The police talked to each other, barked questions at Aaron, who continued to answer in that same calm tone. The longer they remained outside the door, the more terrified Sophia became. All her feelings of safety were trampled beneath the footsteps of the men closing in.

Please, God. Please...

Suddenly, one of the policemen, said, "She's been spotted. Let's go." The men ran down the stairs, leaving the attic silent.

She didn't dare move.

Because maybe it was a trap. Maybe there was a cop sitting right outside, just waiting for them to emerge.

She didn't know. She couldn't know.

She only knew she and Bryan needed to stay right where they were and be as quiet as they could.

Her heart still raced with fear. She focused on Bryan's stubbly cheeks, his dark brown hair. His lips. He was here. He was safe and kind and gentle and warm, and it was ridiculous, but she itched to touch him, feel more than just the palm of his hand in hers.

His eyes opened.

She was caught staring. But she couldn't make herself look away.

He said nothing.

But he lifted a hand and cupped the back of her head. He pulled her in.

And then his lips were on hers. Moving against hers.

She didn't have to go far to tip into his embrace.

His hands wove into her hair. His muscled chest was tight and strong beneath her fingers, and she ached to explore more.

Everything else faded away. Her fears, her worries, her questions...all irrelevant as she reveled in Bryan's nearness. His kiss. His touch.

She never wanted to move from the tiny room or the air mattress. She could spend the rest of her life in Bryan's arms.

He groaned, the sound low and loaded, sending a visceral reaction through her body. She wanted to stay there, where she felt safe and protected, and cherished. In Bryan's arms, she felt like nothing could harm her. Not terrorists. Not police.

But Bryan shifted, and she knew it was time to stop. She felt his desire for distance between them.

Though, maybe it wasn't distance he was desiring, and she was right there with him. Which was why they needed to stop.

She pushed away and met his eyes. They'd smoldered before. There was fire in them now.

Matched by the one inside her.

She rested her cheek against his chest, listening to the rapid beat of his heart.

Wow.

She'd kissed her share of men, but she'd never known a kiss could feel like...that.

If kisses were flames, all those in her past were candlelight.

Bryan's was a bonfire.

A forest fire.

Downstairs, the voices faded. A door slammed. Minutes passed.

And then, there were footsteps on the stairs again, but only one set.

The attic door opened.

"It's me." Aaron's voice was faint through the bookshelf. "They're gone."

"Okay, thanks," Bryan called. "We'll be right out." He pushed himself up to face her and rested his forehead against hers. He chuckled, the sound dark and husky. "I'm trying to figure out if I owe you an apology."

"Did you start it? Or was it me?"

"I think it was me?" Though his tone ticked up at the end, like he was genuinely asking her.

"I think it was mutual," she said. "Are you sorry?"

"No."

It was the intensity in his voice that had her leaning back to meet his eyes.

"I'm not sorry," he said. "I regret a lot of things I've done in my life, and if dragging you into this nightmare harms you in any way, I'll never get over it. But kissing you?" He watched her, seemed to be waiting for her to say something.

She had no words. When he looked at her like that, when he spoke with that kindness—and strength—her emotions all jumbled inside, good and warm and solid and real.

"Kissing you, Sophie, is something I'll never regret."

She felt the same way. She would tell him that, too, if she could get her voice to work. Instead, she nestled against his chest and held on like she'd never let him go.

CHAPTER TWENTY-TWO

Hours later, Bryan was still thinking about that kiss.

That mind-blowing, life-altering kiss.

Which needed to be wrapped up and packed away. He'd have plenty of time to uncrate it and examine it later.

He stepped out of the only bathroom in the house, wearing a pair of too-short workout pants and a too-tight T-shirt. He knocked on the open door and stepped into a bedroom off the hall. "I don't like this."

Standing at the end of a queen-sized bed, Aaron wore Bryan's clothes. He'd shaved his mustache and beard, and he looked younger.

His wife, Mary, knelt at his feet, pinning Bryan's pants up so they didn't drag.

"I do not make this look good?" Aaron asked.

He looked like a kid dressing up in his father's clothing. He was about five-nine, meaning at least four inches shorter than Bryan, and much narrower. He'd shoved something in his shoes to give him a little height, but that wasn't helping much.

From far away, with the wool coat and the knit cap Bryan had been wearing, plus carrying his cane, it might work.

"I don't like the idea of putting a target on your back."

The amusement in the older man's face faded. "If there is a target on your back or mine, I believe it is on mine, no? I am the Iraqi who converts Christians. Hasan Mahmoud cannot be pleased with my existence."

"But he's looking for me."

"He is looking for Sophia. I am only going to lure him away so you and she can escape. Unless you have come up with a better plan."

Bryan hadn't, not in the hours since Aaron had told him what he wanted to do. He and Sophie had been over it and over it, and neither of them could figure another way out of Aaron's house without being seen.

Mary stood and looked Aaron up and down. "It will do."

"Am I so handsome that you can't keep your hands off me?"

She tried to give him a stern look, but Bryan didn't miss the way her lips quirked at the corners. "Be serious, you fool. This is important."

He kissed her cheek, then slid her hand into his and faced Bryan. "Your key?"

Bryan handed him the plastic card that would give him access to the hotel room. Aaron would take his bag as well, though Bryan would keep the laptop and the collapsible cane he always carried in the bag. "The staff are good at remembering faces, so keep your head down."

"I will go straight to your room." He turned to his wife. "Right after I leave, you go."

Mary was headed to the airport. Sophie had overheard enough of their conversation—spoken in rapid Arabic—to know Mary wasn't happy that her husband was sending her away. But she'd agreed to fly to London to stay with their daughter until this was over.

Sophie had explained as much to Bryan, who was glad at least one of them would be far away from this mess.

Aaron would pretend to be Bryan. They were fairly certain the police had all moved on after the alert that Sophie had been spotted—which must've come straight from God. Perhaps there were terrorists out there now, though Bryan doubted it. He figured it was more likely they were staked out at his hotel.

So, after Aaron left, Mary would leave. If anybody *was* watching the house—assuming they bought Aaron's ruse—then they would believe only Aaron remained home.

As long as nobody came knocking in the next couple of hours, Bryan and Sophie should be able to slip out the back.

"You stay there until I contact you," Aaron said to his wife. "Out of sight."

Mary nodded, her face grim. "My part is easy, husband. I will be safe."

Sophie stepped into the room, carrying a couple of reusable bags. "Packed some food for you and us."

"Good, good." Aaron gathered them all together and prayed for help and safety. When he was finished, he stepped away, kissed his wife, and nodded to Sophie and Bryan. "Follow the plan, and it should work."

Should.

Bryan would prefer a little more confidence, but they were dealing with the scant information they had.

Aaron's phone dinged, and he glanced at the screen. "Car's here." He shook Bryan's hand, then kissed Sophie on each cheek. "Trust the God who leads. I will see you soon."

Then he and his wife walked down the stairs. Bryan and Sophie didn't follow, wanting to give the couple a little privacy to say goodbye.

A few moments later, Aaron left for his Uber.

When he was gone, Mary ordered her own car and headed

for the airport shortly thereafter, leaving Bryan and Sophie in the house alone.

Not the best thing, considering their kiss. Every thought of it brought the desire to do it again.

And maybe Sophie felt the same way, because she agreed when he insisted she wait in the hidden room, and he hang out in the attic. The only thing separating them were a few steps and Bryan's commitment not to do anything stupid.

And hers, he assumed.

The sun set, but they didn't turn on any lights in the attic. Aaron had left his office lamp on, and there was a light on in the kitchen, the rooms Aaron might occupy, were he home.

If anybody burst into the house, Bryan would join Sophie in the hidden room. Hopefully, the police—or terrorists—would believe the place was empty.

So they waited separately in the darkness and silence. They'd discuss the kiss later, when they were safe.

It was after nine, the neighborhood quiet, when Bryan and Sophie made their way down to the ground floor.

They bundled up in borrowed coats and gloves and hats. Standing by the door that led to the small garden behind the house, Bryan took her hands.

"You ready for this?"

"I'm ready." Her nod was confident, but he picked up fear in her voice.

"Lord, protect us and lead us. We need You more than ever."

Sophie echoed his amen, and they stepped into the cold night.

Paused, waited for a shouted, *Stop! Police!*

Or a gunshot or...something.

But nothing happened. *Thank You.*

Sophie was empty-handed, and Bryan carried a backpack

Aaron had given him. It held his laptop and the food Sophie had packed. He used his collapsible cane, though he'd rested enough that day that his leg felt strong.

Mary had taken the ivory chest in her suitcase and flown to London with it. Aaron had texted Bryan, letting him know that Mary had gotten on the flight, then texted again when she'd arrived and was safe at their daughter's house.

Aaron was safe as well. He planned to leave Bryan's hotel out a back door in a couple of hours.

So far, so good.

As soon as Bryan and Sophie were clear of the house, they'd be safe as well.

They walked through the backyard and out the gate in silence, then down an alley to a main road.

They turned away from the street Aaron and Mary's house was on and walked three blocks, turned at the corner, and walked another two, reaching a busy intersection.

The hairs on the back of Bryan's neck stood, and he glanced at the faces all around. Nobody seemed to be paying them any attention. So why did he feel like he was being watched?

He and Sophie didn't talk, but they held hands so they looked like a couple.

And because...it felt right to hold her hand. Her hand felt perfect tucked into his.

He inhaled the frigid air, glad to be out of the house.

Most of the shops were closed, but lights from restaurants and bars illuminated the sidewalk. A huge group of people bundled in coats and hats and gloves congregated on a corner, talking to one another in rapid French.

Tourists. Skiers, by their attire.

Another man stood on the sidewalk beyond them.

His eyes zeroed in on Bryan.

Bald head, glasses.

Hasan Mahmoud.

He spoke into a cell phone, then pushed through the group toward them.

"It's him. Come on." Bryan pulled Sophie toward the street.

"What? What are we—?"

"Mahmoud. He's coming."

Her gasp was swallowed up as they dove onto the street, dodging traffic in their dash to the opposite side. Bryan aimed for the subway station another block away.

Chanced a look behind him.

Mahmoud was following.

"Over there!"

At the sound of Sophie's terrified call, Bryan followed her gaze.

Another man, running up a side street toward them.

"Go, go!" He pushed Sophie in front of him. If only one of them made it to the station, it needed to be her.

She bolted. Ignoring the pain in his stupid, gimpy leg, he kept up, knowing if he didn't, she'd slow her pace to match his.

Mahmoud was gaining on them, the second man angling to intercept.

They were within twenty feet of the subway station when a third man stepped from the shadows between them and the entrance. By the looks of him—built and swarthy and glaring their direction—this was another enemy.

Sophie gasped.

Bryan put himself between her and the terrorist and dropped her hand. "Run! Go!"

He barreled into the guy.

The man toppled and fell against the stone wall, obviously taken off guard by Bryan's quick attack.

Bryan managed to keep his feet. He lifted his cane and jammed it down on the man's stomach, hoping between that and the fall, the guy would have his breath knocked out. Then Bryan whacked him in the head.

He started toward the steep stairs leading down to the underground train.

Sophie was standing at the top, eyes wide. "Are you—?"

"Run!" He couldn't help the irritation in his voice, but seriously, what was she doing? Waiting for Mahmoud to catch up?

He followed her down the stairs to the Munich subway—the U-Bahn—leaning heavily on the railing to keep his leg from slowing him down too much.

They'd both put their subway passes into their pockets before they left Aaron's house, so they scanned them quickly, then hurried to the platform.

He looked behind, thinking he'd see Mahmoud and his friends any second. They were coming.

Bryan looked down the tracks. *Come on. Come on.*

Finally, the rumble of the train. It screeched into the station.

Just as Mahmoud ran down the stairs.

Bryan gripped Sophie's hand, and they hopped on. Grabbed poles, and stared through the glass as Mahmoud bolted toward them.

The doors whooshed closed. The train sped out of the station, leaving Mahmoud on the platform, watching them leave with murder in his gaze.

CHAPTER TWENTY-THREE

Sophie was half-asleep, head on Bryan's shoulder, when lights outside flickered in her vision. They'd been riding for hours, stop to stop, town to town, train to train, until they'd finally boarded the last one of the night bound for Berlin.

The S-Bahn train was a little more comfortable than Munich's subway, but far from luxury with its thinly padded seats. Once they'd left Munich, there'd been little to look at outside the windows for hours, just fields swathed in darkness. Now the lights of Berlin brightened the world, despite it being four in the morning.

She pushed off Bryan's shoulder and stretched, peering out at the buildings as they flew past.

"Have a nice rest?" he asked.

"I slept a little. Did you?"

He shrugged. "I'm looking forward to a real bed."

She couldn't agree more. "Did you sleep at all? I mean, not tonight, but last night. Or...Saturday night?" She was too tired to figure out what day it was.

His lips tugged up at one side. "You mean when you were

on the run from terrorists, no coat, no cell, carrying a priceless antiquity?"

"Stupid question?"

"They say there's no such thing, but..." By his smile, she knew he was teasing. "I didn't even try. I sat in the hotel lobby hoping you'd come. And hoping you wouldn't because I was pretty sure I was being watched."

"So you haven't slept at all? In two nights?"

"I'll survive." The word was stretched by a giant yawn.

She started to settle against his side again, but his quiet, "Sophie?" had her turning to him.

"Yeah?"

"Why didn't you run when I told you to?"

Oh. Back at the subway station in Munich, when he'd tackled that terrorist.

"You thought I'd just leave you there, not knowing what happened?"

"If I put myself between you and a bullet, I'd prefer you not hang around and wait for another one."

A bullet? The word had her heart thumping. "I'd prefer neither one of us get shot, thank you very much."

He smirked, not happy. "Between you and danger. It was a metaphor."

"I'd prefer you not use bullets in your metaphors."

"Sophie."

"You really thought I should leave you there? What if you never joined me? What if you'd died?"

"If I had, and you'd just been standing there, then you'd have been taken. Probably tortured until you told the terrorists everything we learned. And then killed. That would be better?"

His words sent acid to her empty stomach. She swallowed. Swallowed again.

"The next time I tell you to run, run," he said. "I can't worry about you and protect myself at the same time. Please."

"But...but I'm not very good at playing the role of damsel in distress."

His eyebrows lowered, and something hot flashed in his eyes, bringing to mind their kiss. But his words brought her right back to the moment. "You're no damsel in distress. You're strong and courageous. And I'm no rescuing hero. I'm just trying to keep us both alive. And because I'm a little bigger than you— and by 'a little,' I mean about a hundred pounds..."

Not even close, but if he thought so, she wasn't going to set him straight.

"Even with my stupid crippled leg—"

"You're not crippled, Bryan. Sheesh, you took that guy down in about ten seconds and didn't even fall."

"If I'd fallen, I wouldn't have been able to get back up, not in time. The point is, I'm more capable in physical fights than you are. So if I tell you to run, run. Please?"

The thought of being caught by those terrorists terrified her. They were aptly named, after all. And all she knew about self-defense was what she'd learned watching action movies.

When she didn't respond, he turned, placed his hands on her face, and leaned in, holding her eye contact. "Sophie, if something happens to you... I don't even want to consider it." The sincerity in his voice, the pleading, had her insides twisting.

How could she run away and let him fight for her?

How could she do nothing? If she did nothing, then...then what was the point in her being there? If she couldn't contribute, then she was useless.

"Please." The sincerity in his tone had her nodding despite her jumbled thoughts.

"But if there's anything I can do," she said, "I want to do it."

"Of course you do." He kissed her forehead and leaned against the chair back as if all were settled.

As if he was glad to be given permission to fight for her.

As if...as if she were worthy of that. But was she? Could she be?

She shook off the questions. She was too tired for deep thinking. What she needed was a good night's sleep, not contemplation about her own personal worthiness.

The train rolled to a stop, and they followed other travelers into the train station. One side of the huge space was filled with ticket kiosks. The other side had coffee shops and stores. The roof was so far above she wouldn't even try to guess how high—three stories, at least. In front of them, a wall of glass overlooked a huge courtyard. She couldn't see that yet, but she remembered it from the one time she'd been here, when she'd come for a mission trip in college. Back then, the area had been packed with people. Now, though it wasn't packed, there were plenty of folks headed for the doors or train platforms. Most of them looked about how Sophie felt—exhausted.

She didn't see anyone who looked like a terrorist. She didn't see anyone who looked like they wanted to kill them. Even so, she said, "Do you think we're safe?"

Bryan took her hand, scanning the travelers around them. "I think, if they followed us on that train, they'd have confronted us before now. Don't you?"

She hoped so but couldn't help a peek behind.

Nobody watched them. Nobody followed.

"I could use a restroom," she said.

He veered toward the bathrooms but didn't go inside, just planted himself near the door like a bodyguard. Which...yeah, she didn't mind his determination to keep her safe.

When she was finished, they headed outside, where she

inhaled the fresh air, happy to leave the stench of diesel fuel behind.

Bryan looked around. "Aaron said we should get a bus."

"Yup." The thought of it made her want to curl into a ball. "Let's not."

They took a taxi to the hotel Aaron had suggested and checked into two rooms.

"We're meeting Aaron at noon," Bryan said. "Let's get some sleep between now and then."

"You're playing my tune." The quip was stretched out on a yawn, earning a grin from the man holding her hand.

He escorted her to her door. When she got it open, he leaned against the wall beside it. "You'll stay here until I come for you?"

"Sure."

His eyebrows hiked. "You promise? If you need something, call me, and I'll go with you."

"I don't want to wake you."

"Sophie." The way he said her name, all don't-argue-with-me, made her smile. "You promised."

She hadn't promised to obey his every command, but she knew what he meant.

He wanted to protect her.

The thought warmed her insides, made her feel...treasured. "Okay." She had to work to keep a pleased smile off her face.

Which was silly. Except...except there was something so... honoring about that.

"You do the same," she said. "I don't want us to get separated."

"Deal." He kissed her cheek, then didn't move until she was inside with the door closed.

Her room was a small, utilitarian space. The bed had one of

those fat European down-filled puffs. She crawled between the sheets, pulled the comforter over her, and closed her eyes.

And thought about Bryan. Their kiss. The way he'd put himself between her and danger, over and over. The way he wanted to keep her safe.

The look in his eyes when he said her name.

As if...as if she were as valuable a treasure as the ivory chest so many people were trying to get their hands on.

As if, to Bryan, her value was even greater.

CHAPTER TWENTY-FOUR

The phone woke Bryan, and he pushed up in the bed, blinking as he took in the space.

Right.

He was in a hotel room in Berlin. Daylight shone through the crack between the drawn curtains.

The clock on the bedside table told him it was after eleven. He'd slept almost seven hours.

The phone rang again, and he snatched the handset. "Hello?"

"It's me." Sophie's voice sounded a lot more awake than his did. "I didn't write down your cell phone number, so..."

"Oh, right." He stretched and yawned. "Did you get any sleep?"

"Yeah. I've been awake for a little while. Took a shower. I thought you might want to do the same before Aaron gets here. Didn't he say noon?"

"Yeah. Hold on." Bryan grabbed his cell and checked the notifications. He'd silenced it before they left Aaron and Mary's house. There'd been no calls from Aaron, which meant either the older man was on his way, or something terrible had happened to him. Bryan decided to assume the best.

There were—he scrolled down—five missed calls from Michael.

"No news from Aaron. I'll come get you in a few." He ended the call and dialed Michael, who answered before the first ring stopped.

"You okay?"

"Are you?" Bryan asked. Demanded was maybe the better word. "What happened?"

"Yeah... I can't tell you."

Of course he couldn't.

"You're okay? Everybody's okay?" Bryan asked.

"One in the hospital, but he'll recover."

Hospital. Meaning Michael had been on an op, and maybe it had gone wrong. Certainly, it'd been dangerous.

"You're okay, though?" Bryan clarified. "Not injured?"

"I'm fine, Bryan. Are you? What's going on?"

"We're in Berlin." He gave his brother the short version of what had happened, starting with the break-in at the museum. Michael listened, never interrupting. Never questioning. Never second-guessing decisions.

Bryan appreciated that. "We got here early this morning," Bryan said, "and I just woke up."

"Okay." There was a long, long pause. Then, "Thank God you're all right. If anything had happened to you..." Did Bryan hear emotion in his brother's words? "Bro, I would not have sent you over there if I'd had any idea you'd be in danger. I thought it would be simple."

"I know. It worked out."

"I'm not sure when we'll be able to look into what you've learned. Brock and I already had it out about the break-in."

"Wait. You knew?"

"Not as it was happening, but after. Where's the item?"

"London." Bryan explained how that had come about.

"Get me an address ASAP. We'll have someone fetch it."

"And smooth things over with the museum so Sophie doesn't lose her job?"

"I'll see what I can do."

"A man died. And they think she did it. You need to—"

"I'll take care of it. For now, her best bet is to stay out of sight."

"Michael, she was just trying—"

"I know." The words came out too loud, frustrated. Michael took a breath. "I can only do what I can do. It'll be taken care of. I just don't know when exactly."

Bryan didn't like that answer but doubted get a better one. "I figured out the string of numbers."

"You did? Tell me."

"They're coordinates. It's a spot in Bavaria on the Austrian border, near Liechtenstein. Aaron believes—"

"How much does he know?" Michael's tone darkened. "I don't love that you brought him into this. You shouldn't have—"

"You should've answered your phone." When his brother said nothing, Bryan added, "Aaron protected Sophie. He hid us from the police when they searched the house. He's proved his loyalty."

"What does Aaron think?" His words were...skeptical, as if the Iraqi man couldn't possibly help.

Sometimes, Michael's arrogance was irritating.

"He said that, back during the war, there were rumors that Saddam Hussein had smuggled weapons of mass destruction out of Iraq and hidden them somewhere. His guess is that the coordinates lead to those weapons."

Michael said nothing for a few beats. Then, "Huh." And more silence.

Bryan put the phone on speaker, tossed it on the bed, and stretched. He opened the curtains to reveal an overcast sky. His room looked over a narrow road, across from which was a brick building that probably looked much like the one he was standing in. He glanced at the cars and pedestrians below, wondering if they'd been followed.

Was anybody watching for them? Waiting for them to show themselves?

"That's...plausible," Michael finally said.

Bryan snatched his cell up. "You think so?"

"Unfortunately. Even if it's not WMDs, it's something worth getting. But the chatter—" He cut himself off. "We'll have someone look into it."

"Will you?" And now whose voice was skeptical? "Because so far, your team hasn't taken the Munich angle seriously."

"This is what we do, Bryan. Trust me."

"Of course I do. The question is when. When will your team turn your attention—?"

"When we can. Soon. We have to deal with the most pressing matter first."

"Meanwhile—"

"We're doing our best," Michael snapped. "Our resources are stretched. We were trying to figure out which city, and it turns out it wasn't a matter of this *or* that, but this *and* that. Here and Munich and other places. We're following a lot of leads. So you're just gonna have to be patient."

"Patient? We're being pursued by terrorists."

"They didn't follow you to Berlin, right?"

"I don't think so. They'd have confronted us before we got to the hotel, don't you think?"

"Probably. In which case, you need to fly back to the States."

"And what about Sophie? What's she supposed to do?"

"Can't she go home—back to California?"

"She lives in Munich. That's her home. But she can't go back there, and I'm not leaving her alone. And if I am being watched, you really want me to go to Shadow Cove? Where Leila is?"

"No." The word came fast. "I mean, I don't think they'll follow, but if you go to Brunswick—"

"So I can put all those college kids in danger? Really?"

"That's highly unlikely."

"Likely enough that you don't want me in Shadow Cove."

"Different. We can't lead your friend to Leila and Jasmine."

Your friend.

As if Hasan Mahmoud were anybody's friend.

"But I see what you're saying." Michael seemed to consider his words, which came slowly. "Do they know your name?"

"Probably."

"How? How would they—?"

"Hasan Mahmoud was at the museum after the break-in, talking to Herr Papp."

"You didn't tell me—"

"I'm telling you now. He was there. They looked like they were acquainted. Not...buddies, but associates. It's possible, probable, even, that Herr Papp told Mahmoud my name."

"Okay." A loud sigh. "Okay."

Bryan could picture his brother pacing, running a hand over his hair.

Thinking hard.

"You can't go home," he said. "You need to stay... Oh, man. I've put you in the middle of this." Another beat of silence passed. "Mom would kill me if she knew."

Bryan couldn't help but laugh. Of all the things to worry about...

Peggy Wright was a force, though.

"I won't tell on you."

"Ha. That'd be a first."

As strange and frightening as this situation was, he didn't hate that he and his brother were talking, joking around like they were friends.

He didn't hate that he was doing something that mattered. That in a weird way, he was fulfilling the dream he'd had as a six-year-old boy, to fight for his country.

And he didn't hate having Sophie by his side, selfish as that thought was.

"Here's what we're going to do," Bryan said. "I'm almost positive we lost Mahmoud last night. If he knew where the WMDs were hidden—"

"We don't know that's what—"

"Whatever. If he knew the coordinates, the place he's looking for, then he wouldn't have bothered trying to find us. Right? He wouldn't have bothered trying to get his hands on the ivory chest."

Michael said nothing, which Bryan took for agreement.

"I don't think he has any idea where we went. So, we're going to go to these coordinates and figure out—"

"Absolutely not."

"What would you have us do then? Stay in this hotel for the rest of our lives?"

"You're not going to those coordinates. Don't be stupid."

"You first."

The slightest chuckle, but Michael was dead serious when he reiterated his plan. "Just sit tight."

"No. If I were the terrorists, I'd assume we'd come to Berlin. If we stay here, chances are good they'll find us."

"If you stay out of sight—"

"For how long? Weeks? Months? Are you footing the bill? Are you going to smooth things over with Bowdoin when I don't show up for work?"

"Right," he said. "I see what you're saying, but that doesn't mean—"

"Let us just go and see what we can find. It'll probably be nothing but chasing those metaphorical wild geese, but it'll give us something to do. And if we do find something, then we can tell you and your team, and you can deal with it. I mean, what if it's...some terrible weapon that can kill millions of people? Don't you think it needs to be found sooner rather than later?"

"Not by you."

Irritation and defensiveness prickled his skin. "Why? Because I'm a cripple?"

"You're not a *cripple*." Michael sounded truly shocked by the word. "Because you're my brother. I want you to be safe."

Despite the anger infusing Michael's words, warmth spread in Bryan's chest.

"I love you, too, man. We'll be careful. Do me a favor and answer the phone when I call?"

A sigh. Then, "I'll do my best. Be safe. Please."

He promised to try and ended the call.

And then second-guessed himself. He didn't have the right to make this decision on his own. His wasn't the only life involved. If he led Sophie and Aaron on this quest and something terrible happened to them...

He'd never forgive himself.

CHAPTER TWENTY-FIVE

A t a knock, Sophie hurried to the door, started to open it, then imagined the lecture she'd have to endure if she did. "Who is it?"

"It's Bryan."

She pulled the door open.

He stood in the hallway in jeans and a fitted forest-green sweater that highlighted the muscles she'd felt in his chest the day before. He leaned on his cane.

Just the sight of him brought back the memory of that moment, in his arms, his lips moving against hers.

Warmth infused her, heating her cheeks.

"Good morning." His voice held a hint of amusement, as if he guessed the source of her blush.

She took in his clothes—and his cane—which he had to have gotten from...

A man moved down the hallway toward them.

"Aaron!" She was ridiculously thrilled to see her friend.

He must've done some shopping because he'd traded Bryan's too-big clothes for jeans and a sweatshirt.

She stepped into the hallway and kissed him on both cheeks. "I'm so glad you made it. Any trouble?"

"None at all." He held out a bag. "I brought Bryan's suitcase and picked these up after I arrived this morning. Mary told me what to buy. It is only enough for the day."

She took the bag and peeked inside. A pale blue sweatshirt and matching sweatpants. Not exactly haute couture, but she'd take it. "Thank you so much."

"There are...um..." He cleared his throat. "Some other things, at the very bottom, which Mary insisted you would need." His cheeks turned bright red.

Beside him, Bryan's grin stretched. "Victoria's Secret?"

Aaron's eyes widened. "No, no. It was bad enough at the normal store, with the women giving me looks like..." He didn't finish his statement, as if just the memory of that excursion horrified him.

She gripped his hand. "Thank you so much. Truly."

"Yes, of course. For you, only."

"Because your wife made you." Still smiling, Bryan turned back to Sophie. "We'll give you a few minutes to change. Call my room when you're ready."

Twenty minutes later, they checked out of the hotel and descended to the parking garage underneath the building, where they loaded into a black Volkswagen Aaron had rented.

The skies were overcast, and flurries blew over the windshield as Aaron drove away from the hotel. Berlin was night-and-day different from Munich. It had been bombed mercilessly during the war, but unlike Munich, it hadn't been rebuilt to recreate what had been there. The structures were more modern, the city more spacious.

Less charming, in her opinion.

In the front seat, Bryan caught Aaron up on their trip, skimming over the way he'd taken out a terrorist in order to get them to the train, as if that were the least interesting part of the journey.

Though that moment had replayed in Sophie's nightmares.

"How about you?" Bryan asked Aaron. "Any trouble?"

"I was followed to the hotel, as we knew I would be. I stayed in the room for many hours. Then, after dark, I called for a taxi to meet me on the next block, thinking they would be looking for an Uber, since that is how you traversed the city. I went out a side door, met the cab, and took it to a train station. From there, I rode the U-Bahn to the airport, bought the cheapest ticket I could find, and went through security."

"Where'd you fly?"

"I did not," Aaron said. "I waited thirty minutes, then rented a car and drove here."

"Wow. Good thinking." Sophie was impressed with his ingenuity. "Do you think you were followed?"

"To the airport, perhaps. But after that, I think not. If I was, then the terrorists are much smarter than I am."

The three of them were safe, for now.

Bryan cleared his throat, turning in the front seat so he could face both her and Aaron. "We need to discuss what to do next."

"We're going to the coordinates, right?" Sophie asked.

"I am not." Aaron caught her gaze in the rearview mirror. "Our granddaughter is sick, and Mary wants me to come to London."

"Is it serious?"

"I think my wife is exaggerating the symptoms to get me out of Germany so I will be safe." He turned at an intersection, following a map on the navigation screen. "I suspect I will arrive in London to find that Dina has only a sniffle." By the slight smile on the older man's face, he didn't mind the ruse. "I would not go if I believed I could help. I do not manage hiking like I did when I was young, and based on the map we looked at, there will be hiking and climbing. I would only slow you down."

"You might slow Sophie down," Bryan said. "I'm not exactly a mountain goat with this stupid leg."

"The Lord will equip you." Aaron spoke as if there were no doubt. "When you are weak, He is strong. But He has made it clear to me that I am to go to London."

"It's a good plan," Bryan said.

"I agree." The more Sophie thought about it, the more she liked the idea of him being out of harm's way. "You can stay there until this whole thing blows over."

"I will not." Normally a soft-spoken man, his voice held iron. "I will go for a few days to make my wife happy and kiss my children and grandchildren. But then I will return."

"You have to stay out of sight." Sophie expected Bryan to back her up, but his lips were pressed closed. "Aaron, you have to—"

"I am confident He will lead me back to Munich soon. I have lived my life for God since He rescued me, and I refuse to stop now."

"But this is different." How could he not see that? "Mahmoud and his people will want to know the coordinates. They could take you, torture you."

"He doesn't know the coordinates." Bryan's voice was grim. "There's no way they could get—"

"That's not the point! Do you not even care? Aaron is my friend."

Frustration and hurt marred his face. "Of course I—"

"Sophia." Aaron's tone was calm. "Bryan and I have already discussed this. He tried to talk me out of my decision, as you try now. But also, he respects that it is *my* decision. If my city and my people are under attack, I will not leave them alone."

"What about Mary?"

"Mary will stay in London until I know it's safe."

So he'd protect his wife, but not himself.

Sophie hated that. But...but she understood. Would she really save herself and leave Bishaaro in danger? Leave Tisa and Koombe to fend for themselves? And all the others she'd met in Munich, people who'd fled tyranny and sought the Lord?

She would return to Munich. Like Aaron, she would face the danger with those she loved. Or try to get them away.

Sophie didn't want to accept it, though. That her friends could be in danger. That she could lose sweet little Bishaaro or her parents. Or Aaron. Or Bryan.

She stared out the window, past the houses and neighborhoods and shops. There were no mountains in the distance here, just flat farmland that stretched for miles.

They reached the airport and all climbed out of the car. After Bryan shook Aaron's hand, the older man turned to her. She wanted to hug him, but she knew that would make him uncomfortable. "Thank you for helping me. I'm sorry I dragged you into this."

His bushy eyebrows lowered. "Do not apologize for trying to keep yourself and others safe. You are where you are meant to be." He took her hands. "No matter what happens, whether you and your friend succeed or fail, you are precious and loved. God smiles on you."

Tears stung her eyes at his kindness.

Aaron kissed her cheeks. "God willing, I will see you soon." He nodded to Bryan, then headed for the terminal.

She couldn't explain her sadness, saying goodbye to her friend as if she might never see him again.

It was more than that, though. It felt like...like everything was going to be different from now on.

When Aaron was safe in the terminal, Bryan said, "You want to drive?"

"Only if you want me to."

Bryan held open the passenger door for her, then rounded the car and climbed in. He entered an address on the navigation system.

She swiped a rogue tear. "Where are we going?"

"I got us a hotel near the coordinates. The town's called Füssen, in Bavaria." He headed toward the airport exit. "It seems like a touristy spot, probably because of that castle."

"Neuschwanstein."

"Right. That seems to be pretty close to our destination." When they reached the highway, Bryan said, "Are you all right?"

She shrugged, not that he saw. "What else did I miss this morning?"

"I talked to Michael, finally."

"Oh, good. He's okay?"

"Said he was. I guess the Munich threat is just one of many right now. He said they don't have enough resources to deal with what we learned yet."

"So they're not coming? Is that why he wants us to go?"

"He doesn't want us anywhere near the coordinates. He wants us to find a place to hide until it's over."

"Really?" She was a little surprised to find out Bryan wasn't going to do what his brother said.

"To be honest..." Bryan shot her a look. "This might be dangerous. I was thinking we could find a place for you to wait it out, and I'll go by my—"

"No way. No way you're leaving me somewhere, alone."

The very thought had her pulse racing. She'd have no idea what he was up to. No idea if he was safe or in danger or...what.

"That's what I thought."

That settled, she asked, "When can Michael and his team get involved?"

"No idea. He is sending people to get the chest from Mary. Aaron called her and let her know earlier."

"Oh, good. That's good."

"They won't return it to the museum, but Michael said he'd try to smooth things over with Herr Papp and the police."

She was trying very hard not to think about her job—or lack thereof. Or that she was wanted for murder. Even if Michael could get the police to focus their investigation elsewhere... "There won't be any smoothing over. I'll be fired. Unless I can get another job, I'll lose my visa."

"Maybe not."

"Even if your brother tells Herr Papp that I took the chest to protect it from terrorists, he'll be furious that I didn't tell him in advance."

"But you couldn't." Bryan sounded defensive on her behalf. "You had no choice."

"There's always a choice. From the curator's perspective, my loyalty should have been with the museum first. Everything else second. Trust me, there'll be no forgiving this."

"I'm sorry. Maybe Michael can find you something else. Or someone can. You risked your life to save others. Even if your boss doesn't see that, God does. He'll lead you."

"He led me to Munich, to the mission. That's where I'm supposed to serve. If I can't serve there, then..." Then who would she be?

"If there's not another option right away, then you'll just have to take a break. Take a vacation." Bryan glanced at her and waggled his eyebrows. "Maine is nice this time of year."

She laughed, but there was no real joy in it. "Maine is no nicer than Germany this time of year." And the world was cold and cloudy outside the window.

"But a break might be nice," he said. "Even if you didn't come to Maine."

"I just took a vacation."

"How long were you gone?"

"Six days. I spent five in Southern California with my parents before I went to see Leila. Now I'm itching to get back to work."

"Six *whole* days?" His voice was heavy with sarcasm. "What a slacker."

"I've never been good at vacations. Or breaks. Or...rest, honestly. I prefer to be busy. Serving. Making a difference."

"Everyone needs to rest."

Not Sophie. Rest made her itchy and frustrated. She liked to go-go-go and then sleep. In the middle, when she had no plans, when there was nothing else to do, she painted.

"But you travel," he said. "I guess you rest then."

"Yeah. But I usually find a place to serve. Like, I told you I ate my way through Italy last summer?"

He grinned. "Sounds like a great trip."

"It was. I loved it. I volunteered at a refugee center while I was there. I wanted to see what they were doing differently and if we could implement any of their practices."

"Huh. So even your vacations aren't?"

"I don't like to waste time. There are so many people in need all over the world. How can I justify not helping? I mean, we were created to work."

"Okay." The word came slowly. "But that kind of thinking can send you into burnout."

"Burnout's an excuse for laziness. Can you imagine people a thousand years ago talking about burnout? 'Oh, I can't plow my fields today. My heart just isn't in it.'" She scoffed. "Burnout is a twentieth—twenty-first—century problem created by pampered Westerners."

Bryan was quiet, though his eyes narrowed, little wrinkles forming at the corner. A mile or two passed outside before he spoke.

"The thing is." His tone was conversational, though she had the sense he was forcing it. "People in previous centuries didn't experience burnout because rest was part of their routine. Sure, on Sundays—or Saturdays, if they kept a strict Sabbath—people would milk their cows and do those daily tasks necessary to keep a farm running, but otherwise, they'd go to church, visit, eat long meals, take naps. Before electricity, after the sun went down, people went to sleep.

"Even today, in most of the world, people know how to rest. Not so in America, and perhaps in other Western cultures. We value money and achievement and stuff. We work, work, work, as if rest were irrelevant. You said God created us to work, and that's true. But He also created us to rest."

"That might be true. But He created me, and I don't like to rest. It makes me feel...useless."

"Why?"

"I don't know." She heard defensiveness in her tone and tried to temper it. "It's just how I am."

"Have you always been like that?"

"Yes." Hadn't she?

Maybe Bryan heard her unspoken question because he said, "When you were a little girl, did you feel that way? Did you feel like you always had to be doing something?"

A memory surfaced. They'd had a swing set in their back-yard, and she used to sit on the swing in the evenings and watch the stars twinkle to life overhead. She didn't even bother swing-ing, which would have at least been exercise.

She'd just sat there, looking up, thinking about how big God was, how small she was, and how it was okay. Because He was watching over her. He had everything under control.

Where had that little girl gone?

She didn't know. After a few minutes, he seemed to realize she wasn't going to answer him. "God knows you, Sophie. He knows what you need. If He closes the door to Munich, then He'll open another at the right time and in the perfect place."

She knew that was true. Even so, the thought of leaving the mission and all her friends there brought not only sadness but fear.

If she wasn't serving—she wouldn't matter to anybody.

After a stop to purchase supplies for the hike the following day, not to mention necessities for her, Sophie offered to drive, but Bryan seemed content to remain behind the wheel. She dozed much of the trip, waking fully when the car slowed.

The sun had long since set. Few lights illuminated the area, most attached to hotels, restaurants, and shops interspersed here and there on the narrow road.

She stretched and yawned. "Are we there yet?" She added just a touch of whine to her voice, eliciting a smile.

"Having fun playing the impatient child?"

"Little bit."

"When we asked Dad that when we were kids, no matter where we were, he'd say, 'Another hour.'"

Bryan turned down a short driveway, and she peered out the window at the structure. Two stories with dark brown siding and a balcony that ringed the second floor. It looked no larger than her parents' house, though, to be fair, her parents' house was larger than most.

"This is the hotel?" she asked.

"This was the only place with two available rooms."

He parked in front of the office. While he grabbed their things, she stretched.

In the center of the first floor, one of the French doors opened, and a man held it for them as they approached. "Willkommen."

"*Danke.*" She passed him and stepped into a brightly lit lobby with a low ceiling crisscrossed with dark beams. Off to one side, a narrow door was opened to a restaurant. The savory scent of meat had her mouth watering.

"Ve are glad to have you," the doorman said in broken English. "You are ze Wrights?"

"I'm Bryan," he said. "Two rooms, right?"

"Yes, yes. Ve have zem ready for you. Zese are all ze bags?" He eyed the single suitcase and paper sacks.

"We had a little mix-up," Bryan said.

"Ah, yes. Airlines are losing ze bags all ze time."

Bryan didn't correct his assumption.

The doorman also served as clerk. He rounded the check-in desk. "If you need anything, zere is a shop down the street vith essentials. It vill open at nine." The man handed them metal keys with old-fashioned wooden fobs printed with their room numbers.

Not exactly the security she would have hoped for, considering there were terrorists out to get them.

They took the stairway to the second floor. Her room was at the end of the short hallway, and Bryan's was on the opposite side.

"You hungry?" he asked.

They'd grabbed a quick snack when they stopped, but that had been hours before. "Very."

"The restaurant is open."

"Give me five minutes?" She let herself into what had to be the smallest hotel room in the world.

A full-sized bed took up nearly all the space. Between that and a deep wardrobe that reached nearly to the ceiling, there was barely enough room for her to pass.

She dumped her bags on the end of the bed, used the restroom, and checked her reflection. Her curly hair was a frizzy mess. She wore no makeup, and the sweatsuit wasn't exactly flattering.

Not that it mattered. It shouldn't matter, right?

She and Bryan had eaten meals together before now. But not since their kiss.

And she really wished she had something else to wear. She considered changing into the jeans she'd bought for hiking, but how pathetic would that make her appear, like she was trying to look good for him? Which would be true, but she didn't want to broadcast it.

Vain as she was, she'd bought some makeup. She decided against changing but ripped open the mascara and applied a little to her lashes, then rubbed lipstick on her lips.

Vanity, vanity. And probably completely unnecessary. He hadn't mentioned their kiss, and neither had she, despite all the hours they'd spent together.

Maybe he went around kissing women all the time. Maybe he'd already forgotten.

Yeah...no. The way he looked at her, the way he talked to her... She knew he hadn't forgotten.

But that didn't make this a date.

Even so, she wet her hands and smoothed her fingers through her hair to tame her crazy curls. When she was done, it looked wet, but better that than her head looking like the end of a Q-tip.

She gave herself a stern glare. "This is not a date. Just two people having dinner. And trying to stop a terrorist attack."

She smirked at her reflection. *Not helping, Chapman.*

Putting aside her strange thoughts, she stepped into the hall and knocked on Bryan's door.

When he answered, he hadn't changed, probably hadn't combed his short, tidy hair, and definitely hadn't added makeup. Even so, he looked perfect. "That was fast." He stepped out, locked his door, and then took her hand in his and started down the hall.

As if, to him, this was obviously a date.

Obviously, they were together.

Obviously...obviously he would hold her hand.

Or maybe this was all an act. The thought raised fear inside her. "Do you think...? Is there any way the terrorists followed us here, do you think?"

He slowed to a stop and faced her. "I don't see how. They weren't behind us on the road. Aaron rented the car in Berlin long after he'd lost them. Unless they just happened to see us... I think we're safe. Why? Did you see something, or—?"

"No, no. I just wondered what you thought."

Bryan squeezed her hand. "I think we're safe here. Let's just relax and enjoy our time together." He continued toward the stairwell.

So, not an act.

His confidence gave her the courage to feel the same way. She walked just a little closer to him. "How's your room?"

"Grand and palatial. Yours?"

"Same. I was thinking of hosting a party."

He held back when they reached the stairs, and she preceded him, taking it slowly. Because maybe stairs were hard for his leg.

The doorman-slash-clerk was the restaurant host as well.

They followed him into the dark space, and she slowed to let her eyes adjust.

The floor, ceiling, and walls were made of stone. The ceiling was arched and gave the sense that the place had been hewn out of the mountainside. Iron chandeliers hung from the highest places, adding a warm glow to the otherwise cold space. The tables were dark wood, each with a glowing candle in the center.

He seated them in front of a window that overlooked a little walled garden lit by tiny white lights.

Bryan spoke to their host. "It's different from the rest of the hotel."

He gave them menus. "The restaurant vas here a century before ze hotel. The hotel was built around it, to accommodate it."

"It's amazing," Sophie said.

"Correct," the host/clerk/doorman said, giving them a crisp nod before he walked away.

Few diners lingered, but the ones who did were casual, their voices and laughter echoing off all the hard surfaces.

A server approached, a different man this time. "Good evening." He spoke excellent English, and Sophie wondered if they were that obviously American—most Europeans argued they could pick out Americans at a glance—or if the other man had tipped him off. "May I get you a drink? Beer? Wine?"

She asked for water, Bryan a Coke, and then they perused the menu.

She was hungry, but she was far more interested in the man who sat across from her, who studied the menu carefully.

"Any suggestions?" he asked.

"If you like sausage, knockwurst is good. I think you had schnitzel the other day."

"What about sauerbraten?"

"A solid choice."

The server returned with their drinks, and they gave their orders. She decided on the rouladen—a thin slice of beef filled with bacon, onions, and pickles and then rolled and seared. Bryan asked for sauerbraten.

When the server left, Bryan said, "I used to think I wanted to be a chef."

"Oh, yeah? Why didn't you?"

"I discovered I don't like to cook as much as I like to eat."

She laughed. "Good reason." But his remark reminded her of the conversation they'd had on Friday before they'd discovered the Byzantine chest. Before all this craziness. "Speaking of what you want to be when you grow up... You never answered the question."

His eyebrow hiked. "Right. In my metaphorical waiting room, what's behind door number two?"

"And three and four... What are the options you see going forward? You mentioned wanting to be a soldier. I assume that's off the table."

"I could've been a sharpshooter if not for my leg."

"No kidding?"

"Weirdly, I'm an excellent shot, something I learned when I used to hunt with my dad and brothers."

"Not a skill you get to use on a daily basis."

That had his lips twisting in a strange smirk. "You'd be surprised."

"Meaning?"

But he shook his head. "It doesn't matter. The point is, even though I wanted to be a soldier when I was a kid, I don't think that life would have been for me, even if I hadn't ruined my leg. I'm a little more...cerebral. Does saying so about myself make me conceited?"

"Only if you think it's a good thing." She infused her voice with humor, garnering a slight smile. It faded, though. In the flickering candlelight, she watched emotions play on his face. Frustration, maybe sadness.

"What are you thinking?"

"Trying to figure out how to answer your question."

She waited, sipping her water, until finally he spoke again.

"Sometimes I worry that I just *want* there to be something else. Am I restless? Maybe I want to walk away from my career because I'm bored. Maybe I'm itching to find something more fulfilling or more exciting or..." He shrugged. "Maybe I just need to learn contentment."

"I don't think that's it," she said. "It's easy for people to keep doing what they've been doing. Maybe not fun or exciting, but easy. If you're so unhappy that easy doesn't appeal to you, then there's a reason for that."

He weighed her words, dipping his head side to side. "Maybe."

"Let me ask a different way," she said. "What do you *want* to be behind those doors?"

"Oh. Well, there's a question." He looked around the restaurant. "I'd love to travel. I love being here."

So did she. With him. "Is that why you got your pilot's license? So you could travel?"

"Yeah. I've toyed with the idea of working for Derrick more. It's a nice side income, but it couldn't replace my salary."

"Expensive hobby, then."

"You're not kidding. Getting the license took a big chunk of my savings. It was fun and fulfilled my dream to learn to fly, but I'm not sure how I can use it."

"So behind one door is travel, maybe flying full-time?"

"It's a possibility." But he didn't seem convinced. "I love the idea of flying all over the world, but not for the sake of flying."

"You want to see the world?" Sophie asked. "Is that the dream?"

"I've thought about opening a shop that sells imported goods. That would give me a good excuse to travel."

"You don't seem the shopkeeper type."

"You're not wrong. People who own stores have to do things like...math." He mock-shuddered.

She laughed. "So *accountant* is out."

"Yup. Scratch that right off your metaphorical list."

The server brought their meals, and the air filled with the heady scent of roasted meat, garlic, onions, and spices.

Bryan's eyes widened at the pile of food on his plate. He thanked the man who'd set it down and asked for drink refills.

After Bryan spoke a blessing over their food, they ate in silence for a few minutes.

Her rouladen was delicious—savory and spicy. The spaetzle —egg dumplings—were soft and mild—her favorite comfort food.

"Where has German food been all my life?" Bryan asked.

"Germany?"

He grinned. "Wow. And I called myself cerebral."

She chuckled. "What else can you see yourself doing?"

He glanced around the space. She wasn't sure what he was seeing as his gaze rested on the tables of diners who remained in the restaurant.

When he looked her way again, he said, "There was a time I dreamed of being a missionary."

She tamped down her initial reaction and said, "Is that so?"

If the Lord led him that way, they could serve together.

Be together.

And she was getting ahead of herself. Way ahead.

Rather than voice any of those insane thoughts, she said, "Tell me about that."

"When I was a teenager, I went on a mission trip to Haiti. I loved it. I loved the people there. I could see myself doing that for the rest of my life. But while we were there, I tripped and fell. Had a setback and had to fly back to Maine early. It felt like...like the Lord telling me I couldn't do that. I have to stay close to a hospital, just in case."

"There are hospitals all over the world."

"Yeah. I know. When I was a kid, I thought that if I wanted to be a missionary, I had to live in a developing country, but I know now that isn't the case. I mean, you don't. Lots of missionaries don't. It's just something I let go because of..." He tapped his leg.

"You use your leg as an excuse a lot."

"An excuse?" His voice filled with irritation. "It keeps me from doing what most people can do all the time."

"I'm not saying it isn't serious. I am saying you can be a missionary with a cane. There are people everywhere who need to know Jesus."

"I realize that." He sounded defensive. "I was just telling you why I didn't pursue it when I was a kid."

"Okay. Sorry."

His mouth slid into a frown. "No. I'm sorry. Just when I think I've conquered that stupid, bitter attitude, it creeps back in. You're absolutely right. If that's where the Lord leads, then it's what I want to do."

"There's no better way to spend your life. You know the scriptures. Go into all the world to share the gospel." One of her favorite songs filled her mind. "To the Ends of the Earth." The lyrics talked about going anywhere—for love.

That was what God had called her to do. It was what God had called everyone to do, wasn't it? "You should definitely—"

"Sophie." His serious tone had her snapping her mouth shut. "I could be a missionary. I could be a pilot. I could be a lot of things. Do you know why I'm an antiquities professor?"

"You lost a bet?"

He laughed, breaking the tension that had risen between them. "I liked history. When I was in college, I accepted that I'd always have limitations. I studied history and, ultimately, antiquities because I decided it was a good career path for me. It was a way for me to set myself apart from my brothers. They know nothing about what I do, and I like that." He shook his head. "Do you hear the problem? *I* like it. *I* decided the path for *me*. For the majority of my life, I was the center of my universe. I didn't consult God. I was angry with God for"—he made air quotes—"'stealing' my dream, for letting me get hurt. As if my pain were the most important thing in the world. I heard someone say once that it's okay to be mad at God, but don't unpack there. Well, I unpacked. I lived there for a long time. Because of that, I disregarded His plans for my life."

Well, that was honest.

"Can you guess why I don't know the answer to your question?"

She considered everything he'd said. "Because God hasn't given you a direction yet."

"Exactly. I've tried life my way. And you know what I got? I have a decent job I don't hate. I'm still trying to repair the damage my bitterness did to my family. I'm alone. And, to be more honest than I probably should, I'm lonely."

Wow. She wasn't sure what to say.

He chuckled, though there was no humor in it. "Way to go, Wright." He spoke with a sardonic tone. "Way to tell a beautiful woman every pathetic fact about yourself."

Her mind caught on the word *beautiful,* surprise and pleasure warming her cheeks. And then she heard the rest of his statement. "There's nothing pathetic about honesty. I admire it."

"The point is," he said, "God's plans are better than anything I can come up with, and I want exactly what He wants. I don't want to settle on an idea and then convince myself it was God's. I'm trying to keep my eyes and options open."

"Is that why you're here, in Munich? You took this..." She wasn't sure how to call what his brother had asked him to do, finally settling on, "assignment? To keep your options open?"

"Sort of." He took a bite of his meal, then a sip of his Coke. "The idea that I might be able to help thwart a terrorist attack, even if I'm just a tiny cog in the machine... I like it. I'm no hero, but I can make a difference."

"Who told you that?"

"That I can make a difference?"

"That you're no hero?"

"Oh." He shrugged. "I don't mean to sound melodramatic. Just that...you know, I've got this bum leg and—"

"There it is again, that sorry excuse of a leg."

He sat back. "Wow."

"Sorry. I didn't mean to offend you."

"Sure you did."

She started to argue, then stopped herself. "Okay. But now I'm sorry I did."

He leaned in. "I've let my injury color every major decision I've made." He looked around and smiled. "Until recently. Here I am, in Germany, pretending my leg isn't a problem. Doing something good, or trying to."

What he'd already done—and was still doing—was more than simply *good*.

And she had a feeling it was just the first step in God's plan.

It was after nine by the time they finished their meals, but Sophie wasn't tired. Maybe because she'd slept in the car. More likely, because she was with this man.

He wasn't perfect, but that was true of everyone. He was honest, though. Honest and humble and eager to follow the Lord. She liked those things about him.

So far, she liked...everything about him.

But he lived in Maine. She lived in Germany. And even if she lost her job and her visa, she didn't plan to live in the US again. There were too many people in the world who'd never heard of Jesus. Sophie's number-one mission was to tell them about Him. God had been very clear about His calling for her.

Which meant, no matter how much she liked Bryan, unless he drastically changed his life, a future with him was impossible.

CHAPTER TWENTY-SIX

Despite his fatigue and his full stomach, Bryan wasn't ready to say good-night to Sophie.

He didn't know what the next day would bring. Maybe they'd find nothing. Maybe they'd find a hidden stash of weapons. Either way, Michael and his team would come to Germany and take over. For Bryan and Sophie, the quest would end soon. He'd go back to Maine. She'd return to Munich.

And be out of his life. Forever?

He didn't want to consider that.

Maybe God was up to something Bryan hadn't figured out yet. Was there any chance that behind door number three was a beautiful curly-haired blonde with striking gray eyes that glimmered in the candlelight?

Was there any chance that God hadn't answered Bryan's inquiries about what his future would hold because He was waiting for Sophie to enter the picture?

Maybe. Maybe she could be a part of his life. Or he could step into hers.

And yeah. He needed to slow down, to stop running ahead

of God. To stop hoping for the outcome he wanted and to work on trusting the One who had it all figured out.

The server cleared their plates and gave them dessert menus. Though Sophie had only eaten half of her meal, she perused the offerings.

"What are you thinking?"

"Have you ever had *Spaghettieis?*"

"Uh...I've had spaghetti."

She ordered it. "With two spoons," she said. "And I'll have a decaf coffee."

Bryan seconded that. After the waiter walked away, Bryan asked, "Not even a hint?"

"You're going to have to trust me."

"Now I'm nervous." As long as they were prolonging their meal... "You've grilled me enough. It's time for me to get some answers about the elusive and mysterious Sophia Chapman."

She laughed. "You're going to be sorely disappointed."

"Tell me about your paintings. When did you start? What is it that drives you?"

"Drives me? To paint?" She shrugged. "Boredom, I guess."

That didn't seem right. A person with as much talent as Sophie had must be compelled by something more powerful than boredom. Yet, she seemed completely sincere. Was she being dishonest with him? Or herself?

The second, he guessed. "You said you're not good at relaxing. Is painting what you do when the rest of us are binge-watching Netflix?"

"You do a lot of Netflix binge-watching?"

"I'm a documentary man."

"Boring historical things, I'm guessing."

He smacked his palms on his chest and dropped his jaw. "I'm offended."

"Oh, please. I'm guessing you get that all the time."

"Pretty much every day. I happen to think documentaries are fascinating."

"You would." She shook her head, fighting a smile. "I never had much use for TV. I've always been artistic, so yeah, when I have time on my hands, I paint." She seemed to be considering more, and sure enough, after a moment, she said, "Sometimes, I do feel compelled to it. When I see a beautiful place, I'll take a photo, then take a few minutes to draw it. And then I'll have this compulsion to paint it."

"I bet it's more fulfilling than Netflix."

"It's mostly indulgent."

Huh. Okay, so... "You said before you don't like to waste time. Does painting feel wasteful to you?"

"Not...really. God gave me talent. It seems I ought to use it. Besides, I give the paintings away when they're finished."

"The one in your living room was...?"

"An exception. I painted it for that spot. I almost parted with it. A friend from the mission told me I should do something like it for the waiting room, and I considered handing it over. But I couldn't force myself to do it."

"The ones you donated are beautiful. I'm glad you kept the big one. It's a perfect reflection of the artist."

She looked down quickly, but he didn't miss the grin she was trying to hide.

"You must have a million ideas."

She looked up, head tilted to the side. "Why do you say that?"

"Because... Well, I guess because you don't finish so many of them. You must get excited about the next project before you can finish the one you're working on."

"Not...really. It's more like I do the part that excites me, the part I have a vision for. And then the excitement wanes, and I move on."

"Oh." A theory formed. "Is there any chance you don't finish them because you don't want to give them away?"

"No." The word came out fast, no uncertainty in it. But then she added, "I don't think so." A moment passed, and she tilted her head to the side. "Huh."

"Maybe?"

"Yeah. Weird. I never realized, but I'll have to pray about that." She met his eyes again, smiling. "If it's true, I can fight the selfish impulse."

"Is it selfish to want to keep something that you conceived of and created?"

"I think so. Don't you?"

"If you kept everything, then maybe. Or, if the Lord told you to give all your paintings away and you didn't, then sure. Did the Lord tell you that?"

"I don't know. I guess I just..." Her words faded, and then she smirked. "I usually like to talk about myself, but this *analyze Sophie* time isn't fun for me anymore."

"Sorry. I'm trying to figure you out."

"I'm far too complex for that."

"I have no doubt."

The server brought coffee, cream, and sugar. Bryan took his black but enjoyed watching Sophie add enough cream to turn the dark brown liquid to the color of caramel and enough sugar to chase any bitterness away.

When she was done doctoring her drink, he said, "You've heard about my family. Tell me about yours."

"It's just my parents and me."

Oh, But... "Didn't you mention a sister?"

"Josie. She was five years younger than I was."

He didn't miss the past tense. "What happened?"

"She had cystic fibrosis. It was...severe. She died at fourteen. I was away at college. She'd been fine the last time I saw her. As fine as she ever was. And then... It happened really fast. My parents didn't even tell me she'd gone into the hospital."

"That's awful." He didn't know what to say. He'd lost his oldest brother years earlier. Though Daniel hadn't actually been dead—and *there* was a long story—they'd all grieved, believing for four years that he was. "I'm sorry you went through that."

"Losing Josie was indescribably hard. We weren't close in age, but we were close. Obviously, it's different when it's a child. My parents have never recovered." She swallowed, and did he see a tear?

Oh, man. He wanted to wipe it away. He wanted to scoop her into his arms and hold her close and comfort her. And it was more than just desire. When Sophie was with him, desire was never far away, always humming beneath his skin, but what he felt now was protectiveness, the need to guard her from anything that could hurt her. To keep her safe and warm and happy and...

Dang. He was in trouble.

"Tell me about your parents. What do you mean, they haven't recovered?"

"Having a sick kid changes everything. When they got married, they talked about having a houseful of children. After being an only child for years, I was excited to have a brother or sister. Of course, I was really little, so I didn't understand. I imagined a bunch of kids my age, little playmates for me."

"Wait. You were there when they got married?"

"Oh. I guess I should back up. My birth father was a Marine. He died in Afghanistan when I was a little girl."

"Aw, Soph. That's terrible. I'm sorry. To experience so much grief, so young."

"I barely remember him. What I do remember is probably a combination of everything I've heard about him and all the photos I've seen. Every once in a while, I'll pick up the scent of something that reminds me of him. Like, he loved lemonade. Just the taste of it on my lips makes me think of him. And he wore this spicy cologne that's not popular anymore. Every once in a while, I'll get a whiff, and then I'll be right there, on his lap." Sadness darkened her features, but she shook it off and forced a smile. "My stepfather is my dad. Mom married him when I was four, and he adopted me."

"I'm glad you have him." Even so, it had to do something to a kid when a parent left and never came home.

And Sophie had lost her sister as well. She'd lost two incredibly important people in her life. That must have affected her.

The server set a bowl of spaghetti in the center of their table, complete with marinara sauce and a sprinkling of Parmesan cheese. He gave them each a spoon and refilled their coffee cups before fading away.

"Um." Bryan looked at her, catching a spark in her eyes. "I'm not exactly in the mood for pasta."

"Try it."

Reluctant, he tested the surface. It wasn't spaghetti. The long, skinny strands gave no resistance as he pushed his spoon through. He tasted the concoction with his tongue, then popped the whole bite into his mouth. Vanilla ice cream. Strawberry sauce. And the little bits of Parmesan cheese were... "Is that white chocolate?"

She seemed to be enjoying his surprise. "You need to dig deeper."

He dug the spoon into the mound of spaghetti-shaped ice cream, grabbed a giant portion, and saw what she meant.

White fluffy... "Whipped cream?"

She grinned, and he ate his spoonful. After he swallowed, he said, "Okay, that's delicious."

"Right? And unique."

He didn't disagree. Maybe Germans were like New Englanders. What was it about cold-weather climates that created ice cream lovers?

Bryan savored the contrast between the cold ice cream and the hot drink.

After a few bites, Sophie wiped her mouth and returned her napkin to her lap. "You asked about my parents. After Josie was born, the dream of having a houseful of kids seemed to fade away. Josie required so much care."

"I bet that was hard for you."

He guessed Sophie had been about to say something else, but she changed tack. "It was hard on *her*. It was hard on Mom and Dad. She was sick. Even her good days were a challenge. She couldn't go to school, so we home-schooled her. I taught her to read."

"Amazing."

"Not really." She picked at the dessert, filling her spoon, but she didn't eat it. "She was the center of our home. Our lives. As it should have been, of course."

"Should it?" At Sophie's raised eyebrows, he added, "Not that your parents shouldn't have cared for her, but you were there too. Did you feel like your needs were met?"

"My needs were unimportant." She snapped the words. "I didn't have a deadly disease."

"Okay."

"It *was* okay." Sophie was getting angry. "Of course my parents focused on her. They had to."

He had a feeling disagreeing would be a bad idea, so all he said was, "Okay."

"What does that mean?"

"It doesn't mean anything, Sophie." But she glared at him, so he tried again. "You had a little sister with serious health issues. Of course that affected the dynamics of your family. You know a lot more about it than I do."

The anger in her expression morphed to something else, something he couldn't read. She looked away, sipped her coffee. Sighed. "They didn't mean to push me aside. I know they loved me."

Not *love me,* present tense. *Loved.*

"It's just that she took up so much of everyone's time. I think they always thought that, when her health was better, they'd focus on me. Mom would take her to the doctor, and there'd be a new treatment or a new...technique, and Mom would act like they'd found a solution."

"There's no cure, though, right?" Bryan didn't know much about the lung disease, but he knew that.

"Right. But, you know, there are always advances. Mom would hear of one and be all bubbly and excited, as if things were about to get so much better. And then Dad would play the *let's not get ahead of ourselves* card, and Mom would get annoyed. And Josie would be the peacemaker, trying to get them on the same page, telling Mom it was all right to hope, telling Dad it was all right to be afraid to hope. She was amazing at seeing into people's hearts. But she was just a kid. She couldn't fix it, and so she'd feel guilty because they were arguing about her."

"What about you? What did you do?"

"Cleared the table. Or mopped the floor. Or dusted. I dusted a lot. I thought maybe if we could just keep the air clean..."

"You had a servant's heart, even as a kid."

The waiter took the empty dessert dish—they'd managed to eat the entire bowl of ice cream/faux spaghetti—and left the check. Bryan barely spared the man a glance when he thanked him.

Sophie seemed to wrestle with what to say next. "I was always into art. Painting, sculpting, whatever I could get my hands on. When I was in high school, I took a sewing class and made a quilt. My teacher thought it was good and entered it in a citywide contest. It won."

"Wow. You're a woman of many talents."

Her lips tipped up at the corners, barely a smile. "There was a ceremony. It wasn't a big deal, really."

"Of course it was. It was a big deal to you, right?"

"I made it a big deal. Which was dumb."

That wasn't what he'd meant at all.

"There were reporters there, and the award came with a scholarship, so there was someone from the local art college that had sponsored the contest. There'd been hundreds of entries." Her head wagged back and forth. "I guess in that respect, it was kind of a big deal." She acted embarrassed to admit it. "My parents didn't come. Mom was home with Josie. Dad promised he'd be there, but he forgot. In fact, neither one of them remembered it until Dad saw my picture in the paper the next morning."

Bryan pressed his lips closed to keep his reaction from escaping. Because really, what kind of parents...?

"He apologized for missing it, of course," Sophie said. "Mom did, too, because she'd forgotten to ask me about it. Josie had remembered, and I'd told her all about it. Mom and Dad were just...distracted."

"Mmm-hmm." He didn't trust himself to open his mouth.

"I'd been so proud of that quilt. But at the end of the day, it was just a blanket. I gave it to Josie, and she treasured it." The memory brought a smile to Sophie's lips. "She was nine or ten, and I guess she looked up to me. She acted like I'd given her something of tremendous value, not just some stupid homemade quilt."

"You *did* give her something of value. You made it. It must've taken you hours."

"That doesn't matter." She tossed the words out as if they were unquestionably true. As if her time and talents were worthless.

Oh, boy.

Don't say it, Bryan.

He had to clamp his lips shut to keep from speaking his mind.

"My parents were far more impressed that I'd given Josie the blanket than they were with the award." Sophie was still smiling.

How could she not see how...off that was? How could she not see...?

"That's what they taught me," she said. "That giving to others, serving others, is far more valuable than serving myself or stacking up accolades. I guess that's why I do what I do. Because I know that when I serve, the Lord smiles on me."

"Yes." He heard the skepticism in his drawn-out word. "I don't disagree."

By the way her eyes narrowed, she wasn't going to like what he said next. And maybe he shouldn't say it.

"What?"

He definitely shouldn't say it. Because it was going to make her angry. But she'd called him out on his stuff more than once. On using his leg as an excuse. Before that, she'd called him on wallowing. And she'd been right.

And if she trusted him enough to tell him the truth, he could do the same. Even if it made her angry.

When it made her angry.

"I'm glad your parents were devoted to your sister and her health." He chose his words carefully. "She needed them. But wasn't there a way for them to care for Josie *and* care for you?"

"They did care. They taught me to love others more than myself. To serve. They taught me what matters."

"*You* matter. Did they teach you that?"

She blinked. "Yeah, of course. When I serve, I'm following the highest calling. They're the reason I do what I do."

He had no doubt about that. "Didn't the heart of a teenage girl matter? Didn't recognizing your talents matter?"

She waved his words away with a flick of her wrist. "You missed the whole point."

One of them was missing it, no doubt. "I'm wondering if maybe, though they appreciated you for serving, they forgot to teach you a few important lessons." He was still trying to figure out how to articulate the rest of what he wanted to say when she plopped her napkin on the table.

"We should get to bed."

Oh.

Okay, then. Maybe challenging the behavior of people she loved was a bridge too far. He could understand that. If someone criticized his parents, he'd defend them.

She gave the leather case holding their bill a glare. "When I get my purse and wallet, I'll pay you back for my portion. And the room, and—"

"Sophie." He laid his hand, palm up, on the table. It was only a few seconds before she slid hers into it. He closed his fingers. "I didn't mean to offend you. It's just that I had such different parents. They would never have missed an opportunity to see my brothers or me being celebrated. It feels strange to me that yours did."

"But Josie—"

"I know." His mother had raised six children—six *boys*. That could've been an excuse. But she'd never once missed what was important. "I had a different upbringing. If I'm judging your parents, it's only because I feel protective of that teenage girl's heart."

She dropped her gaze. "You don't understand."

"I'm sure that's true." When she said nothing else, he squeezed her hand. "Are we okay?"

"Yeah. Sorry. I'm just..."

When it was clear she wasn't going to finish her sentence, he charged their meal to his room and followed her out of the restaurant.

They were halfway up the stairs to the second floor when he realized... "You never explained what you meant when you said that your parents never recovered from Josie's death."

She was quiet until he joined her in the second-floor hallway.

She stopped in front of her door. "Josie died fourteen years ago, but she's still the central focus of our family. As much time as they spend with me, I might as well have died with her." Her lips formed a semblance of a smile, but there was no happiness in it. "There's a reason I don't live near them. From here, I can pretend they're still the same happy couple they were when they got married. I can pretend that...that they still care about what happens to me." No emotion in her face. No tears in her eyes. Nothing but a calm acceptance.

"Oh, honey." He wrapped his arms around her and pulled her against his chest.

She stood stiffly, arms pressed to her side.

"I'm sorry. I'm sorry they don't know how amazing you are."

"It's fine." The words were muffled against his sweater. "Really, I'm over it."

How could a daughter get over believing her parents didn't love her? She hadn't said that exactly...

Come to think of it, she *had*, at the start of their conversation. She'd said her parents *loved* her.

How could they be so...unfeeling? Or had the loss of Josie stripped away everything?

Bryan had no idea. What he knew in the depth of his soul

was that this woman who seemed to struggle to accept a comforting hug was lovable. Whether her parents realized it or not, she was worthy of love and protection and care.

And with everything inside of him, all he wanted to do was prove that to her.

CHAPTER TWENTY-SEVEN

S ophie had gone over the conversation a thousand times since she slipped into her hotel room the night before.

What had she been thinking, telling Bryan all those personal things about herself and her family? Of course he couldn't understand how all-encompassing Josie's illness had been. How could someone who hadn't lived it possibly understand?

She'd thought things would be awkward between them this morning, but when he'd knocked on her door, he'd acted like everything was normal. He'd even kissed her on the cheek before he'd taken her hand to escort her to breakfast.

A kiss on the cheek was more than she'd gotten the night before. And that was probably good, considering how jumbled her emotions had been.

Now she was seated on a bench at a shop near their hotel, trying on yet another pair of boots while Bryan watched from a few feet away, his back to the shelves of shoe boxes. His thin winter jacket was draped over one arm. The other hand leaned on his beautiful cane.

Did he have any idea how handsome he was?

She doubted it.

They'd picked up everything else they needed for this trek on their way from Berlin the day before, including the light blue jacket lying across the bench beside her and the hat and gloves shoved in its pockets. But they hadn't been able to find boots in her size. She'd figured she could wear her tennis shoes, but Bryan had scoffed at the suggestion.

"You need suitable footwear," he'd said at breakfast. "You can't go traipsing over the mountains in sneakers."

He was worried her feet would get wet. Or she'd slip. Because that was the kind of man he was. Caring. Concerned.

All the things she craved. To be the object of someone's affection. To be the center of another person's attention. To be another person's...person.

But not like she'd been to Felix, for whom that meant ownership. Being Felix's person meant he felt he had the right to tell her what to do.

Not Bryan.

The way he'd hugged her the night before had made her want to melt in his arms.

And...push him away.

Which was confusing, but she didn't like that he thought she needed his pity, as if her upbringing had been horrible. It hadn't. She'd learned that she wasn't the center of attention. She'd learned to serve, not be served. Which was why she'd felt so uncomfortable with his hug.

She'd been offended by his pity. But also, she'd soaked it up like a fresh towel tossed into a sparkling pool.

There'd been a moment when she'd seen her upbringing through his eyes and wondered if maybe he was right.

Maybe her parents shouldn't have pushed her aside as much as they had. Maybe...

Yeah, maybe those feelings were useless now. The past was the past. They'd done their best. What more could she ask?

But the night before, in his arms, she'd felt safe entertaining those questions. She'd felt like she could face all that and be okay, just because she was the center of his attention.

Selfish, selfish, selfish.

She hated herself for craving it.

"What do you think?" Bryan asked.

She finished tying the laces on the sturdy hiking boots and stood to test them. "They'll work."

Bryan's lips twisted. Was that frustration? Impatience, maybe, considering this was the third pair she'd tried. She didn't want to be difficult, but the others she'd picked out—because they were half the price of these—hadn't fit.

"Take a few steps. We're in no hurry. Are they going to give you blisters?"

"I'm sure they're fine."

"We don't want your feet to hurt."

Right. Of course. This wasn't about her. It was about getting to the coordinates, finding the stash of...whatever was there, and then alerting Michael.

According to Bryan, they had a "steep hike" ahead of them. Not a climb, but it wasn't going to be a stroll in the park, either. He'd done some research and even talked to someone at the hotel that morning and learned about a trail that would lead them most of the way. For that, she was thankful.

She marched among the racks to test the boots. They were a smidge too big, but her socks were thin. She found a thick, wool pair and returned to the bench.

She tried on the socks with the boots and tested them. "These'll work. I don't want to slow you down."

He lifted his cane, then his eyebrows. "I doubt *you'll* be slowing *me* down. Is there anything else you need?"

"I'm ready."

He paid for her things, and they left the shop. The air was cold—above freezing, though with the cloud cover, it felt chillier. The forecast had predicted sunshine. Liars.

It'd been dark when they drove through town the night before. Now she took in the charming little Bavarian hamlet. She'd never heard of Füssen. Red-roofed buildings were snugged side-by-side, some white, some painted in cheerful pastels. A castle stood on a hill in the center. It was...well, not *reasonably* sized, but more so than the gigantic Neuschwanstein Castle. Between the buildings, she caught sight of low mountains, foothills to the Alps. The roads and sidewalks were clear and dry, but the grass was covered with a few inches of old snow.

"Reminds me of Shadow Cove," Bryan said. "All the different-colored buildings."

She thought back to the seaside town in Maine. She'd only seen it in the rain, but the downtown shops had been colorful.

"I wish you'd seen it on a clear day." He opened the passenger door for her. "It's cute."

"That's where you grew up, right?"

He closed her door and then climbed in beside her. "We grew up inland, on an apple farm that's been in our family for generations. My great-grandfather ran the orchard, but after he died, Grandpa sold most of the trees. He was a physician, like Dad, and didn't have any desire to farm."

"Was the orchard still there when you were a kid? Or did the buyers use the land for something else?"

He entered an address into the GPS, then shifted into drive. "The orchard is still producing apples, operated by another farm in town. Grandpa kept a couple acres around the house. We used to climb the trees."

She could picture little Bryan and his brothers running

among the lanes and lanes of apple trees. The image made her smile. "You were able to climb trees?"

"Yeah. It wasn't easy and took me longer, but if my brothers did it, I was going to do it."

Determined. Or maybe stubborn.

"In the fall, we had to pick up drops. Dad paid us a dollar a bushel." He shook his head. "Talk about child labor."

"Drops?"

"Just like it sounds—the apples that fall before they're picked. Mom would make apple butter and cider and sauce and pie."

"Sounds delicious."

"Well-earned treats after hours of hard work."

"Do your parents still live there?"

"They do. My brothers and I all left for college or, in Grant's case, the army, and then moved away to different places. But a few years ago, Sam moved to Shadow Cove, and then Michael and Derrick followed him. Daniel and his wife are looking for a house near there, too."

"Where is Grant?"

"Coventry, New Hampshire. He's a police detective there."

"And you're in Bowdoin."

"Right."

The way became hillier as they drove away from town. Bryan took the main road, along with all the tourists headed for the castle. But where they turned off, he continued into the low mountains. There was little traffic in this direction. After a few miles, he turned onto a narrower road that wound between two steep, tree-covered hills.

They followed that for ten minutes before he turned into a tiny, snow-covered parking lot that, on a busy day, might fit ten cars. This morning, theirs was the only one there.

Bryan parked, and they climbed out. "You ready for this?"

"As I'll ever be." She zipped her jacket, shoved her knit cap on her head, and slid on her gloves. They swung on their backpacks filled with water and snacks.

"According to Fritz, there'll be a wooden plaque marking the path." Bryan led the way to the back of the small lot, then along the edge.

"Fritz?"

"The clerk. Talked to him this morning. He told me that 'Every-vun comes for zee castle, but zey do not explore zee beauty of Bavaria.'"

She laughed. "That was the worst German accent I've ever heard."

"We all have our talents."

She didn't miss how heavily Bryan was already leaning on his cane. He'd opted for the metal one, leaving the carved one back at the hotel. She considered asking him about his pain but decided not to. What would it help, to point it out? It wasn't as if he would put this trip off until it felt better.

He stopped at a small wooden sign nailed to a tree. Words had been printed on it at one point, but they were faded and impossible to read. He snapped a photo, then tapped a text.

"What are you doing?"

"Sending my location to Michael—and that picture. I called him this morning and told him our plan. He wanted updates." He led the way on the narrow path.

"Any idea when he's going to get here?"

In front of her, Bryan shrugged. "It's impossible to get a straight answer out of him about anything."

The tall pines and leafless trees were stark and beautiful against the gray skies overhead. She itched to photograph them. And then to paint them.

The wintery world was quiet. A few birds had twittered earlier, but even they'd gone silent as the day had dragged on.

She assumed these woods were teeming with life in the summertime, but animals would be hunkered down for the winter. The only sounds were the low thumps of their footsteps on the trail.

They didn't talk much, focusing instead on keeping their footing on the snow-covered ground. Her feet would already be wet and frozen if not for the boots Bryan had insisted she get.

When she got her breath, she'd tell him that, but after a good hour on a gentle slope, the way became steeper. She had no energy for anything but putting one foot in front of the other.

How was Bryan doing it? She'd accused him of using his leg as an excuse, but he sure wasn't today.

She watched the ground in front of her, working to keep up with the man who'd sworn *he'd* be the one to slow *her* down.

A sudden crack snapped her focus to the side. "What was that?"

Bryan didn't answer, though a peek showed he was staring into the woods as well. There was nothing to see but dark tree trunks against the snow-covered slope. Nothing moved. Even the slight breeze had stilled.

The silence pressed around them. What had seemed peaceful before now felt menacing and dangerous.

"Do you think...?" She whispered just loudly enough for him to hear. "Is it possible somebody followed us?"

"I can't imagine how." His voice, too, was low.

Whatever—or *who*ever—had made that noise wasn't moving now.

They stood there, silently, for a minute. Two minutes. They had to be deep into the third minute before Bryan spoke again.

"Sounded like a branch breaking."

"Spontaneous...cracking?"

"It happens sometimes."

She looked at him. "Does it?"

"Snow is heavy. Trees weaken. Look around and you'll see plenty of fallen limbs and branches. Maybe a little animal jumped on one just right, and it cracked."

"So not exactly spontaneous."

"Just unexplained." He turned her way. "It could've been a deer. There're deer out here."

"Did you see one?"

He shrugged. "That doesn't mean it wasn't there."

Didn't it, though?

"If someone was following us," Bryan said, "they'd follow on the trail, not in the woods."

She spun and peered down the narrow path they'd been climbing as if a threat might appear any moment. But there was nobody there.

Bryan's hand clamped on her shoulder. "We left the terrorists in Munich. We have no reason to believe they've followed us."

"Right. Could be police, though. Maybe they're just..."

"Lurking in the woods, in the snow, when there's a perfectly good trail?" She heard teasing in his voice. "I don't think so."

He was right. Of course he was right. After a deep breath and a quick prayer, she turned her gaze back to him. "Okay. Let's go."

"Alrighty then." He trudged onward. Despite his cheerful tone, the peace she'd experienced earlier was gone. This was no casual walk with a handsome woodsman.

She'd do well to remember that.

They climbed almost an hour before Bryan spoke again.

"Whoa. You gotta see this." He held out his hand. When she took it, he pulled her up the last few feet.

When she got her balance, she turned to see what had grabbed his attention and...

Holy cow.

The clouds had burned off, and the sun shone in the pale blue sky. They stood on a ridge that dropped off sharply on the opposite side, giving them a spectacular view of the tree-covered mountain range.

Neuschwanstein Castle glistened in the distance, grand and impressive and gorgeous, overlooking the little village. The castle had to be eight stories high with spires and turrets—everything a castle should be. Beyond it, rolling snow-covered fields led to a wide, blue river.

"Wow."

He grinned. "I saw pictures, but that's so much grander than any picture can capture."

She'd traveled all over Europe. How had she missed this beautiful place just two hours from her home? "Would you mind taking a photo of it? I want to remember this view for later."

"I'll let you use my phone."

While he dug his cell from his pocket, she took off her gloves and hat and shoved them in her pocket. After that climb, she was tempted to shed the jacket too.

He handed her his phone, and she took a few snapshots of the scene, imagining the painting she could create with that in the background. Then she stepped back to get Bryan in the shot as well.

His jacket was thinner than hers and molded to his shape. He'd shoved his gloves and knit hat in his pockets and was gazing at the valley. He'd taken off the backpack and held a water bottle in one hand, leaning on the cane with his other. His shoulders were broad, his back straight. Even from behind, the man was beautiful.

She snapped a couple of photos. When she got home, she'd have Bryan forward them to her. She wouldn't get her job back, but at least she'd have her phone again, eventually.

Well, assuming she wasn't arrested and thrown in jail. But she wasn't going to think about that.

Either way, she'd have these photos to remember this time. This man.

A wave of sadness caught her off guard, and her eyes filled. She swiped the unexpected tears away. There'd be plenty of time to grieve later, when he was gone. When this was over.

She did want it to be over, the scary parts, anyway. She wanted the terrorists to be stopped. She wanted her name to be cleared. She wanted Munich to be safe.

She just didn't want to say goodbye to this man who'd somehow become incredibly important to her.

CHAPTER TWENTY-EIGHT

Bryan turned from the view and caught Sophie staring, not at the castle. At him.

She looked away, but not fast enough.

Was that...? Was she crying?

"Are you hurt?"

She wiped her eyes and held out his phone. "I got a good shot."

"What's wrong?"

"I'm fine. It's just beautiful, isn't it?"

"That makes you cry?" His mom sometimes teared up when she was happy. But that wasn't what this looked like.

Maybe his thoughts showed because she added, "I was just thinking about...all of it."

He took the phone and pocketed it, stepping closer to her. "There's a lot to process. Being chased by terrorists. Your city under threat. Your job."

"Right." She swallowed and nodded as if he'd hit the nail on the head. But something in her eyes told him he'd missed it entirely.

And then he knew—or hoped he did.

He placed his hands on her hips, just below her parka.

She was exactly what he wanted. Was there a chance she saw the same in him?

Her hands on his arms, she looked up, and sure enough, there were more tears in her eyes.

"We never talked about that kiss." And why was his voice so hoarse?

She looked away.

"Sophie." He whispered her name, which brought her gaze back to his. "I feel it, too, this thing between us. I'm not ready... I have to go back, but maybe there's a way—"

"How?"

A single tear dripped down her cheek, and he swiped it with his fingertip.

"I don't know. But I do know God wouldn't bring us together, give us these feelings..." He worried as the word escaped that maybe he was the only one with strong feelings here. But the earnestness in her expression—not surprise, just honest affection, and maybe a little hope—told him she felt what he did. "God wouldn't bring us together to tear us apart. I'm not saying this is a forever thing. But...but it wouldn't surprise me. I can see it. With you."

Her eyes widened, and her mouth formed a little O.

So, maybe he shouldn't have said that. But he wasn't sorry.

Especially when Sophie said, "I can see it too. I know it's early, but...but it feels real."

"Yeah. God has a plan. I don't want us to get ahead of Him. Let's trust Him to work it all out."

"I want to believe it's possible. I never thought... I always thought..." She sighed.

"Tell me."

"I always thought I'd end up with someone like Felix, someone who was as focused on serving people as I am."

Wow. That felt like a direct hit. He dropped his hands, but she gripped his arms and held on.

"Don't. It's not that... Don't misunderstand me, please. I'm not saying... I know the Lord calls us each to our own things. Felix was like me in that his whole life was about helping refugees."

"And stalking you." Bryan probably shouldn't have said that, but he didn't like that she'd brought her ex-boyfriend into this conversation. Which meant...what? She'd declared her feelings for Bryan, yet she was still thinking about Felix?

Surely she wasn't still into that guy.

She dropped her hands and faced the vista. "That's not what I meant. I'm making a mess of this."

The worry in her voice had him shifting to stand behind her. He wrapped his arms around her. "Please explain that, or I'll be making up my own explanations."

She leaned back against his chest. "I always thought I'd end up with someone in ministry. No, that's not right. I always thought I'd end up with someone who placed a higher value on the mission than he placed on me. Even with Felix and the stalking and the demands... It's not about me. It's about him and the mission and the work we can do. It's about him protecting me from... I don't know. My stupidity and foolishness and naïvety."

Bryan hadn't meant his feelings about her ex to escape, but the low growl must've been audible because Sophie said, "I agree entirely."

Which was good, but... "I still don't understand what you're saying."

"I don't know how to be someone's center of attention. In a good way, at least. I don't know how to feel comfortable with someone taking care of me like you've been doing for days. Caring what shoes I have on. Making sure I get a warm jacket.

At the train station, you literally put yourself between me and danger. That was... I've never experienced anybody caring for me like that before. Part of me wants to tell you I don't need it."

"We all need to be taken care of sometimes."

"I know."

"Do you?" When she started to shift away, he snugged her closer. He loved holding her like this. He loved the way she leaned on him. With her in his arms, the beautiful view was even more so. "I was a little kid when I hurt my leg, so I was already accustomed to being taken care of. But as I got older, I came to resent it." He thought of those high school months, being confined to a wheelchair after a surgery. Having to be pushed up handicap ramps. Having his dad or older brothers carry him onto and off the boat that took them to their island vacation home. The long, long route they had to haul him because he couldn't climb the stupid staircase at the boat dock near the house.

Dad, Daniel, and Michael would work their tails off, making sure Bryan missed nothing, and he paid them back with scowls, as if it'd been their fault he was hurt.

"I hated that people had to take care of me like I was a cripple. It made me angry, and I lashed out at everyone around me."

"I'm sure it was hard."

"For them, Sophie. I was just sitting there, being waited on and acting like a jerk. And then one day, my father rolled my chair into the front room at the house, away from the rest of the family. It was after Christmas, and we were back from our annual holiday trip to camp. The decorations were still up, and Mom and my brothers were in the other room packing things away. I'd been sitting in my wheelchair, grousing while everyone worked because I hated that I couldn't help. I hated feeling helpless. Outside the window, fresh snow covered the ground and the trees, which just made me angrier, knowing I couldn't ski or sled or... Anyway, Dad asked me what I thought about Jesus coming to earth as a baby. I probably popped off with some stupid answer. And then he helped me see it in a way I never had before.

"Dad told me that, in Heaven, Jesus is a king. He wears royal robes and sits at the right hand of God. But He shed those royal robes. Did he have to come to earth as a baby?" Bryan shrugged. "Surely, the God who invented the lava lizard and plants that eat bugs could have figured out another way. But Jesus humbled Himself so much that He came to earth, was born in the way babies are born, and then had a teenage mom breastfeed Him, burp Him, and clean His poopy bum."

In front of him, Sophie emitted a little giggle. "I never thought of it that way."

"The King of the world, in the arms of a human girl. He'd come from walking on sapphire tile to crawling across dirt. And needing...everything done for Him. Jesus put Himself in a position where He would've died if others hadn't cared for Him. Think of that."

"So He could grow up"—awe filled Sophie's voice—"perfect in every way, and die for those very same people."

"Exactly." He inhaled a breath, and with the fresh air, took in the scent of Sophie's hair—citrusy and sweet. "Dad told me I could keep being a jerk, or I could humble myself, quit letting my pride get in my way, and be a little bit like my Savior."

"Wise words."

"Hmm. I get that it bothers you to be taken care of, just like it bothers all of us sometimes. I also get that—and please don't be angry with me—your parents only made you feel valued when you were making their lives easier. They only valued you when you cleaned and cared for your little sister. But you need to know that you're valuable, whether you're serving or not, just for who you are. Your very existence makes you priceless."

"Sure, but we were created to serve."

"Yeah." He'd thought about this a lot since their conversation the night before, and he hoped his next question would help her see his perspective. "Was Josie valuable?"

"She was amazing and...so kind and generous."

"Did she serve? Did she make dinners or—?"

"Of course not. She could hardly breathe. She was..." After a few moments, she said, "She was precious."

"She needed people. So do you. So do I. Whether you can serve or not, you're precious. Just like your sister was."

Sophie didn't say anything, and he didn't push it, just prayed she'd understand what he was saying.

They stood in silence for a long moment. And then she said, "Can I tell you something embarrassing?"

"You can tell me anything."

"It's stupid. But with the castle there... I used to read to Josie. Her favorites were these little Disney princess books with knights and damsels. I secretly wanted to be the princess in the fairy tale. You know, the one the hero rescues. I always wanted to be that..." But her words faded.

He shifted to face her. "If you were in that castle, Sophie, I would rescue you. I would risk everything for you because you are worthy."

New tears filled her eyes, but these came with a slight smile. She wrapped her arms around his neck. "You're pretty good at this wooing women thing."

"Well, you know. I don't like to brag."

"It speaks for itself." She tugged him down and kissed him.

And, wow.

Just, wow.

He poured himself into it, into her. He had no idea what the future would bring. No idea what the rest of this day would bring, for that matter. But just like he'd said, she was precious, and he'd give up anything, everything, to keep her safe.

And, God willing, make her his.

It was afternoon by the time they veered from the trail, fighting their way through the woods. After an hour, Bryan wondered if they'd ever actually reach the little dot that marked their target. When it seemed they'd wander the woods forever, he saw an opening in the forest.

An old dirt road. If they'd been in Maine, he'd have called it a logging road—just wide enough for one truck, a road that dead-ended in the middle of nowhere.

He stopped at the edge, and Sophie walked up beside him. "Not that this hasn't been fun, but next time, let's just drive."

"If I'd known..." He checked his navigation, zooming in. "It's not on the map." He switched to satellite view and saw the narrow break in the trees.

He followed its path on his map. It wound down the mountain and ended behind a structure of some kind—a cabin?— that was a mile or so beyond the lot where they'd left their car. So, was this a private road, then? Were they on private property?

Fritz had told him the trail they'd spent most of the day on was used by tourists in warmer weather, so it must cut through public land. But they were off the trail now. So maybe.

He took a screenshot of the map, marked it to indicate the road and cabin, and sent it in a text to Michael, asking him to check who owned the property. It didn't go through. No service up here, of course. That would be way too easy.

At least his navigation still worked.

"Are we there yet?" Sophie asked, doing her bored-adolescent voice.

"Another hour." He took her hand, and they walked down the center of the cleared road. A hill rose on the left and overlooked it.

The road ended abruptly, nothing beyond it but trees, but a narrow trail led into the forest on the right. It was relatively flat, fortunately, considering every step sent fire up his leg all the way to his hip.

He should have brought his crutches. He'd brought the foldable ones from home and had considered shoving them in the backpack, but they would have stuck out. And...yeah, all his talk about being humble enough to allow others to help him just proved what a hypocrite he was.

He hadn't wanted Sophie to see him on crutches. He hadn't wanted her to think he couldn't handle this. So they were in the trunk of the car at the bottom of the mountain, where they'd do him no good at all.

Stupid pride.

The trail they followed away from the road was overgrown, as if nobody had cleared it—or traveled it—in years. But there was definitely a trail, and it seemed to lead straight to the coordinates.

They rounded a bend in the forest and froze.

In front of them stood a rock wall that had to be twenty-five feet high.

He flashed back to the cliff on his family's island. The one he'd tried to climb—and fallen from. The one that had ruined his leg. The one that had almost killed him.

He was adventurous, as much as he could be. He'd spent his life pretending he was whole. He skied. He swam. He hiked.

But he didn't rock climb. Ever.

"Please tell me we don't have to get up that." Sophie echoed his thoughts.

"Let's hope there's another way." After the morning they'd had, his leg would give out.

They walked the ground in front of the monstrosity, picking their way around pine trees and past spindly, leafless bushes.

If his navigation system could be trusted, the coordinates they were searching for were right in the middle of the giant rock. Which made him wonder.

He moved slowly, studying the wall. He reached an evergreen bush that looked out of place among all the bare branches that surrounded it. He'd seen a lot of vegetation on their hike, but nothing like this. He shoved branches out of the way.

"What is it?" Sophie came up beside him.

"Do you see that?" It was a dark spot almost completely hidden by the bush. Leaning on his cane, he shoved his hand past the dark green needles and felt...nothing.

There was a hole. It was too dark to see, but...

"I think it's a cave."

"Oh! That makes sense. Maybe that means we won't have to dig."

He'd carried two handheld spades in his backpack, but using them would mean kneeling, and with the way his leg was aching, that might not be possible. A cave would be much better.

He dug into his backpack, found a hunting knife he'd added to yesterday's purchases, and cut the branches that blocked the way. It took a couple of minutes, but finally, he was able to get a better look.

Ironic that the bush someone had planted to hide the cave entrance had been the very thing that'd made him stop and take notice.

"Let me go first," he said, "just in case."

"Of what?"

The fear in her voice had him grinning. "You don't want to wake a sleeping bear."

Her eyes widened, and he chuckled. "Just kidding. I did a little research on what we'd find up here. There are no bears in Germany. There are some wildcats, but they're rare. Even so, stay here. I'll let you know when to follow." He shoved the knife in its sheath, put the sheath in his pocket, and grabbed the two flashlights from the backpack. He gave one to Sophie, flicked on the other, and ducked inside.

Leaning on his cane, he took his time moving through the narrow and ragged tunnel that was no taller than five feet, maybe a little less. He picked up a musty scent, probably from small animals that made their home here. The air was stale and moist.

A few feet past the opening, the ceiling rose, and he was able to straighten. His flashlight revealed a space a little deeper than it was wide, about the size of the bedroom he and Derrick had shared when they were kids.

"Any lions?" Sophie called.

"I tamed 'em. Come on in."

The flashlight beam appeared a few seconds before she joined him.

"Are we there yet?"

He checked the navigation. "According to this, yeah. The coordinates are right here."

"And yet..." There was nothing but stone—everywhere. "Where's the pot o' gold?"

"We're missing something." He headed to his right, aiming the flashlight at the ceiling, walls, and floor as he moved. He ran his hand along the surface.

Rock, rock, and more rock.

She went the other direction, doing the same.

The silence pressed in. The forest noises—the breeze, the

snaps of twigs beneath their feet, the skittering of small animals —had become background music during their hike. In here, their absence felt heavy, as if they'd left all life behind. All he heard were their footsteps and the sound of his cane tapping the hard ground.

The rock was jagged in most places, probably carved from thousands of years of water dripping through. There were no openings. No hiding places.

It didn't make sense. These coordinates had been etched onto that ivory chest for a reason.

They had led Bryan and Sophie to this place—not a random tree or field, but a cave. A hidden cave near an uncharted road.

Whatever Hasan Mahmoud was searching for had to be here.

"Hey, Bryan." Sophie's voice was low, almost reverent. "Come here."

He crossed the space and stood beside her, studying the wall her flashlight illuminated. There was a space about the size of a piece of paper that wasn't jagged. In fact, it was smooth. And not naturally. There were scrapes across it. Tool marks.

And something else.

He touched a line on the surface that had been etched into the rock, tracing it with his fingers.

"What is it?"

The flashlight cast deep shadows. He aimed his beam a different way and saw a drawing etched into the rock. "Hieroglyphics? But...that doesn't make sense. It's not old enough for that."

"The cave? How can you tell?"

"Not the cave. This smooth place. It's new. There's no patina on it. I mean, not one created from a couple millennia. Whoever scraped this smooth did it in the last hundred years."

"Or twenty," she said.

Right. That timeline would make sense if what they were searching for had been hidden during the Iraq War.

Iraq.

Hmm.

He looked at the markings again and...

"Oh." Could it be that simple? He leaned in, traced the lines again. Symbols, but not hieroglyphs. And not local, not even close.

"'Oh' what?" Sophie asked.

"It's Akkadian."

"Gesundheit."

"Haha. Akkadian is an ancient Mesopotamian language used from about the third millennium BC to about 800 BC."

"I assume you're fluent?"

"Well, maybe not fluent." He propped his cane against the wall. "I can hold my own in a conversation."

"I'm sure there's a big population of ancient Babylonians at Bowdoin."

"Affirmative action. You know how it is." Assuming that it was Akkadian, he tried to work out the first symbol.

There were lines. Arrows—or arrow-like things, but with closed triangles at the ends. There were zig-zags. If this was written, on paper, he could figure it out.

Think, Wright. You know this.

He did know it. It was just that he didn't usually have to read it off cave walls with a flashlight.

And also, it wasn't right.

The symbols, as they were used, were all wrong.

He stepped back.

"Well?"

"It doesn't make sense. It's like...like someone grabbed an Akkadian-to-English dictionary and tried to make words with it. But that"—he gestured to the wall—"is gibberish."

"It must mean something."

She wasn't wrong. "The symbols meant something to the person who etched them. Unless the person was also a student of antiquities, maybe it makes sense that it doesn't make sense."

"That makes sense."

He shot her a grin, then paced the stone floor. "Assuming whoever did that"—he waved toward the wall—"didn't know Akkadian, maybe they just got a dictionary and tried to spell what they were trying to say with the old language."

"Okay."

"But not Akkadian-to-English. If we're assuming this was done by an Iraqi..." He returned to the wall. "You speak Arabic, right? Do you read it?"

"I'm not fluent, but a little."

He worked out the four symbols there. "What does T-A-H-T mean?"

"Down?"

Down. Weird. But okay. Assuming that was an imperative...

He bent, running his hands along the rougher rock surface beneath the etchings. There was another smooth spot almost at the floor. He found another bunch of symbols, did his best to translate to letters, and read them out. Y-U-S-L-L-I-M."

"Hand?" she said.

"Huh? Okay." Almost seemed too easy.

He pressed his hand on top of the symbols. If this were a movie, everything would start moving now, revealing a hidden temple.

And booby traps, so he didn't complain when nothing happened.

But there had to be something. He moved his palm around, looking for...who knew what.

Sophie realized what he was doing and did the same.

Together, they felt around the stone closer to the ground. It was rough, the jagged edges vertical where water had dripped.

He stuck his fingers in every crack.

And then he touched something that felt different. "It's here."

"What is it?"

"A lever, I think." He ran his hand down the stony edge. On the back side, a piece of wood ran the length.

He squeezed and felt the tiniest give. He shifted to get a better angle and squeezed again.

The wood gave way with a thump.

He pulled.

The wall scraped, opening the tiniest crack in the rock.

"Whoa." She sounded awed. "It's a door? A rock...door?"

"Help me out."

Sophie dropped to her knees across from him and stuck her hands in the opening below his. Together, they pulled.

In an Indiana Jones movie, the thing would swing open easily.

And it would be man-sized.

But this was real life. The four-foot-high door barely moved. Bryan pushed his weight into it. Hinges set into the rock squeaked. The door scraped against the floor, raising a discordant screech that echoed off the cave walls.

Why hadn't he bought a can of WD-40? His mother had always claimed that almost everything could be fixed with duct tape or WD-40.

His father, the fix-it guy, would roll his eyes.

Bryan shifted, put his back against the wall beside the opening, and pushed while Sophie pulled.

The opening widened.

"I think I can make it through," she said.

"I'm not sending you in there alone. Keep going."

He was breathing hard by the time they got it wide enough for him to fit through.

Sophie was out of breath, too, as she aimed her flashlight inside.

"What do you see?" he asked.

"It's filled with gold! And the scrolls from the library at Alexandria."

"This isn't *National Treasure*, goofball."

"Is that the Holy Grail?"

He laughed. "Would you just get out of the way? Sheesh."

She did—by going through the hole.

Of course she wouldn't have done that if she'd seen any danger. Even so, his heart jumped into his throat when her feet disappeared.

"You all right?" He dropped to his knees, thankful that Sophie didn't see what had to be a pathetic grimace on his face. Pain shot down to his calf and up to his hip. He fell forward.

Paused to breathe through the throbbing ache.

"Stay there," she called. "Don't come in here. I just need your phone."

Was that fear in her voice?

Despite the pain, he crawled through the hole.

CHAPTER TWENTY-NINE

O f course Bryan hadn't listened to her.

Sophie stepped out of the way of the tunnel, giving Bryan plenty of space to get through and stand. Because he was coming, whether she wanted him to or not.

Holy grail? Not even close. Whatever was in those crates, there was nothing holy about it.

There were four—that she could see. Maybe more behind those, but she didn't plan to get any closer. The cube-shaped crates were about three feet wide.

Bright yellow stickers were affixed to each one.

Those stickers didn't have any words written on them, but they told her all she needed to know. They depicted three circles arranged triangularly and meeting in the center, a fourth in the middle cutting through the three.

She didn't know exactly what the symbol meant, but she knew it was bad. Like, don't-come-closer-or this-will-kill-you bad.

When Bryan cleared the tunnel, he emitted a grunt she was sure he hadn't meant to escape.

"Let me help."

"I got it," he snapped.

"Not feeling very Jesus-like suddenly?"

He looked up, blew out a breath. Rolled over onto his butt and held out his hand.

She grabbed it and pulled. He was heavier than she'd expected, and if he hadn't used his other hand to push himself up with the wall, they might not have managed it.

But they did, and he stood, leaning forward, hands on his thighs. Not getting his breath, though.

"You all right?" she asked.

"Yup." The word was clipped.

True only if *yup* meant *in a lot of pain*.

She wanted to say...something. But there was nothing that wouldn't sound pitying or flippant. She turned back to the crates again. "I'm thinking we ought not to open them."

He stood straight, and like her, didn't step closer. "Why don't you wait for me out there?"

"If it's...contagious or whatever"—her heart pounded with the words as the gravity of the situation hit her—"I've already been exposed. What is it?"

"Dangerous."

"I figured that part."

He walked to the side of the crates, keeping his distance, leaning on the wall and limping. "No other markings."

"So it's a weapon of some kind?"

"Probably. Biological. The fact that they're crated up and marked properly tells me whoever did this knew what they were doing. They wouldn't want whatever's in there to seep out before they could use it. And bioweapons wouldn't be corrosive, I don't think. Not that I'm an expert."

"So you think we're okay?"

"I...think so. I'll talk to Michael, see what he says. Meanwhile—"

"How do you know it's bio?"

"The chemical weapon symbol is three dots in a triangle with lines connecting them to a fourth dot in the center."

"Similar to that, but not circles."

"Right. And the nuclear symbol sort of looks like a wheel with three fat spokes."

She'd seen that one.

He stopped at the far corner of the cavern. This space was a little bigger than the first. "They're stacked two deep. So eight crates of bioweapons, we think, assuming the people who brought them here labeled them properly. And who knows? This whole thing is..." He faced her. "Please wait in the other room."

"I'm not leaving you here alone with those..."

What were they doing?

They'd just found a cache of weapons. *Saddam Hussein's* weapons.

Mass-destruction weapons being sought by terrorists.

This was crazy. They should have run. They should have gotten out of Germany, gotten as far away from here as possible. Her heart thumped and seemed almost audible in the silence. Blood whooshed in her ears.

"Did you hear me?" Bryan's voice seemed to come from far away.

"What?"

He must've heard something in her voice because he closed the space between them and wrapped her in his arms. "We're okay, Sophie. It's okay."

"They're searching for these. What if...?" She looked toward the tiny door, their only escape. "What if they're out there?"

"They're not. We're okay." He held her close, and her heart rate slowed. Yes, they were safe. It was all right. God forbid, if they'd been exposed to something, they'd figure out what and get treatment.

Whatever was in those boxes was packed up tight.

He rubbed her back. "Would you please crawl out? It'll make me feel better. I'll be right behind you. I'm just going to take a few pictures."

"You're hurt. Let me—"

"Princess." He leaned down, his voice a whisper in her ear. "Let me be your knight. Please?"

His sweet, protective tone made her insides melt. "Okay."

He let her go, and she crawled through the hole and into the first cave, half expecting to see terrorists waiting for them.

But the room was empty, bright compared to the other, thanks to the light coming through from the opening that led back to the woods.

A few minutes later, Bryan joined her. She helped him up, seeing a flash of agony in his face as he got to his feet. She averted her gaze, allowing him privacy while he adjusted.

"Get some pictures?" she asked.

"Yup." He snatched his cane. "I need to get to where there's service, fast."

They closed the rock door until it latched, disappearing into the wall, and made their way out of the cave. Again, she half expected to see enemies surrounding them but found nothing but green forest and blue sky.

Bryan tapped on his phone. "I'm marking the location." He took a screenshot of the map and snapped photos of the surroundings. "Might as well make it easier for Michael and his team than it was for us."

He dialed, waited, then shoved the phone into his pocket. "No service. Come on."

They pushed through the woods to the logging road, where he tried to call Michael again. "Still nothing." He continued, practically jogging on the gravel-and-snow-covered ground, though his limp was more pronounced than she'd ever seen it.

"Should we stay on this," she asked, "or head back through the woods?"

They'd reached the spot where they'd emerged from the forest. He paused, seeming to weigh the question. "The trail will take us straight to the car. I'm guessing the road is less steep, but the map shows that it's much longer, winding around the side of the mountain."

"But your leg—"

"Either way, it's going to be hard. If we take the trail, I get the hard over with faster—and sooner get in contact with Michael."

She followed him into the woods, watching him limp from tree to tree, leaning on them with his free hand.

She prayed his leg would hold up.

CHAPTER THIRTY

They'd made it past the ridge and the spectacular view of the castle when they stopped to eat a couple of protein bars and sip from their water bottles.

Bryan leaned against the trunk of an oak tree, thanking God for the moment of rest.

The moisture from that morning had long since dissipated, and the temperature had risen to the midforties, he guessed. He'd already shoved his hat and gloves in his pockets, and his parka was unzipped.

Not that he minded the mild temperature, but the melted snow was making the path slick. The last thing he needed was to fall.

Sophie sat on a rock a few feet away and ate her protein bar, staring into the woods.

She was, by far, the most beautiful creature in the world.

She caught him staring and smiled, the expression almost shy. "You sure you don't want to sit?"

"I don't think I'd be able to get up again."

Her brows lowered, and her smile faded. "How bad is it?"

"It's fine." A lie, but how would elaborating on the throbbing in his leg help?

The last time his leg had hurt this badly, he'd needed surgery. But this wasn't that. On the mission trip in Haiti, he'd been goofing around with some friends and fallen. For a normal person, the fall wouldn't have been a big deal, but he'd banged his leg against a tree and knocked one of the crushed bones in his ankle out of place.

This time, it was just fatigue and overwork that caused the swelling and throbbing. He'd taken four of the ibuprofens he'd stashed in his backpack a couple of hours before, so he couldn't take more of those yet.

"What can I do?" she asked.

"There should be Tylenol in my pack." Which he'd dropped on the rock beside her so he could lean against the tree. He'd get it himself, but that would involve moving.

She dug through and handed him the bottle. He popped three, hoping they would help.

What he really needed was an ice pack and about a week with his leg propped up. At least a couple of hours to let the swelling go down.

"How much farther do you think it is?" This time, no teenager attitude filled her voice, just worry.

"We're moving faster than we did coming up. I'd say another hour."

"Really?" She seemed skeptical at his pat answer.

"An hour and a half at most."

She glanced down the trail. "I can run it faster than that. I can get to the parking lot and call for help. I'm sure there's some sort of...mountain rescue thing around here."

And wouldn't that be a pretty sight—being carried off the mountain on a stretcher like an invalid?

"I can do this." He pushed off the tree trunk, feeling frustrated and stubborn. And annoyed when he had to say, "Hand me my backpack, please?"

She did, and he slid it on, grabbed his cane, and started down the trail.

He needed his crutches. He'd been an idiot to do this without them.

They trudged on silently.

An hour passed, and they still weren't at the parking lot. The pain was getting worse. He could do nothing but watch the trail and pray that God would hold him up.

And then his cane bumped into the knot of a tree root. He pitched forward. Lost his balance. Tried to catch it with his bum leg.

It buckled, and he went down, turning to take the brunt of the fall on his shoulder.

"Bryan!" Sophie crouched beside him, a silhouette against the fading light. "Are you all right?"

He gritted his teeth to keep from snapping at her.

Breathe. In and out. Focus on your breathing.

Surely, the agony would fade. Surely, he'd be able to finish when they were so close.

Moisture seeped through his jeans, melted snow and mud. The cold felt good. He hadn't realized how warm he was in the thin winter jacket.

Though her face was shadowed, he felt her gaze and her concern. "What is it? Is something broken?"

"Just my pride."

"Ah. At least that'll heal. How about the leg?"

He aimed his feet downhill and pushed himself to sitting

and rolled his shoulder. It seemed all right. "Hand me my cane?" It'd fallen a few feet away.

She did and then held her hand out to help him up.

He managed to get to his feet, but pain shot down his leg, and it went out.

Letting out a super manly growl, he released her hand and fell back to his butt.

"What can I do?"

"Nothing. I just need a minute."

"You're sure it's not—"

"I'm not sure of anything." He barked the words, then took a breath. "This isn't your fault." He still sounded angry and tried again. "Really, Sophie. I'm sorry. I don't think I've done anything but overwork it. I was hoping to make it to the car without stopping, but I need to take more Advil. And a few minutes to just...not move. Then I'll be able to make it."

She sat beside him, plopping her bottom on the wet ground. "Maybe."

"Thanks for the vote of confidence."

She ignored his sarcasm, which was kind of her. "Why don't I run down to the parking lot and call for help?"

"By yourself?"

"I'm a big girl, Bryan. I can handle it."

"I know. I know you can." He just hated that she was going to have to. "Some knight in shining armor I turned out to be."

She bumped his shoulder. "Even knights need help sometimes, right? Wasn't that the point of your whole Jesus-as-a-baby thing?"

"Throwing my words back at me?"

"At least I was listening." She waited a beat, then said, "The lot can't be much farther."

"I almost made it but, as Dad would say, close only counts in horseshoes and hand grenades." He hated this. Hated it with everything inside him. "Okay, Princess. There's no need to call for help, though." He fished the car keys out of his pocket. "There's a pair of foldable crutches in the trunk."

"Why are they in the trunk and not—?"

"I know. Stupid pride. Will you get them for me? And take my phone." He held that out as well. "As soon as you get service, resend all the texts to Michael. The sooner he gets the information, the better."

She started to stand, but he tugged her back.

"What?"

He shifted toward her, slid his palm over the smooth skin of her cheek, and kissed her. Just a peck, but he wanted to make it more. "Thank you."

She smiled, the expression soft and gentle and oh, so sweet. "It's my pleasure."

He didn't back away, just wove his fingers into her hair and rested his forehead against hers. "Do me a favor, Princess?"

"Anything."

"Don't become a damsel in distress until I get my leg back under me."

"I'll do my best." She stood, brushed off her jeans, and jogged down the trail and out of sight.

Leaving him alone and helpless, waiting for rescue.

What else was new?

CHAPTER THIRTY-ONE

W as that the sound of a car?

Sophie saw nothing that indicated the road was close, but she was fairly certain she'd heard an engine.

She hated that she had to stop, but the sun had dipped behind the mountain, and it was dark in the shadow of the trees all around. She needed light.

She was digging for the flashlight when she remembered she had Bryan's cell phone. She pulled it from the pocket of her jacket. According to the indicator light, she had service.

Yes!

She tapped in his code and opened the messaging app.

Bryan had sent several texts to Michael over the course of the day, all of which had little red warnings indicating that they hadn't gone through. She clicked the *resend* button beneath each one.

Because of all the photos, they would take time to send. She didn't want to wait. Instead, deciding not to drain the phone's battery, she shoved it back into her pocket and found the flashlight. Following its beam, she continued down the slope.

Finally, there was a break in the darkness ahead, where the evening light still reached. Thank God.

She pushed herself faster and burst onto the parking lot.

Then skidded to a stop.

The rented Volkswagen wasn't the only vehicle. There were two pickup trucks.

Men stood beside them. Watching the trailhead.

One stood out. Bald head. Round face. Glasses.

No!

She turned and bolted back up the trail, running for her life.

But they were coming.

She tossed her flashlight to her right, dove into the woods to her left, and searched for a place to hide. The darkness would cover her. Maybe. *Please, please.*

"Sophia. You will stop running."

His voice was too close.

Men were angling toward her from lower on the slope. Their flashlight beams lit the ground all around her.

Please, get me out of here!

A gunshot split the silence. "You will stop running," a man said, "or I will make you stop."

It was no use.

She was caught.

With the phone, which had screenshots and directions to the weapons.

They were coming. She had a few seconds, no more. She yanked it from her pocket and tossed it toward the far side of a tree, not so hard that they'd hear it land.

It landed in leaves and bracken.

She turned and walked toward the man closest to her. Drawing them away from that phone.

The man who reached her first held a gun in one hand and

smiled as the other gripped her arm. "It's a pleasure to finally meet you. I am Hasan Mahmoud. And you are going to tell me what you found."

CHAPTER THIRTY-TWO

A gunshot echoed through the forest.

Sophie!

Bryan pushed to his feet, hating that he needed to use a tree trunk to do it.

A wave of pain rolled over him. He had to get to her. He had to find out what was happening.

Maybe...maybe it was just a hunter.

Right. Who hunted in the evening, after dark?

If someone were shooting at targets, there'd be more gunshots.

Which meant...

Had Mahmoud found them? How? *How!*

Please, God. Protect her. Get me to her.

While he'd waited, he'd dragged a nearby branch to himself and cut it to use as a walking stick. Now, he leaned on the walking stick on one side, the cane on the other, and descended the path as fast as he dared. If he fell again, he'd be useless.

Every step brought pain, but the thought of Sophie in the hands of that terrorist was pure torture.

It was dark now, but with both hands engaged in keeping him upright, he didn't have a way to hold his flashlight.

Slow and steady, Wright. Keep your feet.

No need to take a header and splat.

Come on, Sophie.

Where was she?

The trail was flattening out. He was almost there.

As if to confirm his guess, he heard an engine start. Was she warming up the car?

If so, she must be safe.

But then another engine roared to life.

What in the world...?

He hurried down the last twenty-five yards toward the parking lot and headlights.

He stopped before he reached the trailhead, watching through the trees. A pickup turned out of the lot, not back toward town but deeper into the woods.

Staying in the shadows of the forest, he caught his breath, scanning for enemies.

He'd heard two engines start. The Volkswagen was gone.

But a pickup truck remained in the lot. Men walked toward the trail. It was too dark to see what they looked like, but Bryan didn't need to.

Mahmoud and his fellow terrorists had taken Sophie...and now they were searching for him.

CHAPTER THIRTY-THREE

Sophie could hardly breathe. It wasn't the small space in the backseat of the Volkswagen or the too-warm air after the chill of outside.

Terror gripped her by the throat.

It was all she could do to pull in a breath and then push it back out.

She focused on that. Breathe in. Breathe out. In and out.

You're still alive.

For now.

Hasan Mahmoud sat beside her. Once he'd caught her, he'd stowed his handgun, unconcerned that she might escape.

Because, really, where was she going to go? It was her against multiple men. Armed men.

Terrorists.

Just breathe. In and out.

The last thing she needed was to hyperventilate. She'd done that once. Nineteen years old, second year of college. She'd been on her way into the library, nearly to the top of the wide marble steps, when her phone rang.

Before Mom could get any words out, she'd burst into tears.

Dad had taken over, giving Sophie the worst news of her life.

Josie, her beloved sister, was gone.

She'd sucked in a breath, and kept sucking. But there wasn't enough air in the world. Her vision darkened at the edges, and she'd felt herself tipping.

If not for a stranger who'd grabbed her, she'd have passed out and fallen down those stairs.

Not this time, though. Despite her panic, Sophie didn't hyperventilate. Nobody was dead. Not yet. But soon...

Soon, she would be.

Her parents would bury another daughter—if her body was found. Or maybe they'd never know what happened.

Bryan would know, or at least guess. *Oh, Bryan.* He'd blame himself. He'd been so sure they hadn't been followed. And...and they *hadn't been.*

So how was Mahmoud here? It made no sense.

Not that it mattered. But she'd rather try to puzzle that out than think about what was going to happen next. What would Mahmoud do to her to get the location of the weapons? How long would she be able to hold out? Long enough for rescue?

Who would come?

Had Bryan heard the gunshot? She'd hoped, as she'd been manhandled to the car, that he'd show up. That he'd see and somehow...

What? What could he have done? Even if he weren't injured, how could he have fought seven men? They had guns. He had a cane.

He couldn't have. Wouldn't have. Because his first priority would be the cache of weapons in the cave. Secure the weapons. Make sure Mahmoud didn't get his hands on them.

Bryan wouldn't worry about rescuing her.

His words came back to her. *If you were in that castle, Sophie, I would rescue you. I would risk everything for you because you are worthy. You are precious.*

He cared about her. When he'd said those words, he'd meant them.

But she wasn't worth more than all the people those weapons might kill. She wasn't worth that much.

Once upon a time, she'd been her single mother's precious child, her highest priority. But then Mom married, and Sophie had been pushed aside. But even though she'd no longer been Mom's highest priority, both Mom and Sophie's new dad had made her feel valuable.

And then Josie was born. Precious, kindhearted, sweet Josie. She took all her parents' time and attention. She took everything, and Sophie had never minded. She loved her sister, just like they did.

But humming in the background was the knowledge that she wasn't anybody's first priority. She'd been replaced.

No matter how much she'd done in her life, no matter how much she'd served, she was...replaceable.

What did the Bible say? There were vessels of gold and silver, and there were vessels for common use. Golden cups for serving the king.

And bedpans.

She'd always been a bedpan.

The kind of vessel that, when it was no longer useful, was tossed in the trash.

A throwaway.

So, there it was.

She would do one more thing to serve the people she loved. She'd hold out telling Mahmoud and his band of thugs where the weapons were.

Make me worthy of this last thing, Lord. Equip me to be like You. To sacrifice myself for them.

Because she had no doubt that, unlike in the fairy tales of her youth, the one Bryan had named Princess was not worthy of rescue. She was going to die.

CHAPTER THIRTY-FOUR

B ryan moved as fast as his bum leg would let him, staying out of sight. Fortunately, there wasn't a lot of brush in the way, and he was able to put a good ten yards between himself and the men before they reached the trailhead.

They moved silently, stealthily.

Bryan lowered the cane and walking stick to the ground, pulled the knife out of his pocket and unsheathed it. He stood behind a tree with his back to the terrorists so he wouldn't be tempted to look and give himself away. The tree wasn't quite as wide as his shoulders, and he prayed they wouldn't swing their flashlights toward him.

They did, though. A beam lit up the ground beside him on both sides.

Did they see him? Had they heard him moving through the woods?

Were they coming?

The light moved. Either they hadn't seen him—maybe his dark jacket and backpack had blended in with the forest—or the terrorists didn't want Bryan to know they had.

He didn't move. Barely breathed. Prepared to fight. Prayed for strength. He wasn't the slit-a-man's-throat type, but he'd do what he had to do.

He listened for the snap of twigs. Steady breathing.

A minute passed. Then two. He heard nothing.

Even so, he didn't move, just lifted prayers for help. For wisdom. For Sophie.

Finally, certain the men had continued up the trail, Bryan dared a peek. Sure enough, nobody was there.

He sheathed his knife, grabbed his cane and walking stick, and took a circuitous route through the forest to the road.

He'd studied the map on his phone enough that he didn't need it now. He could picture the area—not that there was much around here.

If he turned right, toward the castle and the town of Füssen, he'd walk at least five miles before he reached the main road—and "main" was a relative term. After they'd veered away from the castle that morning, they'd left most of the traffic behind. At the pace Bryan was moving, the trek would probably take him five hours. Assuming his leg would hold out. From there, he'd be able to flag somebody down, get a cell phone, call the police, and call Michael.

Probably.

But the men who had Sophie had turned the other direction.

To the left, there was only that small building—a cabin, he'd guessed—behind which ran the road that led to the cave. And nothing else for miles and miles and miles.

The cabin was a mile or so away. He could walk that far.

Maybe the terrorists were there. Maybe Sophie was there. Bryan hadn't seen anything else in that direction. If not, maybe there'd be help.

Should he turn right toward town or left toward the cabin?

Sophie and the terrorists had gone left, and that made the decision for him.

He turned toward the woman he was coming to love. He'd promised he'd rescue her.

But first, he had to find her.

Once he did, he'd figure out a way to keep Mahmoud from getting the weapons.

Thanks to the cane and the walking stick—and the painkillers that'd kicked in—he moved at a decent clip. The moon overhead gave enough light that he could see.

He'd been praying constantly since he heard that gunshot, the requests repeating in the back of his mind. God had shielded him from the two terrorists. God was with him.

Bryan couldn't let himself worry about all the things he couldn't do.

When I am weak, then I am strong.

Less than an hour after he started the trek, a glow of lights shone through the trees in the distance. Had to be the cabin, and the lights told him somebody was there.

As he got closer, he realized *cabin* wasn't the right word to describe it. It was a single-story house in a Tudor style—white with dark beams crisscrossing the front. Wider than it was deep, he guessed it was around a thousand square feet. No curtains or blinds covered the windows, giving him a clear view as a man walked past one.

The house had a steeply pitched roof. A small octagonal window above the front door must be in the attic.

There was a car in the driveway. The car Aaron had rented? Was Sophie here?

When he was closer, he saw a pickup truck behind the sedan.

So...he'd guessed right.

Now what, God?

Had the terrorists already known the whereabouts of the weapons? If so, why go to all the trouble to steal the chest? If not, though, then how did they have access to this house? Had they invaded it? Hurt the owners?

He hoped not, but nothing else made sense.

Because if Mahmoud had followed Bryan and Sophie—or Aaron—they would have ended up at the parking lot at the trail-head. Not here.

Unless Sophie had told them.

An image flashed in his mind. Sophie, being grabbed, harmed, hurt...

Don't think about that.

He needed to focus, and thoughts like that would drive him mad. Or drive him to do something very stupid.

It didn't matter how they'd ended up here. Bryan needed to focus on how to proceed.

Staying in the woods in front of the house, he reached the end farthest from the driveway. There were two windows, neither lit up. Maybe that meant the rooms were empty. If this were a house in Maine, he'd assume those were bedrooms. Were houses in Germany similar?

Probably.

Was Sophie in one of those rooms? The ground fell away here, making the windows too high for him to peek into. He watched for a few minutes and saw no movement within.

He continued his circuit around the house. There was a small backyard, no fence. The gravel driveway continued past the house and ended at a metal swing-gate. Beyond that, the path continued into the woods, not a road, really. Just two snow-covered tracks with a darker line of tall grass and weeds between them.

He took a wide route around the driveway and cars and found a good, thick tree trunk he could hide behind and watch.

He itched to act, to rush in, to save Sophie. But if ever he'd needed to wait for God's guidance, it was now.

CHAPTER THIRTY-FIVE

S ophie longed to stare out the octagonal window at the dark forest and freedom, but she couldn't keep herself upright. She collapsed back onto the splintery floor, her head throbbing.

At least she had a few minutes of peace.

When she and her captors had reached the house just a few minutes after they left the parking lot, Mahmoud had dragged a kitchen chair into the center of the living room and told her to sit.

She had, and the rest of the men gathered around like sentries guarding a dangerous prisoner. Most of them stood behind her. She could sense them watching. Smell their putrid breath. Feel their hate. They had the same dark skin as the Middle Eastern refugees she loved so much. They had the same dark eyes.

Two had stood in front of her. One glared down at her, his arms crossed over a barrel chest.

The other had leaned against the wall beside a window, casual as could be. He held an old-fashioned cigarette lighter in one hand, the kind with a flip-open top. He flipped it open, lit the flame, then snapped the top closed. Flip, grind, snap.

Over and over.

Where the other had hate on his face, this one looked amused, as if he found Sophie only slightly more interesting than the mundane lighter. Interesting, if irrelevant.

He observed her like a person might observe a puppy.

His expression so surprised her that she studied him, and then...

Oh. *Oh.*

She recognized him.

She'd held his hand and prayed with him. He'd been a client at the mission, a man who'd tearfully told her the story of his wife and children's deaths. But he'd looked different then, more...human.

Dariush Shahin. A Christian who'd converted from Islam.

A lie, obviously.

Her realization must've shown on her face because he grinned. "Finally recognized me, I see."

His English was excellent, though when he'd come to the mission, he'd acted as if he only spoke Arabic.

She averted her gaze, an instinctive action. And remembered something her father—her real father—had told her when she was a tiny girl. They'd been taking a walk in their San Diego neighborhood, and she'd seen a big, beautiful dog. She'd started toward it, but Daddy had pulled her back and crouched in front of her. "Never approach a dog without asking for permission. First, from the owner, then from the dog." He'd put his own fist out to let the dog sniff him, and she'd followed his lead. And then Daddy had said, "And never, ever look a dog you don't know straight in the eyes. They take it as a challenge."

This man was a bad dog. Evil wafted off him like the stench of spoiled meat. She'd do her best not to look him in the eyes again.

It all felt surreal, sitting in a cozy living room in Bavaria, a wood-burning stove in the corner with a glass front that allowed her to see the flames flickering inside.

Shiny hardwood floors partially covered by a braided rug. A comfy couch and side chairs perfect for curling up with a good book.

A couple of cups, a plate with crumbs on it. All the signs of a happy home.

And terrorists.

Mahmoud had settled himself on the couch in front of her, resting his arms across its back, relaxed as could be.

"Where is your boyfriend?" His voice was smooth and deep, his accent tinged with a hint of British aristocracy, his tone conversational.

"Who?"

The blow came from her left, a fist against the side of her head.

The world exploded.

She'd toppled over, her chair falling with her. Pinpoints of light sparkled behind her closed eyes.

She hadn't recovered, had barely caught her breath, when men shoved meaty hands beneath her armpits and lifted her and set her back in the chair.

Shahin hadn't moved.

Neither had Mahmoud, who'd watched as if he were enjoying his favorite movie. "I am sorry to be so forceful." The smile on his lips told her the man was anything but sorry. "We are running out of time. Now, where is your boyfriend?"

"He has a bad leg." Her voice shook. She took a breath and tried to rein in her fear.

"I have seen the cane. He was born that way? Crippled?"

"No. An injury when he was a kid. He fell on the trail and couldn't go on." Her voice cracked.

Dariush's lips tugged up at the corners.

"You left him in the woods?" Mahmoud asked.

"To get crutches from the trunk of the car."

Mahmoud's gaze flicked over her head. She heard footsteps, and a moment later, a door opened and closed in the other room.

Mahmoud said nothing, gaze skimming the space as if he were bored.

Dariush didn't take his eyes off Sophie.

A minute or so later, the door opened and closed again. The footsteps approached. The thug didn't step into view, but she guessed he'd found the crutches.

"Thank you for telling me the truth, Sophia," Mahmoud said. "As long as you tell me the truth, you will survive this. How far up the mountain was he?"

"I don't know exactly." Her words came slowly, and Mahmoud's eyes narrowed.

His chin dipped.

This blow came from the opposite side, a fist to the temple. She toppled off the chair.

Stars flashed behind her eyes.

The world spun, and nausea rose.

She forced herself to her hands and knees and vomited what little was in her stomach. Water. A protein bar. Bile.

Fear.

"Clean that up!" Mahmoud's voice came from the far end of a long, dark tunnel.

She was lifted, set in the chair again. She couldn't get her balance back and gripped the hard seat beneath her to keep from tipping over.

One of the men knelt at her feet and wiped the floor. When he stood, he held the filthy towel toward her face.

She flinched away, the scent threatening to have her retching again.

"Stop that," Mahmoud said. "We're not animals."

Weren't they, though?

The thug stomped out of sight. Maybe he returned, but Sophie couldn't keep track of who was where. The room still swayed. It was all she could do to stay in the chair.

"I know when you're lying to me, Sophie," Mahmoud said. "You see, I am much, much better at this than you are. I have interrogated soldiers and spies. I've yet to meet a man I couldn't break. You"—his eyes flicked over her body—"are no soldier. You understand?"

"I wasn't lying." Her words were slurred. "I'm not good at judging distances. I was trying to figure it out."

"How long did it take you to get from where you left your boyfriend to the parking lot?"

"Over an hour." The lie was instant, and before she'd even processed it, she added, "I was worried about him. Jogged when I could."

"You left him where?" Mahmoud asked.

"There's a ridge at the top of the trail where you can see the castle. It was just below that."

She'd left Bryan far, far lower on the trail, and she credited God with the fact that Mahmoud didn't pick up on the lie. She didn't have the wherewithal to know what to say or how to say it.

Mahmoud was right. She was no soldier. And utterly alone.

The world was growing darker, closing in.

If you were in that castle, Sophie, I would rescue you.

Bryan's arms wrapped around her, his breath a warm breeze in her hair.

I feel it, too, this thing between us... Maybe there's a way...

"I asked you a question!" The raised voice snapped her out of the memory.

She cringed, lifting her hands up to protect her head. "I'm sorry, I'm sorry."

But no blow came.

Mahmoud glared at her, lips pressed closed. "You found the location the coordinates led to, yes?"

"Yes."

She just needed to hold off telling him everything. *Help me, Father. Put words in my mouth.*

"Where?"

"It's a cave not far from the road."

"What road?"

"It's behind"—she waved toward the windows—"a cabin. Maybe this one?"

A satisfied expression crossed his features. He looked at Dariush and spoke in Arabic. "Just as I told you. As I always knew."

While they congratulated themselves, she scrambled. What should she say when he asked what was inside? Should she lie? Say it was empty? Tell them about the hidden room?

"This is why we follow you." Speaking to Mahmoud, Dariush's words sounded sincere, but when he turned back to Sophie, she saw something else in his eyes.

She wouldn't name it *loathing*. More like...like he found Mahmoud as irrelevant as he found her.

As if tolerating something far beneath him.

Mahmoud switched back to English. "And what was inside the cave?"

"Crates." Which was true, but not the whole truth. "There were eight, I think."

Mahmoud's back straightened.

Murmurs rose behind her.

Even Dariush's eyes, so uninterested before that, lit at the information.

In Arabic, Mahmoud said, "Quiet." To her, "Describe them, please."

She did, right down to the biohazard stickers. Though she knew she was telling them exactly what they wanted to hear, the men behind her were silent, and those in front of her were more careful to keep their expressions neutral.

"You climbed the trail," Mahmoud said. "Why not use the road, if you knew it was there?"

"We didn't. We came across it on the climb, and Bryan checked his phone and saw where it led."

Mahmoud's expression darkened with anger. She couldn't help the way her shoulders lifted, her back rounding, preparing for pain.

"He has the phone?"

Oh.

She shouldn't have mentioned that.

"Yes."

The word must've come too late.

This time, the blow came from behind, sending her sprawling forward. She tried to catch her fall, but her hands slipped, and she banged her cheek.

Footsteps moved fast.

And then one of the men kicked her.

Pain exploded in her side. She folded up to make herself as small as she could, covering her head with her arms.

"I told you not to lie to me."

"I'm sorry I'm sorry I'm sorry." She felt like a fool, apologizing to this man as if he deserved anything from her. She wanted to stay there, curled in on herself. To close her eyes and pretend none of this was happening. To drift off to sleep. Or to Jesus.

But the men grabbed her and returned her to the chair.

"Let's try that again," Mahmoud said. "Where is the phone?"

"I had it." The words came fast. "I threw it into the woods."

His eyes narrowed. "Why?"

"It has directions to the cave. Screenshots of the map and pictures of the entrance. I saw you and your men, and I didn't want you to find it."

"Did you send those pictures to anybody?"

"There was no service. I was going to when I got to the car, but you were there."

Maybe the texts had sent. She'd forgotten she sent them.

Was Michael on his way?

And what about Bryan? Was he off the mountain? Headed into town for help?

Or stranded, cold and wet and unable to walk?

"Thank you for being honest with me, Sophia." Mahmoud smiled, the expression cold and joyless. "We don't need the phone. We have you. You will take us to the cave." To the men, he said, "Put her in the truck."

A man grabbed her arm and yanked her to her feet. He started to drag her away.

"Wait. I-I don't think...I don't think I'll be able to—"

"Stop," Mahmoud said.

The thug did. He didn't let her go, just yanked her around to face Mahmoud.

"I can find the cave again. But not in the dark. I've only been there once. Bryan led the way. I was just following him. I wasn't watching the trail."

Mahmoud's eyes narrowed. He studied her, frustration clear in the tightness of his lips. "Where is the phone? Could you find that?"

"I don't remember. It was near the trail. I threw it to my right and then ran to my left, where you caught me. I don't really know where that was. Maybe you do?"

Mahmoud didn't catch her lie. Either he wasn't as good as he thought he was, or God was clouding his vision.

Dariush didn't look convinced, but he didn't argue.

"You'd better hope we can find it," Mahmoud said. "And that boyfriend of yours." He spoke to the man who held her. "Put her upstairs."

The guard had manhandled her through a narrow door, up a steep flight of stairs, and into the attic. He'd pushed her inside, then slammed the door.

She heard a lock click, not that she'd have attempted to escape with all those men down there.

An hour had passed since then. Maybe more. She was still alive. For now.

Her one quick look out the window had told what she already knew.

She was alone, surrounded by evil men and, beyond them, nothing but forest. No police were coming for her. There'd be no radio cars with spinning red lights. No CIA agents would rappel through the windows to take out the bad guys and whisk her to safety.

Here I am, Bryan. Rapunzel in the tower, waiting for my knight in shining armor. In the fairy tale, the rescuer was a handsome prince.

And the princess a long-haired beauty, not a curly-haired...
What?

The quiet word resonated in her spirit—a challenge.

What was she going to name herself? A throwaway, as she had earlier?

As she'd always thought of herself?

Irrelevant unless she was serving others. Without value when she didn't perform?

Do I create throwaway people?

She flipped onto her back and stared above through the tiny window, the narrow view giving her a glimpse of treetops and, beyond that, a black sky blanketed with stars.

She was not alone.

Nobody knew where she was. Nobody would be coming for her. But she was not alone.

You're here, God. I know that. I don't have to prove myself to You. I don't have to convince You I'm worthy. You decided that about me a long time ago. Please, save me.

The request felt selfish. She should be praying that God would stop the terrorists from getting the bioweapons and using them. She should be praying for all the innocents those men couldn't wait to kill.

That, too, God. Please. But in her heart, what she wanted more than anything was to get out of that attic, away from the evil men. What she wanted was to live.

Was that so awful, to want to survive until her thirty-fourth birthday?

To want to be rescued?

Jesus had done that for her once. He was her Rescuer. He'd chosen her out of the world and redeemed her life.

Now, she answered the gentle question He'd posed.

You don't create throwaways.

God had formed her and loved her, just as she was.

And God alone got to decide the number of Sophie's days. Nobody could do anything to her outside of His will.

My every thought toward you is good, daughter. You are My favorite.

Sure. But everyone was His favorite.

And why did she do that? Minimize the beautiful things He said to her?

She didn't know how to believe it, but she wanted to.

I am Your favorite.

And she felt His smile.

Tears moistened her scratchy lids.

No matter how this ended, she was going to be all right.

Maybe she'd be rescued from this trial. Maybe she'd be rescued *through* it.

Her parents might not see her value. Mom and Dad might never give her the love she craved. But her God did. And He was here. And nobody could snatch her from His hand.

CHAPTER THIRTY-SIX

S taring at the windows wasn't going to produce Sophie. Or a solution.

Bryan made his way back to the driveway. None of the windows on this side were lit. Peering through one, he saw a kitchen—counters, appliances, a table in the center. No people.

Hopefully, it would stay that way. He moved to the pickup and tried the passenger door. Unlocked. He swung it open.

The dome light came on, and he quickly flicked it off, then searched the cab, desperate for a weapon or a cell phone, or even keys. If nothing else, he could steal the truck and drive to town. Better yet, rescue Sophie, then steal the truck.

All he found was a water bottle, half full. Not that he wanted to share germs with a terrorist, but he'd long since finished the water he'd carried up the mountain. He took a chug, then shoved the bottle into his backpack.

He backed out and pushed the door closed as quietly as possible. At the too-loud click, he ducked, waiting for a reaction from inside.

Nothing.

The terrorists weren't worried they'd be found. They were comfortable here.

He peered into the truck bed. A gray plastic tarp was bunched near the cab, bricks on top of it to keep it from blowing away. He lifted the edge. Shovels and a toolbox filled with everyday tools.

Bryan searched the Volkswagen, found nothing useful, and then popped the trunk.

Dang. The crutches weren't there. Where were they?

Why would the terrorists take them? Was somebody hurt? Was Sophie? Or had she grabbed them before the terrorists came, then dropped them?

He closed the trunk as quietly as possible. Why had he spent years studying ancient antiquities? Had he really not had time for a single *how to hot-wire a car* class?

Not exactly an important life skill for a college professor.

From the house, a hinge squeaked, and then voices carried on the cold air.

Bryan bolted toward the woods and dove behind a tree, landing on his shoulder.

Had he hidden well enough? He dared not look up and draw attention to himself. He stayed still as a stone.

The men were talking in Arabic. Not useful in letting him in on their plan, but at least it would cover any slight sounds he made. He turned to watch as they reached the Volkswagen.

The driver pulled open the door, then looked around, scanning the surroundings.

Bryan dropped his head.

In his attempt to be quiet, he hadn't gotten the door completely closed. The driver had noticed. Would he search for the intruder? Find Bryan hiding just a few feet away?

The thug said something to the other man, who laughed. A door slammed.

Just the one.

Bryan didn't dare check but knew the guy was still looking, wondering who'd opened the door.

Another moment passed.

Finally, the second door slammed. The engine turned over. Bryan watched the car make its way down the long driveway through the woods and turn toward the trailhead and town.

Two fewer men here now.

He crept through the woods, dashed across the driveway, and stayed low until he reached the brightly lit windows. How many were in there? No more than ten, he surmised, based on the two pickups. Assuming three men could fit in the back of the extended cabs.

Two were on the trail, searching for Bryan, he assumed. Two had just left, so four down.

Bryan leaned against the house beneath a window, listening to the low sounds of conversation inside.

Arabic. Another class he should've made time for. Sure, he could read Akkadian. But he'd prefer to understand the terrorists at the moment.

He risked a peek. Hasan Mahmoud was pacing as he talked. Two men stood at attention like soldiers, nodding and yes-sirring him.

Seven men confirmed. Maybe more.

Confident they wouldn't be able to see him with the bright lights inside and the darkness outside, he scanned the space. He wasn't sure what he'd expected—what did the lair of a terrorist look like? Not this place, with couches and recliners and a wood stove.

Arrayed on the coffee table were weapons. Several handguns and a rifle.

Oh, he wanted that rifle.

If he could get his hands on it, that would change everything.

Without it, Bryan could see no way to go up against three men and all those guns with nothing but a hunting knife.

The princess would have to stay in the tower a little while longer. Where was Sophie? Maybe in a bedroom? Or the attic? Or was there a basement? She had to be here somewhere.

He returned to the forest across from the driveway and was praying for wisdom when the door banged open again. A man jogged outside, passing just a few feet from Bryan.

Bryan had the element of surprise, but what could he do? If he killed the guy, then what? More men would come out. They'd know he was there.

No. That wasn't the way. That might be step one in a plan, but Bryan needed to be ten steps ahead.

The guy opened the gate between the driveway and the road leading up the mountain. Preparing the way for when they headed to the cave.

They'd have to take Sophie when they went because, even if she wanted to tell them exactly where the weapons were stashed, how would she describe it? She'd need to be there to show them.

Unless they had Bryan's phone. But if they did, then why would they wait? Why wouldn't they already be up there, loading the trucks in the dark? They knew Bryan had escaped. They didn't know he had no way to contact anybody, so...

No. Sophie must've destroyed the phone, or hidden it. Or refused to give them the password. Which meant they'd need her to find the cave. They'd all head up there eventually.

Bryan would be left here.

Even if he started hiking right now, it would take him hours to get back to the cave. By the time he did, his leg would be useless. And he'd have no idea what was going on here at the house.

He couldn't leave Sophie.

So...what to do?

There was really only one option.

Maybe it would work.

Maybe he'd be caught and killed.

He left his walking stick and backpack in the forest and climbed into the truck bed. Silently, he shifted the bricks off the tarp and crawled underneath, pulling his cane with him. He wrapped his body around the toolbox and shovel.

The uneven metal floor bit into his shoulder and side. Not exactly a bed of roses, but he'd make it work.

He pulled the tarp on top of himself, reaching under it to settle the bricks on the edge. Maybe nobody would notice the extra bulk under the lump.

Help me out, here, Lord. Because if they catch me, I'm dead.

CHAPTER THIRTY-SEVEN

The pounding of footsteps pulled Sophie from sleep. She'd dozed off and on since she'd been tossed into the attic, though between the memories of what had happened, the fear of what would happen next, and the pain in her head and side, she wouldn't exactly call herself rested.

She had no idea what time it was, but a glance outside the window showed the sky was more dark gray than black.

The attic door banged open, and one of Hasan's men stepped in. "Up, up."

She pushed to her feet, and he grabbed her upper arm and propelled her to the stairs.

She held onto the railing as she descended, dizzy and light-headed. Her skull pounded. Her stomach rumbled.

The scent of coffee filled her nose, familiar as an old friend.

A friend among enemies.

The staircase ended in a hallway. The man pushed her toward the kitchen.

Like the living room, it would have been cozy if not for the terrorists. Pine cabinets and formica countertops. Faded linoleum floors and yellow appliances.

Old, but comfortable.

Dariush and another man sat at the table. A third man stood near the door that led to the driveway.

Dariush held the lighter again, flicking it open, lighting it, then closing it. Flip, grind, snap.

"Stop that," Mahmoud commanded.

"Apologies." Dariush slid the lighter into his pocket.

Mahmoud leaned against a counter, sipping from a mug, and addressed her. "Did you sleep well?"

"Never better."

His lips quirked like he found her amusing. "You are ready to show us the cave?"

She nodded, afraid to speak. Afraid of what would happen next.

She would show them the cave because it was her only chance. If the texts had gone through, then Michael knew where it was. Maybe he even knew they were in trouble.

He wouldn't find them here. But maybe he and his team would be waiting up there. Maybe there'd be a rescue.

She'd tell Mahmoud about the cave, but not the hidden door. She was not going to help him kill.

She dared to say, "I could use some food and coffee."

His eyebrows rose, showing he was surprised by the request. Maybe even impressed. He nodded to Dariush, who opened the refrigerator and grabbed a package out.

"Sit," Mahmoud said.

She took a chair that would allow her a view of Mahmoud and the other men.

Dariush plopped a few slices of cheese onto the dirty table along with a glass of tepid water, then sat beside her. His back to Mahmoud, he watched her.

All the men were terrifying, but this one's creepiness

outshone the rest. He showed no fear, no anger, no frustration. Only confident amusement. As if nothing could stop him.

She focused on the food and drink. She hadn't realized how thirsty she was until the liquid touched her tongue. The food settled her stomach. Her head still hurt, but the pain was the least of her worries.

"We did not find the phone," Mahmoud said.

"Oh." Thank God.

"But we found your friend," Mahmoud said. "He is dead."

The words floated in her mind.

No.

That couldn't be true.

Tears blurred her vision. She didn't move, couldn't even think what to do.

Bryan was *dead*?

"He tried to run when my men caught up with him." Pleasure filled the man's tone, taking pride in his thugs, his evil. "Of course, he couldn't outrun them. His body will be ripped apart by beasts, pecked by vultures. If it is found someday, it will be unrecognizable."

She didn't want to picture it, Bryan's body broken and lifeless in the forest.

"He was killed because he tried to escape from us," Mahmoud said. "You, Sophie, do not have to end up that way. You can survive. All you have to do is take us to the cave. We will take the weapons and leave you there. By the time you make your way back to civilization, we will be gone. But if you make it difficult, or if you try to trick us, you will end up as food for the animals, like your friend. Do you want to live, Sophie?"

She nodded. She did want to survive.

Oh, Bryan.

Her heart cracked and splintered and fell to pieces. How

could she go on, knowing what had happened? Knowing what these men planned?

Knowing she was truly all alone.

I would rescue you...

All night long, hope had hummed beneath her fears. She'd believed Bryan was out there, trying to keep his promise.

But he'd been on the trail. He'd had no idea where she was. Had he even tried to find her?

Despair darkened the room. Darkened everything.

Bryan was gone, and she was going to take these men to the cave. And they were going to torture her until she told them how to get the weapons.

Give me strength, Lord. Help me stand up to them. Or take me before I crack.

Because either way, Mahmoud wasn't going to let her live. This would end in her death. But, *please, God*, let it not end with a terrorist attack against her friends.

CHAPTER THIRTY-EIGHT

The air beneath the plastic tarp was warm enough. But the metal floor might as well have been ice. Even so, Bryan had managed to doze a little.

Now, though the tarp was thick and impenetrable, he could tell by birdcalls that morning was coming. He listened to be sure nobody was nearby, then stretched, trying to awaken his limbs just in case he was discovered. He'd like to take at least one guy out before they murdered him.

And there was a grim thought.

He should have kept the water bottle. His mouth was cottony, his stomach growling. His leg ached, and he hoped it would hold his weight.

He and Sophie were up against a whole bunch of armed men. He felt like Elisha's servant, seeing the strength of the army all around. But God had opened the servant's eyes. *"The mountain was full of horses and chariots of fire all around Elisha."*

Bryan had memorized that verse when he was a kid, loving the image of God's army against the enemy, whose force must've looked pathetic facing a host of warrior angels.

Surround us with Your warrior angels, Lord. We need You.

He kept up the prayers as the world awakened. Branches shook as little forest creatures traversed them. Birds twittered and life went on.

And God was good, despite where they were. He was with them, despite what had happened.

Not in my strength, Bryan prayed, *but Yours.*

Help us.

The house door opened with a squeak, and voices carried on the still winter air.

Car doors opened. The pickup shuddered beneath him.

In the middle of the rough sounds, he heard the faintest, "Okay."

Sophie. Awake. Talking. Alive.

Thank You, God.

Not that Bryan had believed they'd kill her. They needed her alive to show them where the cave was. But he was glad for the confirmation.

If only he could let her know he was there.

The engines rumbled to life, both trucks and the Volkswagen. They started moving, not going back toward the main road but forward toward the cave.

Every bump sent pain into Bryan's hip and shoulder where they rested against the truck bed. The vehicles crept along, and he pictured the image he'd seen the day before. This road switch-backed up the mountain, winding around the far side and back.

Thirty agonizing minutes later, the pickup stopped.

The men spoke in Arabic.

Please don't let them get the toolbox and shovels.

If Sophie had told them anything about where they were going, they wouldn't bother to move the tarp until they had the crates.

In English, Mahmoud said, "Lead the way."

He longed to hear Sophie's voice, but she didn't say anything.

Bryan waited for the sounds of their footsteps and low conversation to fade.

He was about to move when he heard something else. Metallic sounds, and then a snick.

The rifle, chambering a round. He'd recognize that sound anywhere.

And then silence. He waited thirty seconds, a minute. Afraid to move but knowing he had to.

Bryan slid out from beneath the tarp, the crinkly plastic making far too much noise. He got clear of it, stayed low, and crawled to the back of the bed.

The sun hadn't risen yet, but it would peek over the foothills soon enough.

Knife in his right hand, cane in his left, Bryan waited for a face, a voice. A demand. A gunshot.

But nothing came.

So far so good.

He climbed out and landed in the dirt between the two trucks. Ignoring the pain that shot up his leg, he moved to the front, peered left into the trees that led to the cave, then right at the low hill on the far side of the road.

A man was halfway to the ridge at the top.

Carrying the rifle.

Bryan dashed into the woods at the end of the road.

His leg throbbing, he moved far enough away that the rifleman wouldn't be able to see or hear him. Nothing mattered at that moment more than getting that weapon.

Stopping Mahmoud.

And saving Sophie.

The problem was, the hill only got steeper. He glared up at

the rock face, memories of the cliff at their island rolling over him. He let them come, then let them fade away.

This wasn't that. And he wasn't a seven-year-old boy trying to prove he was big. This wasn't even the massive rock face he'd seen with Sophie the day before.

He could do this.

He rested his cane against the side of the wall, stuck the knife handle in his teeth like some sort of ninja warrior, and climbed.

It was only about twenty-five feet high. With two strong arms and one strong leg, he managed to get to the top. He hauled himself over it, collapsed onto the damp bracken, and rested. Because as hard as that had been, what came next would be much harder.

Breathing under control, he crept across pine needles toward the ridge overlooking the vehicles. He'd gone about fifty yards when he saw the thug lying on his belly, scanning the horizon through binoculars. Though Bryan didn't see the rifle, he imagined it was beneath the man's right arm, ready to be fired.

If Bryan hadn't climbed from the truck when he did, this man would've seen him. Shot him.

He breathed in the truth of that, breathed out his thanks. And then added a prayer for guidance. He'd never killed a man in cold blood.

He had killed before, but that guy had been trying to murder Sam.

This wasn't that. This was terrorists. Bioweapons. Sophie.

He'd do what he had to do.

Gripping the knife, he crept forward. He had a lot of ground to cover, and the quiet morning and cooing doves weren't exactly raising a racket.

He was within thirty feet of the guy—still undetected—

when he spotted a rock small enough to grab but large enough to do damage. He snatched it. Maybe, if he could knock the guy on the head...

He slipped on a layer of wet leaves.

His foot landed on a hidden branch, and he lost his balance. He gripped a nearby tree to keep from falling.

The man turned toward the sound.

Bryan charged.

But the thug rolled away, taking the rifle with him. No time to aim, but if he got a shot off, his friends would come running.

Bryan whacked the guy in the shoulder with the rock, then kneed him in the kidneys. The man curled to protect himself. Bryan brought the rock down on his head.

Stunned him.

He levered up and whacked him again.

The guy stilled and collapsed onto his back.

Bryan yanked the rifle away. Caught his breath and scrambled backward.

He wanted to see if the man was breathing, but what if the guy was faking?

The thug didn't move.

Neither did Bryan.

A standoff, except maybe one of them was unconscious.

He checked the rifle—a Winchester .22 caliber semi-auto.

Yeah, this would work just fine.

If Michael were here, he'd probably slit the terrorist's throat. Wasn't that the way CIA operatives worked? And Green Berets, too. Grant wouldn't leave him there to do more harm.

But Bryan was no killer.

He grabbed a handful of pine needles, leaves, and dirt and tossed it onto the guy's head. No response. Seemed he was legitimately unconscious.

But not dead, by the rise and fall of his chest.

Bryan hid the gun behind a tree a few yards away, just in case. He readied the knife and crouched beside the guy to search his pockets.

No cell phone. No keys. That'd be way too easy.

He pulled a lace from one of the thug's boots, flipped him over, and tied his hands behind his back. That ought to hold him.

Bryan grabbed the rifle.

Time to stop Hasan Mahmoud and his band of killers.

And rescue Sophie.

CHAPTER THIRTY-NINE

S ophie was in no hurry.

She'd held out hope as they'd driven the rocky path that maybe Michael and his team were waiting to ambush them. But nothing awaited them at the end of the road but a trail that would lead to the weapons.

Maybe Michael was on his way. If she could just stall until they got here, they could stop this.

She hadn't overstated matters when she said she might not be able to find the cave. Following Bryan, who'd held his phone, she hadn't paid that much attention to where they were going.

The path into the forest was overgrown, and more than once she feared she'd veered off the trail.

Now, she stopped again, peering past the trees on both sides. There'd been a giant rock wall. Where was it?

"What is the problem?" Mahmoud simmered with impatience she could practically smell.

"I'm not sure which way to go."

His exhale was heavy, hot in her ear. "I tire of wandering."

She ducked away. "Really?" she snapped. "Because this is a

blast for me." Stupid to use the angry tone, but she was done cowering.

He'd had Bryan killed. And he'd kill her as soon as he had what he wanted. Why would she hurry?

Whatever happened next, she'd face it. Standing up. Shoulders back. Head high. When he knocked her down, even then she wouldn't forget who she was. *Whose* she was. God was on her side. And her real God was a lot more powerful than this man's false one.

He snaked his hand around her arm, but she yanked away. "I can hold myself up, thank you." She marched forward, half expecting to be punished for her impudence.

The chuckle that drifted on the air behind her grated on her nerves.

Not from Mahmoud but from Dariush. He and the rest of the men trailed their leader, all ready to haul out crates and crates of bioweapons.

She rounded a bend and froze. There was the giant rock face in the distance. The sight of it didn't bring calm but terror. As soon as they stepped into the cave, even Dariush's patience would run out.

She moved slowly, carefully. Praying for rescue. For something to happen.

Single file, they walked at the edge of the rock face. She stopped at the shorn bush and stepped aside. "In there."

Mahmoud pushed her out of the way and spoke to one of the men behind her. "Keep an eye on her." Then he ducked and moved into the cave, the rest following.

His roar of frustration echoed on the walls and rumbled through the stone tunnel.

The man assigned to stay with her looked to be the youngest of the group. Smooth skin, patchy whiskers. She doubted he was even twenty. Old enough to fight and young enough to be brainwashed into believing lies. He got in Sophie's face. "What did you do?" He spoke the words in Arabic, and she responded in his language.

"Nothing." Did she sound convincing? "This is the spot."

The man was shoved out of the way. Mahmoud stepped into her space and glared down at her. "Where are the weapons?"

"I-I don't know. They should be there." Her voice shook with fear, which was completely genuine.

He backhanded her, and she stumbled, crashed against the stone wall, and crumpled to the ground.

The young one hauled her up and turned her to face Mahmoud. She backed away but bumped against the stone.

Mahmoud stepped so close she could feel his hot breath on her face. "Tell me where they are. Now."

"They were here." Her voice pitched up. "I swear, they were... You see the bush. The cuts are fresh. The cave is here. Why would I lie?"

His eyes narrowed to slits.

The others watched.

Even the forest seemed to still in the silence.

He leaned down, right in her face. "I will tear you apart."

Don't cower. Don't whimper.

Don't give in.

His hand snaked around her neck. He pushed her against the wall, pressed his body up against hers, and squeezed.

Cutting off her air. Her blood flow. Her thoughts.

She would die here. Now. But she hadn't told him. She'd kept silent.

If she died now, she wouldn't be able to spill the secret.

A shout had Mahmoud's grip loosening.

Dariush sounded triumphant. "I found it."

No!

Mahmoud backed away, then shoved her, hard.

Her head whacked into the rock, and she went down.

Mahmoud ducked into the cave again, the rest following.

Only the young one remained, his gaze flicking from her to the stone entrance. Eager anticipation filled his eyes as if he couldn't wait to put the weapons to use.

Or maybe he was excited to see what Mahmoud would do to her next.

She didn't bother to stand. She'd lie here on the soft ground despite the cold moisture seeping through her filthy jeans. She'd enjoy the feeling of the land, the breath in her lungs.

She closed her eyes. Knowing it was over. Trusting God to do what she'd failed to do.

And to protect her from what would happen next.

CHAPTER FORTY

I t took every ounce of self-control Bryan possessed not to pull the trigger.

He'd wanted to, God help him. When he'd seen Mahmoud put his hands on Sophie, he'd itched to put a bullet in his head.

Shooting Mahmoud then might save Sophie in the short run. But it would ultimately get her and Bryan killed.

And since Sophie had been the terrorist's only link to the location of the weapons, Bryan had believed—or maybe it had been more hope than anything—that he'd back off.

And then the shout came from the cave. One of the thugs must've found the secret door.

He watched as all but one ducked inside.

Whoops of joy filled the air, as if they'd discovered a treasure of great value. Not weapons capable of killing thousands.

Bryan crept forward, never taking his eyes off the man guarding Sophie.

She hadn't moved since she'd fallen. Was she conscious?

One problem at a time.

He lifted the rifle, took the last two steps, and jabbed it hard into the back of the goon's skull.

He toppled, face-first. Started to turn.

Sophie gasped and scrambled away.

Bryan kicked him in the side, then hit him in the head with the butt of the rifle again, hard.

When the guy quit moving, Bryan crouched in front of Sophie.

Her eyes widened, her mouth opened.

He pressed his palm against it and shook his head. He wouldn't think about her two black eyes or the dried blood on her temple.

He helped her up and urged her through the forest away from the path. "Go. I'm right behind you."

She gripped his arm. "Come with me."

"I'll be right there. Go. Please." She looked like she wanted to argue, then gave in. When she started moving, he walked back to the thug.

Bryan took out his knife, prepared to kill him if necessary, and searched his pockets. Somebody had to have keys.

Bryan had checked the trucks and the car, hoping to find them. No deal. And no keys with this guy, either.

Wouldn't want it to be easy.

He hurried through the forest and caught up with Sophie probably no more than thirty yards from the cave. Too close, and too soon, considering how slowly he moved. But she was lumbering, crashing through the woods.

He gripped her arm and whispered, "You okay?"

She nodded, but her eyes were unfocused. He had the feeling she was barely seeing him. Barely hanging on.

They needed to hurry. Any second, those guys would find them.

But Sophie collapsed, falling onto the pine needles.

His heart jumped into his throat. "What is it? What can I do?"

"I can't. Everything is spinning." She rolled over and threw up.

They couldn't stay here. They were too close to the entrance. He needed a good vantage point if he was going to keep the terrorists from leaving.

He covered the vomit with bracken, then helped her up, shifting her to lie behind a couple of skinny tree trunks. She curled into the fetal position.

He picked up an armful of leaves and needles and dumped them on top of her. "Listen to me. Are you listening?"

"Yeah." Her voice was thin and reedy.

"Do not move. They shouldn't be able to find you, but you can't move, no matter what happens. No matter what they say. No matter if they find me and threaten to kill me. Even if they shoot me, you stay right here and don't move. That's your only chance. Understand?"

Her head shifted, maybe a nod.

"I need you to promise."

"I promise."

He leaned down, kissed her forehead. "I love you, Princess. I'm going to get us out of this."

Her eyes opened, met his. And maybe this hadn't been the time to confess his feelings, but...well, there might not be another opportunity.

He pushed to his feet and ran back to the road.

Every step raised anxiety in his chest. The last thing he wanted was to leave her. But if they were going to get out of this, he could see no other way.

Bryan was nearly to the vehicles when he heard an angry shout from behind him. "Sophia! Show yourself, now!"

Mahmoud wasn't happy.

Stay where you are, Princess.

The man said something in Arabic, and his men answered.

Were they looking for her?

Hopefully not. Hopefully, they'd start loading the weapons. Why bother trying to find Sophie? They had what they wanted.

Unless they realized she'd had help escaping.

Protect her, God. Please.

Bryan couldn't let Mahmoud leave with those crates. He wasn't excited about the prospect of walking down the mountain, assuming he and Sophie survived, but he couldn't let the men leave. He stabbed the tires on the trucks and the sedan.

Then he hobbled to the hill and climbed, praying he'd make it to the top before any terrorists broke through the trees. He wasn't moving at Spider-Man speed.

At the top, he glanced to where he'd left the unconscious would-be shooter.

The rifleman was gone, nothing left but the ragged ends of a broken shoelace.

Please don't let me pay for sparing that man's life with my own. Or Sophie's.

He didn't dare lie on his belly like the thug had done, even though it would make him less of a target. He needed to be ready for an attack. And anyway, he wouldn't be able to get back up.

He braced himself against a tree and faced the forest. Waiting.

Angry shouts continued to sound from the woods.

Just give up. Leave her be. Let her go.

Two men emerged from the path carrying a crate.

Bryan aimed at one of their heads but didn't squeeze the trigger.

Cold blood.

Despite the bioweapons and the threat they posed, he couldn't make himself shoot.

A third man hurried past them and opened the tailgate of the nearest truck. They didn't notice the ruined tires.

They loaded the crate and went back for more.

What do I do, Lord?

Should he shoot?

Or wait?

Two more men emerged with another crate.

Again, Bryan got one of them in his sights.

Do it. His silent command was loud in his head. *Do it.*

But he couldn't.

Did that make him a coward?

He was no soldier, no trained killer. He wasn't afraid of those men finding him, not as much as he feared facing God.

Lord, You're going to have to squeeze it for me. Or show me what to do. Because I can't...

A new sound rose. Not a man's shout, but something else.

A triumphant call.

No. Please.

But the worst had happened.

A terrorist—not Mahmoud—stepped out of the forest, Sophie at his side. She was stumbling, unable to even stand up straight.

The man shoved her roughly against a tree. "You come out!" he shouted. "You come out, or I kill her."

Bryan lined the man's head up in his sights.

"Now," he shouted, "or she dies."

The terrorist shoved his hand in his pocket.

Came out with a pistol.

Inhale. Exhale. Hold.

Bryan squeezed the trigger.

The terrorist toppled.

Sophie staggered, nearly collapsed.

"Run!" Bryan shouted.

The other men dropped the crate. Reached for weapons. Looked up at the cliff, but Bryan was hidden in the shadows. He took aim.

Inhale. Exhale. Hold.

Squeeze.

A second man went down.

The other one roared, lifted a pistol toward Sophie.

Bryan set his sights. Breathed. Squeezed.

He landed in the mud beside his friend.

Sophie made it across the road, barely walking at a normal pace, much less a run. Bryan lost sight of her as she neared the hill.

He had no choice now. He had to shoot as many as he could.

How many more? Could he kill them all? *Help me, God. Please. Help her.*

He needed her to get far, far away before the terrorists found Bryan and took him out.

The entire forest seemed to tremble in anticipation.

Another man emerged from the trail at a full sprint, running toward where Sophie had disappeared. Bryan couldn't see her, but he had no doubt the thug could.

He lined the man up.

Inhale. Exhale. Hold.

Squeeze.

The man went down, but more were following. Bryan aimed at the next.

Before he squeezed the trigger, he went down.

What?

Gunshots rose from the forest.

A sound came from beside Bryan. He swung the rifle that

way. No idea how someone had crossed the road, but if a terrorist was coming...

It wasn't a terrorist.

Sophie came into view, seeming unable to keep her feet.

He hurried toward her and caught her an instant before she collapsed. "You should have run away. Down the mountain."

She said nothing, just hung onto him.

"Sit down, Princess. I need to watch for—"

A hand clamped on his shoulder. "I'm friendly."

Bryan twisted toward the voice. Blinked at the figure dressed in camouflage, face painted black.

"Well done." He spoke with a nice, normal Midwestern accent. "We'll take it from here."

He was gone before Bryan could process it.

He knew that man. He'd met him in Greece.

Michael's friend, Stone.

They were here.

Thank You! Thank God.

Bryan held Sophie, breathing in the feel of her, the truth of it. She was alive. He was alive. They were saved. "Are you all right?"

"I didn't know what to do." Her voice was weak and trembly. "I just...I needed you."

"Me, too, Princess. I needed you too." He held her against his chest, breathing prayers of thanksgiving.

There was no way they could possibly have survived. And yet, somehow, they had.

Already, the sounds were changing at the bottom of the hill. The triumphant shouts were coming not in Arabic but in English.

Mahmoud emerged from the forest, hands behind his head, followed by an American suited up in camouflage. When they reached the road, the man kicked the back of Mahmoud's legs, and the terrorist went down to his knees.

Other operatives closed in, guns trained on the mastermind.

The American looked up at Bryan.

Michael.

Bryan raised a hand, and his big brother dipped his head.

Movement had Bryan's gaze shifting to the woods on the ridge.

The rifleman Bryan should have killed aimed a handgun at his brother.

"Watch out!" He pushed Sophie aside. Swung the rifle.

Took aim.

The handgun fired.

An instant before Bryan did.

His brother fell.

Bryan fired again. The bullet hit its mark.

The terrorist pitched forward and landed face first.

An instant too late.

Bryan dropped the rifle and ran down the hill, every step torture, and not because of his leg.

His brother. His brother had been shot.

Michael's teammates gathered around him. Bryan could hear their voices, but he couldn't make out their words. Everything was garbled as if he moved through water.

He pushed men out of the way, not caring about anything but getting to Michael.

He dropped to his knees. *No, no!*

And then Michael's eyes opened. "Man, that hurts."

Bryan couldn't speak. Couldn't do anything but stare, trying to figure out what had happened.

"He's fine."

A man loomed over them, a smirk on his face. Bryan had met Michael's boss, Brock, who added, "He's got more lives than a cat." He shook his head, all *just another day at the office,* and turned to give instructions to one of the other men.

Bryan looked at Michael again. "He missed?"

"Got my vest." He pressed a hand to his collarbone, just above his heart. "That's gonna leave a mark."

Bryan dropped onto his butt, adrenaline seeping out of him, his leg reminding him that it wasn't meant to dash down hills at top speed.

Except, apparently, when it had to.

He dipped his head, took a few breaths. Realized...

Michael was alive. Sophie was alive. He was alive.

They'd done it.

Thank You.

Michael gripped Bryan's forearm. "Hey, bro?"

When he looked up, Michael was looking at him, concern and...something else in his expression.

"You all right?"

"Yeah. Just...yeah. Processing."

"Process this." He squeezed Bryan's arm. "You saved my life."

"He got your vest."

"He'd have gotten my head if he'd had more time to aim."

Right. Maybe.

"You saved a lot of lives today, bro."

"No." Couldn't be true. Bryan wasn't the hero. He was the guy who needed saving.

Before he could come up with a response, Sophie dropped to the ground next to him.

He wrapped his arm around her, holding her against his side. She was safe now, if a little worse for the wear.

"Hey, Sophie," Michael said. "Glad you're okay."

"You too." Her words were weak, but she smiled. She needed medical care and about a month's rest, he guessed. "Bryan saved me."

Michael grinned. "Yeah. I guess that's his thing now." He stood, wincing a little. "Rescuing women, shooting bad guys, stopping terrorists." Michael's grin faded as a cargo van made its way toward them and stopped a few feet away. He turned to look at the crates in the back of one of the pickups. "Saving lives." His hand dropped on Bryan's shoulder. "I never meant for you to get caught up in this. I'm sorry."

"I'm not." Bryan kissed the top of Sophie's head, inhaling her presence. She was alive and well and safe. Getting involved in this had led to him meeting this amazing woman. He'd even had a hand in protecting her. And others.

How could he be sorry about any of that?

Michael regarded him a long moment, then he squeezed his shoulder. "I'm proud of you."

Bryan didn't know what to say. He had nothing but thanks to the One who'd really done it.

Michael headed toward his teammates as if he took a bullet to the chest—or vest, anyway—every day.

"He's right, you know." Sophie leaned back and pressed a hand to Bryan's cheek. "You saved a lot of lives today."

"*We* saved a lot of lives. I couldn't have done any of this without you."

She didn't argue and didn't turn away. "You stormed the castle for me."

"It wasn't a castle so much as a house, and I couldn't figure out how to get you out."

She leaned away. "You knew where I was?"

"Sorry I didn't rescue you last night. I saw no way to get past those men."

"I hoped you were out there, but I didn't... They told me they killed you."

"Aw, man." He brushed the hair away from her face, careful of the bruises. "I'm sorry you went through that."

"You saved me."

He pressed his lips to hers, a gentle kiss. "You're worth it."

Tears filled her eyes. She settled against his chest again.

He reveled in her warm skin, the feel of her, alive and breathing, in his arms.

He'd never call himself a hero. He'd never have managed any of this without a whole lot of help and God in his corner. But somehow, he'd done his part to stop the bad guys.

And win the princess.

CHAPTER FORTY-ONE

S ophie was learning that multiple blows to the head, along with dehydration, lack of food, lack of sleep, and shock, weren't great for the body. After the long ride to the hospital in Munich, during which Sophie had curled up beside Bryan, in and out of consciousness, she'd been poked and prodded by doctors, then taken to a room and told to rest.

She vaguely remembered a CT scan. Or was it an MRI?

Now, pressure on her arm pulled her from sleep, sending her heart rate to top speed. Her eyes popped open, but it wasn't Mahmoud manhandling her. A man seated at her bedside watched a monitor as the cuff on her arm slowly let out air.

"Am I still alive?"

He startled and smiled at her. "You are awake." He wore scrubs and was clean-shaven with chubby cheeks that gave him almost a childlike appearance. He spoke with a thick German accent.

She was too groggy to translate her thoughts into his language. "What time is it?"

"After nine."

It was dark outside the window, so nine at night.

"How do you feel?"

"Okay, I think. Can you help me sit up?"

He pressed a button, and the head of her bed rose.

She'd thought maybe Bryan would be in the room, but the bedside chair was empty.

"He told me to tell you he will be back soon. There is a phone number." The nurse handed her a piece of paper from the table near her bed. "You want to call him?"

She did, but she had more pressing needs. "Can I take a shower?"

A half hour later and feeling human, Sophie climbed back into bed wearing a clean hospital gown. Her hair was still wet, making the chilly room feel colder. She pulled the blankets around her, then rolled the table closer. The nurse had promised to send her food, and it'd been delivered while she was in the bathroom.

She lifted the top off the warm plate. Beef stew and a crusty roll.

Her stomach grumbled. She enjoyed a few spoonfuls of the hearty stew—a little bland, but good after she added salt—and a few bites of the bread.

She was just reaching for the phone to call the number Bryan had left when a knock sounded on the door. It opened a crack. "Mind if I come in?"

Bryan's voice, low and calm, soothed a worry she hadn't realized was there. "I'm glad you're back." She pushed the food table aside.

Bryan moved into the room on crutches.

"How's the leg?"

"Nothing time won't fix. I'll be on these for a while." He propped them against the wall, then gave her a quick kiss.

It felt so normal, as if they'd been together for years.

"How are you feeling?" he asked. "You slept a long time."

"Better."

"Good. In case you were wondering, we weren't exposed to anything in that cave. They tested both of us."

"Oh, good." She hadn't even remembered to fear that.

He wrapped one of her damp curls in his finger, his touch gentle. "You look good."

"You know there's a mirror in that bathroom, right?" She'd had a good long look at herself. One of her eyes was ringed with a dark bruise, the skin around it swollen. The bruise on the other eye was lighter. A bandage covered what must be a cut on her temple.

She looked terrible. Bryan, on the other hand, looked perfect. He'd taken a shower and changed his clothes. If not for the crutches, there'd be no sign of what he'd been through.

No outward sign. But he'd killed people. She figured that wouldn't fade as fast as her black eyes.

He pulled up the side chair and sat.

After everything they'd been through, she felt like she'd known Bryan for years. Not...a week?

No, that couldn't be right.

How could she have fallen in love in a week?

He took her hand and kissed her fingers. "I'm sorry I wasn't here when you woke up."

"Did you go back to the hotel?"

"Different hotel, but yeah. I took a shower and changed clothes." He brushed his fingertip across her cheek. His touch, so tender, was warm on her skin. "He hurt you."

It was probably Bryan's gentle tone and the unspoken question behind it that had tears pressing against her eyes.

"I'm so sorry," he said. "I never should have sent you to the parking lot alone."

"If you hadn't, then we'd have both been taken." She'd been rehashing everything that happened since she woke up, and she couldn't imagine a better outcome than the one they'd managed. "Mahmoud wouldn't have wasted time looking for you. I think... I think his belief that women are less-than—you know, not as smart, not as clever, not as capable—made it easy for me to convince him I wouldn't be able to find the cave in the dark. But if you'd been there, I doubt he would have waited until daylight. Maybe he'd have gotten to those crates before Michael and his team showed up."

"We don't know that. And what you went through—"

"I know." She caught Bryan's hand and held it. "We can't know what would have happened. But we can trust that God was working it all out, just like it was meant to be."

Bryan's lips pressed into a grim line.

"I'm okay. Truly."

As thankful as she was to be safe, those few hours as a prisoner had opened her eyes in a fresh way to the things people endured all over the world.

How many lived entire lives as prisoners, forced to do the will of evil men? Willing to risk everything—their lives, their fortunes, their bodies—just to be free.

She'd always felt a pull to help them. She was more determined than ever to serve those who'd fought and escaped tyranny. The corporate tyrants—selfish and cruel leaders who stole from their people. And personal tyrants—small men who squashed the people around them to make themselves feel powerful.

She gazed at the face of the man she'd somehow fallen for. She should have fought it, but her heart had had different ideas.

It was about to be crushed. Because she cared for him. She loved him. But she had a mission, and that mission hadn't changed.

God, what are You doing?

Why would God bring Bryan into her life, only to make her give him up?

"What is it, Princess?" Bryan leaned in, his gaze flicking from eye to eye as if he might find the answer to his question there.

How could she give up this man who treated her as if she really *were* a princess? As if she mattered.

"Are you hurting?" he asked. "Should I get the nurse?"

"I'm okay. Just thinking how..." But she didn't want to say what she was thinking. She didn't want to risk sending him away one moment before she had to. "How blessed I am."

He continued studying her, and by the press of his lips, he didn't believe her answer for a second. But when she added nothing else, he sat back. "Are you up for some questions? Michael wants to debrief us." He said the words with an amused smirk. "It's weird seeing him as an operative."

"You think?" To her, the weird thing was that he was a CIA agent, not special forces. All suited up, he'd looked terrifying.

Not like his sweet and gentle younger brother. Bryan might not be a soldier, but he was a hero in every way.

The door opened, and then a knock sounded. "Mind if I come in?" Michael called.

"We do mind." This from Bryan. "Go away."

Michael stepped in and looked at Sophie for permission, one eyebrow raised.

"Ignore him," she said.

"I usually do." Michael moved closer, looking not like the soldier but like the man she'd met in Maine. He'd showered and combed his hair and changed into jeans and a navy-blue sweater. Just a nice, regular guy. Even so, she'd never unsee the operative with the AK-47—or whatever that thing had been.

"How you doing?"

"I feel better," she said.

"Sorry I had to take Bryan away. We had some things we needed to take care of, and he was driving the nurses crazy. You ever seen a guy pace on crutches? It's hilarious."

"Yeah, well, it wasn't your...girlfriend." He tripped on the word, giving her a quick look.

She smiled, only wishing it could be true.

"She's fine," Michael said. "Like we told you."

"Thank you, Dr. Wright."

"Not me. The medic assured you..." Michael shook his head, and she had the feeling they'd had this conversation more than once while she'd slept. He focused on her. "You mind answering some questions?"

"I can do that."

Michael gave Bryan a look, tipping his head toward the door. "You wait out there."

"Yeah. No."

"I'm not kidding, bro."

If anything, Bryan settled deeper into the chair. "I'm staying."

She swung her gaze back to Michael, suddenly feeling like she was watching a tennis match.

"We do this in private."

"Not this time, you don't."

She had a feeling the brothers could do this all day.

"It's fine, Bryan." She squeezed his hand. "I'll be okay."

His eyes narrowed, gaze flicking from her to Michael. "I want to stay."

"I'll tell you everything I tell him, word-for-word. I promise."

"Fine." Bryan stood and kissed her on the forehead. He shot his brother a glare, then crutched to the hallway.

"Close the door," Michael called, maybe just to annoy him.

It slammed, and the older brother smiled. "I don't get to pick on him nearly enough these days. It's fun. Brings back memories."

She laughed. "Be nice or I'll tell Leila."

"There's a serious threat. She's little but packs a heckuva punch." Michael's smile dimmed. "Seriously, are you up for this? I'd like to do it now, but it can wait until morning." He eyed her unfinished dinner. "Maybe you should eat and rest."

She was tempted to take the offer. The last thing she wanted was to relive everything. But, as much as she'd gone over the events in her head, she needed to say them out loud, to try to make sense of them. To try to forgive herself for choices that could have gone so very wrong.

The nurse interrupted Sophie and Michael before they got started. He gave Michael a quick look. "Visiting hours are over. The exception was for her boyfriend, but you are not him."

"I have special permission." Michael stood, towering over the chubby-cheeked nurse, and handed him a badge.

The nurse peered at it closely, then handed it back, obviously unimpressed. "Miss Chapman needs to eat and take some medicine."

"What is it?" Michael asked.

"You will wait outside."

"It's okay." She smiled at the protective nurse. "I need to talk to him."

"First, you eat. Then you take these." He plopped a little paper cup with pills on her tray. "For the headache."

"What is it? Not narcotics, right?" Michael gave her an apologetic look. "If so, they'll have to wait until we're done."

The nurse said, "*You* will wait—"

"It's fine." Sophie was too tired to referee another argument. "They're not narcotics, right?"

The nurse glared at Michael but spoke to her. "No, but they will make you sick on an empty stomach."

"I'll take them. I promise."

He slid the rolling table in front of her and walked out.

She started to push the tray away, but Michael said, "Uh-uh. Doctor's orders."

"You sure he's safe? Not trying to kill me or anything?"

Michael grinned. "I admire your paranoia. We vetted everyone with access to your room. He's safe."

"Oh. I was kidding."

"I wasn't." He nodded to her food. "Go on, then. I'll wait."

She finished the now-cold stew and the bread, then swallowed the tablets.

When she was done, he rolled the doctor's stool over. "Why don't you take me through everything that happened after you and Bryan found the crates."

"Bryan told you he fell on the trail? And sent me to get his crutches?"

At Michael's nod, she told him about seeing the terrorists in the parking lot. Trying to run and hide. Tossing the phone.

Her heart raced as she recounted the events. Had she really lived all that? It already felt like she was talking about somebody else. Like those strange, dangerous things couldn't possibly have happened to her.

Sophie Chapman, California girl.

Missionary to refugees.

Victim of terrorists.

Michael didn't take notes, just listened, nodding. When she reached the part where they left the house in the woods that morning, she faltered. She didn't want to tell him this. She was ashamed of it, even though it had all worked out.

"It's okay, Sophie." His voice was soothing. "Go on."

He already knew what she'd done. She just needed to say it and get it out there.

"I took them to the cave. I didn't think they'd be able to get into the hidden room." The words were coming fast. She looked down at her hands, clenched tightly on her lap. "I thought...I hoped you'd gotten the text, and maybe you'd be there. I was trying to lead them into á trap. But also...I was afraid. I knew they were going to hurt me if I didn't, so... It was probably the wrong thing to do. I should've refused. I'm sorry."

"Sophie, listen to me." He leaned forward, and when she met his eyes, continued. "You did exactly the right thing."

Tears blurred her vision. "What if you hadn't come? I never thought they'd figure out how to get that door open so fast. If you hadn't gotten there—"

"We did. We got there because you sent those texts. And then hid the phone from the terrorists. I'm only sorry we didn't get there faster. That wasn't your fault. We should've been there. We got there as fast as we could."

"Why not call the Germans?"

"Yeah. That's the question." He sat back, shaking his head. "It's all politics and...and the arrogance of power. Decisions way above my pay grade—decisions that could've gotten you and Bryan killed. Believe me, they knew how I felt. Not that I'm sorry we were the ones to take the terror cell down." By the way his lips pressed closed, he had a lot more to say on the subject, but he probably couldn't say it to her.

He'd probably said it all and more to his boss already.

"Anyway." He forced a bland expression. "You did great, better than anyone had a right to expect. I'm just sorry you had to go through it. Let's keep going. Once you got to the cave..."

She told him about when Mahmoud found it but not the

weapons, and how he started to strangle her, and then, in the cave, how Dariush found the door.

The man was clever.

She told Michael how Bryan had rescued her from the young thug who'd been assigned to watch her.

"But I couldn't run," she said. "My vision was fuzzy, and I was dizzy and nauseated. So Bryan hid me and told me not to move."

She could still feel the damp ground, smell the stench of the rotting leaves Bryan had tossed on top of her. The moisture that seeped through her jeans had cooled her skin. She'd been covered in sweat and shivering and nauseated and terrified, trying to be silent as men searched.

Unable to quell a wave of nausea, she'd rolled over and retched.

The sound had given her away.

A rough hand had grabbed her, yanked her to her feet. Dragged her into the open. He screamed for Bryan to show himself.

She squeezed her eyes closed and covered her face with her hands as if she could hide from the memory.

"It's okay." Again, Michael used a soothing tone. "You're safe now. Can you tell me what happened next?"

"There was a gunshot, and for a second... He'd threatened to shoot me. And I didn't feel a bullet, but I thought..." She'd thought she was dead, that any second, she'd collapse. She'd feel the pain. "But it wasn't me who was shot. Bryan shot him." She swallowed, trying to get her trembling under control, or at least keep it out of her voice. "The man who'd found me fell, and I staggered and probably would have gone down except Bryan yelled at me to run."

She dropped her hands and took a breath. The worst was

over. "I ran into the forest. I didn't know exactly where Bryan was, but I went toward where I thought he was. All I could think was that I needed to get to him. As if... It's stupid, but at the time, I felt like if I could just get to him, then we'd both be safe. I don't know how I had the strength to do it—maybe I was just running on adrenaline—but I climbed that hill and...and he was there."

The memory was fuzzy from that point on. She'd fallen into his arms. He'd held her, said something. And then he'd pushed her and yelled and lifted the rifle and fired.

"I still really don't know what happened, except Bryan ran down that hill to get to you."

Michael's Adam's apple dipped as he swallowed. "There was a gunman on the ridge we hadn't seen. Bryan had disarmed him, tied him up, and left him unconscious. He had a handgun. Maybe Bryan missed it. Maybe it was in the truck. We don't know." Michael's lips pressed closed, and he shook his head. "Not Bryan's fault. My fault for...all of this. Getting him involved." Michael forced a smile, though she didn't believe it. "I know what happened after that. Let's go back to the house where you were held. What can you tell me about the men? We have Mahmoud in custody. What about the rest of them? How many were there?"

"Seven, including Mahmoud."

A look crossed Michael's face, but he schooled it quickly. "What can you tell me about them?"

"Five were young—early twenties, if that. I'd never seen them before. I saw Mahmoud at the mission the day I gave Bryan a tour. The other man had been a client. Dariush Shahin." She quelled a shudder just thinking about him. "Most of our clients are families. We do get some single women or older people. Dariush stood out because he was a forty-something guy who came by himself. He claimed his wife had died during their escape. I had no reason to disbelieve him, but... honestly, he always gave me the creeps. I couldn't put my finger on it. I thought it was just me being...prejudiced."

Michael's eyebrows hiked. "Haven't you spent your life helping the refugees? How do you call yourself prejudiced?"

"We get ideas about people based on how they look. It's not fair."

"It would be prejudice if you were suspicious of all Middle Eastern men or all men who looked like him or all single men in their forties. But you aren't, right?"

"True."

"What you felt about Dariush Shahin wasn't prejudice," Michael said. "It was instinct. You'd do well to heed those instincts in the future. Often, our subconscious picks up clues we never note consciously. Listen to those clues, Sophie. They could save your life."

A week earlier, she'd have called Michael paranoid. Not anymore. Though most of the refugees she met were peaceful and genuinely looking for a better life, some were liars. Some were terrorists.

The last twenty-four hours had taught her that, a lesson she'd never forget.

"Mahmoud was in charge." Michael paused until she nodded to confirm. "Was Dariush his second-in-command?"

"Mahmoud never sought input from anybody. He issued commands, and everybody just...obeyed."

"Including Dariush?"

"Yeah, except..."

When she didn't finish her statement, Michael said, "Tell me what you're thinking."

"It was like...like a young manager who's forced to work

under an old boss. Dariush never said anything disrespectful, but... I don't know. Maybe I'm reading into it."

"Remember what I said about your instincts? Let's trust them for now. If you had to conclude something about Dariush..."

She wasn't sure what he was looking for. "I guess I'd say that, like an ambitious employee, he acted like he was eager to take over. Or maybe..." In her mind's eye, she saw the smug, arrogant look on the man's face. "More like, he was waiting for what he knew was coming. Like the old boss was about to get the ax, and the young manager had already been given the promotion."

"Huh. Okay." Michael seemed to file that away. "Good analogy. Let's talk about the things they said. What did you hear?"

"Not a lot the night I was with them, but that morning in the kitchen..." Not *that* morning. *This* morning. It was unreal that not even twenty-four hours had passed. "Mahmoud was discussing his plan."

"In front of you? Or did they not know you could hear?"

"I was with them. They'd given me some food and water. They spoke Arabic, but they knew I understood. I'd spoken Arabic with Dariush at the mission."

"He didn't speak English?"

"Claimed not to at the time, but his English was excellent."

"So, educated, you'd guess."

"Yes."

"They knew you understood them but spoke in front of you anyway."

"Right. Not that I'd believed Mahmoud when he told me he'd let me live, but at that point, I knew I was going to die."

Michael's expression turned from all business to sympathetic. "Terrifying."

"I'd made my peace with it."

"I don't think I would have."

"That's because you could fight your way out. You wouldn't give up because you would have had a chance. It was me against seven strong men. I didn't think anybody was coming for me. They told me Bryan was dead."

Michael's jaw tightened.

She'd forgotten that part. "The point is, I had no hope." She heard how that sounded and tried to explain. "No hope that I could save myself, that is. I hoped you would come. And I knew God was with me. But I knew I wasn't going to be able to outsmart them or fight my way to freedom.

"Anyway, one of the young guys asked Mahmoud about his plans. Mahmoud told them he had a buyer for the bulk of the weapons."

"Who?"

She thought back to that moment. Munching cheese. Sipping water. Listening to terrorists plot their evil.

"He didn't say the name, just called him a Russian."

"Did they say anything else?"

"Mahmoud talked about a delivery device for the bioweapons. He didn't say what it was, but I got the sense it wasn't a bomb. They planned to set it off in the market Saturday. No. Not *it*. *Them*. They were going to set *them* off at the market."

"The Christmas market?"

"I think so. At Marienplatz." She imagined the square near her apartment and all the people there. Unsuspecting tourists enjoying the holiday festivities. Listening to music. Eating strudel.

No idea what was coming.

"And they mentioned the mission as well," Sophie said.

"One of the men said he was going"—she emphasized the words —"'to take care' of those who lure Muslims away."

"The mission where you work?"

It was the only time during the discussion that Mahmoud acknowledged her, giving her a triumphant look, wanting her to know his plans for her friends. "He mentioned Aaron by name."

"Aaron Driscoll?" At her nod, Michael asked, "They were going to set off one of their devices there? The bioweapon?"

"I don't know. Maybe? Maybe something else? I had the sense that the kid seemed intent on that part of the job. Like he had a personal stake in it."

"What makes you say that?"

"Just the way he perked up. The seriousness in his tone. You told me to trust my instincts. I guess that's all this was, my instincts."

"Could you identify him?"

Whoa. What? Look at him? Face him?

Her reaction must've shown because Michael said, "In a photo. They're a little gruesome, but it would help."

"I think so."

"Good, good. We'll do that when I get the pictures."

"Anything I can do," she said. "It'll make me feel like less of a victim."

Michael stiffened at the word. "You're alive and free, which is more than we can say for the terrorists. You're not a victim. You're a survivor."

Oh.

Well, then...

Her eyes filled again. Because she felt like...like the opposite. Like she'd done nothing to help. She'd always wanted to be the princess in the fairy tale, but the reality wasn't what she'd thought.

Being helpless, dependent on others.

Admittedly, she loved that Bryan had been willing to risk his life to save her.

But she hated that she'd needed saving. She'd hated feeling helpless.

Even though Michael had told her more than once that she'd done the right things, she felt the opposite. If not for him and his team, she'd have let terrorists get away with bioweapons.

Which made her...what? A servant who failed to serve was...

Worthy. Cherished. Priceless.

Oh.

Right.

That was what the Lord had told her. She hadn't been able to save the day, but that didn't make her any less lovable.

Michael held out a tissue. He didn't seem uncomfortable because of tears, just waited for her to get her emotions under control.

When she did, he said, "Did you hear anything else?"

"I don't think so."

"If you remember anything—"

"I'd like to know what you've learned."

"You're not the only one. Bryan can be annoyingly persistent." If anything, Michael looked impressed. "I wanted to wait until I talked to you to share what we've learned. I'll get him."

Michael walked away, and Sophie settled back on her bed.

Amazing how just saying it all out loud relieved some of the internal tension. Saying the words had made the nightmare feel real. But also, it'd made it less powerful.

She'd learned that after her sister's death. Talking about that time made the memories sting less, and the memories of her sister's short life sweeter.

When Josie died, Sophie'd had nobody but a paid counselor to talk to. Her parents hadn't been able to deal with her grief, not alongside their own. Her friends tried, but they couldn't comprehend what she was going through.

This time, she had Bryan. They'd gone through it together. They could process it together.

Until he went back to the States. And then...and then she'd be alone again.

CHAPTER FORTY-TWO

Bryan was pacing—as much as one could pace on crutches —when Michael stepped into the hallway. Finally.

"Figured you'd be listening at the door," Michael said as Bryan crutched closer.

"Tried to. Stupid thing's soundproof. She okay?"

"She's fine. Eager for you to come back." He stepped aside to let Bryan pass him. "Sit before you fall and crack your skull."

Bryan ignored his brother and entered the room, focused only on the beautiful woman who, despite the bruises and scrapes on her face—and the nightmare she'd endured—smiled at him.

He rounded the bed and pressed a kiss to her forehead. "Was he nice to you? Do I need to beat him up?"

"Not today."

"Okay, good."

Her fingers skimmed his stubbly cheeks. "How are you?"

"Better now. You'll tell me everything?"

"Of course. And you'll do the same?"

"Everything."

Michael cleared his throat. "Not that this isn't fun for me."

Bryan scowled at him, earning a grin. He propped his crutches against the end of the bed and sat. "Spill."

Michael settled on the rolling chair. "When the texts came in last night, we were in the middle of an operation. Otherwise, we'd have gotten there sooner. If it'd been up to me, we'd have contacted local authorities and gotten them up there immediately."

He'd already told Bryan how he'd guessed when Bryan didn't answer his calls that something was wrong. He and his boss had nearly come to blows over what to do next.

Michael told Sophie the short version. "There's a chain of command, and I'm supposed to trust they know what they're doing. Easier said than done when someone I love is in danger."

Bryan's eyes did that annoying prickle thing, emotion trying to work its way out, which only got worse when Sophie squeezed his hand.

He was just tired. And it'd been a heckuva day. And...and yeah, he didn't mind hearing that his brother cared.

"We finished what we were doing," Michael said, "and flew to a private airport near Neuschwanstein. We put together the op in the air. Had to have vehicles delivered, which took some time. We headed up the mountain as soon as we could. We were still getting into place when that guy dragged you out to the road." He nodded toward Sophie. "We weren't close enough to see what was happening, but we heard him yelling."

Bryan guarded against the images his brother's nonchalant words conjured. He'd see that moment in his nightmares for a long time. The man. The gun. The woman he loved.

"I was moving as fast as I could," Michael continued. "We weren't ready, but we weren't about to let him execute you."

Sophie's already pale cheeks blanched.

Bryan shot Michael a look, and his brother lifted his shoulders in a *What? That's what happened* shrug.

Sophie said, "Bryan took care of him."

"Right." Michael punctuated the word with a nod. "The rifle shot had the terrorists on alert, so we hustled in. We hadn't had a chance to secure the woods, which is how Stone missed the guy on the ridge."

"I tied him up," Bryan said. "Should've killed him when I had the chance."

Michael gave Bryan a long, hard stare. After a minute, he said, "I've made the same choice more than once—and nearly gotten myself killed for exactly the same reason. You knocked the guy out. Are you really sorry you didn't kill a man who was already down? Life is precious. Even that guy's life. Even if it had ended differently, I'm glad you didn't."

Michael wasn't the one who'd have had to bury his brother because he'd trusted flimsy shoelaces.

Of course, Michael would've been the one buried, so there was that.

Bryan could live with knowing he'd killed men to protect Sophie and Michael. He didn't know how he'd have lived with having killed an unconscious man.

"You guys know what happened after that," Michael said. "We captured Mahmoud, loaded up the crates, and got them out of there."

"Where'd you take them?" Bryan asked.

"Next question."

"What was in them?" Sophie asked.

"Next question."

"Come on, bro. We risked our lives to protect those crates. We deserve to know. Besides, you have them now. What could it hurt to tell us?"

Michael lifted one eyebrow. Was he planning to stare him into submission?

Bryan wasn't going to back down. They had a right, didn't they? After all they'd been through?

Sophie shifted on the bed, drawing Michael's attention. "I'd like to know if it was worth everything we went through."

"It was."

"Please?" She did that thing women don't even know they're doing, head tilted to the side, eyes wide and hopeful. Bryan wouldn't be able to resist.

Apparently, Michael couldn't either. His jaw loosened, and his shoulders fell a little. "Stays between us."

"I think we've proved our loyalty," Bryan said.

Michael didn't argue. "They've only tested one sample from one crate so far, but... It's anthrax."

Sophie gasped. "Wow. I mean, I knew... I guess I shouldn't be surprised, but somehow, I figured it was going to be nothing. A hoax or... Anthrax is deadly, right?"

Michael nodded. "You said something about a delivery system. Those were the words they used, right? Delivery system?"

"What?" Bryan hadn't heard about that.

"Mahmoud was talking about it this morning," she explained. "How the things would infect everybody at the Christmas market."

"Everybody?" Bryan considered what that meant. "They weren't planning to put it in the water or food, then. That would only infect those who ingested it. Meaning..."

His big brother wore that smirk again. "Go on. You probably know as much about this as I do."

"I did some research."

"Of course you did." Michael lifted one eyebrow, looking at Sophie. "Always with his head in a book, this one."

She leaned toward Bryan but spoke to Michael. "You're just jealous because he's so smart."

Bryan couldn't help the grin. "What she said."

"You wish." Michael rolled his eyes. "Go on, then. Tell us all about it."

"I was just going to say that if they thought the anthrax would infect everybody, then they must've planned to blow it into the air somehow so people would inhale it. Inhalation anthrax poisoning is the most deadly—much deadlier than if it's ingested or touched. Right?"

Michael was nodding, all amusement gone. "It would have been ugly."

"But it's not contagious," Bryan said. "It would be contained."

"To the thousands of people at the Christmas market," Sophie said. "And the panic it would set off."

"Assuming anybody knew it was happening." Michael pushed up from his rolling stool and paced away. "Panic would be bad, but at least people would get out of there. But anthrax is a fine white powder. People might have thought it was fake snow or even fog from a heater." He swiveled at the wall. "Depending on where they put their devices, it's possible nobody would've noticed."

In cold weather, any moisture created fog. People could potentially walk right through the anthrax, maybe even expecting it to be warm. They'd inhale it into their lungs. The powder would get on their skin and clothes. After that, everyone they came in contact with could be infected, people who hadn't even been at the market.

There were treatments—if it was caught early—but no cures. And how many of those medications would be on hand in Munich?

It would have been...devastating.

"Thank God we stopped them." Sophie practically whispered the words. "Thank God."

"Yeah." Bryan couldn't think beyond that. So many things could've gone wrong. Yet here they were, safe. Mahmoud in custody. The other terrorists, dead.

Michael settled on the rolling stool again. "The property you texted about, Bryan, where you were held"—he nodded to Sophie—"is owned by Hasan Mahmoud. Has been for a decade. Up until last summer, it was available for short-term rentals, managed by a local company."

"Let me guess," Bryan said. "He stopped renting it last summer. Probably right about the same time the contents of the donation to the Munich museum were published."

"Bingo," Michael said.

"That explains how he found us. He didn't have to follow us." Bryan focused on Sophie. "All the work we did trying to stay hidden was for naught. He already knew where we were going."

"Close to, anyway," Michael said. "He probably had men in Füssen and the other little villages near the castle. But he had enough manpower and—"

"We weren't even trying to hide," Bryan said. He'd been stupid. Arrogant. So sure they'd lost Mahmoud and his people.

Sophie's head dipped to the side. "But if that's true, then why did he and his men try to stop us at the train station?"

"What's this?" Michael asked.

Before Bryan could explain, Sophie told his brother the story, how they'd run to get to the subway before Mahmoud caught up with them, and then how Bryan had tackled the guy at the top of the stairs.

"Wow." Michael didn't look happy. "You're a regular James Bond."

"I didn't know what else to do."

"No, you did...great."

Bryan decided not to be offended by the tone of surprise.

"But why would they bother," Sophie asked, "if they already knew where we were going?" Bryan was formulating an answer when she continued. "Actually, it makes sense. He wouldn't want to take the chance he might not be able to find us again. And also, he wanted to protect the information, to make sure we couldn't pass it along." She turned to Michael. "Right? He didn't need us to lead him to the cave. He just needed the coordinates. Which we had."

"Makes sense," Michael said.

"Have you learned anything else about that artifact?" Bryan asked. "How the coordinates got etched on it?"

Michael shook his head. "We talked to a guy in Washington who got in touch with the curator at the museum in Iraq. He remembered the chest because it was brought to him right before Baghdad fell. He was told not to display it."

"He wouldn't have anyway," Bryan said. "It was Byzantine."

"Sure. Okay." Michael obviously didn't care about that aspect. "Anyway, this guy thinks they sent it to the museum because they thought it would be safe there. They knew the Americans would tear the palace apart, but they'd probably leave the museum alone."

"But then it was looted." Sophie was nodding as the story came together. "The security guards abandoned it, and the locals broke in and stole thousands of items, including the chest."

"It's a theory," Michael said. "Not sure if we'll ever confirm it."

"How did Mahmoud find out about it?"

Michael glanced at his phone, frowned, and lowered it to his lap. "Thanks to some information Leila was able to provide about Mahmoud, we figured out who raised him and where. He went to school with some of Hussein's most trusted guards. For a time before the war, he was in the inner circle. We believe—and again, it's all theory—that one of those guards told Mahmoud about the weapons and the ivory chest."

"And that it was moved to the museum," Sophie said. "Otherwise, he wouldn't have known where to look."

"That's true." Bryan looked back at his brother. "How would he have gotten all that information?"

"Who knows? I can tell you that Mahmoud was a ghost for fifty-plus years. We didn't even know he existed. He posed as his twin sometimes—Leila's father—who worked for Saddam, so maybe Mahmoud used that connection? And the guards?" Michael shrugged. "We have him in custody, so we should get all our questions answered, eventually."

"Do you know why Hussein would've hidden the weapons in Germany?" he asked.

"He had no connections here," Michael said. "And maybe that's why. There's no way to know." He pulled his cell from his pocket and read something on the screen. "Be right back."

Bryan watched his brother leave. He was worried about what Michael had been waiting for on his phone—and what his abrupt departure meant.

He turned to Sophie. "It's a lot to take in."

"I'm glad we're getting answers. I'm sure your brother would get in trouble for telling us so much."

"He's already in trouble for getting us involved. His boss was furious when he found out."

"He told you that?"

"Earlier, yeah. But Michael isn't worried because... Well, if not for us, Mahmoud would have gotten the ivory chest with the coordinates. He'd have found the anthrax. So as ticked off as Brock is—that's Michael's boss—he's not going to make a big stink about it. That would only magnify his own failures."

"Even so, it can't be good for Michael's career."

Bryan looked toward the hallway. "I get the feeling he doesn't care that much. I think..." He looked back at the woman he'd come to care for. "I think he's ready to be done with all that. To have a life and a family."

"I hope that's true, for Leila's sake."

Bryan did too. Now that he had more information about what his brother did for a living, he hoped Michael would give it up, soon.

"What did you do while I was sleeping?" Sophie asked.

"After they X-rayed my leg and examined me, I rented a hotel room right down the street. Then I took a shower and came back and waited for you to wake up. I would have been here except Michael was back and wanted to debrief me."

Bryan had also talked to his department head and fed him a story Michael had concocted about an illness that had prevented Bryan from making his flight—and from getting in touch sooner. He hated to lie, but there was the whole national security thing. And anyway, if he told the crusty old history professor what'd really happened, the guy would think he was off his rocker.

Bryan had promised to be back at Bowdoin the following week.

The thought of leaving Sophie opened a hole inside him.

And the job he no longer wanted wouldn't fill the void.

He'd been asking God for years what was next for him. Now that question was different. More defined. More... courageous.

Because Bryan had learned something this week. That he didn't have to be a Green Beret or a CIA agent or a physician or...anything special. He didn't even have to be *whole*. God used broken people and flawed people. God used people like Bryan.

All Bryan had to do was stay in the middle of God's will in order to be the hero of his own story.

He just prayed that God's will was big enough for a certain blonde missionary. And that her life was big enough to fit him.

CHAPTER FORTY-THREE

A million questions swirled through Sophie's mind about Bryan and his plans. Was there any way to make this work?

Everything felt so...tenuous, like a spring daffodil facing down a late frost.

Was that all this was? A short-term romance?

There'd been two mind-blowing kisses.

One date in the hotel restaurant.

Most of what happened on the mountain after Mahmoud nearly strangled her was fuzzy, but she would never forget Bryan's whispered words. *I love you, Princess. I'm going to get us out of this.*

But what kind of love was this? The spring-bloom kind—a flower that would last a week or two and then fade away?

Or the rosebush kind. The kind of love that, with proper care, could grow and blossom for years?

For a lifetime.

She didn't know. She only knew that, even if it was a daffodil romance, she wasn't ready for the frost to kill it.

The door opened, and Michael stepped back in carrying her purse and dragging a pink-and-brown suitcase.

A very familiar suitcase.

"Pretty," Bryan said. "Matches your eyes."

Ignoring him, Michael sat by the bed and spoke to Sophie. "We went to the museum and got your things. And a couple of my teammates went to your apartment."

"I can see that."

"Whoa." Bryan pushed to his feet. "You did what?" He turned to Sophie. "I'm sorry. I had no idea."

Michael didn't even spare him a glance. "Bryan told us that your place was broken into last week."

"Felix, my ex-boyfriend. He said somebody else did it, but I thought..." She turned to Bryan. "Except you weren't sure it was Felix."

"I didn't know."

"Bryan told me about it," Michael said. "His theory was that Mahmoud had done it. After the break-in, the curator—"

"Herr Papp," she said.

"Right. Papp was quick to believe you were guilty of the break-in at the museum, if not working alone, then working with an accomplice. We found out today that only your badge and the guard's accessed the doors that night."

"Oh. I don't understand. Unless Gunter let them in. But they killed him, so..."

"It wasn't Gunter," Michael said. "Your badge and fingerprint accessed the door to the storage room a little after nine, which must be when Mahmoud and his men got in."

"I didn't let them in."

"Of course not." To Michael, Bryan said, "Can Papp be trusted? He and Mahmoud were pretty chummy when I saw them after the break-in."

"We accessed the security system," Michael said. "And I

questioned Papp myself. He said Mahmoud reached out to him a few weeks ago and offered to make a sizable donation to the museum in return for a private showing of the artifacts. Papp refused."

"Why?" Bryan asked.

"I can guess," Sophie said. "That would be against the rules. And Papp is a stickler for the rules."

Michael was nodding. "He claimed Mahmoud showed up after the break-in expressing worry about the items, as if he were a lover of ancient Babylonian artifacts."

"Herr Papp would be respectful to a potential donor," Sophie said, "no matter what the circumstances."

"So if only Sophie's badge was used that night, then..." Bryan spoke slowly, seeming to put it together. "You think her intruder broke in to her apartment to get access to her badge?"

Michael looked at her. "Was your badge there?"

"I only carried it when I was at work. I didn't take it to the States with me. So Felix was telling the truth?"

"I think so."

"He's still a creep, Sophie." Bryan sounded almost angry. "He might not have done that one thing, but he did follow you. He confronted you at the restaurant. I don't want you to forget—"

"I know." She took his hand and squeezed. "Don't worry. I get it."

He visibly relaxed, his shoulders dropping. "Okay. Sorry. I didn't mean—"

"I get it."

Michael cleared his throat. "He won't be bothering you anymore."

His tone had Sophie turning her attention back to him. "What do you mean?"

He shot a look at his brother. "Uh, Bryan told me a little

about what he's been up to. We needed to make sure our theory was correct, so I sent a couple of my teammates to have a chat with him. He confirmed that he didn't break into your place. After some questioning, he admitted that he'd been keeping an eye on you, meaning *following* you. We had to make sure he wasn't working for anybody."

Her gaze flicked to Bryan, who asked, "Who would he be working for?"

"Mahmoud, or his people. We needed to be sure nobody had paid him to keep an eye on you." Michael smirked. "But no. He's just your run-of-the-mill stalker. We, uh, educated him in the proper way to treat women. There might've been a few promises to keep our eyes on him. Nobody does stalking like the CIA does stalking." He winked. "Not that we can make good on those threats, not officially, anyway, but don't tell him that. He should leave you alone from now on."

Sophie didn't know what to say. "I'm a little...wow. Thank you for doing that. That means...so much."

"That's awesome, bro," Bryan said. "Wish I could have been a fly on the wall."

Michael chuckled. "I'll see if they got a video."

Bryan's grin faded. "Going back to the terrorist, though... You think Mahmoud or one of his people broke into Sophie's place. But they couldn't have stolen her badge"—he looked at her—"because you still had it, right?" At her nod, he said, "They must've cloned it, which they could do with the right equipment. But what about the fingerprint?"

"Probably as easy to get an imprint of that as cloning the magnetic strip," Michael said. "I've heard of people using regular glue. Don't know if that works, but it's not as hard as you'd think." To Sophie, he said, "We went to your apartment to look for evidence. The more we know about Mahmoud and what he's been up to, the faster we'll be able to get information from him."

"Is he being taken back to the States?" Bryan asked.

Michael's lips pressed closed. He shook his head. "Next question."

Before Bryan could argue, Sophie asked, "What's in the suitcase?"

That brought a real smile. "One of our team members is a woman. She picked up a few things she thought you'd want. Toiletries, clothes."

"I appreciate that, but I'm going home tomorrow, so..."

His smile stiffened at the corners. He pulled his phone from his pocket and tapped on it. Averting his gaze.

Her heartbeat quickened. "I *am* going home tomorrow, right?"

"You were going to look at some pictures for me."

Sophie didn't want to think about why Michael wouldn't look at her. Or answer her question. "Okay."

"Pictures of what?" Bryan asked.

"The terrorists." Michael held his phone out to Sophie.

Bryan swiped it. "Is that necessary?"

Michael glared at his brother. "I wouldn't ask her if it weren't."

"She's been through enough."

Sweet of Bryan to try to protect her, but it wasn't necessary. "It's fine." She held out her hand. "Really."

Bryan gave her the phone, then leaned close and watched as she scrolled through the photographs. They weren't gruesome. No blood. Just gray faces and lifeless eyes.

Young men who could have spent their lives in so many good ways but had chosen hate and evil and death. Two were curly-haired, two had straight hair. One had shaved his head.

Some with darker skin, some with lighter. In death, they didn't look frightening or threatening. They looked young and...sad.

She'd forgotten her task and backed up to one of the curly-haired men. "This is the one who was going to target the mission."

Michael glanced at the image. "Good."

But before he could take the phone back, Sophie realized... She started swiping again. Slowly.

"Where is Dariush?" She looked at Michael. "He's not here."

"Who?" Bryan asked. "Who is Dariush?"

"One of the terrorists. He was a client at the mission." To Michael she said, "Is he in custody?"

Gently, he took the phone from her hand. "Unfortunately—"

"Where is he?" Her voice was too high. "I don't understand. You said—"

"Dariush escaped."

"What are you saying?" Bryan's volume rose. "One of them got past you?"

"How?" Unlike Bryan, Sophie's voice was barely a whisper.

"I don't know." Michael slid his cell into his pocket. "Like I said, we weren't in position yet. We had to move fast. My guess is, when the shooting started, he figured out what was happening and ran. As soon as you told me there were seven men, I knew we had a problem."

Of all the people to escape...

Dariush Shahin. The craftiest of them all.

"So now what?" Bryan asked. "You guys are going to find him, right?"

"We're working on it." Michael sat on the rolling stool again. "One of my teammates has been looking into him since you told me about him. Your instincts are spot-on. He's very dangerous."

"But you're going to find him, right?" Her heart raced as if he might walk in the door. "Soon?"

Michael's head dipped and rose, slowly. "He knows who you are, Sophie. He knows where you live."

"What are you saying?" Bryan asked.

She was afraid of the answer.

"I'm sorry." Michael sounded genuinely grieved. "You can't stay in Germany."

"What? No." She wanted to stand. Maybe she could talk Michael out of that ridiculous statement. She started to flip the covers aside, then realized she wore nothing but a hospital gown. Frustration filled her voice. "I don't want to leave."

"I know."

"Even if I lose my job, I don't have to leave right away, and by the time my visa expires, I'll get another one. This is... This is my home."

Bryan didn't tell her not to worry or to calm down or that it would all be okay. He just gave her hand a little squeeze.

"I'm sorry." Michael ran his palm over his head. "I'd apologize for getting you involved in all of this, but you were involved long before I sent Bryan here. If our guess is right about them using your credentials—and it is, even if we can't prove it—they'd already planned to use you to get into the museum. To pin the theft on you. And I'm guessing, to kill you when it was over."

Oh.

That thought raised terror in her throat. She worked to swallow it. Where would she be if not for Bryan? And Michael and his team?

She should be thankful she was alive. And she was. Truly. Even so, it felt like she was losing...everything.

And yet there was that hand holding hers. The man gazing at her with such tender concern.

So...not everything.

Michael had barely moved, as if bracing for her reaction.

It had been the longest day of her life. But she'd survived it. She was still...well, not standing, but sitting up. Alive and recovering.

"Is that it?" she asked. "Or is there another shoe dangling?"

"All the shoes are on the floor now." Michael stood. "I'm sorry about all of this."

"Is she going to have to hide? Change her name?" Bryan asked. "What happens next?"

Michael addressed her when he answered. "You should be safe in the States. Dariush Shahin might carry a grudge against you for thwarting his plans, but he's not going to continent-hop to hurt you. He's got more important things to do."

"Like try to kill my friends," she said.

He didn't argue. "He's on the run. We've got every law enforcement agency in Europe looking for him. Until he's captured, you need to go to the States."

"What if you never find him?"

Michael's lips tipped up at the corners. "We're very good at what we do, Sophie. Now that he's on our radar, it's just a matter of time."

She appreciated his confidence, but meanwhile, what was she supposed to do? Leave the city she loved, leave all her friends. Run and hide?

Everything inside her balked at the idea.

She wanted to argue. To tell Michael she was going to stay, no matter what dangers existed. The refugees had endured great danger to get free. She could endure some, couldn't she? Aaron was going to.

Michael held her gaze until a low buzz had him sliding his phone from his pocket. He glanced at it, then put it back. "Do you have any more questions for me?"

She had a million questions, but Michael couldn't answer most of them. "Is it all right if I tell Aaron what happened?"

Michael seemed to weigh the words.

Bryan said, "He risked his life to help us. He's safe."

"You cannot tell him about the bioweapons," Michael said. "But you can tell him the mission was a target and that Dariush was in on it."

"Okay," she said. "Thank you."

"You'll be around tomorrow," Bryan asked, "if we have any more questions?"

"If not, you have my number." To Sophie, Michael added, "Anything you need."

"Thank you."

He smiled. "Don't thank me. If not for you"—he lifted his gaze to his brother—"and you, I don't know what would have happened. You two risked your lives—and saved so many." He reached out toward Sophie, seemed to hesitate, then dropped a hand on her shoulder. "God saw this coming—all of it, right down to your next move. I don't know His plan, but I know He has one, and it's good." He nodded to his brother and walked out.

She stared after him for a long time, considering what he'd said.

God's plan versus hers. If she had to choose, she'd take God's plan every single day.

Bryan was quiet beside her, maybe giving her time to process.

"Sit with me?" She patted the bed beside her.

His eyebrows hiked. "I'm pretty sure that's not allowed."

"What are they going to do, kick me out?" She scooted over.

"Not you," he said. But he toed off his shoes and reclined beside her, on top of the covers.

He slid his arm around her, and she cuddled against him, resting her head on his chest. It felt...perfect.

Like she was meant to be right in that spot, in his arms.

He kissed the top of her head. "What are you thinking?"

"I'm in shock, I think. I'm not sure how to feel about leaving Germany. But your brother's right. God knows what He's doing."

"I'm sorry this happened."

She considered that. Was she sorry?

Sorry she'd gone up against terrorists? Sorry she'd thwarted their plans?

How could she be?

"I came here to serve the refugees," she said. "And I did that for years. And now...now I guess I had a small part in saving some lives."

"More than a 'small part,' Princess."

Princess.

He'd been calling her that since she'd confessed her silly childhood fantasy. She could ask him to stop, but she liked it. She liked being Bryan's princess.

"I don't want to think about what would've happened if not for you," he said.

"And you."

"Hmm." The low sound rumbled in his chest against her ear. "We make a good team, you and I."

A week before, she hadn't even known this man, and now she couldn't imagine her life without him.

She had no idea what the future would bring. She didn't even know where she'd be living in a few days. But she had a very strong suspicion that the man holding her was going to be part of whatever came next.

So, alongside her grief, anticipation sparked.

God was up to something. And soon enough, she'd find out what.

CHAPTER FORTY-FOUR

B ryan parked outside Webb's Harborside in downtown Shadow Cove a little before six on a Saturday in early December. He hung the handicap tag from his rearview mirror to justify the close parking space, stepped from the car, and grabbed his cane. His leg was almost back to normal, but he wanted to save his strength for after dinner.

He headed up the walkway, which was clear of the snow that'd fallen that morning, blanketing the state in fresh powder. The last time he'd been here, Sophie had been talking on the phone in the cold and rain. He'd thought her beautiful, if a little dimwitted.

He couldn't have been more wrong—about her wits, that was.

The storm had moved out, leaving the air crisp and cold and tinged with the scent of the wood fire burning inside. Stars twinkled in the midnight-blue sky, even more glorious than the Christmas lights blanketing tree trunks and outlining the roof of the restaurant and the surrounding businesses. Waves crashed against the rocks in the harbor across the street.

It was perfect, as if Shadow Cove and all of Maine—and perhaps even God Himself—were on board with Bryan's plan.

Now, he just needed to get Sophie to agree.

The day she was released from the hospital, he'd said goodbye to her at the Munich airport. She'd flown to her parents' house in California. He'd returned to Maine. Though they'd made no plans to see each other again, they'd talked every night since, sometimes for hours.

The more he got to know her, the more he loved her. And yeah, he was still using that word, even if he hadn't confessed his feelings again after the one declaration on the mountain.

In the last couple of weeks, he'd gotten caught up at school and prepared for exams. He'd smoothed things over with his department head.

Now it was time to smooth things over with Sophie.

Not that they'd been arguing, not really. She'd initially agreed to leave Germany, but now that some time had passed, she'd started talking about going back. Aaron was there, after all, even though he knew he was a target.

"Why should I stay hidden while he puts himself in danger?" she'd asked on the phone a few nights before.

"You're not him." Bryan had kept his tone even, though frustration with the Iraqi man still hummed. Not that it was Aaron's fault Sophie felt she needed to follow in his footsteps. If Aaron wanted to risk his life, fine. Power to him. But Sophie didn't need to live in Munich to serve God. "Is that what God is telling *you* to do?"

"I don't know yet. I just know...I can't stay here."

He didn't want her to stay in California, either.

Inside, the restaurant, like the rest of Shadow Cove, was decorated for the coming holiday. A Christmas tree in the corner twinkled with white lights that reflected off red glass balls and ornaments of various shapes and sizes. More lights were wrapped around pine greenery that framed the windows and doors. Festive music played from speakers overhead, barely audible over the conversations of locals and tourists enjoying the view of the Atlantic through the windows. The moon glowed over the dark water, glimmering on the waves.

Bryan had made a reservation and asked for a table by the fireplace. He followed the host and took the spot facing the door.

A few minutes later, Sophie stepped in and scanned the space.

Wow.

He'd forgotten how incredible she was. Gorgeous. Radiant. She wore a pale pink sweater beneath the puffy parka she'd worn in Munich. A white scarf hung around her neck and matched her gloves. Her dark jeans flared a little at the bottom and made her look tall and slim, especially with the boots that stuck out beneath them.

Her eyes were bright, her cheeks healthy and pink from the chilly air, the bruises that had marked her face gone.

She caught sight of him and smiled.

He stood and, when she approached, opened his arms.

She stepped into them, and he held her, inhaling her floral perfume and the fruity scent of her shampoo and the essence that was simply Sophie.

With her in his arms, everything felt right again.

They stood like that for a long time. And then she sighed and backed up. "Hi."

"Hi." He bent to press a kiss to her lips, just a light peck that ignited a desire for more. He pulled out the chair for her, and she sat. "Did you have a fun day?"

"Yeah. Leila and Jasmine and I went to the outlets in Kittery and did some Christmas shopping. Did you get your exams graded?"

"Most of them." He'd wanted to meet Sophie at the airport in Manchester the day before, but his exam schedule had made it impossible. This morning, rather than rush down and steal her away from her friends, he'd decided the wiser move was to grade the exams so he could relax and spend more time with her.

And Leila, in on his plan, had wanted to spend the day showing her around the area.

The server came, and they ordered drinks, then settled into conversation as if nothing had changed.

He'd worried maybe things would be awkward. He and Sophie had grown so close, so fast, and in the midst of crazy circumstances. After two weeks apart, his feelings for her hadn't lessened, and if her radiant smile was any indication, she was right there with him.

When the server returned with their drinks and asked what they wanted to eat, they hadn't even looked at the menu. He was about to ask her to come back when Sophie said, "If I get a lobster roll, do I have to take the meat out of the shell? Or does it come...de-shelled or whatever?"

"The meat comes on a bun with mayo," the waitress said. "But if you just want lobster, we can remove it from the shell for you."

"Is that so?" Sophie turned to him, eyebrows raised. "So you're saying I don't have to break it apart all by myself?"

The waitress looked from Bryan to Sophie, maybe trying to figure out what she'd missed. "Um, no?"

Bryan laughed. "Admit it. You had fun."

"Fun? That thing almost killed me." Sophie shook her head and spoke to the server. "I'll have the lobster, without the shell and icky...green stuff."

"The tomalley," Bryan said.

Sophie wrinkled her nose in disgust, which only made her look cuter.

Okay, so he could've told her she could ask the kitchen to remove the meat from the lobster. And okay, maybe he'd not done it because he'd wanted the excuse to talk to her. To get to know her.

He'd apologize, except he wasn't sorry. And by the way her eyes sparkled, she wasn't angry.

He ordered surf and turf and handed the menus to the server.

He and Sophie chatted about everything and nothing until their meals were served. After they dug into their food, Bryan asked, "How was your time with your parents?" Every time he'd tried to broach the subject over the phone, she'd brushed him off, but he'd felt her tension.

Her smile faded. "I told them what happened. Not everything, of course. Your brother was very clear on what I could and couldn't share. I told them I'd been held against my will and rescued."

Amazing how so few words could encompass what she'd been through.

"They must've been horrified."

She looked toward the fireplace a few feet away.

Bryan studied her profile in the reflection of the flickering flames, the way her lips curved into a frown.

"They were horrified. But not like you'd think. Dad lectured me about my safety and how I need to be more careful."

"What? It wasn't your fault."

She lifted one shoulder and let it drop. "I was there. I shouldn't put myself in dangerous situations. Don't I know how much it would hurt them if something happened to me?"

Bryan pressed back against his chair. "He said that?"

"That was nothing. Mom practically wailed. Which is why Dad acted like he did, because I'd caused Mom distress. So he had to comfort her, which he's been doing ever since Josie died."

"Wait. Your dad comforted your *mom*? What about you?"

She shrugged. "I cleared the table. I was halfway to the broom closet when I realized what I was doing, falling right back into the same pattern. They freak out, I try to make their lives easier, to make myself small and insignificant. To justify my existence by serving."

"When I call you Princess, I don't mean Cinderella."

Her smile was sad. "Mom has stayed mired in grief. Dad tiptoes around her, trying not to set her off. She's his priority, which... I mean, she's his wife, so I get that. There was a time he treated me like a real daughter, but I realize now that he doesn't see me that way. Probably hasn't since Josie was born, though he tried to pretend."

Bryan wove her fingers between his own, offering connection and comfort.

"When I was little, Mom was fun-loving and joy-filled. But Josie's death changed everything." Sophie shook her head. "No, not her death. Her life. Her illness. But Josie's been gone a long time. Mom could choose to heal, if she wanted to. People do it. She could see a counselor or go to a grief support group. She could press into her relationship with Christ. I'm not saying it would be easy. But wouldn't it be better than what she's doing?"

Bryan nodded but said nothing, giving Sophie the time and space to finish her thoughts.

"She won't even consider it. It's like she doesn't want to get better. I used to feel sorry for her, but on this visit I saw everything differently. Mom's refusal to get better has harmed not only her, but Dad and me too. She makes herself and everyone around her miserable. I mean, our God is a God of joy, don't you think?"

"Of course He is," Bryan said. "'Strength and joy are in His dwelling place.' That's in Chronicles. And in Nehemiah, 'The joy of the Lord is your strength.'"

"Exactly." Sophie picked at her lobster but didn't take a bite. She set her fork down. "Mom can't see past her own grief. She can't see...me. So the fact that I could've died... She made it all about her."

Bryan had to press his lips closed to keep from saying the word that came to mind.

Selfish.

The exact opposite of her daughter, who was giving to the point of self-sacrifice.

And the opposite of his own parents, who loved Bryan and his brothers so well. And would love Sophie the same way, when the time came.

"I'm sorry your parents don't realize the treasure you are."

"They're doing the best they can. I need to stop expecting more from them than they can give. It's okay."

"It's not, really. But you have a God who died for you. Friends who treasure you. And a man who sees you as the beloved princess you are."

Her eyes filled, tears sparkling in the firelight. "That's very sweet."

He kissed her hand. "And very true."

The conversation turned to more pleasant topics as they finished their dinners. Bryan paid the check, and they stepped into the cold night. "Will you walk with me for a few minutes, or is it too cold for you?"

She seemed to take his question as a challenge, wrapping her scarf around her neck. "I can handle it."

He took her gloved hand in his free one and leaned on the cane with his other. They rounded the corner and headed up Shadow Cove's touristy district.

Shoppers filled the sidewalks on both sides of the wide, divided road, moving in and out of stores, swinging baskets, some munching popcorn or sugared nuts sold by a street vendor.

Bryan and Sophie meandered past souvenir shops and boutiques. The strong scent of leather wafted out of a leather-goods store when a customer pushed the door open. Another store carried the cloying stench of a thousand scented candles.

Every storefront was decorated for the holiday. More than one piped Christmas music outside, filling the sidewalk with a festive air. Wreaths hung from streetlamps, and fake reindeer made of metal and twinkling lights munched snow in the grassy area between the lanes running up the middle of Center Street.

"Leila was telling me some of her wedding plans," Sophie said.

Bryan laughed. "Oh, yeah. Michael was thrilled when Mom talked her into letting her help plan it. He was hoping for a small ceremony before the end of the year. But now Mom's involved."

"They're going to have it where Leila works, right? We drove up there today. It's a beautiful spot." She walked a few steps, then added, "She asked me to be a bridesmaid."

"Oh, good. You said yes?"

"Of course. So I'll be back in April."

He shot her a look. "Back from where?"

She shrugged and tugged him toward a bakery display window. Scents of chocolate and yeasty goodness wafted from inside as Sophie gazed at cookies and cakes and loaves of bread, nestled alongside fudge and saltwater taffy and maple candy.

"You want something?" he asked.

"No. It's just..." She continued on the sidewalk. "It's charming."

"You like Shadow Cove?"

She looked up at him. "Who wouldn't? It's lovely."

He figured a lot of people wouldn't like it, especially when the temperature hovered in the midtwenties. Most California girls would be complaining. But that wasn't Sophie's way.

Despite the grief she'd suffered—losing her father when she was so young, then losing her sister. And really, she'd lost her parents, too. At least she'd lost the parents she should've had.

Yet she'd found a way to be happy. Even now, having been chased away from her home, she was happy.

He loved that about her.

They reached a little park at the top of the hill. The town had erected a Christmas tree in the center, and it sparkled against the night sky. A paved and cleared path wound around it. There were picnic benches scattered throughout, but the couple of inches of fresh snow kept other visitors away. He urged her in that direction, away from the crowds.

She studied the tree, its lights reflecting in her eyes.

He prayed for courage and started the conversation he'd wanted to have all night. "I want to talk to you about something."

She looked at him, expression open and curious. "Okay."

He stopped and faced her. "I don't want you to go back to Germany."

Her smile faded. "I know."

"Not just for your safety. That's the biggest thing, of course. You won't be safe there until Michael and his team find Dariush Shahin."

They'd gone the entire evening without mentioning that particular elephant in the room, but he wasn't going to tiptoe around it.

"I understand there are risks. But Aaron is there."

"Aaron feels that's where God wants him. Do you feel that's where God wants you?"

She looked down. Her shoulders lifted and fell. "I'm not

ready to abandon my work in Germany. And I can't do nothing."

With a finger under her chin, he urged her face up until she met his eyes. "You can rest for a little while, Princess. It's okay."

"I'm not very good at that."

"I know. But if you're not feeling the Lord urging you back there, then you shouldn't go. You understand that, right? Sometimes He wants you to wait. Sometimes waiting takes the greatest faith of all."

"Ugh." She stepped close and rested her forehead on his chest. "I feel useless when I'm not working."

He wrapped her in his arms. "You're priceless, no matter what you're doing. I think maybe He wants you to learn that lesson."

She didn't agree, but she didn't argue, either, which he took as a good sign.

"Speaking of waiting... You remember that metaphorical room I told you about, where I've imagined myself waiting?"

She looked up at him. "The one with all the doors?"

"Yeah. All the doors and all the options I refused to investigate until God gave me His direction."

Her eyebrows rose. "My interest is piqued. Did He open one?"

"A crack," Bryan said, enjoying the metaphor. Enjoying sharing it with Sophie. "I have an idea of what's on the other side."

"And?"

He swallowed the worry that tried to silence him. He'd prayed enough. He wasn't going to let fear or pride silence him.

"The thing is, Princess... It's not just that I don't want you to go back to Germany. I want you to stay here. I already cleared it with Leila and Jasmine. And of course Michael's on board."

Confusion clouded her expression.

"I want you to stay with the twins until the wedding."

"Stay with them?" Her eyebrows hiked. "The wedding isn't until April."

"You'll be safe."

"What would I do?"

"Whatever you want. You can volunteer—there are plenty of organizations in Portland that could use your help. Or get a job. Or just...paint. Rest. Pray about what's next. Because the thing is... That open door... I don't know everything on the other side of it, but I got a very good look at one thing."

"Yeah?"

"It's you."

Her eyes widened. And maybe she would have stepped back, but he held her hand and wasn't letting go. "I know you and I aren't...official or anything. If you stay, then we can date and get to know each other." He needed to be careful here. He needed to not say too much and scare her away.

But she was looking at him with such...openness. Curiosity. Wonder. And wow, she was beautiful, and he just couldn't stop himself.

"I want to spend time with you. I want to be with you and pray with you and...and I want you to feel about me the way I feel about you. Which...it's okay if you don't right now. But what I said to you on the mountain—you probably don't even remember, but—"

"I remember." Her voice was soft and tender, as if she'd held his words close all that time.

Was he making a total fool of himself? Maybe she'd let him down easy, tell him it was just the adrenaline and the moment and what they felt wasn't real.

Maybe not for her, but it was real for him.

He swallowed and started again. "I've been praying, and I know we don't know each other very well, and I could be way off. But I feel like this"—he held her hand against his chest—"is a forever thing. A God-ordained thing. Not just you, but the timing. All of it. I turned my back on the calling God put in my life a long time ago because I was afraid I wouldn't be good enough. I used my brokenness as an excuse. I'm done with all of that. I'm ready to go where God leads. I already told the department head I'm leaving at the end of the school year."

"You're quitting your job?"

The least important part of what he had to say. "I don't know what God has after that. I'm just going on faith here. But the more I pray about it, the more I know God wants me to pursue His plan. To pursue...you."

He forced his lips closed and waited for a reaction.

She blinked up at him, studying him with those big gray eyes. "That's a lot to take in."

"I don't mean to pressure you. There's no—"

"Okay."

"Good." Not what he'd hoped, but at least she hadn't rejected him outright. "Pray about it, and we can talk whenever—"

"No, I mean... Okay. I'll stay. I had to leave California. I had to get away from my parents. I wanted to come here, but I didn't know what was next. I had no idea... Yeah, I could go back to Germany, but that's not what God wants for me. I know that. But He gave me no other idea what to do. And now I understand why." She tapped Bryan's chest, and a grin spread across her lovely face. "I'll let you pursue me, Bryan Wright. In fact, I think I'll enjoy that very much."

Joy exploded inside him. He hadn't expected that reaction. But God was always exceeding Bryan's expectations.

He dropped her hand to wrap his arm around her. "I think I'll start now then, if you don't mind." When he got no answer except raised eyebrows, he lowered his head and kissed her.

She opened up to him, sliding her hands into his open jacket and around his back, tugging him closer.

Everything faded—the festive music, the chatting tourists, the cars driving past. The cold no longer mattered. Nothing mattered except Sophie's warm lips moving against his. A kiss filled with promise and forever.

Desire warmed him, a warning to slow down. He forced himself to end the kiss, studying her face to ensure he hadn't overstepped a boundary.

But she smiled. "So far, I like this pursuit thing. Let's keep doing it."

And those words just added fuel to the fire the cold air wasn't extinguishing. He hugged her to his chest. "You're killing me, Princess."

"You started it."

"Hmm. I guess I did."

He held her, not ready for this moment to end.

"Hey, Bryan?"

He backed up just enough to meet her eyes. "Yeah?"

"What you said on the mountain?"

"That I love you?"

She blinked, maybe surprised he'd stated it so bluntly. "Yeah. That. I didn't have it in me at the time to say it back."

She'd been dizzy and nauseated, still catching her breath after nearly being strangled by a terrorist.

"Lousy timing on my part. I just wanted you to know, in case..." He shrugged. "You know. Anyway, you don't have to say anything."

"I love you too."

Oh.

Her words were a balm. A warm breeze. A haven he wanted to spend the rest of his life curled up in.

"Even if it's too soon," she said, "and even if it doesn't make sense. That crazy experience in Germany... That was just the beginning of our story."

"If that's the case..." He rested his forehead against hers. "I can't wait to read the next chapter."

The End...

...for now, but there is one more chapter, and you won't want to miss it. Check out the *Sheltering You Bonus Epilogue*. You can download it at https://www. subscribepage.com/finding_you. If you have trouble, reach out to me at https:// robinpatchen.com/connect/ and I'll see if I can help.

Okay, now... the end.

Of Bryan and Sophie's story, but for Jasmine and Derrick, it's just getting started. Because Jasmine is carrying Qasim's child, and he's not about to let her go.

Turn the page for more about *Sheltering You*, Book 4 in the Wright Heroes of Maine.

(Be gentle with me—this is unedited and might be a little rough.)

One more thing before you go...

This Christmas, join me on a trip back to Nutfield in a brand-new novella, *Sleigh Bells and Stalkers,* that features Daniel (the little boy from *Innocent Lies,* who's a college student now.) The story will be just one of the novellas in the *Christmas in Nutfield* boxset. Stay tuned for more information about the other novellas.

Now, turn the page for more about *Sheltering You.*

SHELTERING YOU

After escaping Iraq with her twin sister, Jasmine seeks refuge from Qasim, the terrorist she was forced to marry. She's determined to carve out a safe haven in this peaceful coastal town for herself and her unborn child. But her polygamous husband's relentless pursuit threatens to shatter her fragile world, leaving her with nowhere to hide.

Enter Derrick, a guardian angel in the guise of a friend.

Drawn to Jasmine's quiet strength, Derrick vows to shield her from harm, even as the boundaries of friendship blur into something deeper. Unaware of Jasmine's secret, he agrees to help her rescue and hide another Iraqi refugee woman and her younger brother in the US. Derrick will do anything for Jasmine, his heart yearning for a connection she refuses to embrace.

All the while, Qasim is closing in.

He took Jasmine as his second wife for one reason, and she carries that reason her womb. Once his heir is born, nothing will stop Qasim from bringing him home to his beloved first wife and disposing of Jasmine—and he will take out anybody else who stands in his way.

Join the Wright Heroes of Maine for an edge-of-your-seat international romantic suspense that takes you on the run with a heroine in hiding, a secret baby, and unrequited love.

DEAR READER

Novels often begin with a simple question... *What if?*

This story is no different.

I'm old enough to remember the 2003 Gulf War, when the US and allies invaded Iraq to topple Saddam Hussein's government. At the time, intelligence services in America and other nations believed Hussein had stockpiled weapons of mass destruction. After all, Hussein had used WMDs against Kurdish and Iranian civilians during the Iran-Iraq war in the 80s. Moreover, he and his government repeatedly failed to cooperate with UN weapons inspectors and to comply with UN sanctions.

Why would they do that, unless they had something to hide? And what else would they be trying to hide from weapons inspectors but WMDs?

But by the time coalition forces marched into Baghdad, no WMDs were found.

Which begs the question... What went wrong?

It's generally believed these days that there were never any WMDs at all—that all the intelligence coming out of Baghdad was simply...wrong. That's possible.

This story was written with a different supposition, and the simple question of *what if...?*

What if Saddam Hussein was one step ahead of us?

What if he had a plan?

What if those weapons are still out there, somewhere?

Of course, *Finding You* is a complete fabrication. There is zero evidence—as far as I'm aware, anyway—that any WMDs were squirreled out of the country and are now hidden in a cave in Europe. But isn't it fun to imagine?

(These things are so much more enjoyable in fictional form than real life, aren't they?)

Other notes: Most likely, a mission aimed at serving the refugee population in Munich wouldn't be within walking distance of Old Town, but I wanted the story to stay in a small area.

Though there are mountains near Neuschwanstein Castle in Germany, the particular mountain referred to in the story, along with the hiking trail and cave, are fabrications.

This story was so much fun to write and made me yearn to visit Germany and the Alps again soon. God bless and thanks for reading!

Robin

ALSO BY ROBIN PATCHEN

The Nutfield Saga

Convenient Lies

Twisted Lies

Generous Lies

Innocent Lies

Beautiful Lies

Legacy Rejected

Legacy Restored

Legacy Reclaimed

Legacy Redeemed

Christmas in Nutfield

Amanda Series

Chasing Amanda

Finding Amanda

ABOUT ROBIN PATCHEN

Robin Patchen is a *USA Today* bestselling and award-winning author of Christian romantic suspense. She grew up in a small town in New Hampshire, the setting of her Coventry Saga books, and then headed to Boston to earn a journalism degree. After college, working in marketing and public relations, she discovered how much she loathed the nine-to-five ball and chain. She started writing her first novel while she home-schooled her three children. The novel was dreadful, but her passion for storytelling didn't wane. Thankfully, as her children grew, so did her skill. Now that her kids are adults, she has more time to play with the lives of fictional heroes and heroines, wreaking havoc and working magic to give her characters happy endings. When she's not writing, she's editing or reading, proving that most of her life revolves around the twenty-six letters of the alphabet.

Made in the USA
Las Vegas, NV
20 March 2025

19874329R00216